The Sliammon Escudo

The Sliammon Escudo

GEOFFREY R. TIGG

Rushing Tide
M E D I A

The Sliammon Escudo
Copyright ©2014 Geoffrey R Tigg

ISBN: 978-1-939288-51-6
Library of Congress Control Number: 2014933430

This is a work of fiction. Names, characters, places, and incidents are either the product of the author's imagination or are used fictionally, and any resemblance to actual persons, living or dead, business establishments, events, or locales is entirely coincidental.

Rushing Tide
M E D I A

Published by Rushing Tide Media, Imprint of Wyatt-MacKenzie
Contact: grtigg@rushingtidemedia.com

Dedication

This story is dedicated to my daughter Danica Elizabeth Tigg

"Family is not an important thing, it's everything."
MICHAEL J. FOX

NOTE: A character list can be found at the back of the story.

Preface

A tall, lanky, young man sat cross-legged on a large granite rock on the stony shore of Gibson's Beach, watching the beautiful sunset slip away on the last day of August. Harwood Island loomed a mile away to the southwest across the Strait of Georgia and, further south in the distance, the northern tip of Texada Island appeared as a hazy, gray mass that contrasted with the orange and red sky of the late summer evening.

Dillon Point soaked up the smells of filleted spring salmon barbequed on open fires in the Sliammon village up the road, not far from where he lived with his mother. His First Nations peoples had lived along these shores for over a thousand years, and Dillon embraced his culture and traditional way of life. Native life had been molded by time, and modernization had crept into their lives. He sat silently, thinking about his adventure that was to begin in a few days. He knew the time would eventually arrive for him to leave the life he knew so well. He also realized that he needed all his inner strength and spiritual training to help him through this next step in his life passage.

His mother had given him an old diary bound with a deerskin woven tie, and Dillon had placed the book carefully between his folded legs.

The Sliammon peoples are a close community, and family units often lived together in wooden houses. Dillon Point's family was small. He and his mother lived with his grandparents in a modest bungalow at the edge of the village. Dillon was knowledgeable about Sliammon heritage, but knew little of his own family history.

He often thought it strange that his mother did not want to talk about their family story. He was always told the right time would come one day for him to learn about his heritage.

Today was that day. The diary he now possessed belonged to his grandfather, Walter Smith, a Caucasian anthropologist. This revelation had shocked him. The love affair between Walter and Dillon's grandmother Gloria-Louie was a closely guarded secret, known only to his mother and grandmother.

In the spring of 1975, Walter came to study and document the culture and history of the Sliammon First Nation peoples. He lived in the community, learned their language and ways of life, and recorded his observations and teachings. He was thirty-one at the time, unmarried, and became attracted to Gloria—a beautiful, seventeen-year-old Sliammon First Nations woman. Dillon's mother told him that Gloria and Walter hid their affair, but Gloria became pregnant in November of that year. Walter decided to leave the Sliammon community in December before Gloria's pregnancy was common knowledge. Gloria had been promised by her parents to a local man, Brett Paul, many years earlier, and Gloria decided to marry Brett rather than bear an illegitimate child.

Dillon looked down at Walter Smith's diary as he mulled over the story his mother, Robbie-Paul Point, had told him. She was the illegitimate daughter of Walter and Gloria, and she had been given the diary by her mother the day she became betrothed to David Point. Neither Brett nor David were aware of the affair with Walter Smith or the two gifts that Walter had given to Gloria to remind her of his great love and affection for her; she had received the gifts the night in December when Walter left the Sliammon community.

Walter couldn't stay. He felt his immediate departure was best so that Gloria could marry Brett and give their child a Native father. The gifts from Walter were placed in a wooden, carved box and hidden away, only to be opened when Gloria felt in the mood to connect with Walter. She would read passages from the handwritten diary and would smile, as the entries rejuvenated her past memories and reminded her of the love they had shared.

The worn diary was one of the gifts from the wooden box. His mother told Dillon that he was now worthy to know the secrets of the diary, and she hoped it would comfort him on his journey to the big city. Dillon was nineteen. After finishing his first year of university in Powell River, he had chosen to take his second year at the University of Victoria on Vancouver Island. His passion to advance his business skills and knowledge of First Nations cultural studies had earned him a scholarship through a Sliammon and University of Victoria joint program.

Life for the Sliammon people was about to dramatically change. The band members had negotiated a new treaty with the government. This treaty required the Tla'amin to take greater control and accept fiscal responsibilities, which meant the band needed educated and competent members. It was an opportunity of a lifetime; with the encouragement of his mother, Dillon apprehensively decided to leave the community to pursue his destiny.

Much of the story about his grandmother and Walter Smith remained unknown. Dillon rubbed the deer-leather binding between his fingers, struggling with thoughts about what other surprises the pages might contain. He wondered if answers to questions he had yearned to know since childhood would be revealed, or if they would remain only in the memory and heart of his mother and Gloria. He wanted to remain in Sliammon to learn the truth of his heritage in the company of his family, but it was too late. He was puzzled why his mother had chosen this particular moment to speak of his family heritage; her answer was that the spirits had told her it was the right time, and he was man enough to handle the truth contained in the diary.

Dillon decided he wasn't ready to unwrap the binding and explore the story, not today anyway. He thought perhaps that his mother was right; it would be a comfort during his forthcoming exciting—and terrifying—journey to Victoria.

⋈

"Hey, guys ... wait for me," Adrianne Padrino yelled, as she waved her arms at a man and teenager sitting on the deck of a thirty-six-foot Grand Banks yacht docked at Granville Island.

The nineteen-year-old woman walked toward the end of the wooden, planked pier. She hadn't combed her hair after a day of swimming at English Bay. Her smile radiated as she approached the well-kept yacht and lithely jumped aboard the swimming platform at the stern of the boat.

"We'd never start without my favorite girl," Adrianne's father replied, turning to greet his daughter. "I'm just getting the barbeque started. I have your favorite, a de-boned leg of lamb, for tonight. How was the beach?" Her father ran a hand through thick, ebony, neck-length hair; his dark anthracite-colored eyes watched his daughter as she walked across the rear deck of the boat.

"Absolutely crazy, Dad … bodies everywhere. The last weekend before school goes back into session brings out the sun worshipers in full force. What did you and Lex do?" she asked, walking toward the galley to see her mother, Lia.

Alexander was her younger brother by three years. Everyone called him Lex.

"Adrianne, come and help with the salad," Lia requested, when she heard her daughter climb down the cabin stairs. "Your dad and Lex were boating around False Creek most of the afternoon. I'd appreciate some company." Lia was a soft-spoken woman with tanned skin, bright topaz eyes, and curly chestnut hair.

"Where's Grandpa Frank?" Adrianne picked up a knife to chop tomatoes.

"He's sitting in the company's office, likely reading the newspaper. You know he loves hanging around that place. It makes him feel like he's still part of the company. I'll send Lex to get him once your dad gets that lamb on the grill."

"Do we have any bookings for Labor Day weekend?" Adrianne reached for a cucumber.

"I know there was a booking for a party of four, but I think I heard your father mutter something about a possible cancellation." Lia looked up from crumbling the feta cheese. "Are you ready to move into the Victoria house tomorrow, Adrianne?"

"It'll be okay, Mom. I'm looking forward to sharing the house with a group of students," Adrianne replied with a smile. "Besides, everyone moves off campus after the first year."

♓

Selina Archie's face was solemn as she sat at the bedside of her mother, Clara-Meyers, in their home overlooking the Salish Sea. Selina had left Sliammon two years previously to move to Victoria to make a name for herself as an artist. At twenty-two, she was talented and determined. Her father had died three years ago, and, with the progression of her mother's terminal lung cancer, Selina was torn about her decision to move away from the family and community.

"Selina," her mother whispered in a barely audible, labored voice, "I have a special gift for you, my daughter. It is time."

"Time…." Selina replied, as a tear formed.

"Yes, time to mend fences with my friend, Gloria-Louie Paul," Clara rasped.

"Mom."

"No, Selina … listen to me." Clara inhaled a shallow breath. "A family secret I promised your father on his deathbed that I would never reveal."

"What secret?" Selina leaned over to hold her ear close to her mother's mouth.

Clara labored to breathe before she replied, her strained eyes fixated on her daughter. "Time because Dillon Point is leaving the Sliammon … just as you did … to create a better life."

"What secret, Mother? What does Dillon Point have to do with it?"

Clara inhaled with a sucking sound. "Take the jewelry box on the dresser. Your father made a necklace for you." Clara's eyes widened as she struggled to speak. "It's time to give it to you, I … I …."

Selina glanced over at the carved wooden box. "Is the secret about the necklace or jewelry box, Mother?"

"It's a secret, not even Cecilia knows." Clara closed her eyes.

"Mom." Tears streamed down Selina's face. "Mom!"

One

Dillon rose at five thirty to catch the bus to the Powell River airport, even though his flight wasn't scheduled to leave until after nine. His mother heard him gather his things. She began to cry when he kissed her goodbye at the front door.

This was his first flight. He was exhilarated when the plane charged the runway. He watched his village shrink into a dot as the aircraft rose from the runway and gently turned south toward Vancouver International Airport—the first stop—on his trip to Victoria.

The sun was hot as it pierced the mid-day scattered clouds, as Dillon finally got off a bus at his final stop, and walked a few blocks to an address on Charles Street. He stopped outside a two-story house, with freshly painted, green, wood siding, a wide wooden staircase to a covered front porch, white-detailed window frames, and a red, shingled roof. A manicured front lawn added to the charm and character of the Victoria home. A sun-bleached red Jeep parked in the side driveway implied that at least one of his roommates was there. He pulled his suitcase onto the porch and rang the front doorbell.

"Just a moment." Dillon heard laughter and footsteps creak across a wooden floor.

"Hello, I'm Josh. My, my, you look exhausted. Come in … come in." Josh didn't move, staring at Dillon. "Niki, one of our roomies is here."

"I'm Dillon Point." He grabbed the handle of his pull suitcase.

"Hi, I'm Niki," a blond, fair-skinned man appeared in the doorway. "You're the first to arrive."

Dillon pulled the suitcase into the foyer and slipped off his backpack. "Where's the bathroom? It's been a long trip."

"Around the corner here and through the sitting room. It's under the staircase just before the kitchen." Josh was still eyeing Dillon.

"He's better-looking than I thought he would be, Josh," Niki whispered, as Dillon disappeared around the corner.

"Don't get any ideas, Niki. I don't like to share … but he sure is hot, though. I love his hair in that little pony."

Dillon found Josh and Niki sitting on a sofa watching a cooking show on television when he returned from the bathroom. "I should unpack. Where is my room?"

"Both bedrooms are upstairs. Niki and I share the large master bedroom on the main floor. Since you're here first, Dillon, you get to choose which room you'd like," Josh replied. "I think the room on the left side of the hallway has a better view of the ocean. Other than that, they have identical layouts."

"Okay, thanks. We'll visit later."

A worn, wooden staircase led directly upstairs from the front foyer. The years of rental tenants showed on the walls as Dillon climbed the narrow steps. Boards creaked under his weight. The stairs led to a landing with a door at each end of the narrow hallway. He opened the door on his right a crack for a quick peek inside. There was a bare double-sized bed, with sheets and blankets placed on the mattress. A shabby green dresser, a bedside table, and a lamp lined the wall toward the end of the room. An oak rolltop banker's desk, a wooden chair, and a silk tree were crowded into an alcove next to a door with green and red stained-glass squares.

Dillon left his suitcase in the hall. He separated the blind louvers covering the window. It overlooked the neighboring house and the driveway below. He released the blinds.

Dillon grabbed his suitcase and walked down the short hallway into the second bedroom. The room was furnished the same as the other room, except the layout was reversed. This room had an old cream-colored brocade-framed mirror and the walls were covered in remnants of scotch tape and tiny pinholes. He pushed the blinds apart; the view was of the neighboring house's roof and a garden below.

Dillon opened the balcony door and caught a glimpse of the ocean. He closed the door, pitched his backpack on the bare mattress, and went to take a closer look at the bathroom.

It was a shared walk-through bathroom with entrance doors from each bedroom. Dillon checked that each door lock worked and, satisfied, he returned to his chosen bedroom.

He pulled up the wood-framed window to let air into the hot and stuffy room. He sat on the edge of his mattress.

The doorbell announced a visitor. Dillon heard Josh's high-pitched voice. "I've got it." Thumping feet ran across the floorboards below.

Dillon put his suitcase on the bed and began to unpack.

"Hey, Dillon, come down and meet Adrianne." It was Josh's unmistakable voice.

Dillon walked to the center of the hallway, and looked down the stairs before descending. He saw a slim brunette with shoulder-length hair pulling her suitcase into the foyer.

"Hi, I'm Adrianne Padrino." The brunette closed the front door. "Josh told me on the phone you guys lived here last year and you needed two new roommates. I'm looking forward to meeting everyone."

"You and Dillon Point will live here with Niki and me. We're excited to have you, Adrianne," Josh said, as Dillon reached the bottom of the staircase.

"Hi, I'm Dillon," he said shyly.

Niki turned towards the sitting room. "We can get to know each other better after you both are settled. Josh has agreed to cook tonight. He's quite the Italian chef. Come down for drinks when you're unpacked. Josh wants to see the end of this cooking program first. Adrianne, you have the room on the right upstairs."

Adrianne and Dillon started upstairs, as Niki settled at the end of the sofa by Josh's feet.

"I'll take your suitcase, Adrianne," Dillon offered.

"That's so sweet. I've a bit more stuff in the trunk of my car. I'll get it and meet you upstairs."

Dillon stood at the bottom of the staircase and stared at the exotic girl's toned body, dressed in a light summer skirt and halter-top, as she walked outside. He grabbed her bag and left it on her unmade bed.

He returned to his room to unpack. His bedroom was still hot. Dillon yanked off his shirt, dropped it onto the dresser, and walked to the window to pull it up further. A few bags dropped on the bedroom floor next door. He turned when he heard a bathroom door open at the end of the room.

Adrianne kicked Dillon's bathroom door partially closed, and he heard her sit on the toilet.

"Have you been here long, Dillon?" The toilet flushed and water ran in the sink. "You got any towels in there, Dillon? I haven't unpacked mine." She pushed open his bathroom door with her foot, shaking her wet hands, and noticed Dillon hadn't unpacked his bags, either.

"Air-dry will have to do. It's like being on the boat." She looked round his room. "Is that all the stuff you brought?"

"That's it. I had a long trip and couldn't bring anything else. I'll buy what I need when I figure it out. I've no idea what the weather's like here, but I think I'll need cooler clothes," Dillon replied. "I live up the coast by Powell River. It's colder and windier there."

Adrianne studied the attractive, muscular young man with light-golden skin, long black hair tied in a ponytail, narrow eyebrows, and a pronounced nose.

"I know it rains a lot more up the coast. My parents' company has a business branch in Comox, and I've been there a number of times. It's beautiful and peaceful on that part of the West Coast." She paused, still studying his physique. "I'll let you get settled. I need to unpack, too." She disappeared through the bathroom.

Dillon started to pull things from his suitcase. He wondered about sharing a bathroom with Adrianne. He hadn't lived with girls before, other than his mother and grandmother. His heart pounded at the thought. He wasn't sure if it was nerves, stress, or something else. She was attractive, and her body and alluring eyes were hard to ignore. She was unlike any young woman he had met, and his reaction to her was something he had never experienced before, either.

Although Adrianne had more to unpack, she was finished before Dillon. She joined him in his room as he started to make his bed.

Adrianne walked to the other side of the bed to help him pull the bottom mattress sheet tight.

"You got a computer in that stuff?" she asked.

"No. The community center at home has a couple of computers for everyone to share. I studied and did my assignments there, but I'll have to buy one now." As he tossed part of the top sheet in her direction, his heart began to pound again when he inhaled the scent of her subtle perfume.

"I can help you choose one if you like. You should get a Mac, like mine." She passed him a blanket.

"We had Windows XP at the center. We never have the new version of anything." Dillon bent over to tuck the blanket under the mattress and glanced at Adrianne's shapely legs.

"That's not a problem. The Mac is fully compatible; most of the main programs will work the same. We should meet at the campus store tomorrow, and we can look together."

"What's taking so long?" Josh yelled from downstairs. "It's time to party and get acquainted."

Dillon stepped toward the door. "I guess we'd better join the others downstairs."

"Niki and I are having white wine. Would you like a chardonnay or something else?" Josh asked when the new roommates appeared. "I know it's early, but it is Labor Day and we party when we're not studying. School starts this week; then work, work, work."

"Wine is okay, but do you have something less oaky tasting, like a Sauvignon Blanc?" Adrianne asked. She put her cell on the coffee table and sat in a tub chair.

"Certainly." Niki got off the sofa. "We have red, too, if you prefer. Dillon?"

"I'll have the same as Adrianne." He sat in a leather chair by the window.

"Two blancs, then," Niki called from the kitchen. "Dillon, tell us what brings you to Victoria. Josh told me you're going into second year."

"I'm studying business administration and First Nations studies. I finished my first year in Powell River, and won a scholarship to take my second year at the University of Victoria. I want to bring new skills to my community. When a new treaty between my people, the Sliammon, and the government comes into effect, I want to be part of the financial accountability and local stewardship." He watched Niki pour the wine. "This is my first time living away from home."

"How do you like your room? Niki and I spent this summer fixing up a few things in the house, and we added a silk plant in each of your rooms. We thought it made the place more inviting," Josh said, finishing his wine. "Niki, could you refresh my wine, please?"

"You were right about the view," Dillon replied, as Niki handed Adrianne her wine.

"Can you cook, Dillon?" Niki handed Dillon his wine.

"I can cook on a stovetop, but I prefer an open fire or barbeque. I am good at cooking seafood and deer steaks," Dillon answered.

"I'm Greek, so I make dishes like lamb, spinach pie, and Greek salad," Adrianne said, sipping her wine. "I'm in my sophomore year and taking business administration, too. I also want to study tourism. I hope to take over my dad's diving company one day. I have a passion for the ocean."

"The ocean's a passion of mine, too, Adrianne. I grew up on the waters around my village. The Sliammon have lived off the land for centuries. Understanding our environment is key to our survival and way of life." Dillon took a sip of wine. "What about you two, Niki?"

"Josh and I are in our second year of the nursing program at Camosun College. We met in our first year, and were attracted to each other the moment we met. We do everything together, and spend a lot of time at Starbucks and the library. It's a tough course load and demands hours of labs and assignments. Don't expect that you will see much of us during the week."

"What happened to the roommates you had last year? This is a great place. It's better than most of the rentals I saw on the Internet," Adrianne asked, as she studied the two young men who held hands on the sofa.

"We had two girls last time." Josh shook his head. "I think living with gay guys became a problem. I don't know for sure, but I think maybe their boyfriends had the problem, not the girls. Anyway, we stay to ourselves most of the time." Josh stood up.

"I'm doing Italian tonight, so I'd better get started. Everyone will have to make their own meals during the week, and maybe we can alternate cooking on the weekends. Come, Niki, I need help."

"Before you go, I want to take a photo. Dillon, you join the guys." Adrianne grabbed her cell from the coffee table.

⋇

This was Dillon's first experience with alcohol. He had avoided that vice after seeing friends wasted after drinking at bars in Powell River. The white wine loosened his natural reservation, and he became more comfortable talking to Adrianne as the evening progressed. She had her share of wine, too. They finished a second bottle and part of a third before they realized Josh and Niki had retreated to their bedroom.

"Some party. I hope we don't party every night … I'll never get my work done." Dillon slurred his words slightly, looking at Adrianne as the pair lay on the wooden floor. "I like Josh and Niki."

"They seem like fun. I don't know why they don't study here, but that means it will be quiet for us." Adrianne looked back at Dillon, studying his face with inquiring eyes.

Dillon blushed for a moment, then suddenly blurted out. "My mom gave me a diary yesterday that belonged to my grandfather. My family heritage is a mystery to me. My mother never spoke of it, even though I asked many times when I was growing up. She said I was man enough now to know the truth about the family story. I want to know about the past, but then again, I don't." Dillon rambled on. "She told me she was an illegitimate baby, and that my grandmother married my grandfather to keep it a secret." Dillon paused, and looked into Adrianne's eyes. "Would you like to read the diary with me?"

"Sure, Dillon, if you'd like me to. Are you sure you want to share it with me? It sounds private."

"I need a friend; someone I can to talk to about whatever's written. I like you, Adrianne, and feel comfortable with you … is that okay?" He anxiously held his breath while he waited for her reply.

"Yes, of course. I like you, too."

Dillon got off the floor and held out his hand to help her to her feet as she asked, "Have you read any of the diary yet?"

"No, but I've thought about it most of the time since I left home. I can't imagine what's written inside that I need to be a man to understand. I found my chosen guardian in a dream—the spirit of the wolf—when I was twelve. That's when the village boys go away from the village for their spiritual training at puberty and learn to be good men. I was considered a man by the Sliammon community when I returned, so I don't know why my mother waited until now to tell me about the diary." His head spun as they stumbled upstairs.

Adrianne sat on the edge of Dillon's bed as he found his backpack and pulled the diary from the front pouch, placing the book beside her.

Adrianne picked up the journal and undid the leather tie. She opened the front cover. A photograph fell to the floor. "I'm sorry."

Dillon slowly bent over to pick up the picture and peered at it for a moment. "I think this is a picture of my Grandmother Gloria-Louie Paul when she was young," he said. "This white man must be Walter Smith. It is his diary."

Adrianne took the picture from Dillon and examined it. "Your grandmother was young when this was taken. Walter's quite a bit older. When do think this was taken?"

"Nineteen seventy-five, I believe. My mother said Walter came to the Sliammon community to document our heritage and language that year. You can see a totem pole in the background. What are they holding in their hands?"

Adrianne brought the photograph closer. "I can't make it out. Maybe it's something like a locket." She put the photograph on the bed and turned her attention to the diary.

The pages were tattered. Adrianne was careful when she opened the book to look at the first page. She flipped through a few pages. Some were torn and others were smudged from handling over the years. "Well, Dillon, we certainly won't be the first to read what's written in here," she remarked. "I'd rather start this another time. I'm wiped out."

"It's been a long day for me, too. Maybe we can find time tomorrow after dinner. We better buy groceries, too."

"I'll pick up something at a supermarket on the way home and make dinner for both of us." Adrianne closed the diary. "Tomorrow," she said, and placed the diary onto the mattress next to Dillon.

He picked up the photograph. He watched Adrianne walk through the bathroom corridor and heard the bathroom door close behind her. He sat quietly for a moment, slid off the bed, and placed the black and white photograph between the glass and frame on the mirror that was hung over the dresser.

Two

Dillon, always an early riser, had finished his cereal and toast before seven on his first day of school. He didn't feel too bad considering the amount of wine he had consumed the night before. He didn't hear anyone else up when he left the house to catch the campus-bound bus.

The university was a twenty-minute bus ride northwest of his house. Dillon was energized as he walked around to get oriented. It was a community unto itself, with over seventeen thousand undergraduates. Dillon was daunted by the number of students; his Sliammon village had fewer than four hundred people.

Dillon's first class started at nine thirty. Adrianne had promised to meet him at the campus bookstore an hour before class. He checked the time on his cell phone; he had another thirty minutes to find the building. His thoughts turned to Adrianne, and the new campus experience faded into the back of his mind. She was beautiful. He knew he had been instantly attracted to her.

She seemed to have her act together and was easy to talk to. He was impatient to see her and checked the time again. He found his destination wasn't far from the bus loop, and sat on a bench outside the bookstore to wait for Adrianne. He opened his backpack, found his course and textbook requirements list, and quickly scanned the information. He had to purchase a computer as well, all before his first class. He glanced at his cell phone again. The line of students waiting for the bookstore to open was growing.

Adrianne showed as promised. "Hey, Dillon," she called. She walked over to where he was seated. "I was going to give you a ride this morning, but you'd already left when my alarm went off."

"That's okay. It hadn't started to rain when I left, and I enjoyed the bus ride anyway. I didn't know you were going to drive every day. Parking's expensive, isn't it?" he asked, rising from the concrete bench as the bookstore opened and the line of students dissolved inside.

"I won't drive every day, but I have to lug all my textbooks back to the house so I thought the car might be easier. My first class is at nine thirty, so we'd better get started. The bookstore's a zoo the first week of classes," she said, as they entered the glass swinging door. "We'd better get the text books first. The computer section won't be as busy. Do you have your course list?"

"Sure do."

She took the list from Dillon and skimmed through the requirements. "We've got two classes together. Let's grab those books first." She snatched his hand. "Come on," she said, and darted toward a row of bookshelves at the back of the store. "They're already out of the used ones, so we have to buy these," she said, pulling texts from the shelf and handing them to Dillon to carry. "I have to go to the commerce section, and you need the indigenous studies area." She pointed to the corner on the opposite side of the store. "Find what you need and meet me at the computer counter at the back of the store."

Dillon juggled the handful of books and headed directly toward the computer department. "Can I leave these texts here for a couple of minutes? I'll be back to buy a computer once I get the rest of my books," he asked.

"Sure, no problem," the clerk replied. "First time at UVic?"

"Yeah," Dillon replied over his shoulder, as he rushed to the area as directed by Adrianne. "I've got a class in forty-five minutes."

Dillon met Adrianne at the computer counter, his arms loaded with course materials. She had reached the counter first, and had already spoken to the computer technician.

"I've ordered what you need, Dillon: a MacBook Air and the Office pack. Is that all right? I thought we'd run out of time otherwise." She smiled at his efforts to carry the course materials without dropping the whole lot onto the floor. "You can pay here, and we can pick up the computer stuff after class."

"Great, thanks." Dillon put his armful of materials on the counter. He fished out his wallet, extracted a new credit card, and handed it to the clerk.

"The young lady asked if I could keep everything here until you come back later around noon. I'll note on that on the receipt. I promise to have the computer set up by the time you return. She's told me which apps to install."

"Thanks for your help …." Dillon paused to look for the man's name tag.

"Bruce," the clerk interjected, handing Dillon the receipt.

"Bruce ... great to meet you, Bruce. I'm Dillon Point." He shoved the receipt into his pocket.

"Come on, Dillon. We have 'Professional Skills Development' together across campus. I hate being late."

☓

"Sorry I'm late, Amy. I had to stop off at Vanessa Jewelers to have gold jewelry appraised that my mother gave me this weekend." Selina was breathless when she arrived at the counter of Munro's Books. "I'll need a valuation before I can cover them under my home insurance policy."

"That's okay, we haven't been busy yet. How's your mom?"

"Not so good. I think I should've stayed, but the doctor couldn't give me a timeframe. He said that she didn't have much time left. The cancer has spread, but I just can't just sit and wait. It's awful, but her sister in-law Cecilia is spending what time she can with Mom. Mom knows her time is near. That's why she gave me her family jewelry. I dread every call on my cell these days."

"Everyone at Munro's is here for you if you need anything, Selina. I know you have an art exhibition later this month, too. Don't get stressed over it all."

"Thanks. I'll put my stuff in a locker and join you in a moment." Selina hurried toward the employees' room in the back.

☓

Firth Coin and Rarities was situated on Store Street in a two-story commercial building built in the late 19th century during the Klondike gold rush days. Hamish Firth had selected the tourist-rich area for his shop, which bordered on Market Square, when he moved to Victoria in the spring of 1980. He was making a fresh pot of coffee in the back room when he heard the tinkle of his doorbell announcing the arrival of a customer.

Hamish was fifty-five years old, of Scottish heritage, and almost six feet tall. His full graying hair and eyebrows, along with the lines on his light-complexioned face, showed his age despite his thin-framed body.

"Good afternoon, Monica. It sure is miserable outside. Come, get out of the rain," Hamish said to the middle-aged woman who he had known for years. "I understand you have a unique piece of jewelry you want me to look at."

"It was dropped off this morning. I believe its value may be much more than the workmanship and gold content. I'd like you to take a look and let me know if the piece has historical value." Monica pulled a carved wooden box from a brown-fiber carry bag. "My customer wants an appraisal for insurance. Can you have it back to me tomorrow?"

Hamish opened the box with a West Coast First Nations carving engraved on the lid. He stared silently, his hazel eyes fixated as though he was in a trance. He leaned over to take a closer look. He suddenly stopped, regained his thoughts, and glanced up at Monica. "There are two pieces in here, Monica. Do you want an opinion on both?" he asked, as she placed a sheet of paper on the counter.

"No, thank you, Hamish. I'm interested in the necklace. I didn't want to separate the pieces as there is a slot for the gold key in the box. Please sign this receipt, and I'll be on my way."

Hamish studied the paperwork for a moment, noted that both pieces were listed, and signed the document. He closed the lid of the wooden box. "Usual fee?" He pushed the paperwork toward Monica.

"Yes, of course, Hamish. Let me know when you're finished." Hamish watched Monica dart out of the store toward a parking lot across the street.

He took the box and bag into his office in the back. He placed the fiber bag at the foot of his wooden desk and put the carved box on his desk. He scribbled "Selina Archie - 1226 Rudlin Street" in a notebook.

Hamish gazed at the two pieces for a moment before he carefully lifted out the necklace. Three ingots of solid gold dangled from the center of a wide gold chain. The ingots were long and narrow and stamped with unusual round markings. There was a square stamp bearing an "M" with a small case "o" at the end of each ingot. He continued to study the ingots and located another round stamp with a "P." To the right of that mark, there was a larger stamped "V."

He exhaled when he noticed a crowned stamp bearing the monogram PVS. He knew the significance of the monogram from long years of research: the Spanish quinto minted during the reign of King Philip IV.

Hamish rubbed one of the ingot bars between his fingers. He put the necklace back into the box. How had Selina Archie come by the necklace? It was a question he meant to have answered.

The coffee aroma interrupted his concentration. He got up and poured a cup. Leaving it black, he sat back down, took a sip, and reached for the golden key. It had its own specific indention in the center of the box, surrounded by the necklace. In all his years, he had never seen anything like it before.

The key was definitely of West Coast Native design, with a whale fluke at one end. One side was flat and the other studded with small diamonds, set in the same-carat gold as the quinto ingots.

Hamish replaced the whale key and leaned back in his office chair. He took another sip of coffee, pondering the situation. He needed to know the origin of the quinto ingots, but couldn't be personally involved.

The back room of the coin shop office was veiled in silence as Hamish considered a course of action. He finally picked up the telephone.

♓

Adrianne was in the kitchen cutting boneless chicken breasts into cubes while Dillon watched. "We're making chicken souvlaki and Greek salad," she said. "I like to put these chicken pieces on a wooden stick mixed with vegetables and barbeque them, but we don't have a barbeque so I'll sauté them."

"There are lots of things here that we don't use at home," Dillon remarked. He picked up a bottle of extra-virgin olive oil. "Extra-virgin. How do you become extra-virgin?"

Adrianne laughed. "Don't just stand there; cut this cucumber into small pieces." She handed the knife to Dillon. "When we eat at my place, we use lamb instead of chicken, but lamb is expensive on a student's budget."

"I've never had lamb, but I'd like to try it. We have deer, goat, and bear at home. What's that stuff?" Dillon asked, watching Adrianne pull the lid off a plastic container.

"Feta cheese." She crumbled a handful into a bowl. "Bear—that would be interesting." She glanced over at Dillon. "I saw you trying out your new computer earlier. What do you think?"

"The Mac system is sure different than Windows XP. It'll take me a while to figure it out. The touch pad is cool, but I need practice." Dillon watched Adrianne work on the salad. "Need more help?"

"Yes, please. Cut those tomatoes into pieces and put them in the bowl. It took time for me to learn the Mac too, but everyone says it's the machine for students these days … it's light and fast." Adrianne paused, working on her salad.

"Hey, Josh, do you know the password to connect the computers to the network in the house? Dillon and I need to sort that out today." Adrianne spoke loudly over the music playing in the sitting room.

"I've no idea. Niki's the computer guy. I'll ask him." Josh turned down the music on the MP4 player.

"What are you going to cook for us tomorrow, Dillon?" Adrianne asked, as she returned to preparing the salad.

"I don't know yet. I'm more comfortable cooking outdoors than inside. I'll have to think about it. I haven't bought anything." He paused and sighed. "I guess I should've thought about that when we stopped at the supermarket earlier."

"We were in a hurry after we picked up all your stuff from the bookstore." Adrianne turned on the stove and placed a skillet on the front element.

"It's great you invited us to eat with you tonight," Niki said, as he and Josh entered the kitchen. "The secured network name is 'Rossbay' with a capital 'R,' and the password is 'togetherness,' all lowercase. Do you need me to help you set up the computers?"

"Thanks, Niki, I'll try it myself first later. Is there anything you or Josh can't eat?" Adrianne poured extra-virgin olive oil in the pan.

"We'll eat and try anything. We're becoming home chefs, so we're adventurous with our diets." Niki placed his arm around Josh.

Dillon glanced over at the two young men. He wasn't sure what he thought about their open relationship, and it was too awkward to ask. "Dinner looks ready. I'll put the salad out."

"Do you have a busy schedule this term, Dillon?" Niki asked, while he watched Adrianne scoop chicken into a bowl.

"I'm taking a business minor with undergrad indigenous studies. My first class begins tomorrow. I want to see if the professor can help me find my grandfather, Walter Smith. My mother said he was a professor at the university in the seventies."

Josh gave Dillon a curious look. "I didn't think there were First Nations professors back then. I mean …."

"That's okay," Dillon said. "My grandfather was white, not First Nations." Dillon repeated the tale of his childhood and the diary.

"Sounds mysterious to me." Josh raised his eyebrow.

"I don't know what the big deal is, but I guess I'll find out." Dillon took a deep breath. "Let's eat."

♓

A knock shattered Hamish Firth's thoughts as he sat in his back office. He looked at his watch as another knock on the glass door drew him from his seat.

"I'm coming." Hamish turned on the lights in the front room. He saw a heavyset figure through the front door glass, huddled under the covered front entrance.

Hamish unlocked the shop door. "Eduardo, you're later than I expected."

"The Tsawwassen ferry terminal was packed, and I missed a sailing. Damn, it's wet." Eduardo's Mexican accent was thick. "I hit rush hour in Vancouver. I need a drink, amigo." Eduardo's damp, black mustache accentuated his round face.

"I've got scotch in the back. Give me your wet coat and have a seat." Hamish helped Eduardo take off his coat. "I'll take your cap, too, my friend."

Eduardo sat in a brown leather easy chair while Hamish hung the wet coat on a peg behind the door. "You said you've a job for me, but didn't say why you can't handle it yourself."

Hamish pulled a scotch bottle from a cupboard above the coffee maker. "This will warm you up, Eduardo." He poured two double scotches into crystal glasses. "This job is more suited to your talents." Hamish handed Eduardo his drink and sat behind his desk. "The job's here in town, and I can't be connected in any way."

"Delicate?" Eduardo took a welcome sip of scotch. "What do you want me to do?"

"I need information about this gold necklace." Hamish opened the wooden carved box that sat on his desk. "I need to know where these gold ingots came from. I want you to get the information from the owner, a Selina Archie. I wrote down her address for you." He pulled a slip of paper from under the carved box and pushed it across the desk.

Eduardo glanced over at the necklace. He focused his dark, coal-black eyes on Hamish. "Just information?"

"The information is more important than the necklace, but I want the necklace as well."

"I can understand the necklace, but why the information?"

"Let's just say it's a pet project of mine. An historical mystery."

Eduardo shifted his eyes back to the contents of the box. "What's that thing worth anyway?"

"I'd say in the range of thirty-five grand. The key is irrelevant." Hamish took another sip of his scotch as he studied his friend's reaction. "I'll give you ten grand if you get me the information and the necklace. Easy money for a couple nights' effort."

Eduardo picked up the slip of paper and held out his glass. "Ten? Got another shot of scotch?"

"Yes, ten. I agreed to return these items to the jewelry store that's doing the appraisal for Ms. Archie tomorrow. You can go from there." Hamish refilled Eduardo's glass and his own. "I know only what I've told you about this Archie woman."

"This isn't what I usually do, Hamish. I get your product from legitimate sources, but don't ask questions about my suppliers."

"So you tell me, but you're a scrounger and you know people with useful skills in your line of business, Eduardo."

"I should stay at your place so there is no record I'm here." Eduardo gulped down the remaining scotch.

"I agree. I'll close up and meet you there."

♓

"It's turned into a miserable night." Adrianne followed Dillon into his bedroom. He turned on his bedside light, and Adrianne walked to the bedroom window to gaze out. "Do you want a ride tomorrow? I have 'Fundamentals of Marketing' at eight. You'll be drenched if this downpour continues."

"I'm used to the rain, but I'd appreciate the ride." Dillon put his backpack on the bed. "Can you help me set up the wireless network on my computer? We can read some of my diary afterwards, if you'd like." He pulled his new computer and the diary from the bag and put them on the bed.

Adrianne turned away from the window. "Here, I'll show you." She opened the laptop. "You should put a user password on this, Dillon." She keyed in the home network password. "We'll do the same thing tomorrow at school, and you'll have wireless access at the university."

"I'll play with it later." Dillon pushed the laptop to the bottom of the bed and picked up the diary. He propped up his pillow at the headboard. "You might as well join me." He patted the bed.

Adrianne grabbed Dillon's second pillow and settled beside him. He moved himself closer to Adrianne, untied the leather string, and opened the diary. He noticed a scribbled note, smudged and faded, on the inside front cover. Dillon read it aloud:

No words can express the sorrow of leaving you, my love. You said you understand, but that doesn't ease the pain. I leave you this diary of our time together; the events are burned into my soul and being. I hope you find comfort within. With all my love, Walter.

Dillon was tense, unsure if it was because Adrianne lay close to him or because of what he might discover in the diary. He turned to the first entry. Adrianne intently followed the careful well-formed handwriting as Dillon read the passages.

Monday May 5th 1975;

Just arrived in Sliammon village, less than two miles north of Powell River. Larry Louie will be my translator and language teacher during my stay here. It's late afternoon, and the spectacular flight from Victoria took about two hours, including the stop in Vancouver. I was invited to stay at Larry's home and given a room in the back. Larry's wife Faye-Elliott doesn't speak English, but their seventeen-year-old daughter, Gloria, has good command of the language. I've made my first entries in my research notebook, and described my first native salmon meal, an outdoor celebration of my visit. I look forward to tomorrow.

Tuesday May 6th 1975;

The Sliammon people call themselves 'Tla'amin.' It is pronounced 'Kla Ah Men' in the Coastal Salish language of mainland Comox. The village is on the rocky and sandy shores of Georgia Strait. It has a mild and rainy climate, as attested to by today's light drizzle. Western Red cedar, Douglas fir, Sitka spruce, and Western hemlock trees dominate the forests. There are a few broad-leaved maples and red alder, but the Arbutus trees are the most interesting with their reddish and smooth-textured bark. I was treated to fresh, barbequed yellow-eyed rockfish tonight. I learned that 'ɫɛɫɛnƏm' means barbecuing fish.

Dillon skipped a few pages:

Sunday May 11th 1975;

I spent most of the day with Gloria Louie. She said the Sliammon people have a strong sense of community and are taught social behavior at a young age. A person's behavior, reputation, and the status of one's family are of prime importance. Gloria said traditional marriages take place after puberty, but the man must be successful to support a wife before he can marry. The decision about marriage is made by the girl's parents. Marriage combines both families, and they cooperate economically. Brett Paul has been selected as Gloria's future husband and her parents expect her to marry next spring.

Dillon closed the diary. "Gloria-Louie Paul is my grandmother." He thought for a moment. "In 1975 she was seventeen. I wonder how old Walter Smith would've been."

"Is Walter Smith still alive, Dillon?" Adrianne asked.

Dillon was again lost in thought and didn't answer.

"We can read more tomorrow. Maybe you will learn more about him," she said. "Perhaps your professor can tell you about Walter, too."

Three

Eduardo Dominguez sat in his black Escalade down the street from Selina Archie's home. None of the houses on the street had private driveways.

A man in his late twenties left the yellow, wood-clad house from the basement suite around seven. He dashed through the rain to a white Fiesta and exited the street at the other end. It was almost eight, and the heavy rain had not subsided.

Suddenly his patience was rewarded. A woman stepped onto the front porch from inside the house, and locked the door. Eduardo turned on the windshield wipers to get a clearer view of the woman who was short and looked in her early twenties. She began to walk in his direction. A raincoat and hoodie covered her head and a portion of her face.

He squinted, but couldn't distinctly make out her features. It appeared she had First Nations characteristics. She was on the other side of the street. He crouched down as she rushed past to her destination. He watched her in his rearview mirror as she turned the corner toward Pandora Avenue, a busy artery with public transit.

Eduardo waited until nine to see if anyone else appeared. He dialed a number on his cell phone, and pulled out from his parking space as the phone rang his intended party.

♓

Hamish pressed the door buzzer at the doorway to Vanessa Jewelers. Monica looked up from behind the glass counter in the shop and pressed the security release.

"As promised, Monica, I've completed my appraisal." Hamish placed the brown fiber bag on the counter.

"Come to the back, Hamish, and tell me your findings." Monica pushed a swing door to allow Hamish to pass behind the counter into an office in the back. "I appreciate your promptness." Hamish pulled an envelope from his coat pocket and placed it on the desk. "My invoice and written appraisal."

Monica removed the wooden box from the bag and placed it on her desk. She opened the box and checked the contents. She extracted a folder from a wooden tray on the desk. She withdrew a document and handed it to Hamish. "Please sign and date the return receipt. Is the necklace of historical value, as I suspected?"

"It sure is," Hamish answered. "The long strips of gold are 22-carat ingots made in 1659 in Mexico City by, I believe, the Spaniards. They have the monogram 'PVS' that was minted for Philip IV. They are associated with the 'quinto del rey,' a lucrative royal tax requiring everyone to pay the king the equivalent of one-fifth the value of all their income and assets. The ingots have a stamped 'V,' indicating their weight equaled five Spanish ounces. The two large stampings are of the obverse rim of an eight escudo coin piece, a Spanish colonial coin. Those types of escudos were minted in Mexico and

Bogotá." Hamish took a breath and then continued. "I don't know how your client got hold of these ingots. The only documented source of ingots like these on this continent came from a Spanish galleon, the Santa Regio, which was discovered off the Florida Keys in the early 1970s. I called the necklace the 'quinto necklace' in my appraisal. It was difficult to provide an appraisal due to its uniqueness, but I valued the necklace at thirty-five thousand dollars."

"Intriguing, Hamish. What about the gold key?" Monica opened the envelope.

"As you instructed, I didn't examine it with any detail. It doesn't have the same historical context, other than that it's made with the same grade of gold as the necklace. It is unusual because its design has a flat side. The diamonds are of good clarity and grade. You'll have to set the appraisal on that piece."

"Fair enough." Monica scanned the documents she had removed from the envelope. "Your fee seems reasonable, considering the detail you provided. I'll settle up at month's end."

He signed and dated the receipt document. "Thanks for your business, Monica. Let me know if I can be of further service."

⋈

Dillon attended his first "Aboriginal Peoples of BC" class, and decided to talk to the professor after the lecture. He waited for the hall to clear, walked to the front of the amphitheater, and introduced himself.

"I'm from the Sliammon village, north of Powell River. I'm interested in locating a Walter Smith, who was documenting our culture and language in the mid-1970s. I wonder if you could help me."

"I know of him, but I have never met the man. He was a professor here at the university years ago. He's authored a number of books."

"Are you able to obtain information about his whereabouts or how I might contact him? I've a personal interest in his time at Sliammon."

"I'll see what I can do, Dillon. I'm glad to see you taking an interest in your heritage."

"Thank you, Sir. My heritage is important to me."

⨯

The rain eased off by the time Eduardo reached a construction site in Rock Bay, a suburb north of Victoria's downtown core. A building had been demolished to make room for a new high-rise condo development that would have a spectacular view of the Gorge, a strip of waterway connected to the Victoria harbour.

It was situated close to a drug-addiction rehabilitation building complex on Ellice Street. Eduardo had been told that the Rock Bay establishment had addicts looking for an easy buck. He had a meeting arranged with Chaz, a youth willing to do a break-and-enter for cash.

Eduardo had been assured Chaz was able to perform the assigned job and that, for substantial remuneration, his drug addiction wouldn't interfere. Eduardo trusted his source, and since there wasn't time to make alternate arrangements, he proceeded with caution.

A cold front had pushed out the rain. A chilly fog began to rise from the warm waterways and ocean, quickly engulfing the edge of the waterline as Eduardo waited for Chaz. It was late afternoon. Eduardo listened in the eerie mist, surrounded by a stand of trees, for the footsteps of his guest. His eyes darted around, searching, and then he heard the telltale sounds.

Footsteps came closer—not hurried but steady—and got louder.

"Hey man, you Eduardo?" A male voice pierced the thick mist. "Mason sent me."

Eduardo saw a scrawny, anemic-looking figure emerge from the fog. He couldn't clearly make out the features of the man dressed in a hooded coat that partially concealed his face. "You think you can keep your shit together if I give you a job?"

"Mason told ya I could, right?"

"Mason isn't paying you, and there's no second chance. Can you leave the drugs at home?" Eduardo asked sharply, as he inspected the unshaven youth with wiry, dirty-blond hair.

"Man, I'm in rehab. Ya want me to do a B&E?"

"You'll be on your own, and I don't want anyone hurt." Eduardo considered whether the kid was capable of doing the job. "It must be tonight."

"Piece of cake, man. What's the deal?"

"I want a gold necklace that has three long, dangling, gold bars with stamped patterns. I also need to know where the woman got the necklace. The target should be bringing it home tonight. That's it."

Chaz looked at fat Mexican. "You're not the B&E type," he said sarcastically. "What's it worth to ya?"

Eduardo considered the price for a moment. "Five hundred cash … only if you get the necklace and the information from the woman."

"Do I meet ya here later?"

"No. Here at seven tomorrow night."

"I want somethin' now—say fifty in small bills."

Eduardo hesitated, pulled his wallet from his rear pants pockets. "I have thirty bucks. That's it."

"Okay. Where's the job?"

Eduardo fished in his pocket for a scrap of paper. "Here's the address and your down payment." He handed over the cash and piece of paper. "Time's moving on. I'll take you a block from the place and drop you off. You're on your own from there." Eduardo grabbed the kid's arm. "Don't screw with me, amigo."

Chaz grinned and stuffed the cash and piece of paper into his pocket. "Not a chance, man."

"There's one more thing you should know. There's a guy living in the basement suite. He drives a white Ford Fiesta. You may want to watch for him."

"And the girl?"

"She lives in the main house. I think she takes transit. I don't think there is anyone else, but I can't be sure. She is First Nations, I think."

"Ya, okay. We better get going. I want to get there before anyone shows up."

♓

Selina knocked on the door window at Vanessa Jewelers. It was past closing, but the owner had agreed to meet with Selina after she finished work at the bookstore. She stood in the cool night and knocked on the glass again. The shop light came on, and Monica looked through one of the front windows before opening the door.

"Come in." Monica locked the door as soon as Selina had entered the store. "The fog is early this year. Come into the back office so I can review the appraisal with you."

The carved wooden box sat on top of a fiber tote bag and a white envelope was placed in the center of the desk. Selina sat down, pulled back her hoodie, and waited for Monica to take her seat.

"I looked at your necklace and decided that I needed another opinion before completing the appraisal. The markings on the gold pieces seemed unique, and I thought the piece might have historical value besides the gold and workmanship value." Monica opened the envelope. "I was correct. This necklace dates back to the 1650s when the Spaniards were in Central America. It's been appraised at thirty-five thousand dollars."

"Thirty-five thousand," Selina said, her forest-green eyes wide.

"The information is detailed in your appraisal, and the necklace is listed as the 'quinto necklace.' The other piece, the whale key, is made of the same 22-carat gold as the necklace. A coincidence, I suspect. It has no historical value, so I've priced it at fourteen hundred dollars." Monica handed over the appraisal document. "You will see that each appraised item has a photograph. It's part of my standard package."

"I would never have guessed. These pieces belonged to my mother, and I have no idea how my father got hold of Spanish gold. He was a jeweler before he died, but he never left the Powell River area." Selina said. "I appreciate your extra work on this evaluation."

"I suggest you get these pieces insured at your first opportunity." Monica said.

"I'll call my insurance broker first thing tomorrow." Selina watched Monica open the box to display its contents and then place it inside the fiber bag.

Monica prepared to lead the way from the office. "I'd love to hear the story if you ever find out the history of the necklace."

♓

Dillon had a big grin on his face as he put together a new hibachi barbeque on the back porch. The barbeque required briquettes—which was a new experience for him—but he was happy at the prospect of cooking outdoors.

"Ranger Dillon." Josh had come outside to see what Dillon was doing.

"I want to give everyone the outdoor flavor and there wasn't a barbeque, so Adrianne bought one."

"That's not a gig for me, man. I'm a city boy. I work with ovens and gas stove-tops. The biggest cooking adjustment I've had to make here is using electric burners. We'll be calling you Barbie Man."

"It's the only way to go." Dillon poured black, dusty briquettes into the cast-iron tray. "We don't use these things at home, though." He paused to look for the can of lighter fluid. "Adrianne told me to put some of this stuff on these chunks and ..." Dillon squeezed the small can, "bingo." He lit the fuel with a match and a flame erupted. "Whoa ... I'll have to watch that next time."

"I hope we don't need a fire permit for that thing. Anyway, here's your wine. Niki thought you might need one." Josh laughed and handed a glass of pinot blanc to Dillon. "This wine is perfect with seafood."

Dillon carefully poked at the heating coals, then looked up from the hibachi. "You like prawns? I know they are expensive down here, but I love these things."

"Sure ... everyone likes prawns." Josh left Dillon to his task.

"Niki, leave that biology stuff until after dinner and have a glass of the wine Adrianne bought," Josh said, as he walked through the kitchen. "I think we should leave outdoor cooking to Dillon."

"The coals should be ready in about thirty minutes. Some are already white." Dillon returned to the kitchen, where Adrianne was making a broccoli salad. "I wonder if Josh has ever had anything barbequed in his life. It sounds like he hasn't." Dillon shook his head. "Don't you find that strange for a budding chef?"

"Yes, a little." Adrianne stopped to get a glass from the cabinet. "Prawns definitely go with wine … pour me a glass while I work on this."

♓

Chaz watched Eduardo's black Escalade disappear into the fog, a couple of blocks away from his Rudlin Street target. He walked to the light on Pandora Avenue hoping neither tenant was home. It was early in the evening, but the increasing density of the fog allowed him to see only across the street, and the traffic light was a red blur.

He had worked this area before and knew that the homes were modest, built close together, and their age made entrance a simple matter. Normally there were no security systems, and trees and shrubs were overgrown.

Some homes were lit and others were in darkness as Chaz peered through the fog to determine the color of the house at 1226. The street was quiet and the house in question was dark.

He slipped between a hedge and the side of the house. It was wet and muddy from the earlier rain in the day. The basement lights were off. He sighed, relieved that the downstairs' tenant wasn't home.

Chaz surveyed the yard and carefully stepped onto a wood staircase that rose to a deck at the back. It creaked a little. He stopped and listened in the growing darkness. Lights were on in the house behind him, and he peered through the fog to see if anyone had noticed the noise. He inhaled sharply, held his breath, and swiftly reached the back door.

He quickly inspected the back of the house and discovered an open window. He peered through, but couldn't see inside. He placed his fingers under the wooden window sill and inched up the frame. He stuck his head inside and noted the room was a tiny dinette off the kitchen with nothing to impede his entry.

He pushed the rest of his body through the window and landed on the floor with a thump. He lay on the floor for a moment, then pulled back his hoodie and poked his head up to the window to peer across the back yard.

All was silent. He stood with his body hugging the wall. He pushed the window frame down, leaving the opening as he had found it, and slipped into the kitchen. He unlocked the back door, and his eyes began to adjust to the dark room.

Chaz rummaged through a drawer, found a paring knife, and slipped it the back pocket of his jeans. He looked around the kitchen and spotted an avocado in a bowl. He grabbed it, placed it in the pocket of his hoodie, and pushed it outwards. It bulged as expected.

He headed for the front room. He glanced about, noticing there was only a sofa, a flat screen television, and an artist's easel supporting an unfinished painting, accompanied by a padded chair and a table full of paint tubes. He heard footsteps on the front porch, then the sound of a key inserted into the front door lock. He sharply inhaled as his eyes darted about the room, looking for a suitable place to hide. He slipped back through the kitchen and stood stiffly against the wall in the dinette.

Chaz pulled his hood up to hide his face. He placed his hand in his pocket, grabbed the avocado, and pushed it forward. He held his breath as his brain raced to decide what to do. The front door opened and closed. The sitting room light was turned on, its glow flowing through the kitchen and across the floor close to where he stood in tense silence.

Selina took off her coat, hung it in the hall closet and walked into the kitchen. She turned on the light and placed the brown fiber bag onto the kitchen counter. Chaz's heart pounded as he stood stiffly by the wall in the next room listening to the woman's every move.

He saw her shadow cast across the floor as she headed for the kitchen sink. He knew her back would be to him, and he darted out from his hiding place to seize her from behind. He covered her mouth with a scrawny hand, "Shh … don't make a sound. I have a gun, but I don't want to hurt you." Chaz paused for a moment. "If I release my hand, you promise not to scream?"

Selina nodded her head in agreement.

"Don't move from that spot," Chaz ordered. He removed his hand and grabbed the knife from his back pocket. "I have a knife." He flashed it in front of her face. He whispered in her ear, "Where's the necklace?"

"Necklace?" Her voice shook.

"Don't screw with me. I can find it after I slit your throat if you wish."

"In the bag on the counter behind you. How do you know about the necklace?" She regained her composure.

"I'm asking the questions. Where did you get it?"

"It's a gift from a friend. The gift card is in the box. I'll get it for you if you like," she answered.

"I'll do it myself. Stay put. Face the window and take off your earrings and ring. Place them on the counter next to you." Chaz moved away from the woman, and glanced backward for the bag. He spotted it, and backed towards the counter while he watched the woman to ensure she did as she was told. He watched Selina as she began to take off her earrings with trembling hands, but didn't notice that she caught a glimpse of him as he was momentarily reflected in the black window. He grabbed the bag and pulled out the carved box.

"Native? Family friend? What gift card?" Chaz opened the box and peered at the necklace and gold key and glanced at Selina as she placed her earrings and ring beside her on the kitchen counter. He reached for the necklace, but heard a key being inserted into a lock downstairs and momentarily glanced across the room toward the sound. Chaz became distracted— only for a second but Selina realized this was her chance.

She kicked the man, aiming for his crotch. Chaz dropped the wooden box as Selina screamed and the necklace shot across the kitchen floor into the other room.

Chaz grunted as the avocado dropped to the floor from his hoodie. He looked up at the woman as she kicked him again in the side, and ran into the front room toward the door screaming for help.

"Shit." Chaz grabbed the whale key that lay on the floor by the kitchen door and the jewelry on the counter. "Damn bitch." He shoved the pieces into his jeans pocket and bolted out the back door. He heard the man in the bottom suite open his door and the woman screaming on the front porch as he darted along the back hedge and into the neighboring yard.

Chaz worked his way through a break in the fence as the yelling stopped and the night went silent. He hobbled into the front yard of a home that faced busy Pandora Street. The fog was thick, but he noticed the dull yellow sign of an approaching bus. He darted across the street as the traffic light changed and sprinted to the bus stop a block away. He pulled his hoodie up over his head when he stopped to catch his breath. Chaz boarded the bus, cognizant of the wail of sirens in the distance.

⧓

Dillon sat next to Adrianne on his bed, holding the black and white photograph he had removed from the mirror frame. "I was thinking about everyone at home in Sliammon while I was setting up the hibachi," Dillon said. "You thought whatever my grandparents were holding looked like a locket, but I don't think so. Take another look."

She took the photograph. "You're right." Adrianne replied, peering closely at the photo. "It looks like some type of coin. It's got strange markings but I can't make them out. It doesn't look like our Canadian or the American coins. I've seen most of the shipwrecks on our coastline, too, while diving with my dad, and I've studied treasures that have been discovered in sunken ships. That coin looks Spanish to me, Dillon."

"It can't be Spanish. This photo was taken in Sliammon. What would the Spanish be doing up the BC Coast?"

"The Spanish were here, Dillon. Our company takes people on diving expeditions around shipwrecks. There's a Spanish galleon in Bute Inlet. Maybe even pirates could've been here."

"My mother never mentioned a coin or anything like that."

"From what you tell me, she hasn't mentioned a lot of things," she retorted. "I could pull up websites to show you the Spanish were here."

"No, not tonight. I'm a bit tired." Dillon took the photo from Adrianne.

⧓

Selina sat in her front room and gave her statement to a pair of Victoria Police constables, while another constable gathered evidence from the crime scene. Her downstairs neighbor had left her apartment after he gave his short witness account.

"I don't know what he intended to do after he got hold of my jewelry. He threatened me with a knife and said he had a gun, but I never saw it." She took a sip of water the police had given her. "He did know that I was bringing home the necklace and the whale key. I hope you get it back, constable."

"You must keep your windows and doors locked when you're not home, Ms. Archie. No neighborhood is completely safe from druggies and thieves these days," a constable said sternly. "You're lucky you weren't injured."

"Yes, Sir. The house gets stuffy on damp days, but I understand. We don't have this type of problem at home. Mom will be upset that I lost her special key. I can't tell her."

"We'll arrange to have a detective team talk with you tomorrow and see what we can do. I'll ensure that they receive your statement and tonight's official report. Bring the jeweler's appraisal with you and notes about the earrings and ring. We're going to take the necklace to check for prints, but I suggest you obtain insurance on it immediately. This doesn't sound like a random B&E. Someone is desperate to have that necklace. Put it in a bank safety deposit box at your first opportunity."

"That's it, Sergeant," a uniformed officer said, as he entered the room. "I'm done here."

"Here's the receipt for the necklace to confirm that I have taken it with me." The sergeant signed a piece of paper and handed it to Selina. "Lock up when we go."

⋈

Chaz couldn't believe he screwed up a simple heist. He was stressed, fumbled in his pocket to check that he had the jewelry, ensuring himself that he hadn't lost any during his escape. He changed busses at Douglas Street and tried to mingle amongst the late-night crowd while he waited for his bus. He hunched in his bench seat in the dimly lit bus to hide his face.

It was a few blocks from the bus stop to his apartment. He walked toward a poorly lit street corner and eyed a figure in the gloomy shadow of the street light. He suspected it was a man who frequented the spot, waiting for drug customers—drugs Chaz was more than familiar with.

Chaz was tempted to calm his nerves and ease his pent-up frustration with a little hit. Did he possess the inner strength his rehab counselor assured him that he did? He thought of everything that went wrong. Mason. How was Mason going to react to the botched job? He wanted to feel good. He sauntered over to his supplier.

"Still haunting the neighborhood, are you, Sammy?"

"Chaz. I didn't think you were supposed to talk to me, or so you said last time we met." Sam Queen's eyes were cynical behind thick black glasses. "I got a deal on ecstasy or do you want coke?"

"How much are the pills? I'm still tryin' to kick the coke."

"For you, ten bucks each. I'll give you six for fifty." Sam glanced around furtively in the fog.

"I was goin' to meet this Eduardo guy." Chaz placed his hand in his pocket and fumbled around, sorting out the jewelry with his fingers. "But I need them pills more. Can I trade this?" Chaz pulled out the gold key. "It's worth more than fifty bucks, but I'd rather give it to you than the Mexican."

Sam snatched the key from Chaz. "You doing a little after-hours shopping, Chaz?" Sam inspected the key. "You think I'm a bloody pawn shop? As a favor for a past customer," Sam shoved the whale key into his pocket and counted out six pills. "Don't take them all tonight."

Four

It was seven in the morning, and Detective Senior Constable Jamie Steele was already seated at her third-floor office desk typing a summary report of a case she had closed the evening before. Her office sat in a new three-story concrete building. Sun streamed through the window.

Jamie Steele was a twenty-five-year veteran of the force and had worked her way through the ranks. At forty-eight years old, she still loved what she did, and liked being one of the few senior detectives in the group.

The first week of September often brought new blood into the department. Her latest partner had been transferred the week before. She hoped she wasn't going to be saddled with a rookie. Her boss, Inspector Stephen Harris, appreciated having a seasoned detective on his team. He respected her experience and tenacity. Jaime thought this was merely an excuse to assign her the latest inexperienced recruit.

Jamie had never married. The Victoria Police Department was her life, and she knew everyone by name and their stories.

Stephen Harris had been her boss for the last six years. He was tough, but Jamie also thought he was kind and honorable—not that she would admit this.

Jamie took another sip from her Starbucks coffee and leaned back in her chair, contemplating the last statement she had written.

"Good morning, Jamie," a cheery voice came from outside of her office, breaking her concentration. "Wasn't the fog unbelievably thick last night?"

Jamie rose from her chair and poked her curly, red head out her door. "Hey, Darcy. I heard that patrol was busy with accidents and B&Es last night. Any news on my new partner yet?"

Constable Darcy Lyndon, who was Jamie's boss's executive assistant, was bright and intuitive. "You know I can't tell you that, Jamie."

Jamie moved to the side of Darcy's desk. "Come on, you must know something," she persisted, as Darcy logged onto her computer.

"Good morning, Detective Steele," Inspector Harris said in a monotone voice, as he appeared behind the two women. "You complete that report for me yet?"

"Good morning, Sir. I'm just proofreading it before I send it to you. I was just wondering, Sir …."

Harris who knew all too well what Jamie wanted to ask, so he smiled and entered his office. "Send me that report, Detective. I have another case for you."

"Yes, Sir." Jamie returned to her office.

"Darcy, come into my office, please," her boss said sharply, "and close the door."

Darcy grabbed a notepad. "Busy last night I hear, Sir," she said as she closed his door.

Inspector Harris's large executive office was on the southwest corner of the building. It was outfitted with a lacquered pine desk and credenza, and had a round pine conference table with four chairs. The walls facing the inner office were glass, and had narrow metal blinds.

Constable Lyndon took a chair in front of Harris's desk, and waited for her lanky boss to sit.

"Did Detective Steele need your help with something, Darcy?"

"I was ...." She noticed a big grin on his face as she started to reply. A knock on his glass door interrupted her explanation, and they both glanced up at the tall woman standing outside.

"Detective Kennedy's early. I thought she would be with personnel longer," the Inspector said as he stood. "Please let her in, Darcy."

Darcy went to open the door.

"Detective Tammy-Jean Kennedy, reporting for duty as directed, Sir." The woman spoke stiffly as she walked toward the inspector's desk.

"Welcome aboard, Detective-Constable Kennedy." He held out his hand.

"Sir, thank you, Sir." She shook his hand.

"Detective Kennedy, this is my assistant officer, Constable Darcy Lyndon. She will help you get settled this morning."

Tammy-Jean turned to Darcy. "Constable Lyndon. Good to meet you." Her tone was formal as she offered her hand for Darcy to shake.

Darcy shook the woman's hand and said, "Welcome to the VicPD."

"Detective Kennedy, would you please take a seat at the conference table? Darcy, please ask Detective Steele to join us and bring me a department orientation kit."

The inspector thumbed through blue folders on his desk while he waited. He selected one and placed the rest back into the pile. Jamie entered his office.

"Detective Steele, meet your new partner, Detective Kennedy. Take a seat and we'll have a little chat." Inspector Harris opened a drawer in his credenza.

The two women shook hands. "Welcome aboard. I'm Jamie."

"Good to meet you, Jamie. I'm Tammy-Jean, but I prefer TJ."

Darcy returned to the office and placed a brown envelope on the inspector's desk. She left, closing the door behind her.

The inspector added the envelope to the other articles in his hand. "It's always a pleasure to welcome a new member to my team." He placed the materials on the meeting table and took a seat. "The department is fortunate to have an experienced and competent detective join our group, Jamie. Tammy-Jean comes to us from the Canadian Forces National Investigation Service in Esquimalt. She's completed her latest tour with them and elected to resign from the navy to join us at VicPD." He paused for a moment. "I have assigned Detective Kennedy as your partner while she becomes orientated with our practices, processes, and protocols. She will have the vacant desk outside your office. You two can begin your first assignment as a team by investigating this B&E." The inspector took the blue folder from the table and slid it toward Jamie.

"Here is your official VicPD shield, Detective." He handed a blue box to TJ. "There is a form in this package. I need it completed and returned to Darcy before you begin your assignment." He passed the package across the table while TJ opened the box. "Check out a weapon and place your shield number and the weapon's serial number on the form. Darcy can help you. After that, you two can get started on your first assignment."

"Yes, Sir. Thank you, Sir." TJ pulled the new detective five-point, silver-star shield from the box.

Inspector Harris rose from his seat. "Again, Detective Kennedy, welcome to our unit. You two are dismissed."

"Once you've sorted out what you need to do, we'll review this case file, TJ," said Jamie.

"I shouldn't be long," TJ replied.

Forty-five minutes later, TJ lightly rapped on her new partner's door and walked in to stand rigidly in front of Jamie's desk. Her dark brown hair was pulled into a tight bun. Everything about the woman was austere. "What's our case?"

"Take a seat, TJ. We have a B&E case in Fernwood. Let's talk for a minute before we head out. I'm impressed. CFNIS. That's an elite group. Whatever caused you to leave, TJ?"

"My parents died in a car accident about ten years ago. I had joined the navy a couple of years earlier. My only family is my grandmother, who is 83 and lives alone in Esquimalt. She is having difficulty getting around and doing everything for herself. I knew the right thing to do was resign to look after her. Besides, I'm not married, and being away on tour duties most of the time doesn't work well in building relationships outside of the forces. Another reason to rejoin civilian life."

"Right then, we should make a great team. We have a B&E where a young woman was assaulted last night and jewelry was stolen. One piece, an expensive necklace, was recovered after the assault, but there are less valuable pieces missing. According to this report, we have prints from the necklace, but forensics hasn't run them yet. The woman fought off her attacker, and the perp escaped in the fog before one of our units arrived. I've contacted the vic at work, and she is expecting us to meet her there."

TJ looked somewhat disappointed with the case description but said nothing.

The detectives took the elevator down to the basement level. Jamie pressed a security lock fob and an unmarked Dodge Charger beeped. The pearl-colored, four-door Charger was new and sleek, with aluminum sport wheels.

"I've had this baby for a few months. There're only a couple of new ones in the fleet." The Charger roared to life. "Our vic is a Selina Archie. Our responding team to the 911 call says she was held up at knifepoint. The report states the perp threatened Ms. Archie with a gun, but no gun was found on site. We're headed for Munro's Books on Government Street, where the vic works."

"I know that bookstore in Old Town. It's a famous landmark. Jamie, did Ms. Archie catch the perp in her house during the robbery?"

"The report states that she thinks he was waiting for her, and that he was specifically after the necklace later recovered at the scene."

"He must've been pissed he didn't get it," said TJ. "Her story should be interesting. Here's our destination."

The pair entered a neo-classical, gray-colored stone building with majestic stone pillars.

"We're looking for Selina Archie. She's expecting us," Jamie told the clerk at the front counter.

"She's helping a customer. I'll go get her for you."

"This place has been around forever." Jamie looked around the high-ceilinged main floor. "It has such atmosphere."

"Hey, look at this. Ms. Archie is an artist, and she is having a fundraiser and exhibition in a couple of weeks." TJ picked up an advertisement from the counter.

"I'm Selina Archie. Amy said you were asking for me. Can I help you?"

Jamie pulled out her police shield. "I'm Detective Steele and this is my partner Detective Kennedy. I called you this morning about your assault and robbery last night. Is there somewhere that we can talk in private?"

"There's an employee lounge in the back where we can talk." Selina glanced around the bookstore. "I haven't told anyone here about last night."

Jamie began the conversation in the employees' lounge. "We read the report from the responding constables last night and an initial report from forensics. I understand your attacker was after something specific—a gold necklace. What can you tell us about that?" Jamie pulled out a small black notebook and a pen as she watched Selina pour coffee into a mug.

"The man was specific, Detective. He knew I brought home a necklace last night. My mother had just given me the necklace on the Labor Day weekend. I have no idea how he knew I had it; in fact, only a few people knew. Anyway, he demanded I give him the necklace and asked me where it came from. Don't you think that strange, Detective?"

"Who knew that you had it?" TJ asked.

"I told Amy I was at the jewelers that morning, but didn't give her any specifics about the necklace. The jeweler who did the appraisal ..." Selina paused to sip her coffee, "the jeweler said she had had a second opinion on the appraisal because she thought that it had some historical value. She was right. The necklace was made with gold bars from the 1600s."

Selina walked toward the lockers. "The police told me last night to bring this to work today. It's the appraisal of both the necklace and a gold whale key that my mother gave to me. I thought I should get insurance coverage so needed the appraisal, and I hadn't yet had an opportunity to put the jewelry into a safety deposit box after having it appraised." Selina opened a locker, fished around in her purse, and extracted an envelope. "Here's the appraisal. I hope that you're able to recover the key. The gift has special importance to my mother."

Jamie took the envelope and removed the appraisal. "Thirty-five grand." She handed the document and envelope to TJ. "At least we have a photo. I assume this other item, the whale key, was one of the pieces taken. Your statement indicates you also lost a pair of earrings and a ring."

"The intruder demanded I remove my earrings and ring while he checked that the necklace was in my father's wooden box." Selina took another sip of coffee. "I don't think those pieces are valuable, even though they were made by my father many years ago. I don't have appraisals, photographs, or written descriptions of those, I'm afraid."

"Do you remember anything else about the intruder that isn't in your statement?"

Selina played the event back in her head. "I did get a glimpse of his face, at least a part of it. The night was so dark that the kitchen window reflected like a mirror. I saw his reflection when I was removing my earrings and the man moved backwards to the necklace. It was only a flash really, and his face was mostly covered by a gray hoodie. His face was unshaven."

Selina looked at Jamie. "I was so terrified about what he might do after he got the necklace, that all I could think about was how to get away. He said that he had a gun, but I didn't see it. When Mr. Simpson came home and put his key into the lock, the noise distracted the guy for a split second. After I kicked him, I didn't see any more of his face. I just ran and screamed." Selina's eyes began to tear up.

"Okay, Ms. Archie, that's good enough for now. Here's my card. Call me anytime if you recall anything else," Jamie replied. "We'll find the man. The whale key is unique, so I'm sure that it will turn up. We'll see our way out."

♓

"Eduardo, you should've got the necklace last night." Hamish Firth was still annoyed. "You're crazy to trust a junkie with the quinto."

"You brought me in to handle this, so let me handle it. I told you last night I was concerned about the fog and being seen at the time of the heist. I thought it was better to conduct the transaction today. Besides, I didn't want to freeze my ass waiting. I was assured the kid could do the job."

"We can't change it now. You said seven tonight, right?"

"Yeah, seven. The meet is a block or so walk from the kid's place, so he has no excuse for a late show. I expect to be back by seven thirty. Are you expecting the cops to call today? They'll be poking around looking for leads. I'm sure they know you've seen the necklace."

"Hopefully, they think it's a random heist. The cops might come nosing around because of the appraisal value and because it was stolen right after it was picked up. It was a timing risk, but there was no other option. Anyway, there's nothing to implicate me. I'll be ready for them if they show."

Hamish looked at Eduardo. "You watch your ass while you're picking up the goods tonight. The cops could be watching the kid if they figure out he was involved."

"I'll leave early and scope out the place to be sure the kid's alone. I'll check for an alternate route out of the area, too. In the meantime, I have work to do. You're not my only client."

"Call when you have the quinto, Eduardo. We'll have a late dinner to celebrate."

♓

Sam Queen hadn't slept much the night before. He had tossed and turned thinking about the gold whale key he took from Chaz. He knew that he scored on the deal, but with further thought, decided it would be best to get rid of it for cash. He was positive it was stolen. Its uniqueness made it too hot to hold onto. Sam was in the drug business—nothing else, including purloined jewelry.

He put on his black-rimmed glasses and inspected his hair and beard in the mirror. He was pleased his image reflected that of a sophisticated businessman.

It was late morning. The sun was burning off scattered clouds and remnants of fog from the night before. Sam knew it would be foolish to pawn the diamond studded key, so he looked for a street vendor on Government Street who he knew would be setting up at the foot of Bastion Square for the daily parade of tourists.

"Cassy, getting ready to push some stuff I see," Sam said, while a girl in her late teens concentrated on setting up her wooden display box.

The girl looked up. "Best deals in town. I cut off the 'Made in China' labels and pass this stuff as my own. I get by."

"I won this in a poker game last night, and I need the cash to pay a debt." Sam pulled the gold key from his pocket. "These are real diamonds ya know."

"Cubic zirconium they call 'em. Don't bullshit me, man." She stopped what she was doing and took the item from Sam's hand. "Likely gold plate, too. It is different, though."

"Give me two hundred. You can get plenty more from a rich tourist." Sam thought she might be right about the quality.

"I sell on the street; not in one of those fancy shops, Sammy. It's cool, but I can't pay you that kinda money and make a profit. Find someone else."

"Say … one hundred and a quarter. That's a steal."

"Ninety-five or go check out a pawn shop. There's a few around here."

Sam pondered the offer. He knew the key was worth more than that, but going to a pawn shop was definitely out. Cassy could sell it to a tourist and the thing would disappear.

"Deal." He pretended to look disappointed.

♓

"The pawn shops were a bust, TJ. I thought our perp would've unloaded the jewelry immediately."

"I suppose it's seldom that easy, but I don't have much experience with B&Es and jewelry heists. I usually handled larger crimes when I was with the CFNIS. Anyway, I'll bet our perp took transit after the heist. It would've been the quickest way out of the area. The report says our guys found footprints in the wet ground running along the back of the house and next door. It seems he panicked when Ms. Archie screamed. He didn't stop to look for the necklace that fell on the floor. If the necklace was the prime target, the kid must've freaked. What time was the 911 call logged?"

"Seven twenty-two. The closest transit would be on Pandora Avenue. Maybe the bus driver will recall something—good idea. The main bus depot is on Gorge Road. Let's catch the driver before he begins his route."

A middle-aged man was seated in a crowded control room, surrounded by computers and radio gear, when the detectives entered the bus dispatch center. They presented their badges. "We need to talk to the driver who had the Pandora Avenue route last night."

"What time and was the bus going east or west?"

"We're not sure, but I suspect the westbound bus at about seven thirty around the Fernwood Road stop."

The dispatcher keyed in letters on his computer and stared intently at the results. "That would've been Tim Chambers." He spoke into an intercom microphone. "Tim Chambers, please report to the dispatch office."

A short, heavy-set man in his mid-fifties, appeared in the doorway. "You called?"

"The detectives want to have a word with you. Don't take long. Your route begins in less than ten minutes."

"What's this all about, Detectives?"

"Do you recall picking up a male passenger at the Pandora Avenue and Fernwood at about seven thirty last night?"

"It was foggy, and I was running behind schedule. Fernwood ... yeah, some kid in a gray hoodie who looked agitated. He slumped in his seat and stared out the window most of the trip. He kept his hoodie wrapped around his face. He stayed on until I reached the end of the route. He's probably a junkie kid who stays at the rehab place on Ellice. I get them kids all the time, and he had a monthly pass."

"Did he get on with anyone else?" Jamie asked. Her cell phone rang before the bus driver could answer. "Excuse me." She pulled the phone from her jacket pocket. "Steele."

Everyone was silent until she finished. "So, was he alone or did anyone meet him when he got off?"

"Not that I recall. There were few people out in the fog, so I'd remember."

"Thank you for your time. You were helpful." Jamie watched the man leave the room.

She spoke to TJ. "We got a hit on the prints taken from the necklace. One of them belongs to a Charles Collins. He has a rap sheet for B&Es and drug possession. His last address is 535 Ellice Street. He has to be our guy. Let's go."

In less than a couple of minutes the Charger was parked in the street across from a four-story blue and gray metal-clad building. A Victoria Police squad car and an ambulance were parked outside the brick entrance. "TJ, pull out a pair of rubber gloves from the console. This may be a crime scene." The detectives approached the squad car.

"Constable Taylor, what's going on here?"

"Hey, Jamie. Some kid ODd. We got a 911 call fifteen minutes ago. One of the kid's neighbors became concerned when Charles Collins missed his rehab session this afternoon. Apparently Charles hasn't missed a session in over three months. He's on the third floor."

"Sounds like our guy just ODd, TJ."

The front door of the building was blocked open with a wooden doorstop. Jamie glanced at the security door entry keypad, then instinctively looked up to the overhang over the front door and noticed a small video camera. She waited for TJ to pass through the door and followed her inside.

"We better take a quick look about before the body's moved, if it hasn't been already." She pressed the elevator button.

Jamie and TJ found a pair of paramedics preparing to remove the young man's body when they reached room 311. "Hey guys, Detectives Kennedy and Steele. Could you wait a few minutes while we take a quick look around? This man is a suspect in a B&E and assault last night."

"Sure, Detective. He's not going anywhere."

"TJ, see if you can find the jewelry. If the pawn shops don't have it, maybe it's still here." Jamie pulled on a pair of rubber gloves. "A bachelor suite—not many places to stash stolen goods."

TJ pulled on a pair of rubber gloves. She asked the uniformed constable who was standing by the door, "Was the door open or locked when you entered?"

"Locked, Detective. We got a key from the superintendent downstairs." He studied the attractive woman. "You Jamie's new partner?"

"Yes, I'm TJ," she replied, while she continued to look around the room. "I started today."

Jamie entered the bathroom. TJ turned to the two paramedics. "Either of you check his pockets?"

"No, Detective. We didn't have cause to do that. You want to check?"

"Yes, please unzip the bag."

The flap was pulled back and TJ knelt on one knee. She momentarily looked at the unshaven face of the scrawny man. "What a waste," she muttered, then patted the front pockets of his dirty blue jeans. "Jamie, I've got something."

Jamie reentered the room and saw her partner had jewelry and a pill in her fist. "Are all three pieces there?"

"No, only the earrings and the ring. There's no gold key."
She slipped her hand under the corpse and searched the back
pockets. "Nothing else here, Jamie." She got off her knee.
"Thanks, you can close it up again."

"I doubt it's here, then." Jamie pulled off her gloves. "TJ,
bag what you found and I'll show you how to register the
evidence when we get back to the office. "Thanks boys, we're
done here."

Jamie waited for TJ to join her in the hall. "I saw a video
cam at the front door. It looks like part of a security system.
Check it out to see if there's any footage of visitors last night.
We'll narrow down the time to view it when we get the time of
death from the coroner."

♓

Dillon waved at Adrianne as he entered the swimming
pool area of the university aquatic center. Adrianne was
perched on the lifeguard observation tower waiting for the last
of the swimmers to finish their laps.

"I'll be down in a few minutes," she called, and waved
back.

He sat on the spectator bench, watching the swimmers,
and thought about his last class in indigenous studies. He was
surprised when Adrianne tapped him on his shoulder.

"Lost in thought, Dillon?"

"No," he replied, "well, yes, I guess so," he admitted,
embarrassed that he hadn't been paying attention to her.

"I was thinking about the black and white photo. Aren't
you just a bit curious about the coin in the picture?" Adrianne
asked, as she walked toward the women's change room.

"I'm more interested in what my grandparents were doing
with it—if it was really a Spanish coin. It obviously meant

something special to them. Maybe there's more about it in the diary."

"Perhaps," Adrianne said. "Do you know how to scuba dive?"

"Scuba dive? No, but I'm a good swimmer. Why?"

"The thought of the Spanish coin, and possibly, an undiscovered wreck gave me an idea. We could look for it together," she said. "The ships are usually hundreds of feet below. You'd need to be certified. It's best to obtain certification before open water diving so you should take the PADI course. I'll help you with the non-water portion of the program when we get home today. What do you think?"

"I think I like your idea," Dillon answered. "I was going to take you for a burger at Felichas, unless you've already organized something at home."

"I was going to make a quick salad," Adrianne said. "I'd rather have a burger."

⚓

It was seven thirty. Eduardo was chilled as he waited for Chaz at the agreed meeting place. Eduardo had been in the area for over an hour, checking that no police were hidden, expecting a clean bust. "Damn." He checked the time on his cell phone again, now becoming concerned that Hamish was right and that he shouldn't have trusted a junkie. The evening was cold and clear, and the light of a crescent moon reflected off the stillness of the water. Eduardo kept walking in the shadows along the gorge waterfront to stay warm.

All was quiet with no foretelling footsteps. Eduardo took a deep breath and sighed as he again looked at his cell phone. "Shit." He shook his head and dialed a number from his contacts list.

"Mr. Perez," Eduardo began, then realized it was an answering machine. He started over at the beep. "Mr. Perez, your man Chaz hasn't showed up for our meeting, and he didn't complete the job I paid you to arrange. Find out what happened. I'll call later."

Eduardo keyed another number. His brain searched for the proper words. "Hamish, Eduardo."

"I was getting worried, Eduardo, it's well past seven thirty."

"Yeah, well ...." Eduardo couldn't get the words out.

"Your guy didn't show, did he, Eduardo?" The tone in Hamish's voice said it all. "I knew it. Damn it, Eduardo, you said that you had it under control ... you said ...."

"I'm an antiquities dealer, Hamish. I don't do this stuff. I have to trust people in my line of work. Sometimes shit happens." He was becoming angry at Hamish, rather than Chaz.

"Come to the house and we'll go out for something to eat. Tomorrow you can poke around and find out what happened to your guy. Maybe he got high and missed the meet."

"I'm sorry, Hamish. I'll try to fix it."

♓

"I passed." Dillon bellowed so that Adrianne could hear him in her bedroom. "How are you doing on your assignment?"

"Passed?" She grinned as she joined him in his room. "I see you've already pulled out the diary."

"It's getting late. I want to go through a few passages tonight." He opened the page to the marker.

Adrianne settled on the bed next to him.

Sunday May 25th 1975.

I spent another Sunday with Gloria. She said ⁿc̆ɛ́c̆haθɛ́c̆' means 'I honor you.' Gloria is mature for a seventeen-year-old. She looks after herself well and is fit and strong. Her jet-black, long, silky hair is usually tied in a ponytail and bound with an animal skin woven rope. She is shorter than I, about five feet six or so, and has an alluring smile. I love listening to her gentle voice and her laughter brightens up our conversation. We went to Atrevida Reef today and swam in our underwear to collect butter clams. Her body aroused me.

I smelled the salmon cooking on the fires in the village when we returned with our catch. Larry straddled the clams between logs by the fire, and I watched them steam in the moisture of their shells. Gloria gave me the Tla'amin name 'qoqoq' today. It means 'white owl.' It was a full moon tonight, and the brightly painted carvings of the totems contrasted against the darkness of the forest. It seemed somewhat eerie.

Dillon flipped through pages and read another entry:

Saturday October 11th 1975;

Today Larry and Gloria took me chum salmon fishing at Sliammon Creek, just north of the village. It's spawning time, and the river was full of the red-skinned fish rushing up-river. The smoke-dried flesh is a winter staple food. Most of the women stayed in the village, filleted the fish, and hung the flesh on sticks to smoke dry in front of the fire.

Dillon turned to another page and read:

Sunday October 19th 1975;

> *Another Sunday with Gloria. I have been looking forward to my day with Gloria all week. It is the only day we spend alone together. My new word for today was 'qomqɛt.' She kissed me and whispered the word in my ear. I must admit I was aroused with her caress, but not surprised. We have grown close and try hard to conceal our attraction from everyone in the village. She placed her hand on my heart and said 'ʎukʷɛnƏs.' She told me she doesn't love Brett Paul and wants to be with me. She whispered 'χaʎnomɛč, I love you,' and left me in the full moonlight of the evening before I could reply.*

"I can see where this story's going, Dillon." Adrianne gave him a languid kiss. "What do you think?"

Dillon squeezed his legs together. He wanted to make love to her, but he had to control himself. He didn't want to destroy their friendship. "I'm surprised Walter wrote all that stuff, but I feel his emotions flow from the pages." Dillon pretended to stretch his legs.

Adrianne noticed his struggle, but didn't comment. She kissed him again, lingering longer and more brazenly, then pulled back. She heard the gay roommates arrive home and their voices downstairs. "It's late. I'll pick up some diving gear in the morning, so you'll have to bus to class," she said as she got off the bed. "Meet me at the pool after class and we can begin your underwater training."

Dillon was relieved that she left. He stood up and adjusted the crotch of his pants. He pulled up the blinds. The moon shone brightly in the clear night sky. His thoughts were consumed with how much he wanted Adrianne.

He closed his eyes and tried to relax. Adrianne's perfume drifted though the bathroom door, and the inviting odour filled his consciousness.

Five

"You're in bright and early, TJ." Jamie's partner was seated at her desk reading a manual.

"I wanted to start on this orientation package."

Jamie placed her coffee on the desk and sat down. "Are you getting settled with your grandmother?"

"It's an adjustment for both of us. I've been using her car. She still has her license, but I'd rather she doesn't drive. She isn't happy and wants me to buy my own vehicle."

"You have to be a lead detective to get a department car, but I suspect it won't take long to reach that point with your credentials." Jamie took a sip of her coffee.

"In the meantime, I have to figure out a compromise with my grandmother. She's accustomed to independence." TJ closed her manual. "What's the plan for today?"

"We're off to the morgue to see if our B&E guy, Charles Collins, was a self-administered overdose or a homicide. I'm suspicious about this death because of the missing whale key and the botched necklace heist. I had a conversation yesterday with the inspector after you went home. He wants us to look into the death. He's given the case to us since it's related to our current assignment."

"It doesn't seem likely Charles was working on his own. Ms. Archie stated that Charles knew about the necklace because he specifically asked for it. Based on what Ms. Archie told us yesterday, we should focus on someone at either the jewelry store or the guy who appraised the necklace."

"Let's do the morgue first to get a timeline on his death and an opinion on the cause of death from the coroner."

⋈

Adrianne left the Charles Street house early to pick up scuba gear from her father's diving operation at the West Bay Marine Village in Esquimalt.

On the way to the marina she drove past Victorian-style homes strung along the waterfront. Second World Diving BC was located in a boathouse at the end of the wooden dock. Adrianne climbed aboard and entered the sliding-glass office door.

"Hey, Nathan, I need a couple of tanks and diving gear for a few days," she said to the diving assistant. "I'm helping a friend get certified." She checked tags on the tanks stacked in a rack.

"Boy or girl?"

"Boy." She pulled a cylinder from the rack.

"You should bring him around so I can meet him. How are your roommates?"

"We get along. I like living in the house better than on campus." She pulled out another cylinder. "Any bookings for this weekend?" she asked.

"One. A young couple who needs recertification before they vacation in the Caribbean. Need help with the gear to your car?"

"Sure," Adrianne said.

"Your parents met this guy yet?"

"No, it's not a big deal ... just a guy friend," she replied. "We might go to Race Rocks tomorrow. I'll call you."

"Let me know, and I'll schedule one of the Zodiacs. Now let's get this stuff loaded."

⯛

The morgue was located in the basement of Royal Jubilee Hospital.

"I've never been to a morgue," TJ remarked, as the pair entered the building. "I've never been involved in a murder case. I worked on drug smuggling, naval misconduct, and terrorism files."

"It was a bit of a shock the first time I visited the coroner's lab. It's interesting once you get past the human body element," Jamie said, as she pressed the elevator button.

"Good morning, Dr. Sanders. It's been a while."

The overweight coroner looked up at Jamie in the doorway. "Detective Steele. I saw your name on the report about my OD customer. New partner?"

"Meet TJ. We started together yesterday. This is her first visit to a morgue."

"There's a first for everyone in this profession," said Dr. Sanders.

"What can you tell us about Charles Collins?" asked TJ.

The coroner flipped a sheet over the corpse he was examining and walked a few tables over. He uncovered the remains of Charles Collins. "I found a great deal of ecstasy in his system. It was ingested orally. By the track marks on his arms, he was likely a cocaine addict, but there were no traces of coke in his blood. There was no evidence of a struggle, other than bruising in his groin area and lower back. He has abrasions on his arms and face, likely from bushes."

"Any evidence he was forced to take the pills?" TJ took a closer look at the victim.

"No, a typical overdose case. According to the toxicology results he ingested about five pills, based on the typical 20 milligram pill. Two would be more than adequate to induce a high, so the dosage he took was excessive. Most drug addicts would know this or the supplier would tell a new user."

Jamie agreed the amount of ecstasy taken was unusual for a long-term drug addict. "What's the estimated time of death?" she asked.

"I'd say around 22:30 last night. I'll have my report to you by late this afternoon."

The detectives left the coroner's office. "The bruising makes sense from the statements taken at the B&E scene. This sounds like either an intentional OD or one taken under duress. So if intentional, why?" Jamie asked TJ.

"Because he screwed up and didn't get the necklace he was hired to steal. We know Collins went specifically for that piece. Overdosing was preferable to facing whoever hired him."

"That makes sense, TJ, but the extreme overdose bothers me. Somebody was pissed Collins didn't get the quinto necklace. Let's pay a visit to the jeweler."

♓

Dillon waited for his "Aboriginal Peoples of BC" lecture to finish, and then approached the professor.

"Sir, have you had an opportunity to look into Walter Smith?" Dillon asked.

"Why, yes, I do have information for you." The professor reached into his briefcase. "My contact provided this, but told me Walter's been retired for some time. He's still living in Victoria." He handed Dillon a folded scrap of paper.

"I really appreciate your help."

"Please pass on my best regards when you speak to Dr. Smith," the professor said, as he started to pack up his lecture materials. "I hope you find what you're looking for."

Dillon finally had a lead on his mysterious grandfather. He pulled out his cell phone.

"Hello, Dr. Smith's residence. How may I help you?"

"I'm looking for a Dr. Walter Smith, the anthropologist."

"Dr. Smith is unable to come to the phone right now. Is there something I can do for you?"

Dillon hesitated, and then answered, "Yes, madam, I'm his grandson. I wish to visit him tomorrow. Is that possible?"

"I didn't know he had a grandson. He'll be here, but it's unlikely he'll remember you. He's not well, and his memory is poor."

"I'd like to come anyway."

"That's fine. I'll expect you then. Good-bye."

Dillon hung up the phone. "Yes!" he yelled out.

♓

Adrianne was waiting poolside for Dillon. She had reserved—after wheedling the manager—a portion of the deep end for the remainder of the day.

She sat with her feet dangling in the water, dreaming of discovering a new shipwreck on the West Coast. She had explored the well-known diving destinations around Vancouver Island and up the coastline. Many were spectacular, but a new discovery—that would be something else.

She turned to see Dillon waving his arms.

"My professor gave me Walter Smith's address and phone number. We can go tomorrow," he blurted, almost breathless.

"Tomorrow?"

Dillon didn't notice her surprise.

"I had planned something else, but we can do it Sunday. Let's focus on getting this diving prerequisite completed."

"I don't know what to say to him, Adrianne. He probably doesn't want to be involved with my mother and me," Dillon paused, and his face reflected his thoughts. "Maybe I shouldn't go."

"Of course you should. You may never get another chance," Adrianne said. "I had planned to take you to Race Rocks tomorrow, but Sunday may be better."

"An ocean dive?"

"Don't get ahead of yourself. You need to complete the introductory diving program first today, or we can't go."

♓

It was noon. Chelsea Roberts was at Bastion Square to get away from the office and eat her lunch outside in the warm Friday weather.

"Beautiful jewelry for a beautiful woman like you," a teen-aged girl called, as Chelsea approached the entrance of the quaint square. Chelsea paused to look at the collection, picked up one of the pendants, and then placed it back. "I don't know …." She began to walk away.

"I have a unique, diamond pendant. It'll look wonderful on you," the street vendor pressed on. "All you need is a gold chain."

Chelsea stopped and turned. The vendor extracted a gold whale-like key from the clutter. "This piece belonged to a friend's mother, and she asked if I could sell it for her. She said that it has real diamonds. It's a bargain at one hundred and fifty."

Chelsea took the gold pendant and examined it. "Real diamonds—" She paused to take a closer look. "I'll give you one hundred cash."

"It's solid gold and the diamonds are authentic. It's a steal at one hundred thirty-five."

"I still have to put on a chain." Chelsea scrunched her face. "One hundred twenty-five. That's my last offer. That's all my tip money from last night."

The vendor sighed. "Okay." She held out her hand for payment.

Chelsea found a bench seat in the square, unwrapped her purchase, and examined it again. She glanced at the time on her cell phone.

In less than ten minutes Chelsea stood at the counter of Aurea Gems. "Could you put a gold chain on this for me?"

"It needs a clasp first so that it will hang on a chain. I can have it ready for Monday and you can select a chain then."

Chelsea dug out her wallet from her purse. "Okay. Thank you."

♓

Jamie turned her police car onto Broad Street, a narrow road with artistic designs troweled into the surface. She pulled into a parking stall of reddish brick. TJ pressed the security buzzer at Vanessa Jewelers, and a woman inside buzzed in the detectives.

"Can I help you?"

The detectives showed her their shields. "We're investigating a robbery and would like to ask you about an appraisal you performed for a Selina Archie. Here is a copy of your valuation." Jamie pulled an envelope from her jacket pocket and placed it on the glass counter.

"A robbery?" She looked surprised as she opened the envelope. She scanned the sheet inside. "The quinto necklace and gold diamond-studded key. My customer picked these articles up after closing on Wednesday night."

"And you are?" TJ asked.

"Monica Davies, store owner. Were these stolen?"

"Ms. Archie was attacked and assaulted at her home Wednesday night. The intruder absconded with the whale key. He was interested in the quinto necklace, but didn't get that piece." TJ said. Monica put the appraisal onto the counter. "Did anyone in this store besides you know that you had these pieces of jewelry?"

"No, I run this store by myself. This appraisal was performed by Firth Coin and Rarities. I use Mr. Firth for pieces that I think may be rare or of historical value. I want to ensure my customers receive an accurate valuation."

"Did you see anyone following or watching Ms. Archie when she brought you these pieces or when she departed with them on Wednesday night?" Jamie asked.

"Ms. Archie dropped off the jewelry here first thing Tuesday morning just as I opened. I didn't see anyone of note, but I was focused on opening my store," she replied, looking pensive. "There was heavy fog Wednesday night. I saw Ms. Archie to the door and watched her leave as I locked up."

"Can you think of any way the intruders would've known Ms. Archie's home address?"

"No. That information is confidential and is only noted in my computer and printed records." Monica shook her head. "Of course, her name and address were on the receipt Mr.

Firth signed when he took possession of the two pieces, but I took the transfer documents back with me."

"Do you engage in business often with Mr. Firth?"

"I receive estate jewelry and other rare pieces about a dozen times or so each year. I trust his judgment and valuations. He's been in the business for over thirty years."

"Here is my card if you think of anything else. Thank you." Jamie placed the envelope in her jacket inner pocket.

The detectives returned to their car. "What do you think, TJ?"

"I didn't get the sense she's involved. Let's see what Mr. Firth has to say for himself."

Five minutes later the detectives arrived at Firth Coin and Rarities. The glassed storefront windows had powder blue-colored wood frames.

Ding, ding, a small doorbell rang as the women opened the door and entered the store.

"Be with you in a moment." A voice with a thick Scottish accent drifted from the back room. Moments later a man approaching six feet tall with salt and pepper hair appeared. "Can I help you fine ladies?"

"We're Detectives Steele and Kennedy. We would like to have a few words with you concerning a case that we're working on," TJ replied. "We understand you appraised two pieces of jewelry for Vanessa Jewelers earlier this week."

"That's correct. A rare gold necklace and a gold diamond-studded key. Why?"

"One of those pieces was stolen." TJ closely watched his reaction.

"I assume the quinto necklace was taken. In my view, it's the only one worth stealing," Hamish said casually. "I also assume you saw my appraisal. I didn't bother to price the key as it has no historical value. I left that judgment to Monica."

"Did you give the necklace that name—'quinto'?" Jamie asked. She gazed at jewelry and artifacts inside a glass case. "I noticed you called it that in your appraisal, too."

"The major pieces of the necklace were 22-carat gold ingots that were minted in Mexico for the Spanish King Philip IV in the mid-1600s. Quinto is the name of a royal tax back then, so I thought it appropriate to name the necklace as such." Hamish smiled.

"You had a special interest in the necklace?"

"Not really. It's what I do—handle historical items. I become interested if one is as rare as that necklace."

"Rare because?" Jamie asked.

"Gold ingots with those particular stampings have only been found on the Santa Regio, a sunken Spanish galleon off the coast of Florida."

"Have you seen ingots like these before?" Jamie looked up from the glass case at Hamish.

He momentarily paused, "I don't believe ingots like these have been seen here on the West Coast. I often conduct extensive research when I appraise pieces such as the necklace. I assumed the owner of the necklace purchased the ingots through the Internet."

"Did anyone else know you had those pieces here, Mr. Firth?" TJ asked, catching his slight hesitation.

"I work alone. I run a specialty business. I rely on my experience and the Internet to appraise and locate goods." He glanced at Jamie who was strolling around the store. "I returned the two pieces to Monica in person late Wednesday morning, I believe." Hamish's tone became stilted, and he looked slightly agitated. "If the quinto shows up here, I will call."

"It was the gold whale key—not the necklace—that was stolen, Mr. Firth." TJ noted the surprise on Hamish's face. "Did you know the name or address of the person who owned those pieces?"

"I worked for Monica. She had contact with the customer," he replied curtly. "Not me."

"Ms. Davies indicated the name and address of her customer was on the receipt you signed. Do you recall that?"

"I never noticed. I checked the listed goods and signed. Are you suggesting I was involved in the robbery of the key?"

"The key wasn't the objective of the heist—the quinto was. As you said, it was the piece with historical value." The shop was silent for a moment. "Thank you for your time." Jamie placed her card on the glass counter and stared at Hamish. "We'll call if we need to talk to you again, Sir." She abruptly left the store.

TJ met Jamie out by their car. "The guy goes to the bother of naming the necklace and then pretends he has only a casual interest. You see his reaction in there?" Jamie asked.

"Sure did. I think he has a greater interest in the necklace than he admitted," TJ replied. "Where do we go from here?"

"We should let Ms. Archie know that we recovered her earrings and ring. I know she wants the gold whale key, but we're out of leads at this point."

"We can't close the case—even though we've identified the burglar—until we recover the gold key. Someone paid Collins to steal the quinto necklace. My money's on Firth unless a better candidate shows."

⚓

Dillon and Adrianne were stuffed from their meal at the campus pub and were now sprawled on Dillon's bed.

"This diving program is brutal, Adrianne. I'm exhausted. Doing it in one day is crazy."

"You got that right, but you did it. Come on," she poked his shoulder, "let's read the diary. I'll bet I know what happens."

"We know part of the ending." Dillon climbed off the bed to get the diary from his backpack.

"Let me. I want to read some, too." Adrianne took the book and found the folded corner that marked their last place. She flipped pages and discovered one with a torn upper corner and a penned star. "Hey, this page has already been marked."

Monday 3ʳᵈ November 1975;

The weather was foul today. A gale started to blow up the strait at noon, and the villagers prepared for wind and driving rain. The howling wind and pelting rain on the wooden roof encouraged everyone to go to bed early. Windows rattled and the sound of things torn from the ground was intimidating as I prepared for bed and made my notes before the loss of light. I hope the villagers don't find too much damage in the morning.

Tuesday 4ᵗʰ November 1975;

I didn't hear Gloria creep into my room last night. The sound of her footsteps was drowned out by the blistering racket of the storm outside. I couldn't see her face, but felt her as she snuggled into my bed and wrapped her arms about my body beneath the bedcovers; I knew she was scared. She turned to me, kissed my lips, and removed her clothes. She whispered 'χaλnomεč' a number of times and ran her hand slowly down my chest to my crotch to arouse me. She slid her smooth body on top of mine. No one in the house could hear with the clamor of the storm as she straddled my body and eased me into her. 'Just love me,' she spoke, encouraging my seed to flow. Just love me. We made love a second time before she left my bed. I looked at her this morning, but didn't say anything. She flashed me a big smile and left me to do my business with her father. I loved her passionate desire and intimacy, but she is only seventeen. I know she will bring shame onto her family if anyone discovers what we did the night before.

The diary entries aroused Dillon. He put his arm around Adrianne's waist and turned to gaze into her captivating eyes.

She placed the diary beside her. She turned her head and studied Dillon's deep, dark glistening eyes that scrutinized hers, looking for something. They hesitated. Dillon slowly moved his lips toward hers, their eyes now locked together. He kissed her soft, alluring lips, and passion welled up. She returned the kiss, raising her hands to his head, and caressed his soft, smooth, black hair. Her tongue slipped between his lips. She felt his hand caress her shoulder, pulling them into a tighter embrace.

The time for words was gone. Dillon could feel her racing heart as he placed his hand on her sweater-covered breast. She sharply inhaled, but didn't stop his advance, and ran her hand along his chest feeling his pounding heart.

They both stopped moving, searching for something in the other's eyes. Adrianne pulled off her knitted sweater and his t-shirt while he sat transfixed by the soft features of her face. She ran her fingers through black chest hair that contrasted against his golden-colored skin.

Dillon closed his eyes to savor the aroma of her subtle perfume on her skin, its scent stored in his memory. He moved his body to her touch, lifting his hands to caress her firm breasts through her sheer bra. He held his breath as her hand slowly slid down his bare chest, occasionally stopping to play with his hair, and continuing on its journey past his navel.

Blood rushed through his veins as he pulled himself closer, kissing her while he fumbled to unclip the front of her bra. She was amused at his struggle while they embraced, leaving him to his challenge.

She unbuttoned his blue jean pants and pulled the zipper down. She felt her bra finally release and the narrow straps slip loosely over her shoulders. Dillon slid his hand under a loose cup and caressed the breast with the palm of his hand. She sensed his inexperience, unzipped the side of her summer white skirt. She closed her eyes as Dillon kissed her neck and continued to caress her breast, running the palm of his hand over her stiffening nipple, sending tingles down her spine. She savored his gentle touch as sensation bolted through her body craving more of his caress. She took his hand and guided it under her loosened skirt.

He felt the silky touch of her lace panties as his hand slipped across the top of the material. He ran a finger along the edge of her panties around her inner thigh. She spread her legs to accommodate his touch. His fingers searched for a passage under the restraint of the material.

The downstairs door opened and banged shut. "It's us." Josh's voice broke the mood, and Dillon and Adrianne both yanked their hands out from each other's underpants.

"Josh and Niki," Dillon whispered. He looked terrified he would be caught partially undressed in his bedroom with Adrianne.

Adrianne snatched her top, zipped up her skirt and ran toward the bathroom. Her unclipped bra flopped over her breasts. The door closed behind her.

Dillon zipped up his pants. His arousal was still fed by throbbing blood; he was frustrated and wanted to make love with Adrianne. He cleared his throat. "I'm up here reading. You're home early for a Friday."

"It's been a long day. We're going to the Paparazzi Nightclub. You two want to come with us? It's not just a gay bar." It was obvious Josh was excited. "It'll be fun."

"Maybe another night." Dillon tried to regain his composure. His disappointment at the interruption lingered.

Dillon stared at the closed bathroom door. He hoped Adrianne would come back, but she didn't.

Adrianne looked at her almost naked upper body in the bathroom mirror. She was flushed, aroused, and disappointed. She removed her bra, skirt, and lace panties. She looked again at her nude body in the mirror and smiled.

Dillon contemplated going to Adrianne's room to satisfy his passion He inhaled her sweet perfume that lingered in the air. He ached for her, but instead, forced himself to accept that he would have to wait for another opportunity to make love to Adrianne.

He thought about the entries in his grandfather's journal; how his grandmother Gloria must have wanted Walter and how much Walter wanted her. He could relate to the passion they had shared. His mother had been right; he wasn't ready for the diary before. He hadn't been mature enough to know the passion two people could share.

Dillon began to consider words that weren't in the diary, what Walter must have felt and didn't express in the written lines. He looked at the closed bathroom door again, and decided to get ready for bed.

♓

Selina worked on an unfinished painting that she promised herself would be completed for the fundraiser. She felt better now that she had updated her insurance policy to cover the quinto necklace, and hoped the police would soon recover her golden key. Selina stopped working, her focus distracted by how her mother would react to the incident. She decided against telling her mother. She hadn't been injured, and it was only jewelry.

Her cell phone rang as she sat and stared at her canvas. The phone rang a second time. She answered, "Hello."

"Selina, it's Aunt Cecilia. Sorry I'm calling late."

"Is Mom okay?" she choked out, suddenly tense.

"She's failing, Selina. The doctor recommends that you come for the weekend. I'm working a prescheduled charter tomorrow, and I can't spend all day with her. It's critical you come as soon as you can."

"Yes, of course. I'll be on the first flight out tomorrow morning. Get some rest, Aunt Cecilia."

Six

Eduardo found Hamish with a coffee, looking out at his magnificent ocean view. Clouds were accumulating, and the weather report warned of a storm that would engulf Victoria by noon.

"Up early, I see. Still thinking about your conversation with the cops?"

"I couldn't sleep. I became annoyed, and it shouldn't have happened. I knew the cops would come."

"One thing's for sure. The kid paid to do the job didn't get the quinto. I doubt he got the information you wanted either. It doesn't matter what happened to him or the key."

"The cops can't connect me to the heist, but the kid could connect you, so be careful. I think we should focus on the Archie woman ourselves."

"I purchased a disposable phone before I started to deal with Perez. I left him a voicemail Thursday night to find out what happened to Chaz." Eduardo poured a cup of coffee. "I haven't called Perez back yet."

"That conversation will be interesting. You need to get to the girl and find out where she got that necklace. You created this mess, so fix it."

"I'd better check what Perez has to say." Eduardo dialed the number. He listened a few moments before he said, "I called Thursday night and left you a message about Chaz. What's the story?" He was silent as he listened to Perez.

"Stupid, I'd say. You'd better be more careful who you recommend next time. You owe me now, Mr. Perez." Eduardo slammed the phone down on the coffee table. "It seems as though Chaz ODd the night of the heist. That solves that problem."

"As far as I'm concerned, it's good news. We can focus on the girl." Hamish walked toward the kitchen. "You were going to comment on how you're going to get the quinto information."

"Since I won't be paid for obtaining the necklace, maybe I should just go back to Vancouver. I've got my own business to run, Hamish, and this looks like a waste of time. Who cares where the damn thing came from?"

"Because I think there are more gold Spanish ingots somewhere on the West Coast. I don't believe that whoever gave Ms. Archie the quinto purchased the ingots on the Internet just to make a necklace. The value is destroyed if they are altered. There's another explanation, and I want to know what it is."

Eduardo thought about the possibility. "You're the expert, Hamish. If you want my help, we need a new arrangement. I've already invested time in this and have nothing to show for it."

Hamish pondered his answer. "I must stay at arm's length, Eduardo. The cops are already suspicious about my interest in the quinto." He returned to staring out the window at the ocean. "Two grand a day for your efforts and ten percent of the value of whatever is found."

"I expect that to be ten percent of nothing, but the two grand a day will work until we determine if there's anything to pursue. I've been here for four days. The daily rate applies from the day I arrived, Hamish. I want that payment before I go any farther. I don't usually engage in this type of business."

"Sounds reasonable, Eduardo. What's your next step?" Hamish wore a calculating smile.

"Ms. Archie takes transit to work. I'll follow her on Monday morning and see where that leads me. The more I know about her, the better our chances of finding where the necklace came from."

♓

The rain poured outside as Selina sat crying with her aunt in her mother's house in Sliammon. The weather had turned bitterly cold for an early September day on the west coast. The rain reflected the solemn mood of the pair as they grieved the death of Clara-Meyers Archie. It was family time, and there was only Cecilia and Selina. Neighbors and friends would visit later, but now it was a time to make peace with the woman who had fought excruciating pain her last few days.

"I didn't get here in time, Aunt Cecilia," Selina sniffed, her eyes red from tears.

"She passed faster than expected in the end, Selina. It's better than the pain and suffering caused by that awful disease. She's gone to be with your father."

"I feel so bad, not just because she's gone, but … but I lost it, her gift she gave to me the last time I was here. She was going to explain, but now I'll never know."

"What are you talking about, Selina?" Cecilia asked. "You lost what?"

"Mom said something about a secret, one you don't know about. She promised Dad. I lost the key ... it's so ... so," she tried to explain through the flow of her tears.

"Secret? About your father, Selina?" Cecilia frowned.

"I don't know, something about mending fences with Gloria-Louie Paul." Selina wiped her tears with her shirt sleeve. "She said it was time because Dillon Point is now a man ... and ... and starting his life like me. What does that mean, Aunt Cecilia?"

"This isn't the time to talk about this. Make peace with your mother now, and things will work out," Cecilia replied softly, placing her arm around her niece. "It will be okay."

⧓

Dillon sat in the passenger seat of Adrianne's Mazda sports car as the pair headed for Ross Bay. He couldn't wait to meet his grandfather, Walter, but all he could focus on was Adrianne and how he felt about her. Neither of them had talked much that morning, not knowing what to say about the night before.

It wasn't long before Adrianne was driving past Ross Bay Cemetery looking for Earle Place Road. She turned the vehicle onto the street and began to concentrate on the house numbers. "You ready, Dillon? Here it is."

Walter's Victorian home needed upkeep and repair. It was a 1920s bungalow on a quiet street lined with mature oak trees, which were now beginning to show fall colors.

Adrianne parked the Mazda on the street outside the house, and she and Dillon walked to the front porch and rang the doorbell.

An elderly woman opened the door to the visitors.

"I'm Dillon Point. I called earlier. I am Dr. Smith's grandson."

"Come in. I'm Christina, the caregiver." The woman opened the door to let the guests enter.

"This is my friend, Adrianne Padrino. We haven't come at an inappropriate time, have we?"

"Come into the sitting room. I told you on the telephone that Dr. Smith isn't well. His memory is poor these days. It comes and goes." Christina led the pair into a bright front room. "Please, take a seat, and I'll fetch him."

Dillon glanced over at Adrianne as the two sat on a floral-patterned loveseat. Dillon placed his backpack beside him as the pair looked around, waiting for Christina. The room was tastefully decorated with a calming, inviting charm.

"These are the guests I told you about, Walter," Christina said quietly. She led him by the arm to a seat. Walter was sixty-eight, but looked more like eighty with balding gray hair that rimmed his head, and anemic-colored skin. He smiled with a blank stare, and sat quietly where Christina had placed him.

Dillon returned his smile and pulled Walter's diary from his backpack. "Do you recall this, Dr. Smith?" Dillon asked, with the book in hand as he walked toward Walter. "I'm your grandson, and this is your diary of the time you spent with the Sliammon."

Walter stared at the tattered book for a moment. "Yes, I remember that book. It's about Gloria. I loved her," he said in a frail voice. "I left her by herself with our unborn child. I was a coward …."

"Gloria is my grandmother. My mother is your daughter." Tears began to form as Dillon looked at the shell of a man.

Walter's eyes were fixated on the floor. "Secrets ... the book of secrets," he mumbled almost inaudibly, and then said no more.

Dillon gave the man a hug, returned to the loveseat, and looked up at Christina as tears ran down his cheeks.

"I'd better take him back to his room." Christina touched Walter's arm.

Dillon and Adrianne watched as Christina led Walter slowly from the room.

After they disappeared, Dillon wiped his tears with a tissue. "I'd hoped for more, but I'm glad I got to see him." He sniffled as he placed the diary back into the backpack. "I think we should go. I don't want to overstay our welcome."

Christina smiled sympathetically when she saw the two waiting for her in the front foyer. "Have a safe journey."

"Thank you, Christina. This was a special moment for me. I appreciated the opportunity to see him and your kind hospitality."

Dillon put his backpack in the back seat of the car and solemnly waited for Adrianne to climb into the driver's seat.

"Are you all right, Dillon?" Adrianne asked.

He didn't answer. She turned on the engine and pulled from the curb, leaving Dillon with his thoughts.

"Less than a month ago, I thought Brett Paul was my grandfather." Dillon turned to face Adrianne. "Everything's complicated. My mother said there were answers in the diary, explanations to questions I've had since I was a child. Walter is incapable of providing those."

"It's sad isn't it, Dillon ... feeling regret. Love is a powerful emotion."

"The sight of the diary jolted his memory, even though just for a moment." Dillon sighed. "Secrets ... loving her and leaving her. How do you do that? Abandon the woman you love and your unborn child?"

"I don't know … maybe something happened, Dillon. Maybe he had no choice." Adrianne drove toward their house downtown.

♓

"Selina, the coroner said that we should plan your mother's funeral for next Friday. I'll handle the arrangements, and you let me know when to pick you up at the airport." Cecilia appeared in the sitting room where Selina was alone with her thoughts.

"Aunt Cecilia, I was wondering if you know what happened between Gloria-Louie Paul and my father. I assume that was the secret she talked about."

"As your mother said, I don't know. I tried to get your father to tell me many years ago, but he said it was a private matter between him and Brett Paul. It happened a long time ago, in the mid-1990s, when you were about four or five."

"I don't get the reference about Dillon Point either—that he's an adult and building a life just as I am. It makes no sense."

"Whatever it was, no one in the community knew about it. You know how gossip works around here. It's impossible to keep secrets long." Cecilia stood by the window and gazed at the pelting rain. "The winter storms are coming early. I had to cancel my charter last night. Just as well, I guess."

"Now that Mom's gone, losing the key makes me feel sick. It was special to her in some way, but now I may never know how."

"A key to what?" Cecilia frowned, then became lost in thought. She turned back to Selina with eyes lit up. "A gold key with diamonds … like a whale fluke on the end, flat on one side. That key?"

"Yes, that key. It was in a box Mom gave to me last week. The box had a gold necklace and the key inside. Do you know what was special about it, Aunt Cecilia?"

"Yes, I have one just like it. Your father gave it to me and asked me to save it for your wedding day, Selina. I put it away many years ago. I'll have to find it. It came with a wooden carved box I think … it was a long time ago. I'd forgotten all about it."

"Please look for it, Aunt Cecilia. Maybe I won't need my key after all."

♓

Dillon propped a couple of pillows on the headboard next to Adrianne to read his diary. The storm had moved in with a vengeance, and the evening was ugly outside. "I'd like to see what Walter's story tells me about what he said about secrets. That seemed a strange thing to say."

Adrianne pushed close to him, laid her head on his chest, and didn't know what to say. "It's likely about their love affair. He said he thought he was a coward. That's the secret in his mind, Dillon."

Dillon tried to ignore the scent of her perfume and her closeness.

Wednesday 5ʰ November 1975;
> *A group of men in the village had been fishing on the southern tip of Harwood Island and found a man half-dead from exposure on Vivian Island. The man was taken to a house where the village spiritual leader lived and was put into a bed. The poor man was delirious. I was asked to see the man while a doctor from Powell River was called. I couldn't help, and I*

couldn't make sense of his rambling words. The ravaging Monday storm must've caught the man off-guard and his boat was lost in the storm. Today was cold and clouds moved in, threatening another episode of heavy rain. I decided to check on him later in the day.

I spoke with the survivor again later today when the doctor from Powell River finally showed up. The doctor ordered the sailor moved to the hospital in Powell River, and an ambulance was called. I was at the man's bedside while we waited. He was wrapped in blankets and weak. He tried to grab my arm and speak. I couldn't hear him so I brought my ear close to his mouth. He whispered that he, his brother, and another man were on a schooner headed for Campbell River when the gale caught them by surprise. They tried to head for shore and hit a submerged rock that damaged the hull. The wind blew the ship toward Vivian Island where the schooner apparently broke into pieces and drifted further north up the channel. I felt bad when I told him that he was the only survivor. He closed his eyes for a moment, whispered 'Diablo' a number of times, and then didn't speak any more.

The paramedics arrived and placed him on a stretcher as he regained consciousness. He still wasn't doing well, and the doctor said he sustained many injuries, as well as extreme exposure. The man stared at me, indicated with his hand that he wanted to say something. I didn't know what to do and leaned down to hear his labored voice. He whispered he had something for me, and he struggled to give me a gold coin from his pocket. No one saw him pass it to me. He told me there were hundreds more in the hull of the schooner. The bounty was his gift to me for my help. I asked him what 'Diablo' meant, but he was too weak to answer. He died later this afternoon on the stretcher before he reached the hospital.

I told no one of our conversation or of the gold coin. I've decided to wait to speak with Gloria when we meet on Sunday. I know I have strong feelings for her. I think I love her, but don't know the right thing to do or say.

Thursday 6th November 1975;
The Chief called his council together today. They agreed with the Tla'amin desire to bury the sailor on Harwood Island with their ancestors. The sailor has no identification. They believe it's the right thing to do because he died on their lands. Gloria's parents talked briefly about the decision at the evening meal, and were proud that the Tla'amin could give the poor mariner a proper burial. It was bitterly cold today.

Friday 7th November 1975;
The weather was dreadful today. All I could think about was telling Gloria about the mariner's secret.

Dillon couldn't concentrate on the story anymore, and he placed the diary on the floor. He leaned back over and embraced Adrianne, moved to kiss her soft lips as he felt his arousal increase.

Adrianne gently pushed him back. "That reading didn't last long. The story's just getting interesting."

"You're all that interests me right now, Ms. Padrino." Dillon tried to kiss her.

She slightly pulled back. "I was thinking while you read. We should find out more about the coin that Walter writes about. I'll bet it's the one in the black and white photograph." She sat up. "Get me your computer, Dillon."

"Right now?" He wanted to cuddle with Adrianne and consummate what they hadn't finished the prior night.

"Yes," she said, knowing what was on his mind.

Dillon sighed.

Adrianne placed the laptop on her legs and began keying. "Let's see ... coins." She waited for the search results.

Dillon climbed onto the bed and peered over her shoulder. Firth Coin and Rarities' website page appeared at the top.

"This guy's local. I'll take a picture of your black and white on my cell and email it to him. Dillon, grab the photo from your mirror frame."

Dillon scrunched his face, did as he was asked, and placed the photograph on the keyboard.

Adrianne took the snapshot, attached it to an email and typed a short text. She passed her phone to Dillon "You read it and send it if you're satisfied."

I'm interested in the coin in this photograph. Your website states you are an expert on antiquities and rare coins. What can you tell me about the one in this photo? Please reply to this email address.

Dillon pressed the send key on her phone.

"You never know, Dillon, it might be worth it."

"If it makes you happy, I'm happy. How about a kiss now?"

Seven

Hamish was up early, even though it was Sunday. The clearing morning sky looked magnificent from his luxury home with its panoramic, oceanfront view, overlooking Trial Island and the calm ocean. The property was situated in prestigious Oak Bay and was only ten minutes from downtown Victoria.

He sipped his coffee, pondering the disappointing loss of the quinto. He was trying to quash his anger with Eduardo. Eduardo had no clue why the loss was so important, and Hamish had no intention of disclosing his obsession with the Spanish ingots. The necklace confirmed his suspicion that at least a portion of the Santa Regio treasure had made its way to the west coast.

"A million dollar view, amigo." Eduardo interrupted his friend's contemplation.

"Eduardo. I was thinking of something pleasant to do today." Hamish walked back into the house to sit at his laptop on the kitchen island. "How about we take the yacht out for a spin? It's been three years since I've done that. Just let me check my emails first."

"Sounds fun. I've got some business of my own to attend to as well."

Hamish grunted. "I better look at this on the computer monitor."

"What's that, Hamish?" Eduardo asked, as he placed a coffee pack into the coffee maker.

"Just a moment, Eduardo," he said in a distracted voice.

Moments later, Hamish scrutinized the monitor. "Can't be." Hamish turned to Eduardo. "Could you do some research for me? I need to know if the Spanish were around these parts in the mid-to-late 1600s."

"Hamish, you should know if they were. You're the expert."

"I thought I did, but I need to be sure. The quinto necklace is made of ingots from Mexico for King Philip IV. Perhaps some of tax gold came up this coast and it hasn't been discovered yet—or no one has admitted it for some reason. Just see what you can find out. I have something else to investigate."

♓

Adrianne parked her Mazda in the private stall designated "Second World Diving BC" in the West Bay Marina parking lot. "You can always tell Sundays. The parking lot is full."

The pair, carrying the diving gear, headed for the marina's floating dock. Adrianne climbed aboard the boathouse and knocked on the office sliding door.

"I've got your Zodiac ready to go." Nathan gave Dillon the once-over.

"Nathan Lenox, this is Dillon Point, the friend I told you about."

Dillon shook Nathan's hand. "This is my second open-water dive, and I'm pumped."

"Private lessons and all, Adrianne," Nathan remarked with a smirk. "You sure you don't want me to come along? I've got nothing going on until later in the day."

"We'll be fine, Nathan. We left the used tanks on the dock, but we'll take the rest of the gear with us."

"The weather's going to close in later, so be back by lunch time. Call me on the radio if you need me."

♓

Selina tried to concentrate on a painting she needed for her art exhibition, just two weeks away. An envelope with Selina and *χaλnomɛɂ* handwritten on the front was on a table littered with tubes of oil paints, some with open caps. She knew the writing was her father's. She had brought the envelope home, along with the jewelry box, the week before. It was still unopened.

She put her paintbrush down and gazed at the envelope. The writing was bold and strong, and not that of a man with chronic arthritis in his hands—arthritis caused by his jeweler occupation.

It was obvious the letter inside the envelope was written many years ago. She was unsure if she wanted to read the message. Her mother had never spoken of the envelope, and Selina wondered why not. Her thoughts wandered to the cryptic conversation she had had with her mother—their last words before she died—about mending fences and Dillon Point.

Selina recalled her fortunate circumstances growing up, and how difficult it had been for Dillon. She didn't know him well as they were two years apart in age, but everyone knew that his mother, Robbie-Paul Point, had struggled; his whole family had struggled for that matter.

Selina sighed, and turned her attention away from the envelope. Somehow it didn't seem right to open the message with the whale key missing. She decided to await recovery of the key by the police first. She hoped it would be soon.

♓

Hamish Firth had an enlarged picture on his office computer of the black and white photograph he had received from Adrianne Padrino. The focal point of the photograph had the image of the coin enlarged and showed only blurred features of the surface. The image sat in the corner of the screen, and Hamish tried to compare the markings on the coin to other images that were displayed on a reference website. It was definitely an escudo minted in Bogotá around 1656, the same as those found on the Santa Regio, he concluded.

He leaned back in his leather chair. He had several questions, for which he had no answers. Why was there an escudo in a First Nations community? Why was the First Nations girl with an older white guy? Who was the white man and why was he there? Why did the escudo and the quinto necklace show up at the same time?

Hamish tapped his fingers on his desktop, then got out of his chair. He walked into the sitting room where Eduardo was working on a laptop computer. "Eduardo, find any Spaniards up here in the mid-to-late 1600s?"

"The earliest records of the Spaniards in this area are about the mid-1700s. It is said there was a Spanish mine east of Harrison Lake. The natives said that they saw ships with great white wings. Many historians believe the Spanish were there in search of gold. A Spanish wreck can be found as far north up the inside passage as Bute Inlet."

"The only other information about Spanish explorers is about José Narváez, a Spanish naval officer and explorer, who was around the Pacific Northwest in 1791. That's it, nothing earlier."

"Other than pirates coming up here to stash their loot, the quinto ingots must've originated from back east then," said Hamish.

"Are we going out in your yacht, Hamish?" Eduardo looked at the changing weather outside. "I still have some work to finish."

"Maybe another day."

♓

"Race Rocks was awesome," Dillon said, as the pair sat in the Princess Mary Pub situated beside the parking lot of the marina. "I can't believe those basket stars, giant red urchins, and anemones. You can't see that where I live without scuba equipment."

"It's one of my favorite spots. Race Rocks is considered by some to be one of the best cold water dive sites in the world."

Adrianne changed the subject and commented, "We haven't talked about what we read in your grandfather's diary the other night. Have you thought about what he wrote about the sailor and the coin he was given?"

"I'm curious what 'Diablo' means, and what my Grandmother Gloria has to say about all of this."

"It sounds Spanish to me." Adrianne decided to leave the discussion alone until later.

She was intrigued by the schooner and the mystery of lost gold coins in the shipwreck. She had made many dives around local shipwrecks, but none that weren't well known and thoroughly explored. The thought of a new, undiscovered shipwreck was exciting, and she was going to find it if it existed.

Her mind wandered to Dillon. She liked him—not merely for her interest in the coin mystery—but she didn't want to admit it to him just yet.

⚓

Hamish tried to reconcile Eduardo's information with his own thoughts. The facts weren't meshing. Hamish pulled a notepad out from the front of his drawer and scribbled a note:

Call Dr. Wallace Redding first thing Monday morning. Check if he's available for a meeting on whether he can identify the white guy and location in the black and white photo.

⚓

Dillon was surrounded by textbooks on his bed. He had an assignment due Monday morning and he hadn't started yet. He knew he was distracted by Adrianne and Walter's diary. He had to focus on his studies. Adrianne was busy, too, thankfully.

He had promised Adrianne to spend more time on the coin mystery the following weekend, but that plan required that he call his mother.

"I was wondering when you were going to call, Dillon. How are classes?"

"I'm having a great time here, Mom, and learning a lot. I can't talk too long. I have an assignment due tomorrow. A friend and I plan to come to Sliammon next Friday to stay overnight."

"That's okay, but isn't it expensive, Dillon? You need your money for school."

"My friend is paying for the trip."

"Don't you have classes on Fridays?"

"That's when my friend wants to go, Mom. I can catch up on the weekend."

"Okay, Dillon. I'm excited to see you and meet your friend. See you Friday."

"Love you."

Eight

Jamie exited the elevator and noticed TJ was already working at her desk. "Up with the birds, I see." She placed her Starbucks coffee on her partner's desk. "What brings you in so early on a Monday?"

"I'm working on the Collins OD case, and thought I would look at the video for that night," TJ glanced up at Jamie. "The coroner said the estimated time of death was around 22:30. There was a visitor who came to the door at 23:35 according to the date and time stamp. The visitor had an entry code, though." She paused, "The same person left seven minutes later at 23:42."

Jamie pulled around a chair so that she could view the computer monitor.

"The visitor had his coat pulled up around his face as though he knew where the video camera was, and all I can make out is shapes because of the fog."

"The time frame fits. Seven minutes would've been long enough to threaten Collins and force him to take an overdose.

The responding constables said Collins' door hadn't been forced open, though. It would've been shit luck if Collins' door hadn't been locked. Maybe our unknown suspect was expected."

"I figure that, since Collins screwed up the heist and whoever funded the B&E was pissed because Collins didn't deliver the quinto, there may have been a planned meeting to develop a back-up plan. The meeting went nowhere so Collins was terminated for his incompetence. I'm looking into known associates of Collins to see who might've hired him."

"Great work, TJ. I'll update the inspector to let him know that homicide hasn't been ruled out, and that we're continuing our investigation. I think he was going to give us another assignment this morning." Jamie picked up her coffee and headed for her office.

"Oh, I almost forgot. The lab report on the pill found in Collins' pocket was on my desk this morning. It was a 20mg ecstasy, so that's consistent with the coroner's toxicology findings. No surprise there," TJ called after Jamie.

♓

Eduardo sat at the back of the Pandora Avenue bus headed for downtown Victoria. Downtown businesses opened at nine on workday mornings, so he assumed that Selina would likely catch the eight twenty bus at the Camosun Street stop. If she didn't show, he had ten minutes before the next bus, and he was prepared to get off and wait for the next one. He was relieved when she climbed aboard and found a seat close to the front.

Selina eventually stood to get off at the corner of Fort and Government. She exited from the front and Eduardo exited from the back doors, along with a group of other passengers.

It was a warm, sunny morning. Eduardo kept his distance as he followed Selina from the opposite side of the street. She knocked on the front door of Munro's Books of Victoria and waited to be let in. He looked for a nearby coffee shop to plan his next move.

♓

Hamish was in the back room of his coin shop. Even though his business didn't rely on tourists, he always opened at the same time as other stores in Market Square. He had built a solid reputation since he'd started out. Coins and antiquities were a lot more profitable than most of his business friends realized. He suddenly remembered that he had planned to call Wallace this morning.

Hamish dialed his friend at the University of British Colombia.

"Hamish, my friend, how's business?" Wallace asked, with a strong Scottish accent.

"Holding with the economy, Wallace. I must get out there and see your new exhibition, but you know how time rushes by."

"Come soon, Hamish, and I'll buy lunch. What can I help you with?"

"I'm doing some research on BC First Nations artifacts and trying to identify a man in a black and white photograph. It seems he worked with the First Nations quite a number of years ago. I'm going to email you the photo. I'll wait until you get it."

The line went silent for a moment, then Hamish heard the phone being picked up.

"That man is Walter Smith. He was studying BC First Nations' cultures and languages in the seventies. I think he did some work at the University of Victoria, too. He published a number of books on First Nations' heritage in the Lower Mainland and the North Coast. I believe he retired years ago."

"Could you ask around to find out where he is now, Wallace? I'd like to talk to him as soon as possible."

"Sounds important. Anything you can you share with me?"

"It's likely a wild goose chase, Wallace, but I need to check out my information before I say anything."

"Sure thing. I'll make a few calls and get back to you if I can find anything. Remember about lunch …."

Hamish put down the phone, and thought about what Walter Smith likely uncovered in the seventies. Hamish knew there was more to the photograph than anyone suspected. He recalled the early days after he had opened his first shop in Gastown.

He walked to a corner in the cluttered back room. The black banker's safe looked like any other collectable, but it wasn't. Hamish rotated the dial a number of times, pulled down the chipped, chrome handle, and opened the heavy door. He reached into the back of the bottom shelf, moved aside an engraved Soviet pistol, and extracted one of ten gold ingots impressed with Spanish stamps.

He brought it to his desk and placed it on the copy of the black and white photograph that he'd made from Adrianne Padrino's email attachment.

Hamish pushed aside a coffee that was now cold, and reached for a half-full bottle of scotch. He poured some into his glass, sat down in his chair, and stared at the five-ounce, oblong-shaped bar of 22-carat gold. He had purchased five gold ingots in 1977 from a Mexican man who said he needed emergency cash.

It had been a highly unusual transaction, but the ingots had intrigued him, and he remembered how ecstatic he'd been with his opportune purchase. Hamish sobered when he remembered the Mexican's appearance two years later in the summer of 1979 with five more bars, saying he needed money for a new baby on the way.

Damn, stupid Mexican. It was an accident. Hamish had just wanted to know the Mexican's source, but the Mexican had pulled a Soviet handgun. Hamish shuddered. The pool of blood, the sightless eyes, the Mexican's gray-toned skin. It was as clear today as it was all those years ago.

Hamish sighed, and put the ingot back into the safe and locked it. There was more to the ingots. Maybe the Padrino woman had the clue that had always eluded him. Hamish pulled out an address book. He put the call on speaker phone.

"Geek IT Services."

"Is this Jack Bryce?"

"Who's calling?"

"My name is Hamish. I was given your name by a mutual friend. I need your special services."

"What kind of services?"

"Nothing too complex for your skills, I understand. I received an email with an attachment. I need you find out everything you can about the person who sent the email."

"Not a problem. Five hundred dollars and cash payment by debit to my business account. That work for you, Hamish?"

"Five hundred's a bit steep, but I hear you're skilled and also discreet. I will have the funds to you in an hour."

"Send me the email you want traced. I'll get back to you later today with whatever I find."

Hopefully Wallace Redding would come through, too. Hamish finished his glass of scotch.

⊁

Chelsea Roberts couldn't wait for her break at Brasserie L'ecole. She was anxious to get her new necklace from the jeweler. She had to be back to work before the big rush that usually began at eleven thirty during the week. Mondays were no exception.

She hustled to Aurea Gems. "I'm here to pick up the whale key pendant you fixed for me so that I can wear it as a necklace." The woman disappeared for a moment, and then reappeared with the pendant. "It's beautiful. Do you need a chain for it?"

"Yes, please."

The clerk chose a selection from a cabinet behind her. Chelsea decided that a slender chain suited the pendant best.

The woman threaded the chain through the new whale key clasp. "We looked at this piece. It has real diamonds and is made with 22-carat gold. That's unusual these days."

"I didn't expect that. I bought it from a street vendor not far from here."

⊁

"Detective Kennedy, we've been given a few more days to wrap up this Collins case." Jamie stood by her partner's desk. "What have you uncovered about possible suspects for this potential homicide?"

TJ looked up from her computer monitor. "Well, the only person I think could've been involved, is the guy who helps rehab people like Collins. His name is Mason Perez. Mr. Perez has hovered mostly under the radar, but he's got a rap sheet for small time stuff that includes assault and a DUI, nine months ago."

"That's it, TJ?"

"Yes, but he was in a perfect position to find Collins a job—a B&E job. Perez would know if any of the rehabs were capable of pulling off a B&E and robbery."

"You think that Collins was capable? He screwed it up, TJ."

"Perhaps his track record was better. The circumstances described in the B&E report indicate to me that Ms. Archie was lucky, and Collins got caught in a bad moment. He could've been competent for the job."

"Keep checking on Perez. Let me know if you find enough to justify a discussion with him."

"Working on it." TJ turned back to her task.

♓

Hamish was happy. Dr. Wallace Redding had provided a phone number for Walter Smith.

"I'm looking for Dr. Walter Smith, the anthropologist."

"Dr. Smith can't come to the phone. Is there something I can do for you?"

"I'm an historian, and I'm interested in Dr. Smith's research from the seventies. I would like to talk to him about some specifics, if I may."

"I'm sorry, Sir, but Dr. Smith is unable to recall anything these days and is in poor health."

"Oh, I'm sorry. Are there any notes or memorabilia about his work that I may look through? It's important that I confirm my research."

"No, there's nothing like that here," Christina hesitated, "but …."

"You said, but?"

"His grandson was here and has a diary," Christina said, but then thought better of discussing Walter's business on the phone.

"Grandson. How would I contact—"

"Sorry, Sir. It's not my business. Good day." Christina hung up.

Damn woman. Diary ... the kid with the photograph.

♓

Eduardo realized that loitering outside the bookstore wasn't getting him closer to the information Hamish wanted. What was Hamish really after? Why was finding out where the quinto necklace came from so crucial? How could it be more vital than the necklace itself?

He decided to see what he could find out about Selina from the employees inside. His hope that she would leave the store was futile. He would have to be creative in not drawing suspicious attention to himself or his inquiries.

Eduardo entered and wandered around the open space, almost mindless of his objective for being there. He looked up at the two-story-high ceiling that looked like it had been designed by the Romans, then stood for a moment to study the large fabric banners hung on the walls. He didn't spot Selina, so he sauntered toward the main counter where a clerk was busy on a computer. He paused as he approached the desk and noticed a framed photograph of Selina on the stone service counter. He casually picked up the frame and studied the now-obvious advertisement.

"That's one of our staff, Selina Archie," the woman said. "She's an artist in her spare time, and is putting on a fundraiser to raise money for a skills program for her First Nations community. We don't usually advertise non-book-related events, but we wanted to support her."

"I think it's wonderful to help others." Eduardo mentally recorded the name of the gallery. "I'll try to attend." Through the corner of his eye, he saw Selina coming from the back of the store. He replaced the frame and walked toward the exit.

♓

"I like this 'Organizational Behavior' class," Adrianne remarked, as she and Dillon left the lecture hall. "Let's grab a coffee at the Biblio Café before heading home."

"Me, too. It'll help me with my community work when I return home," said Dillon.

Adrianne was taken aback. "You're going to go back to Sliammon when you graduate?"

"Of course. The community needs leaders when we finalize our new treaty and …" His voice trailed off when he noticed Adrianne's expression. "But things could change by the time I graduate."

Adrianne realized why Dillon backtracked. "I've got my plans, too. I'll run my dad's company. Maybe do my own thing for a while first, but as you said, circumstances can change." Neither said anything for a moment.

Adrianne changed the subject. "I got an email from the coin guy during class. He said the coin is called an escudo, and it was minted for the Spanish in the mid-1600s. He asked where the photo was taken."

"I wouldn't bother to answer him. You found out what you needed, although we probably should learn more about the escudo. I looked at the flights to Power River for Friday. How early did you want to leave?"

"I thought we could visit Comox first on Thursday. We have a diving operation there. You could get more diving experience, and then we can take one of our boats across the strait to Power River. The float plane from here would be fun."

"Sounds like a blast. I told my mother I was bringing a friend. My mother will love to meet you, and you could learn about my community." He stared at his coffee on the round table. "We live a simpler life at home, Adrianne ... and they'll make a big deal about your visit."

"What kind of big deal?"

"A beautiful girl with me from the big city ... questions ... our way of life." Dillon apprehensively studied Adrianne's sparkling, amber eyes. "I've never brought a girl home before."

"I can hold my own; I'm a big girl. Maybe we should read more of the diary before we go, so that I can understand if the story comes up."

"Walter's view about the Sliammon and ..." Dillon said quietly, lost in thought for a moment. "I don't know why I commented about that—maybe him being an outsider."

Adrianne comprehended the implication. "Will they have a problem with me because I'm not First Nations?"

"No ... I don't know ... I see your kindness, your heart and—" Dillon tried to explain, but was interrupted.

"I get it, and I can deal with it, Dillon. It'll be no different when you meet my parents." Adrianne gave him a peck on his cheek. "I'm excited to meet your family."

"Me, too." Dillon had no clue how his family, or the community for that matter, would react. He wasn't sure of himself, either.

♓

Hamish was content to sit in his office sipping scotch from a crystal glass. He was lost in thought as he slowly rotated the glass in his hand. He was pleased that Eduardo had a solid lead on Selina Archie's background.

An art exhibition was an excellent venue to obtain details about her heritage and family. Hamish wasn't content to wait another few weeks, though. Eduardo would be at the gallery the following morning. He pondered which First Nations community was to benefit from the fundraiser. While he was thinking about the exhibition, his phone rang.

"Mr. Firth, Jack Bryce. This a good time to talk?"

Hamish put his scotch on his desk, and pulled a notebook towards him. "Perfect time. What do you have for me, Mr. Bryce?"

"I've determined from Adrianne Padrino's Facebook page that she is nineteen, slim, and has shoulder-length brunette hair. She is in her second year at the University of Victoria in a business program. She shares a house in Ross Bay with three men, one a First Nations possibly and two Caucasians."

"Do you have an address for the Ross Bay house?"

"I checked the back rental listings for Ross Bay and matched the property from the advertising photo and the Facebook pictures. The house address is 2012 St. Charles Street." Jack hesitated a second. "I conduct surveillance as well, Mr. Firth. Is there anything specific you are looking for concerning this woman?"

Hamish didn't answer for a moment as he weighed the offer. "You might be helpful. I'm interested in a diary that perhaps belongs to the First Nations boy. I want information on that diary or anything to do with Spanish coins—escudos to be exact."

"A diary and coins—escudos? That's it?" Jack asked.

"This is a private conversation. Anything concerning this matter, you talk to me exclusively. Is that understood?"

"Sure, client privilege. Now for a reasonable fee, Mr. Firth. Five hundred a day for two hours a day, including incidentals, until you terminate my services by email. I require payment one day in advance. Agreed?"

"I agree on the conditions, but you have to report via email or phone call every day—immediately if the information is critical in your opinion. No messing with me, Mr. Bryce."

"I'll contact you tomorrow." Jack hung up.

"Eduardo, would you like a drink? It's near cocktail hour." Hamish found Eduardo engrossed in computer work in the sitting room.

"Thanks, amigo. A scotch will be fine." Eduardo placed his laptop on the leather sofa. "I've poked around the Internet to see what I can find on the Spanish ingots. As I'm sure you know, there was a manifest found in 1987 that listed cargo carried by the Santa Regio, a Spanish galleon shipwrecked off the coast of Florida. It had ingots like the ones in the quinto necklace and escudo coins."

"That's right. I read about the manifest when I was doing the research on the ingots of the quinto necklace," Hamish repeated as he poured scotch from the mini bar. "I didn't bother reading the detail concerning the manifest, though."

"The manifest listed other articles like the 'Necklace of Kings' and something called the 'El Rey Dorado,' which translates into the 'golden king.' The entire wreck has been explored for years, and apparently, a number of items on the manifest were never recovered, including the Necklace of Kings and the El Rey Dorado." Eduardo accepted the glass of scotch. "I know an expert, Pirro Marco, on Spanish shipwrecks."

"There's a debate whether the El Rey Dorado is a myth. I've read about it for years. I wonder what Marco thinks," Hamish said. "I've heard of him. He's a Colombian national who lives somewhere in Florida."

"He's from Sincelejo, a city on the Caribbean coast. I've never met him face to face though, and I think he might be retired," said Eduardo.

"A toast to you, and your fine day's work." Hamish raised his glass.

"I bet the ingots in the quinto necklace came from an Internet sale of the goods from the Santa Regio, Hamish. Don't expect anything else, my friend."

Nine

Jack sat in his yellow, rusty VW camper van early Tuesday morning watching the beautiful heritage Victoria house on St. Charles Street. The sun began to burn off the scattered cloud cover. It was a perfect day, while he sipped his Starbucks latté and waited for the occupants to leave for school. Jack was a third-year computer science student at the University of Victoria. He was a slight twenty-three-year-old, with a typical, computer geek appearance.

Two men he had seen on Adrianne's Facebook photos left the house on foot laughing and holding hands.

His patience eventually paid off. Adrianne Padrino and the First Nations boy left, wearing backpacks and holdings hands, as they walked toward Fairfield Road.

Jack knew from Adrianne's Facebook profile that they were students; therefore, the house would be vacant for hours. He got out of the van and slid open the passenger side door. Inside was a brown leather bag. He hauled out the bag, surveyed the area, darted across the street, and ran past the two vehicles into the backyard. He sped down the concrete stairs to the basement and plastered himself against the wooden door until he was satisfied that no one had seen his arrival. The staircase above shielded him from the view of neighboring houses.

He pulled a plastic case with his lock-picking tools from his inside coat pocket. In less than ten seconds, the door was unlocked and Jack was inside the basement. He stood in the musty and poorly lit room and surveyed the area.

All was silent. Jack hunched in the low-ceilinged room and crept up the stairs. He paused at the top. The silence remained unbroken. He carefully turned a brass knob and entered the main floor.

He checked the main floor bedroom, picked through a few items on the dresser; it was obviously the gays' room. Floorboards creaked as he crossed the floor and climbed the upper staircase, but he was unconcerned.

He chose to first search the room that was to the right at the top of the staircase. The door was open. The books and framed photographs indicated that it was the girl's room. He rummaged in his bag and placed in the foliage of a silk tree in a corner a minuscule, wireless, video camera recorder pointed in the direction of the bed.

It wasn't long before Jack repeated the same process in Dillon Point's room. He took a picture on his cell phone of the black and white photograph pressed between the mirror and the frame of the mirror. He thoroughly searched for the diary, but came up empty-handed.

Jack returned to the main floor to search for the cable and Internet modem. He split the cable and inserted a digital box.

He shoved his tools into the bag and walked downstairs to the basement. He looked out the door window for neighbors and, seeing no one, exited the house to return to his vehicle. He double-checked that he remained unseen, pitched the bag onto the passenger seat and started the van. All he needed now was a network password.

♓

It was late morning by the time Eduardo located Dales Gallery in downtown, historic Victoria. The gallery shared space in a brick building with windows that overlooked the busy Chinatown life that attracted locals and tourists. The bright red door, set into a white, wooden frame, buzzed as he entered the art gallery. The brick wall that ran the length of one side of the gallery was hung with framed art. A large placard on an easel advertised Selina Archie's upcoming event.

"Good morning. I see that you noticed my fundraiser featuring an upcoming First Nations artist. I represent both established and emerging artists." A female voice floated from the back of the gallery.

Eduardo walked around, pretending that he was interested in the art. "A First Nations' artist exhibition in Chinatown. That's quite a culture mix. I'm looking for something like this." He pointed at one of Selina's pieces. "Do you have an information brochure about the artist?"

"Certainly." The woman walked over to a desk stacked with paperwork. "Selina's Sliammon and lives close to Powell River. Her art is fresh and inspiring."

Eduardo took one of the brochures. "Maybe I'll come to the show and purchase a piece."

The woman checked her watch. "I must close for lunch. I have an appointment with the artist. I hope to see you at the show."

"I'll do my best to make the showing," Eduardo said.

♓

Dillon was finished with his class and was deep in concentration studying course materials while he waited for Adrianne to join him at Mac's for a quick bite.

Her touch on his shoulder made him jump.

"I didn't mean to sneak up on you," she said.

"I've got a quiz on this stuff in a few days and I block out things when I concentrate."

Adrianne waited for Dillon to place their order. "I spoke to Dad today, and he's making the arrangements for our Comox trip."

"How's he doing with you sharing a house with a bunch of guys?" Dillon watched her expression.

Adrianne laughed. "Adjusting. I reminded him I'm almost twenty and a big girl now." She looked into his eyes. "We are Greek Orthodox Catholic. Values are different here in Canada now than what my parents experienced as young adults in Greece."

"My community's values are old school, too—not that I don't agree with most of them." Dillon's food order was called.

Adrianne waited for Dillon to return with the food, then resumed the conversation. "Values and young love don't always align." She twisted the cap open on her bottled drink, "Look at Walter and your grandmother—"

Dillon interrupted, "Are you suggesting that ...."

"No, I was just commenting on what I think our parents think." Her face was a little flushed.

"I've no idea what my mother will say when we share my room overnight."

"We're sharing your room?" Adrianne's eyes widened.

"There are no extra bedrooms. I suspect she is setting up something for me on the floor. I didn't tell her my friend is a girl." Dillon kept his voice low so that the people at the next table couldn't hear.

"Are you going to tell her before we arrive or wing it?"

"Would you ask your mother or father first?" Dillon asked.

"I think I'd talk to my mom. I'll wait to see how you work that out first. Then I'll give you my thoughts."

"Chicken," Dillon grinned.

Adrianne decided it was time for a change in conversation. "Do you have time to read the diary tonight?"

"Yes, of course. We need to read more before going to Mom's." Dillon took the first bite from his sandwich, but would have preferred to kiss Adrianne.

♓

Selina spotted Caroline Larose at a street corner, waiting for the traffic light to change. "Caroline," she called. The woman turned around sharply. "Oh, Selina, I thought I was going to be a bit late. A customer came in just as I was ready to leave. He seemed interested in your work. I wouldn't be surprised to see him at your exhibition."

"I hope so," Selina replied, as the two women reached the Brasserie L'ecole. The hostess showed them to the table Caroline had reserved.

Caroline asked Selina, "Will you have all your pieces ready in time for the show? We agreed on a dozen, at least," as they took their seats.

"I think so, I'm working on—" Selina was interrupted by the waitress with the menus. "May I bring you ladies a drink?"

Selina looked up at the waitress and gasped.

Caroline glanced at her and ordered two French chardonnays. As the waitress walked away, Caroline turned her attention to Selina. "What's wrong?"

"That waitress … she's wearing my whale key," Selina said, as she fumbled in her purse. "I know it's mine … my father made it. Damn, where did I put that card?"

"Selina, what are you doing?" Caroline asked, as the white wines were placed on the table.

"Would you like to order now?" the waitress asked, her pen and notepad at ready.

"Could you give us a few minutes, please? We'll have a bit of wine before we place our order. Thank you," Caroline replied, and waited for the woman to leave once again. "Selina?" she said, in a low voice.

"Here it is," Selina muttered, disregarding Caroline and placing a business card on the table. "Just give me a minute, then we'll talk." Selina dialed the number on the card on her cell and turned toward the wall. "Detective Steele, it's Selina Archie," she spoke softly. "I'm at the Brasserie L'ecole on Government Street. My waitress is wearing my whale key. I'm sure of it. Can you come right now?" Selina nervously inhaled and listened, then disconnected the call.

Caroline stared at her guest at the table. "Selina, what's this all about?"

Selina took a sip from the wine glass to calm herself before answering. "I was robbed by a punk in my house a week ago. He stole some jewelry including that whale key our waitress is wearing. I called the police detective who's handling my case, and she said she would be here as quickly as she can. We're to remain calm and act as if nothing is wrong. Okay?"

Caroline sipped her wine. "You're kidding, right? Are you sure that necklace is yours?"

"Only the diamond key. It never had a chain on it. My mother gave it to me just before she died. I must get it back."

The waitress appeared again. "May I recommend today's special—asparagus salad—to start while you decide on a main course?"

"Certainly, that sounds delightful," Caroline said. "Two please. That's a beautiful pendant you're wearing."

"Thank you! I bought it from a street vendor."

Selina hunched down in her seat. "What are you doing?" she whispered.

"Just making conversation. Relax, the cops will be here shortly. Oh, look, I'll bet that's them."

Jamie and TJ casually walked over to join Selina and her table guest. Selina made the introductions.

"Are you absolutely sure the waitress is wearing your diamond key, Selina?" asked Jamie.

"Pretty sure, Detective. You've seen the photograph on the appraisal. You look."

The waitress appeared with the two salads. "I see two more have joined you. May I get you something to drink?"

Jamie looked up and smiled as she studied the whale key necklace. "Just water for us, please. We're not staying long."

Jamie watched the waitress's movements for a moment, then got up and followed her to the back of the restaurant. "I'm Detective Steele," she said, as she produced her shield. "Is there somewhere private we can talk?"

"Not really. We're busy today. What can I do for you, Detective?"

A small bell chimed. "Chelsea, order's up."

"I'm investigating an assault and a robbery. What's your name?" Jamie watched the waitress's body language for her reaction.

"Chelsea Roberts. What does that have to do with me, Detective?"

The small bell rang again, "Chelsea, your orders are up." The tone was impatient.

"How about you give me that necklace and serve your table. I'll wait back here."

"My necklace? Just while I serve that order, right?" She unclipped the chain and placed it into Jamie's hand. Chelsea glared at the detective for a moment, then grabbed the two plates from the back kitchen counter.

Jamie and TJ watched Chelsea stride down the narrow aisle and place the plates in front of two men at a table close to the front of the restaurant. She spoke to them for a moment, then she returned to the back where Jamie waited.

"Do you have a receipt for this pendant, Chelsea?" Jamie asked, trying to keep her voice down.

"No, I don't. I purchased the key from a street vendor at Bastion Square last Friday and had a chain put on it. You never get a receipt from those people. Why?"

"Can you describe this street vendor?"

"She was in her late teens, I think. I didn't pay much attention to her. I've seen her at Bastion Square before. The woman at Aurea Gems—where I had the chain put on—said I got a really good deal. May I have my necklace back, please?"

"A golden key just like this one has been reported as stolen. I'll need to take it with me and check to see if this is the one that was reported. Is there anything else you can tell me, Chelsea?"

"Stolen," she sighed. "No, Detective. I'm out of a lot of money if I don't get it back."

"I'll have a discussion with the street vendor, and then we can go from there. I'll check out your story and get back to you." Jamie placed the necklace in her pocket and walked back to her table.

"What did she say?" Selina asked, while she stared at Chelsea.

"I have possession of the key. I will check out her story and confirm that this is your property. We'll get back to you, Ms. Archie." Jamie glanced over at TJ. "Let's go."

Chelsea watched the two detectives leave, and then marched up to Selina and Caroline's table. "I want you to know that I didn't steal that whale key. I bought it fair and square."

"I'm sorry, I know you didn't steal it, but it's mine. It was stolen last week. I think we're finished here. Please bring the bill." Selina rose from her seat and rushed out of the restaurant as other patrons watched in silence.

Jamie and TJ were crossing the street when they saw Selina dash out of the bistro. "I guess she won't be going back to that place for a while. We'll have to follow up on the Perez hunch later. Let's see if we can find the street vendor at Bastion Square," said Jamie.

It took some time for Jamie to navigate the one-way streets and find a parking space in the Bastion Square Parkade. "TJ, any ideas how a street vendor got hold of an expensive piece of jewelry?"

"I thought that most of the stuff those people sell is cheap stuff from China or something they made. Maybe our vendor pushes stolen stuff when it's too hot to pawn," TJ replied, as they exited their vehicle.

"I don't know. I've seen the young girl Ms. Archie described for a number of years now in Bastion Square. I've looked at her stuff, and she has never been suspected of fencing stolen goods in the past."

Bastion Square was a small area and it didn't take long for the detectives to scour the entire place. "It's long past noon and the lunch hour traffic is back at work or home. I don't see our girl today. We'll have to come tomorrow sometime late in the morning, when most of the vendors set up for the day," Jamie remarked, when the two detectives met at the front entrance of the square.

"Let's get Vanessa Jewelers to have a look at the key. They did the original appraisal so they will be able to confirm whether or not this is the same piece."

"Good afternoon, Ms. Davies," TJ greeted Monica.

"What can I do for you two today? Find your assailant yet?"

"Not yet, but we're getting close. We think we have Ms. Archie's whale key, but we need you to verify it's the same piece you performed the original appraisal on."

"You can leave it with me. I'll take a look for you later."

"I need a signed receipt and a written report, too."

"Certainly, I'll get the paperwork. I should have your report early tomorrow afternoon."

Jamie placed the whale key and chain on the counter.

"It's had a chain added." Monica looked up. "Does Ms. Archie want it removed?"

"I don't know. Just do the verification, and she can make that decision if it's hers. Otherwise we need to return it to the owner, whoever that may be."

♓

Adrianne had brought pillows from her bed and propped them against Dillon's headboard. She lay in a silk robe with a matching pink nightshirt underneath that skimmed her thighs, barely covering her panties. She waited for Dillon to come from the bathroom.

Dillon usually slept naked, but came out of the bathroom wearing his briefs and shorts. His secret hope was that the diary reading would lead to some post-discussion intimate touching.

"You sure you want to read the diary tonight?" Dillon asked softly, as he snuggled close to Adrianne. "We could do something else."

"Yes, I want to read it. I'm interested in your grandfather's story."

Dillon picked up the diary and flipped to the marked page. He handed her the tattered book, but his thoughts were focused on the girl beside him.

Adrianne began to read:

Saturday 8th November 1975;

We buried the sailor today. The villagers said that the man's soul left his body and went to the land of the dead. The corpse was washed and placed in a wooden burial box, which was set in a rock crevice on Harwood Island, that villagers called 'A7geyksn.' They told me they named the island 'A7geyksn' because it looks like a pointed nose. The body had to be facing away from the village, and they took it to a place at the northern tip of the island where Tla'amin have been buried over the years. I wasn't able to see Vivian Island from the burial place. I said nothing during the ceremony. I feel connected to the poor man somehow—maybe through the coin gift—or maybe just by how the Tla'amin had accepted him.

Sunday 9ᵗʰ November 1975;

I looked forward to being with Gloria; it was our special day together and no one suspects we are lovers—at least, I don't think so. We went to a large granite rock on the stony shore of Gibson Beach and watched the beautiful morning sunrise. The weather had cleared and Harwood Island loomed only a mile away to the southwest across the Strait of Georgia. I ached to tell Gloria the mariner's secret. I also ached to caress and kiss her, but knew that we had to find a secluded place first. I told Gloria about the schooner that was destroyed in the gale and showed her the coin that I was given. I placed my camera on the rock and took a picture of us holding the golden coin. I wanted to capture the moment we shared about the gift. She said that it was a sign of good fortune that we shared.

We decided to take a boat to Vivian Island to see if there were clues that would lead us to the coin cargo. We lied to Gloria's father and said I wanted to go back to Harwood Island and explore for a while because there hadn't been time the day before. He looked at me as though he knew that his daughter and I were lovers and we were planning to find a hidden spot, but he didn't say anything.

The sun streamed through the broken clouds as we left on our three-mile journey to Vivian Island. It was late morning before we reached the tip of Vivian Island. It is small compared to other islands in the strait, maybe only a thousand feet in length or so. The surrounding shoreline is rocky. Sea lions and their pups watched us as we slowly navigated around the island. The tide was low and the water clear; I watched below the surface for granite boulders. We saw a few remnants of the schooner wreckage scattered on the southern shore of the island. We scouted around in the boat, but there was little debris left by the storm to indicate where the accident took place.

Dillon saw Adrianne's intense concentration. He wondered if he should kiss her the next time she stopped reading. He listened to her soft, intoxicating voice:

I saw it then—fragments of the schooner's wooden hull that had been ripped apart. I focused on this area and saw shimmering golden reflections bouncing sun rays back from the rocky slope of the island. The wreckage was about five feet below the surface. We knew we didn't have long before the tide began to rise. We struggled into rubber wet suits and climbed into the icy water. We gathered scattered coins and put them into socks I had brought. There were hundreds of coins the size of quarters. Most of the bounty was lying in small wooden boxes, for which we were thankful. It was past one in the afternoon by the time we had recovered all the treasure.

We climbed back into the center of the boat, stripped off the wet suits and wrapped ourselves in warming blankets to avoid hypothermia. We kissed and clung to each other while we talked about what to do. A decision was made not to take our discovery back to the village as Gloria was concerned the treasure could harm their way of life. She wanted us to take some time to think about what to do. In the interim, we decided to hide the coins in a location no one would discover if a search was launched for the bounty. There was a sizeable crevice between two smooth boulders on the other side of the island that would be submerged at high tide. We put on our wet suits and stuffed our sock-filled treasure into the crevice, camouflaging it with smaller rocks. We returned to our boat to wait for the incoming tide to ensure it flooded our hidden cache.

Adrianne stopped reading for a moment and sat with eyes wide open. "Oh my God," she said, and then realized she clutched Dillon's arm. She let go. "Sorry, I'll carry on." Her voice was louder as she read.

Dillon inhaled sharply, and he withheld his thoughts on the revelation as she continued:

> *Gloria and I hugged and kissed under the blanket warming each other with our body heat. We made passionate love on the boat floor, and we languished in the afterglow.*
>
> *I remember my secret love—Vivian—how you changed my life. I love Gloria, and shall leave you, my Vivian, to tease another. It is a cross I'll bear as I watch the playful sea lions on the north point, nosing at the open crevices of the rocks and croaking in laughter.*

Dillon was overwhelmed by the words of lovemaking, and the obvious passion that oozed from the passages and overshadowed the story of the discovered treasure. He sensed the raw emotion between the lines and it seized his being. He took the diary from Adrianne's hands, marked the page, and embraced Adrianne, touching her as he envisioned Walter had caressed Gloria.

"Dillon." Adrianne breathed his name as his hand slipped under her night shirt and fondled her breast. Her heart raced when his lips pressed against hers, and his other hand ran over her panties.

"What should we do?" She inhaled shallow breaths, reacting to his touch.

"Do? Make love … like them."

"That's wasn't what I had meant, but …."

⚓

It was much later than Jack had planned when he parked his camper van a block away from the St. Charles Street house. He was seated in front of a communication module, with computer monitors and electronic devices he had designed to access Internet connections. He pulled a beer from a plastic cooler and turned on his equipment. The monitors showed no images, so he launched a program to search for the wireless signal from the planted devices.

He took a gulp of his Canadian beer. Suddenly the monitors displayed images from the two camcorders planted in the silk trees. He corrected the video images and focus of the units in the bedrooms. Jack leaned back, beer in hand.

Adrianne's room was empty, but Dillon's room was of more interest. He watched the couple seductively touch each other. He heard Adrianne say Dillon's name and saw her push his hand away. She pulled up her panties and got out of bed. He lost sight of her. Jack groaned and leaned back when he saw Dillon shake his head and call "Adrianne ...." in the direction of the bathroom door.

Deprived of his entertainment, Jack examined the monitor closer. A tattered notebook lay on the floor. Jack pulled out his cell phone to call Firth.

"Jack Bryce here with the first report. The surveillance equipment on the Padrino woman is installed, and I have confirmed it's operational. I'll contact you tomorrow with my next report." Jack hung up without waiting for a reply.

Ten

Jack decided to skip his morning class to enable recording for the webcams. To his mind, payment from Firth for watching bedrooms was a bonus.

He lived in a rental bungalow on Waterloo Road, a quiet area close to the university and Camosun College. His roommate kept to himself and seldom had visitors; it was an ideal situation for Jack.

Jack's desk in his bedroom was cluttered with monitors, computers, recording devices, and external hard drives. He keyed the network name and password into a script. He executed the script code and, moments later, his monitors displayed the video feed from the cameras at the St. Charles Street house.

He had a clear view of each bed and a partial view of the bedrooms. The conversation between the pair was audible as they prepared to leave for classes.

Jack had one last task to complete before he, too, left for school; he activated the motion detectors on the cameras. The recordings would automatically run when the sensors detected movement.

♓

Jamie and TJ sat in their vehicle outside Hampton Court—a new, four-story condominium complex in Burnside. "Hopefully we can talk to Mason Perez this morning. The rehab center said he wasn't at work today," TJ said, as she prepared to exit the vehicle. "Apartment 407."

The women waited at the building entrance while the buzzer vibrated once, twice, three times.

"It appears he's not home," Jamie remarked, "Let's visit the street vendor. We can follow up on this guy later."

It was mid-morning when the detectives reached Bastion Square. The teen was setting up her jewelry display at the entrance of the square. The detectives walked briskly toward her.

Jamie introduced herself and displayed her badge. "I understand   you sold a whale key to a woman last Friday." Jamie pulled a photograph of the key from her inner jacket pocket. "What's your name?"

"Everyone calls me Cassy. And, yeah, so? I sell lots of stuff. I've got a legit permit to sell my stuff here, Detective."

"You don't have a permit to sell stolen goods, Cassy."

"Stolen? Who says it was stolen? I bought it from a guy I see around here sometimes. He needed cash in a hurry to pay a debt. He said he won it in a poker game. I got a good deal and made a few bucks when I sold it to the woman. I stole nothin'."

"You know the name of the guy?"

"Sammy. A short, stocky guy with thick, black-rimmed glasses."

"You'll have to come down to the station and look at mug shots. Pack up your stuff. We'll decide if we're going to charge you with selling stolen property or not when we see what you come up with."

It was nearly noon before Cassy positively identified Sam Queen from a file of known local small-time drug dealers. Jamie and TJ decided Cassy wouldn't be charged for her role in selling the stolen jewelry, but Cassy had to return the one hundred and twenty-five dollars to compensate the victim for her loss. It was considered a lesson by the police, and Cassy reluctantly accepted the warning to be more attentive to her street deals.

Cassy was still grumbling about being screwed, whining that she was a victim as well, when Jamie and TJ dropped her off at Bastion Square. "Watch what you sell in the future, Cassy, if you want to stay out of trouble," Jamie said, as the teen slammed the rear door of the detectives' vehicle. "Teenagers. It's always someone else's fault."

"I wouldn't know anything about that," said TJ. Her cell phone rang. "Detective Kennedy." Her discussion was brief. "A squad car's picked up Queen. Forget lunch. Let's see what he can tell us."

The detectives were in the elevator when Jamie's cell rang. "Steele. Great, thanks. Sure, tomorrow. Thanks for your prompt help, Ms. Davies."

"Vanessa Jewelers?" TJ asked, as the elevator opened to the third floor.

"Yup. The whale key is the genuine article, and we'll have our report in the morning. You were right. We'll give Ms. Archie the good news later, but first, let's see what Mr. Queen has to say."

The detectives entered an interview room. It was furnished with an oval pine table, four black fabric-covered chairs, and a cabinet against one of the side walls. The front of the room, which faced the interior of the office space, had a glass wall and door.

Jamie eyed Sam as he sat silently at the table. "You may go now," she told a uniformed constable by the door. "TJ, keep our boy company for a moment and I'll be right back."

TJ was a bit surprised, but she pulled out a chair and sat down. She studied the man in silence as she waited for her partner to return. Sam didn't move and continued to stare down at the table with a blank look on his face.

Jamie reentered the room and pitched a folder onto the table, but remained standing. She scrutinized the man who looked at the folder cover. "So, Sammy, still pushing the drugs?"

"Says who? I'm not in the business anymore, Detective." He looked up from the folder at the red-haired woman.

"We've got you on assault, a B&E, and a home robbery this time, Sammy. You're not going to deny that, too, are you? We know you did it. Confess and make life easier for all of us."

"That's bullshit and a lie, Detective. I don't do that shit."

"We have evidence to the contrary." Jamie reached over to open the folder. "We have a sworn statement that you sold this gold whale key to a street teenager. That trinket links you to a larger heist in Fernwood on Wednesday, September the fifth."

Sam inspected the whale key photograph. "I did no B&E. I found that key thing in the fog that night. I guess someone lost it, and I lucked out."

"Found it in the fog that night—don't give me that crap, Sammy. I couldn't even see my own feet in the dark that night.

Try again, or I'll charge you with the assault and the B&E." Jamie's tone became threatening and louder. "I'm sure if we go to your place we'll find drugs, and we'll add trafficking to the list. So?"

"Okay, okay. I got that whale thing from Chaz on Ellice Street. He lost it, man, and begged me to help him. He was freakin' out, so I gave him some uppers to help him cope, ya know. He gave me that key."

"You just happened to have uppers? Don't you mean ecstasy, Sammy?"

"I said uppers, and I'm stickin' to that. I know Chaz overdosed on something the next day, but I don't know what. All you've got is my statement."

"Did you call anyone to tell them you gave Chaz … uppers, Sammy?"

"No, I didn't call no one. I wanted to help poor Chaz and I thought my girl would like the key, so we traded. That's it." Sam looked at Jamie, then across to TJ. "Can I go? You got nothin' on me."

Jamie stared intensely at Sam for a moment. "Yeah, sure, bugger off. But, Sammy, I'd be careful walking around with a pocket full of uppers. You know what I mean?"

Sam hurriedly rose from his chair and disappeared around the corner.

"Uppers," TJ said. "That was a bullshit story if I ever heard one."

"Yeah, well, we don't have enough proof to charge him for the ecstasy, and we got the story we wanted, so I'll take it. I didn't get the sense that Sammy had a motive to whack Collins, either." The detectives strolled down the hallway. "The question still remains as to who hired Charles Collins and whether his OD was accidental or not."

⚓

The partially cloudy day had capitulated to heavy rain when evening set in. Dillon and Adrianne cuddled in Dillon's bed as a flash of lightning lit up the darkness outside.

"I've never liked these storms," Adrianne said. A boom of thunder rolled overhead.

"I like them," Dillon replied, as a flash of lightening lit up the bedroom window another time. "These weather patterns are common at home. I've always liked nature's intense moods."

"I've talked with Dad again about our trip to Comox. He'll make arrangements for us to be picked up at the float plane dock."

"Did you tell him that we are going to Powell River so that I can cast my council vote?"

"No, I didn't go into details, Dillon. He's concerned about me taking the Zodiac across the strait at this time of year, so I didn't want to complicate our discussion."

"How does he feel about us sharing the same hotel room?" Dillon asked, as another thunder clap echoed.

Adrianne cowered closer to Dillon. "The room has two beds. I said that we would come to dinner on Saturday, and he can meet you then." She inched further under the covers when lightning brightened the room. "I talked to Mom. She said that she would have a chat with him because I said we'd like to stay overnight Saturday, too."

"Stay over?"

"We're going to stay at your mother's, aren't we? So, what's the big deal?" Adrianne poked him under the covers. "Besides, there's a spare room."

"No cuddles at our parents' houses," Dillon said.

"Sorry I freaked last night, but I guess I wasn't ready. Your grandfather's love story sure did get the hormones racing, though." Adrianne grinned. "I want to hear more of the diary story, Dillon." She glanced at him, and asked, "You haven't said much about Walter's story about the coins. Aren't you excited?"

"I'm more fascinated with the love story between Gloria and Walter than the coins. Gloria's passion for Walter … the circumstances. I'm interested about what happened to that love, not the coins. I understand Gloria's concern about taking what they found into the village. I really do."

"You're a romantic, Dillon Point." Adrianne kissed him on the forehead. "Do you believe that the coins are still hidden in the crevice?"

"It's been a long time … more than thirty-five years. My mother must've read the diary numerous times. She and grandmother could've done anything with them over the years. Those diary pages are well worn. I wonder what my mother thought I would do after reading it."

"I think she wanted you to know the truth about your heritage without having to tell you herself. The whole thing must be emotional for her; your grandmother loving another man … a man not of her community. The pregnancy …."

"I thought you wanted to cuddle, not talk about the diary. And maybe …" Dillon put his hand under the bed covers, "we're prepared this time."

"It's stormy, and I'm settled in. The diary can wait."

♓

Jack reconnected his Internet session and entered the username and password to access the video cameras in Dillon and Adrianne's bedrooms. He viewed the feed from Dillon's room for a moment. He selected another icon on his desktop and keyed in a password at the prompt. Two additional video players appeared, and he activated the play sequence. He fast-forwarded the video recordings to zip through the footage. He paused the player in Dillon's room, as he slowed the relay from Adrianne's. He watched her undress to slip into a warm pajama top and bed shorts.

He returned to the live feed from Dillon's room and saw them playing under the covers. He grunted, then played the earlier recording from Dillon's room. He watched segments, whizzed though others, and then slowed it down again.

He suddenly stopped the feed, rewound the short segment he was viewing, and pressed play again, listening attentively. His report to Firth would be of interest today; they planned to go to Comox and Power River this weekend.

Hamish and Eduardo were surfing the Internet for information on the Santa Regio. Hamish had told Eduardo about Cielo Gonzalo, who was accused in 1972 by his partner, Robert Capland, of stealing from the Santa Regio shipwreck bounty. Nothing had come of the accusations because the authorities couldn't prove the allegation.

"There's nothing here about Gonzalo Cielo's suspected accomplices. He did a great job in keeping the heist quiet—if it even happened." Eduardo stretched his back.

"What have you found out about the El Rey Dorado noted in the Santa Regio manifest?" Hamish asked.

"It's documented that the origin of the legend of El Dorado is associated with the native Muisca peoples of Colombia South America. The Muisca were the Chibcha-speaking peoples in the 1500s, which split into three different regions. The Zipa, one of those groups, was in the Bogotá area."

"The Zipa are said to have offered gold and other treasures to the Guatavita goddess. A ceremony took place on the appointment of a new ruler who covered his naked body with gold and precious jewels, and rafted out into a lagoon. The raft was heaped with gold and emeralds. The gilded Indian tossed all the gold and emeralds into the lagoon as an offering to the goddess as part of his coronation ritual."

"Other similar ceremonies were also recorded but they didn't mention the El Dorado."

"Yes, Eduardo, I'm aware of that story. It's also written in the El Carnero chronicle by Juan Rodríguez Freye in 1638, I believe."

"El Dorado means gilded person in Spanish, and El Rey Dorado means the gilded king," Eduardo continued. "The Zipa imported their gold from other regions of their territory. It was abundant and the preferred material for making most articles. The stories of a 'city of gold' attracted Spaniards seeking the location of the stash, but the Indians found ways to rid themselves of the ambitious foreigners by providing misinformation that sent the gold mongers in other directions—far from the actual source, of course. El Dorado eventually became the name of the hidden city of gold."

Eduardo turned and faced Hamish. "Historians concluded years ago that El Dorado is a myth and never existed; but the myth says the El Rey Dorado is the key or map that describes where the 'city of gold' is in truth located."

"So, when the El Rey Dorado was noted on the manifest of the Santa Regio, it was assumed that the historians were wrong and that the golden city and its treasure did actually exist," Hamish said.

"Exactly, amigo, exactly. No additional proof has been identified since then, as the El Rey Dorado was never found."

"I suspect Cielo targeted the El Rey Dorado, and he offered the other loot to his accomplices for the riskiness of the heist," Hamish thought aloud. "That missing cargo could've ended up anywhere."

"If the heist took place, there's been no chatter for more than thirty-five years. An item like the El Rey Dorado, or even the stolen coins and other treasures, surely would've surfaced by now. I think the El Rey Dorado has been lost all this time, or someone has it but doesn't know what it is. Either way, the escudo in the photo may be the clue to the bigger prize."

"That sounds on target, Eduardo. We need Walter Smith's diary. If Smith did find a portion of the Santa Regio cargo, the diary may reveal what he did with it. Scotch, Eduardo?

"A fine idea, amigo, thank you."

Hamish poured two double-sized shots from the bottle stashed in his credenza. His mind was in the summer of 1979; he now realized the significance of the transactions made all those years ago.

Hamish dialed a number on speaker phone. "Jack, where's the information I paid you to provide? I expected something from you by now."

"I was just about to call you, Mr. Firth. Dillon, the Native boy who's tight with Adrianne Padrino, is going to Comox and Powell River this weekend with the girl."

"So?"

"I'm not sure. Something about a coin, but they didn't say exactly. The Padrino girl and the Native kid are becoming an item."

"I don't care about that. Keep a watch on them, and keep me informed." Hamish ended the call and reached for his computer.

"Something about a coin … if the photograph Padrino sent me had Walter Smith with an escudo, we need to see what we can find out about Walter Smith."

"Walter Smith, Hamish?" Eduardo asked.

"Yes. I didn't tell you I identified the white man in the black and white snapshot." Hamish pulled his keyboard closer. He typed "Walter Smith" into Google and waited for the results.

Eduardo sat up in his chair to look at the results. "Click on the link on published works."

"Hmm … works published between 1975 and 1978 about Comox, Sliammon and Comox. Haida is too far north, so he must've been in either Comox or Sliammon," Hamish said.

"Sliammon?" Eduardo asked.

"A First Nations community outside Powell River, and across the strait from the town of Comox. Here, I'll show you." He pulled up a map of the British Columbia coastline.

"It looks rather desolate for hunting Spanish gold from the 1600s, especially this time of year in Canada … Dios."

Hamish laughed. "Winter hasn't even started up there yet, Eduardo. You'd better track those kids if they're leaving tomorrow."

Eleven

Dillon and Adrianne tried to leave the house without waking Josh or Niki. It was Thursday, and they had agreed to skip classes and take an early flight to Comox. They were preoccupied, making sure that they didn't miss their flight, and they never noticed they were watched.

Eduardo trained opera binoculars on them as backpacks were loaded into the Mazda while he sat in his black Escalade.

The sports car weaved its way toward the Victoria waterfront. Eduardo ensured he stayed only far enough behind to keep the sleek vehicle in sight. Eduardo was a few car-lengths from the target car when it turned into a parking lot off Wharf Street. He parked in a space a number of slots further down, and watched the two youth pay for parking. He waited until the gear was unloaded, and the pair rushed toward the waterfront docks. Eduardo bolted from his vehicle and keyed in his parking space in the meter.

He trailed the pair into the Harbour Air Seaplanes ticket terminal. They were at the counter momentarily while Adrianne showed their online tickets. They rapidly exited the terminal.

Eduardo scanned the flight board for the next plane to Comox. He walked to the counter. "A ticket to Comox please."

"A return fare, sir?" the agent asked.

"Sure, Sunday afternoon." He could always change the return ticket later.

The clerk processed his payment and handed him a boarding pass. "You'd better hurry, the fight is scheduled to leave in five minutes."

Eduardo was relieved to join the passenger line just as boarding for the float plane began.

"Buckle up. It's likely to be a bumpy ride today," said the pilot. "Last night's storm pattern is still travelling through the Comox area. I'll have an accurate weather picture at our stop in Vancouver."

The pilot taxied into Victoria Harbor. Adrianne saw Laurel Point Park to her left as the pilot made final adjustments before take-off. Eduardo clutched the armrests as the plane taxied over the choppy water of the inner harbor heading due west.

Dillon watched out the porthole-shaped window as the float plane rose from the water surface and began its ascent toward Esquimalt. The plane bobbed and bounced as the fixed-wing aircraft cut its way through the westerly wind.

"There's no view like it," Adrianne said, as she settled into her aisle seat. "I love travelling from the inner harbor. It's more interesting than the airport in Sidney."

"Your dad is kind to pay for our trip, Adrianne. I'm so excited to get to see my mother." Dillon grinned as the aircraft continued its bumpy ascent, banking northward to its cruising altitude.

Adrianne looked at the other passengers. The plane was almost full. Most passengers were travelling to Coal Harbour in Vancouver.

Comox-bound passengers typically left on Friday mornings for a weekend of sports or fishing. Across the aisle a stocky man sat frozen in his seat, clutching his armrests as the small plane continued to bounce around from turbulence.

"Not having fun?" Adrianne asked. The man's teeth were clenched, and his eyes fixated on the seat in front of him.

He glanced across the aisle. "I hate small planes, señorita. This bumpy weather isn't helping."

"Are you a tourist?" Adrianne asked.

"No, señorita. I live in Vancouver, but I don't like to fly." The round-faced, mustachioed Latino grimaced.

"Returning to Vancouver, then."

"I'm going on a fishing expedition running out of Comox." His tanned, brown knuckles turned white as he grasped the seat arm tightly. "I hear that it's good in Comox, no? Are you and your boyfriend going to Vancouver, or fishing, too?" The plane took a heavy bump. The man tensed further, clutching the armrest as though his life depended on it, and his foot strained against the seat frame in front of him.

"Sorry, folks," the pilot called into the cabin. "I'll try to get above this unsettled air. Stay fastened in your seat."

"No, we're going to Comox to go diving." Adrianne turned her attention to Dillon, who was watching out the window as the plane flew north over the Strait of Georgia towards the lower mainland.

"The view's spectacular up here." Adrianne leaned over him to look out his window and told him, "I've arranged a short dive at Hornby Island for later this morning, weather permitting. Flora Islet is a wonderful place to practice diving because of its shallow waters; the series of underwater terraces are amazing."

"Sounds like a blast."

♓

Jamie sat in her office, with her ever-present Starbucks latté, reviewing the activities of the day with TJ. "You know the inspector has given us until today to wrap up the Collins case. I know it seems extreme to us that our vic would commit suicide because he screwed up the heist, but murdering him seems even less likely to me."

"I've seen all kinds of violent acts performed for non-performance, Jamie. You toe the line, do what you've been told to do, and deliver. That's the military frame of mind, so why not in this case? Collins was expected to snatch the quinto necklace and he didn't."

"The video of the visitor at the Ellice building does make a person wonder. The time of night is right, and a seven-minute visit does point to a reasonable scenario. We'd better find Mason Perez today. I think we should swing by Vanessa Jewelers and pick up our report and the whale key on our way to Burnside. I'd like to get that piece of jewelry back to Ms. Archie and close that loop."

♓

Eduardo was happy with his feet on the ground again. The water landing in Vancouver was bad enough, but repeating his unwanted adventure was downright unpleasant. The flight to Comox had been rough, and he didn't look forward to the return flight Sunday. He watched Adrianne and Dillon leave the aircraft with their backpacks. He stood on the dock as the two kids were picked up.

He knew from the conversation he'd overheard that the pair was planning on a short diving trip at Hornby Island. He considered his best course of action. Eduardo frowned and turned toward the pilot. "I hear there's a diving outfit in town. Who should I contact about getting in some scuba diving?"

"Second World Diving Company's the main one in town. They have an office on the dock further down the waterfront. You could also check into the Kingfisher Oceanside Resort and book an excursion at their concierge desk," the pilot replied as he stood on the wooden wet dock. "It's the largest hotel around here, and most of Second World's clients stay there."

"Who would I call if I want to go fishing?"

The pilot was preparing for his return flight, checking a log on a clipboard.

"There're a few in town, but the most popular this time of year is Comox Charters. They do both ocean and freshwater trips, and their customers usually return with a good catch."

"Sorry, one more thing." Eduardo interrupted the pilot's attention again. "Where can I get a taxi?"

"Our office can help you there."

Eduardo headed toward the flight office to call a taxi and book a hotel room. He was glad to be walking.

♓

Mason Perez sat in an interview room on the third floor of the Victoria Police Department's Investigation Services Division. It was his first time on the third floor. He tried to maintain his image as a cool dude in preparation for his interview with Detectives Kennedy and Steele. In his mid-twenties, he was tall, slim, and fit. He slicked his black hair back, and was gothic in his all-black attire and sunglasses.

The moment arrived; the detectives entered the room with coffee in hand. TJ set the porcelain coffee cup on the oval table next to Mason, and took a seat across from him.

"Mr. Perez, I understand that you are contracted by Addiction Victoria to assist patients in finding part-time work. Is that correct?" Jamie asked.

"Yeah, that's right. I help people find work, and I stay connected with the employers to ensure that there are no problems." Mason removed his sunglasses. "I earn my fee, Detective."

"Did you help this man find work?" Jamie asked. She showed him a photograph of Charles Collins.

"Yeah, Chaz. I found that guy work a number of times. He was clean for months and was a reliable worker. I understand he overdosed a week or so ago. It's tough struggling with addictions."

"Did you help him find work on Wednesday night, the 5th of September?" Jamie asked.

"Night work? No. I seldom locate night work for these people."

"Did you visit Mr. Collins that night at his apartment, then?" Jamie leaned over the table.

"I, ah—"

"I'll help your memory, Mr. Perez," Jamie interrupted. "We have you on video at Collins' place Wednesday night at just past eleven. Did he have something you hired him to deliver? Don't tell me it was just a social call."

"Yeah, I was at his place that night. I wanted to talk about a job I had arranged for him, to find out if it was working out.

His door was open, and I found him dead. I figured an OD, so I split."

"You just split. You didn't call 911. Why not?"

"I didn't want to be involved. Who knows what the rehab center would think if they found out I arranged a job for him, and I didn't check how it was going. Chaz was getting his life together. I didn't think I needed to babysit him." Mason glanced over at Detective Kennedy. "I got the call, went to see what got screwed up. That's it."

"Got screwed up? What took seven minutes to check out? That's a considerable amount of time for a guy who just split." TJ invaded his space, resting on her elbows towards him.

"I was deciding what to do, I guess. I didn't touch Chaz 'cause I didn't want to disturb anythin'."

"Were you looking for something, Mason? Maybe an item from a heist you hired Chaz to do for you that night? We know about the heist, so don't bullshit us," TJ rapid-fired questions.

"Heist. What heist? I ... I know nothing about a heist," Mason's voice rose. "I got a call from a guy who needed someone reliable to do an easy job. Chaz was the most reliable of the bunch I work with, so I sent him."

"This caller have a name?" Jamie observed Mason's body language.

"No name. I got a cell phone call on Wednesday after lunch, I think. We had a short discussion about what he wanted. I arranged the meet between him and Chaz. I got an envelope of cash for my trouble. I figured Chaz was getting his act together and could look after himself. I never thought about it anymore until I got a message from the guy the next night. He said Chaz didn't complete his task. I was told to talk to Chaz and report back. I already knew what happened. I didn't have the guy's number anyway."

"You didn't have the number for the person who wanted the report?"

"No. My call display showed an unknown number. I received another call on Saturday." Mason slid his cell across the table. "You check."

Jamie picked up the phone. "I see an unknown-number received call on Wednesday at 1:26 in the afternoon, and the second on Thursday at 7:34 p.m. There is another on Saturday at 8:12 in the morning. Was that the same guy?"

"Yeah, I told you he wanted a report. He called me on Saturday morning. I told him Chaz overdosed. He was really pissed, said I should select my people better and hung up."

Jamie passed the cell phone back to Mason.

"How did that unknown caller find you in the first place, Mr. Perez?" TJ asked. She twiddled the pen in her hand.

"I don't know. He said a mutual friend gave him my number. I had things tentatively set up with Chaz about three that Wednesday afternoon. I went to get payment at the waterfront construction site at David and Turner. I got the money as agreed, so I told Chaz the job was on. I was concerned about him, so I went to his place about eleven thirty, like you said. I don't know why he would want to OD."

Jamie sighed, looked at TJ. "I recommend you check out jobs before you pass them on. We could charge you as an accessory to the B&E and assault that Chaz committed." Jamie turned to face Mason, "You caught a break this time … you can go."

⽊

Selina lounged on her sofa with a glass of white wine. Thoughts of her mother and father streamed through her mind while she gazed at the whale key and her father's unopened envelope on the table. She picked up the whale key encased in a ziplock bag.

Selina spared a thought for the unfortunate waitress. She pulled the plastic ziplock open and extracted the key. She examined it. It was obvious the key fit an unusual lock.

Her gaze wandered toward the envelope. She put the key down and picked up the envelope. She ran her fingers around the edge, uncertain if she wanted to open it or not. She looked at her father's writing and his words of love on the front. Selina wondered why her mother had withheld the envelope, and her mother's last words came to mind. Selina sighed, picked up the whale key and envelope, and walked upstairs to her room. Today was not the day to open the envelope.

She withdrew the box containing the quinto necklace from her dresser drawer and opened it. She studied the necklace for a moment and placed the whale key into its designed place. Selina folded the envelope, placed it inside the box, and closed the lid. Perhaps when her exhibition was over; right now, she had pieces to complete.

♓

The evening was still overcast and cool when Dillon and Adrianne returned from the Kingfisher Restaurant. The ocean was dark and the hotel's patio room lights barely pierced the darkness.

"That was a remarkable meal, Adrianne. It's awesome your company has an exclusive arrangement here." Dillon opened the door to their waterside suite. "It will be different in Sliammon."

"This is a beautiful place to stay ... there's nothing else like it around," Adrianne replied, and opened the bar fridge. "Wine? There's a bottle of white."

"That's a great idea. What a romantic place." Dillon walked into the kitchen to join Adrianne.

"Don't get any ideas." Adrianne pushed Dillon away. "I'll look after the wine, and you bring your diary and we'll snuggle on the sofa to read a few passages."

Dillon went to the bedroom to fetch the diary. Adrianne opened the patio sliding door that overlooked the ocean, and inhaled the fresh, salty, ocean air.

Dillon put the diary next to the glasses of wine, then flopped onto the sofa. "We shouldn't let this romantic place go to waste."

"It won't." Adrianne closed the door and picked up her wine. "Read to me."

Dillon saw the twinkle in her eye and smiled, "Sure."

Adrianne laid her head on Dillon's lap. "Ready."

Monday 10th November 1975;

I spent all last night thinking about Gloria and her concern about the treasure. I respect her wishes to think about our options before bringing the gold back to the Sliammon. I decided to take my film into Powell River for processing today. I saw Gloria for only a short time this morning. I wished we were able to talk about our great love for each other. Brett Paul had been invited for dinner by the family fire, likely as a reminder to Gloria about her commitment to him. He brought a piece of bear meat. I found it a welcome change from the frequent fish meals of the last few days.

Dillon skimmed a few pages and started to read again:

Sunday 16th November 1975;

I collected my photographs late yesterday afternoon. I couldn't wait to share them with Gloria. I placed a black and white photo in my journal and asked Gloria's mother Faye-Elliott for a small tie to wrap around the book so the photo wouldn't fall out. Today we took the small boat back to our secret place. We decided to name the place 'qoqoq'—white owl—the name Gloria has given me. The smooth granite rock was about five feet directly in front of our chosen hiding place. We decided to chisel a totem image on the backside, facing the island. It was freezing and a strong wind blew across the strait. We didn't make love, and I felt empty. We haven't talked much since Brett came for dinner. I saw Gloria was struggling with her emotions, torn between her family commitment and me.

Wednesday 19th November 1975;

Gloria found a few moments to talk to me this evening. She told me her period was late, which has never happened before. She looked worried and her words 'haʔǰigənəm' burned into my thoughts as she pointed to her womb, indicating she might be pregnant. I told her not to worry and wait a few more days until she was sure. We would talk about how she felt on Sunday, and we'd make a plan for the hidden treasure.

Dillon closed the diary. "This story is sad. I know how it was in those days, commitment was everything … and family." Dillon looked down into Adrianne's deep, golden eyes as she looked at him from his lap. "Not really much different today."

Dillon sighed as he watched Adrianne leave the room for the bathroom. He wanted her with him—not just for sex—but just to touch her, share time with her. He was filled with emotion connected to the diary, and to the dilemma of the love that oozed from the pages. He felt the passion Walter felt as he wrote the lines on the page; he felt the frustration, the want. The words reflected Dillon's life and his situation: wanting a woman and not knowing if they would be together in the end.

"Dillon," a seductive voice drifted from the bedroom, "I've got a surprise for you."

Dillon rose from the sofa and moved towards the alluring voice.

His heart started to beat quickly when he saw the erotic brunette standing at the bedroom door, leaning on its frame. She had a devilish smile as she posed in black, high-heeled shoes and a sheer, black-mesh teddy, tied with three pink ribbons. Adrianne's hair fell over her shoulders, her lips were a deep shade of pink, and dark blush accentuated her cheeks. He was enraptured with her outfit that was covered in pink polka dots.

Adrianne motioned him forward with a wiggling forefinger. "Do you like it?"

"Adrianne … wow." He stripped off his shirt and dropped it to the floor. "I … you're …." He fought for appropriate words as he approached Adrianne. Her perfume lingered in the air. He didn't need encouragement as he drank in her aroma, but Adrianne had other ideas. She took his hand and led him to the side of the queen-size bed.

The room was lit by three mini palm-sized travel flashlights scattered on tabletop surfaces. Adrianne had closed the heavy window drapes. An iPod softly streamed romantic guitar music.

He could almost taste her as his nose touched the fabric of her lingerie. The sound of the music wound its way through his consciousness while he savored the gift Adrianne offered. It was a gift he would never forget; a gift only Adrianne could give. Adrianne silently drew him to her.

Twelve

Eduardo sat in a corner booth of the intimate bistro in the Kingfisher Oceanside Resort enjoying a complimentary coffee and croissant while he waited for Dillon and his girlfriend to appear. The frequent sound of military fighters from the Comox Air Force Base, practicing flight maneuvers, disrupted the serenity of the sunny morning, but didn't distract Eduardo's thoughts of the day ahead.

Dillon and Adrianne stopped at the front counter, slid a room key across the desk, and headed toward the front lobby entrance.

Eduardo slipped a five-dollar tip under the plate of his unfinished meal. He snatched his coat from the back of his chair, dashed out of the restaurant, and located the pair waiting for a taxi outside.

"Good morning. I didn't know you were staying here," Eduardo said, catching his breath. "I'm late for a fishing excursion. May I share your cab if you're going to the marina?"

"Sure can," Adrianne agreed. "Which excursion did you decide to take?"

"Well …." Eduardo struggled to find a plausible answer when the taxi arrived. Eduardo got in the front passenger seat without answering the question. Adrianne and Dillon piled into the back, holding their backpacks on their laps.

"Where to?" The cabbie looked at Eduardo, who waited for the back passengers to answer.

"Second World Diving, dock three, please," Adrianne said.

"And you, Sir?" the cabbie turned toward Eduardo.

"That'll be close enough for me, too."

"Sir," Adrianne said as the cab turned onto the highway, "the fishing tours leave from dock one."

"Yes, señorita, that's right. Dock one then, please."

Eduardo had hoped his silent, fellow passengers would talk about their day's plans; they were halfway to the marina. Eduardo realized he needed to encourage conversation. "Going diving?"

"Yes, my boyfriend's working on his certification," Adrianne said, and then fell silent.

"You know these waters?" Eduardo asked.

"Pretty well. It's the perfect time for fishing for coho and chum salmon. The coho is a game fish. You'll have fun," Dillon said.

"So I'm told." Eduardo was frustrated.

"Dock one," the cab driver announced. "Enjoy your day."

Eduardo handed the cabbie a twenty-dollar bill and got out of the cab. He accepted the kids' surprised thanks.

The cabbie pulled away from the curb. Eduardo grunted as the cab headed toward the second destination, a short distance down the street.

He walked to a shed converted into a dockside office and poked his head in. "Can I rent a boat for the day?"

"You got a valid boating license?" the attendant asked.

"No," Eduardo replied. "I need a license?"

"In British Colombia you must have a current boating license to take one of these boats out. You'll have to go with someone who has a license if you don't have one," the elderly, bearded man explained gruffly. "You could take one of our charters if you want to go fishing."

"I don't want to fish, amigo. I … need to track a couple of kids."

"Track some kids? That's not we do here, mister. We do fishing excursions." The elderly man frowned.

"How much for a personal fishing excursion?"

"We've only one boat left today. See that thirty-three foot Grady-White? It's one hundred per hour, with a minimum of four hundred. You have to be back before dark. The boat's booked for tomorrow, and I don't want that boat out in the strait at night, anyway."

"You take Visa?"

"You betcha."

Dillon and Adrianne entered the diving company's dockside office.

"Good morning, Chuck."

"Adrianne! It's good to see you; second-year university, I understand. I have all your gear ready." He held his hand out to Dillon. "I'm Chuck Williams, the manager out here."

"I'm Dillon. Adrianne is helping me with my diving certification."

"Chuck's like family, Dillon." Adrianne gave the middle-aged man a hug. "We won't be back until tomorrow afternoon, Chuck. We're diving at Saltery Bay, and then we're going over to the Malahat Wreck. Dillon's mother lives in Powell River. We're staying overnight with her."

"That's right," Dillon added. "Adrianne arranged this trip so that I can see my mother."

"Be careful—the weather's unpredictable this time of year." Chuck pulled keys from a pegboard. "Your dad's not that cranked about you being out by yourselves."

Adrianne took the keys. "I know. I'll keep in touch with you on the CB."

"You'd better. The Zodiac is at the end of the dock, outfitted and ready. Have fun and be safe."

"Yes, boss." Adrianne saluted.

"You'd think this was my first time out in a Zodiac," Adrianne muttered to Dillon.

Adrianne tossed her backpack into the center of the twenty-one-foot Zodiac that bobbed on mildly choppy waters. She helped Dillon aboard and climbed in after him. "Put the backpacks in the cabin, Dillon. We don't want everything soaking wet." She untied the lines from the dock and the boat began to drift away.

"Take the front seat." Adrianne stood at the controls, turned the key, and a pair of sixty-horsepower outboard engines roared to life. "We're going to Saltery Bay to visit a mermaid."

Eduardo found Harry Winters on the bridge of the Grady-White. "Reel Burn" was stenciled on the boat's stern.

"I understand we're not fishing today, Mr. Dominguez. This'll be an expensive sightseeing tour," Harry said, as he hung up the CB radio microphone.

"Well, it's not exactly sightseeing. I need to watch those kids who are leaving in that boat over there." Eduardo pointed to the Zodiac cruising into the strait.

"Watch some kids?"

"I work for one of the kid's father, and he wants me to keep an eye on them without them noticing. Can you do that, Mr. Winters?"

"It's your money. We'll see where they go, and maybe drop a line in the water. The coho's running hard." Harry fired up dual Suzuki two-fifty-horsepower outboards. "We out-power the Zodiac. We'll have no problem keeping the kids in sight."

Eduardo settled into a cream-colored, leather captain's seat inside the boat's cabin and hoped the kids returned before dark. He hadn't checked out of the hotel; his laptop and air tickets were still in his room.

"There's a beer in the cooler in the back if you like; five bucks each. I keep it stocked 'cause most guys like a beer while fishing." Harry said, as he throttled the boat ahead to shadow the Zodiac.

♓

Eduardo's rented fishing boat trolled for salmon up and down the coast along the inside passage of the strait between Powell River and as far south as Westview. Harry Winters was pleased with the three coho caught, but Eduardo was more concerned with watching the Zodiac moored at the Powell River marina.

It had been a long day observing the Zodiac occupants, and the effort of appearing to be coincidentally trolling near the divers without directly watching them had been tiring. It was late in the afternoon.

"We must be back before dark, Mr. Dominguez. It's almost an hour back to Comox. The strait can get rough this time of year."

Eduardo was reluctant to leave while the two youth were still moored at Powell River. He recalled the girl had slipped a room key to the hotel's front desk attendant as the two rushed to meet their cab. "Can you drop me off in Powell River?" he asked, as Harry began to pull in the fishing lines.

"Sure, if you want. You'll have to find you own way back to Comox to pick up anything that's still over there." The middle-aged captain continued to reel in the lines.

"Damn," Eduardo muttered.

"Well, what will it be Mr. Dominguez?" Harry asked, as he headed to the bridge of the boat. "There is a ferry between here and Comox, but I don't know about hotel availability in Powell River these days, as it's fishing season."

"Go back to Comox, I guess," Eduardo decided with a sigh. "I have all my stuff there anyway. Can I book you for an early departure in the morning?"

"I'll have to check with the office. I believe this boat's booked already, but the larger forty-foot Grand Banks we have was available this morning. It's more expensive than this Grady-White for a day." Harry throttled the fishing boat ahead.

"Let me know what's available, but I want to leave at daybreak so we're back here early, before the kids leave the marina."

"I'm no stranger to early mornings, Mr. Dominguez." Harry turned west toward Algerine Passage.

Adrianne and Dillon were at a bus stop with their backpacks, waiting for a local bus to arrive. Dillon was accustomed to taking the bus from Powell River to Sliammon, but he was nervous. He had never been to Sliammon with a girl who wasn't local. Powell River was a small town and folks talked. It was Friday; he hoped his school friends weren't on the five thirty bus.

A green bus with "Scuttle Bay" written on a placard pulled into the stop. A pair of squeaky doors opened.

" Dillon," the driver smiled as he studied the Caucasian girl, "back from the big city are ya?"

"Visiting my mom, Pete," Dillon replied. He put two dollars into the fare box and headed toward the back of the nearly empty bus. He placed his backpack onto the floor, then slid across to the window side. Adrianne sat beside him and placed her backpack in the aisle. She looked at him, but said nothing as the bus pulled from the stop.

"Have fun today?" Adrianne asked, as the bus turned and headed for the highway.

"Yeah, it was great," he replied in a low voice. He turned his attention to look through the side window. "I've always wanted to see the Malahat, and Mermaid Cove was so cool. I'd like to do that one again some time."

"Do you realize you completed your diving certification today?"

"No, I never even thought about that. I loved every minute of it though ... well the diving, anyway." Dillon smiled for the first time since he had gotten onto the bus. He took Adrianne's hand and they sat without another word until the bus reached the outskirts of Sliammon.

"We're the second stop," he told her. "It's time to get ready to get off."

"Harwood Drive," announced the driver. "See you when you leave, Dillon. And you, Miss."

The pair pulled their backpacks over their shoulders, as Adrianne looked around the community of homes that sat on a hillside overlooking the ocean. The residences were a conglomerate of two-story or ranch style houses, constructed from cedar or clapboard with painted siding.

Dillon held Adrianne's hand. They walked along Harwood Drive toward the waterfront until they reached a turquoise, single-level house at the top of the hill. He squeezed her hand and led her along a broken concrete walkway toward the well-kept small home.

Dillon knocked on the door, turned the doorknob, and entered at the sound of a dog barking.

"Come in, Adrianne, we're expected." Dillon smiled to reassure her.

"Tan … it's Dillon," he called from the entranceway. He was greeted by a mid-sized dog.

"ƛatom." Dillon rubbed the dog's head.

"Dillon," his mother rushed to the front door to give him a big hug. "Oh! You must be Dillon's friend." She tried to mask the surprise in her voice. "Dillon didn't tell me that his friend was a young woman."

"Mom, this is Adrianne. She is one of my roommates in Victoria. Adrianne, this is my mother, Robbie-Paul."

Robbie glanced quickly at Dillon, then smiled at Adrianne. "Just call me Robbie. Welcome to our home. Come sit." The dog tried to nuzzle Adrianne.

"ƛatom." Dillon's mother spoke sharply. The foxy-looking dog was jet black, with a white patch on its chest, erect, pointed ears, and had web-like paws. He immediately turned and walked into the kitchen.

Dillon took Adrianne's backpack from her hand and placed it in the hallway with his. He led her into a room furnished with a collection of unmatched chairs and sofas, some wooden and some covered. A wood-burning fireplace had a fire burning, and the smell of cedar filled the air. A log had been cut lengthwise, and it served as a mantel that held numerous framed photographs. The walls and floor were wood cedar plank. A worn tapestry carpet was spread in front of the screened fireplace.

Adrianne sat in a yellow-padded wooden armchair and looked at her surroundings. Dillon sat next to her in a similar chair. "ƛatom is the name of my dog. It means 'wolf' in Tla'amin. Are you okay here for a moment? I'll see what my mother's doing." Dillon rose from the chair. "Tan," Dillon called, and headed in the direction the dog had disappeared.

Adrianne hadn't thought much about Dillon's life in Sliammon. She felt out of place sitting in the room by herself. She wondered what Dillon's mother thought of her. She wasn't First Nations, and she knew nothing of their heritage and customs.

She always thought herself adventurous, but this was different. She took in the uncluttered, simply furnished room and felt a sense of calmness as the fire crackled beside her.

"Adrianne, Dillon's rude to leave you here by yourself. Would you like to join me in the kitchen and meet the others? Dillon will just be a moment."

"May I use your bathroom please? I need to clean up first."

"I'll show her, Tan," Dillon reentered the room. "We'll join everyone in a moment."

"Yes, of course."

Dillon took Adrianne's hand to lead her down a narrow hallway that led to the bedrooms. "Middle door, to the left. I'll see you in the next room on the left when you're finished."

Adrianne washed her hands, and took one last look in the mirror. She plastered on a smile, opened the door, and walked to the next room beyond the bathroom.

"You okay?" Dillon sat on his double-size bed.

"Are we sleeping together in here?" Adrianne whispered.

"I just spoke to my mother about that," he replied in a low voice. "I guess I should've told her about you earlier. It's okay we're in the same room, but I'll be sleeping on the floor." He scrunched his face.

"You sure?" Adrianne asked, trying to speak quietly.

"She said so. I've brought our stuff in here. Let's visit everyone else." Dillon got off the bed and took Adrianne's hand.

"Everyone else?" Adrianne held Dillon back from pulling her. "How many people live here?"

"Besides my mom and me, my grandmother and grandfather. It's common for Sliammon families to live together. Mom's room is across the hall. My grandparents sleep in the room across from the bathroom."

"I'd bet the dog sleeps with you, too."

"He'll be on the floor. I think he misses me. He won't be a bother."

"Who is Tan?" Adrianne asked.

"That's 'mother' in Tla'amin." He towed her down the hall to the kitchen.

Robbie introduced Adrianne to Dillon's grandparents, Gloria-Louie and Brett Paul.

Robbie was filleting a large coho salmon. "Father's barbequing the salmon, and we'll have carrots and baked potatoes. Do you like salmon, Adrianne?"

"I love all seafood, Robbie," Adrianne replied, as she watched the woman effortlessly separate the flesh from the bone. "The weather's coming in. Do you barbeque in the rain, too?"

"We do all year, child," said Gloria. She examined Adrianne closely. "You're an attractive girl, Adrianne."

"Thanks. I think it's my Greek heritage."

"Robbie tells us that you share a house with Dillon," Brett interjected. The large-boned man had light brown, thinning hair and dark russet brown eyes.

"Yes, there are four of us and we have some classes together at the university. Dillon and I have a lot in common and have fun together." Adrianne tried to read the elderly man's round face.

"Dillon's coming back to Sliammon after he finishes business school." Gloria looked for a reaction from Adrianne after her pronouncement. "Bright boy, my grandson." She stood beside her daughter, preparing carrots.

"I'll check on the fire," Brett rose from his wooden chair.

"I'll call when the salmon is prepared," Robbie said.

"Dillon, we were all at Clara-Meyers Archie's funeral on Harwood Island earlier today. She passed away from cancer, leaving only her sister in-law Cecilia-Archie Windsor and her daughter Selina," Robbie said.

Gloria continued to study Adrianne.

"Selina was a couple of grades ahead of me, I think."

"Nice girl," his mother casually remarked.

"I heard you say something about heritage, child," Gloria interrupted. "Dillon tell you much about his heritage?"

Dillon interjected, "We've been reading the diary you gave me, Tan." He glanced at his mother.

Gloria and Robbie looked at each other and then eyed Dillon. "Together?" Gloria asked. She put a weathered hand on her mouth.

"We've read some." Dillon looked to see if Brett was still outside tending the fire. "Has Grandfather Brett read the diary?"

"He knows nothing of it, Dillon." Gloria snapped as her head turned to the door that led outside. "It's my story and your mother's, not his. Only the three of us know about the existence of that diary, besides Walter." Gloria paused, "Four now, I guess."

"We should talk about it later then." The tension was awkward, and Dillon sought to diffuse it.

Dillon's mother washed her hands in the kitchen porcelain sink. "Come, you two."

Robbie snatched Dillon's hand and led the pair down the hall to her bedroom. "Come in and sit." She closed the door.

"Grandmother Gloria and I will talk to you two further about the diary later." Robbie put her hand over her mouth and tears began to form in her eyes. "I wanted to tell you, my son, the many times you asked about your heritage when you were a young boy. It's complicated and scandalous, especially for your Grandmother Gloria." She regained her composure. "You had to be an adult first; you see that, don't you, Dillon?"

Dillon smiled. "It's explicit, but there is such a sense of their love together—not just the sex—but their passion. We haven't finished it yet."

Dillon's mother opened her stuffed closet and rooted through the top shelf. She pulled out a wooden box, sat back on her bed, and lifted the carved lid from its base. "The diary was originally in this box, left by Walter Smith—my father—as revealed in entries of his diary."

Dillon sat beside his mother and placed his hand on her knee. "Adrianne and I went to visit Walter in Victoria, Tan." Tears welled in Dillon's eyes. "He's ill now, lost his memory. He recalls nothing really … maybe a faint spark for a moment and then it's lost." Dillon inhaled. "I can't tell Grandmother Gloria. I know how she felt about him. It's so sad."

"I'll tell her when it's right, Dillon. She'll love you for finding him," Robbie said. She pulled a Spanish escudo from the bottom of the box. "I thought you should see this now, my son." She handed him the coin. "This is the coin that was in the black and white photograph Walter placed in the front cover of the diary."

"The diary says that there are many more like that, and it isn't clear where the coins were hidden, Robbie," Adrianne said. She examined the unusual markings and the large impressed cross on one side of the coin.

"The story's with the diary, Adrianne. Of course, your grandmother knows exactly where they are, Dillon, but she could never decide what to do. It's your destiny to decide, my son. You have to judge what is best when you find Walter's gift. It's part of your heritage, Dillon. Your grandmother and I want it to be your choice," Robbie paused for a breath. "We didn't want to just give you the coins as we believe that the journey to discover them will help you discover yourself, too, my son."

Dillon studied the coin, flipping it over a few times in his hand, and then passed it back to his mother. "You keep this one; it's yours from your father. I'll return the diary, too, when Adrianne and I have finished it; it really belongs to you and Grandmother Gloria."

"Yes, that's true, my son." Robbie dropped the coin inside the empty wooden box and replaced the lid. "Let's go and visit with the others."

⊁

Jamie was sitting in her office with TJ. It was the end of the day, and she had just returned from Inspector Harris's office. "The boss says we will be assigned a new case on Monday morning. He doesn't think it's worth our time pursuing the individual who orchestrated the Selina Archie heist. We recovered her jewelry, and Collins is dead."

"I'd like to know who hired Collins, and I'm concerned about Perez, too. It's hard for me to believe he doesn't know who paid Collins. Perez may not be the type of man who should look after the welfare of rehab people, either."

"We don't have any proof to pursue him, just like Hamish Firth. I didn't get good vibes about him, either," Jamie replied, turning off her computer. "So, how was your first week as a civilian?"

"It started off slow, but got interesting. It's quite a transition."

"I'll see you bright and early Monday."

⊁

Adrianne and Dillon decided to go to bed early. Dillon felt apprehensive sleeping with Adrianne in his own room, knowing every sound travelled though the walls of his mother's house. Adrianne trotted into Dillon's bedroom wearing a long, cotton, Snoopy sleeper and matching panties. X̣aƚom was curled up at the foot of the makeshift bed on the floor that had been intended for Dillon.

Dillon looked perturbed as Adrianne closed the door to his room. "I see you already have a roommate. What are you doing?" she asked.

"Just fussing with something, that's all. That's a far cry from last night's outfit." He pulled his hand from under his pillow with embarrassment written on his face.

"Never judge a book by its cover. There might be surprises like Walter's diary. Fussing about what?" She leaned over and ran her hand under Dillon's pillow while giving him a wet kiss.

"Adrianne," Dillon spoke in a barely audible whisper, as he watched her pull out red condom packages and hold them in the palm of her hand.

"This'll be interesting," she remarked and placed the square packs back under his pillow. "Hoping for the tooth fairy, or something else?"

"Shush." Dillon climbed into his bed wearing only his briefs. Adrianne climbed in beside him and cuddled close to him on the cramped mattress.

"Pretty tiny bed." She giggled while he leaned over for the diary from the bedside table.

Dillon held his breath as he heard his mother walk down the wooden hallway and open her bedroom door. "Behave, you two."

Dillon and Adrianne lay in the bed without moving until the muffled sounds of his mother faded. Dillon started to laugh and rolled over with the diary in his hand. The howling wind and rain outside drowned out most sounds within the house. Dillon was happy about that and relaxed.

"This is too weird," he whispered. He opened the diary to the marked page and felt Adrianne cuddle closer. He smiled and skimmed through pages.

Saturday 13th December 1975;

    I went to our large granite rock on the stony shore on Vivian Island in the rain. The weather was rapidly moving in from the south, and A7geyksn loomed only a mile away in the mist of the early morning. I thought about the wonderful times I spent with Gloria, navigating the reefs around it. 'Ayhus' is Tla'amin for double-headed serpent, and I hope it can protect our secret. The weather was threatening like the gale of the November day the sailor met his fate, running up the strait, tearing past Texada Island through Grant Reefs and Aythus. I feel stranded like that sailor must have felt, knowing his dream wouldn't be fulfilled—tragically desperate for another chance he knew would likely not come.

Sunday 14th December 1975;

    It has been six weeks since Gloria conceived my child that will be delivered around the end of July. She still doesn't show, and we are running out of time to decide what to do. She wants me to stay and live with her in the Sliammon community, but I know I don't want that life, even with her at my side. The community would have difficulties accepting me and our relationship, so I told her tonight I have decided to leave the village. She was upset and told me that she would have to talk to Brett about our affair and her pregnancy. She hoped that he would still marry her and keep the secret from her parents and the community. She left in tears. I knew that it was the last Sunday that we'd spend together. I felt that I had betrayed our love, and that I didn't have the internal fortitude to stay and work things out. I started to pack tonight.

Dillon stopped reading when he heard his mother open the bathroom door. He knew she didn't spend long getting ready for bed and placed the diary quietly on the bedroom floor. He rolled over, turned out the small bed light, and turned to kiss Adrianne. "Adrianne! What are you doing?"

The flushed toilet and Robbie's fading footsteps gave Adrianne confidence as she pulled off her long cotton sleeper. She placed it carefully at the bottom of the bed in case she needed it urgently. The stormy night and sleeping with Dillon reminded Adrianne of the passage in Walter's diary of Gloria creeping into Walter's bed and making love under the roof of her parents' house. The vision excited her.

"Shush." Adrianne slid back under the bed sheet and gave Dillon a moist, encouraging kiss.

Thirteen

Eduardo decided he had to arrive at the Comox marine dock early. The cab driver looked half-asleep as he put Eduardo's bag in the backseat of the yellow cab.

"You must be goin' fishin'. No one else gets out of bed this early in this town. Dock one I guess, mister?"

"Yes, a great day to catch a coho." Eduardo was tired himself and thought fishermen on the west coast were crazy. Eduardo dragged his butt out of the cab, handed the cabbie twenty dollars, and waited for his bag in the cold at the end of dock one.

"Fishin' is better in the rain, anyway. The coho love the dreary weather." The cabbie yanked Eduardo's suitcase from the backseat. "Storm's comin'."

Eduardo found Harry Winters waiting in his booth. It was still dark and rain clouds smothered the morning light as it started to lightly drizzle.

"Good morning, Mr. Dominguez. The forecast isn't encouraging this morning. Are you sure you still want to go to

Powell River?" Harry asked, as he drank hot coffee from a thermos cap.

"Yes, that's the deal. Rain or not, I'm afraid."

"Okay, then. Our customer changed his mind about which boat he wants due to the weather forecast, so the Grady-White is available. It'll be rougher, and we might be forced to turn back earlier than predicted if the weather turns ugly. Here's a slicker so you don't get soaked."

"That works for me. Thank you." Eduardo pulled the yellow, plastic rain shell over his head.

ℋ

Dillon was awakened in the morning by the water splashing in the shower in the bathroom next door. It was early and still dark as Dillon cuddled Adrianne. ƛatom perked his ears up as he heard the pair move about.

Dillon whispered in Adrianne's ear, "Good morning."

Adrianne's eyes popped open, and she realized where she was. She hunted for her sleeper. "Get your shorts on!"

"Good morning," Robbie called through the door after she vacated the bathroom.

"Morning, Tan." Dillon pulled a fresh pair of briefs from his backpack. "Man." Dillon fumbled getting his feet through his briefs, and Adrianne laughed, watching the comedy as Dillon tried to yank his shorts over his nude butt.

Adrianne sighed, relieved they were dressed. She slipped into the bathroom leaving Dillon to straighten the bed.

He waited for an indication that Adrianne was engrossed in cleaning up, and darted out to look for his mother. She was in the kitchen with his grandparents, preparing breakfast in her bathrobe. Dillon greeted his grandparents, and then asked Robbie if she had a few minutes to talk.

His mother gave him a slight grin. "My bedroom." They went into her bedroom and Robbie closed her door behind them.

Dillon hugged his mother. "I understand now how difficult it was for everyone. Do you think Adrianne and I have a chance? You know—the culture thing."

His mother took a pensive breath before she answered, studying her son's face. "She's a lovely young woman, my son. There are definitely cultural differences ... you both need to be brave if you want to be together. Your love for each other must be strong, and you both must make sacrifices. Your grandmother Gloria thought that she was ready to make the sacrifice, but Walter knew in his heart that he was not."

Robbie looked into Dillon's inquiring eyes. "Have you talked to Adrianne? You are so young. You haven't known her long, my son. Is the bond between you strong enough?"

"I don't know. I'm sure I do want to be with her, but we haven't talked about our feelings for each other in that way yet. Would you accept her being with me?"

"It's not about me. It's about you two. Remember that love and sex aren't the same thing. Follow your road of discovery first; then, you may know the answer to your question."

It was past nine when Dillon and Adrianne returned to the Zodiac. Dillon had cast his votes for chief and council. Adrianne had booked a mid-afternoon flight so that she and Dillon would be in Vancouver in time to have dinner with her parents. The early morning drizzle had turned to rain. Adrianne pulled a pair of lifejackets and rain slickers from the boat's equipment box.

"We'd better get these backpacks into a protected place. I think the diary should be put into a Ziploc bag."

"I don't have a Ziploc bag, Adrianne."

"Give me the diary, then. I'll put it with my stuff." Adrianne opened her backpack and unzipped a plastic bag that held her dirty underwear. She pushed the book into the bag and zipped it closed. Dillon stared at her. "I keep my dirty stuff away from my clean stuff … okay?" She grinned.

"By the look of the weather, we'll be lucky if we have dry clothes for the plane ride back to Vancouver." Adrianne started the twin outboard engines. "You cast off the lines."

"What's the plan?" Dillon asked.

"We have a couple of hours. I think we should take a look around Harwood and Vivian Islands, and then out to Savary. I'll take photographs and video with my cell phone of the coast lines and surrounding waters. We can review it all later on our computers. Once we get a better idea of the possible places that Walter and Gloria stashed the escudo coins, then we can study the area before we come back."

"I'd like to see if we can figure out where the sailor shipwrecked on Vivian Island, likely on the southern shore," said Dillon.

Adrianne pointed the Zodiac westward to Harwood Island.

"Hey—you better take over. They're on the move." Eduardo was steering while Harry Winters visited the head. The rain had started to pelt down as the wind drove the weather pattern northward up the Strait of Georgia. The swells were increasingly higher, and Eduardo wasn't sure he was enjoying this ride. He certainly didn't want to steer the boat any longer than he had to.

"I got the helm," Harry took hold of the wheel as the boat continued to yaw and roll. "It's gettin' rough. You'd better hang onto something so you don't get tossed about."

"It looks like they're heading to Comox," Eduardo said. The Zodiac cut through the rolling waves heading west between Texada and Harwood Islands. "Let's hang back a bit so they don't notice we're following."

"We can go slightly south down Malaspina Strait and turn back around at Blubber Bay on Texada if you like, but the sea will be rougher going into the wind."

"Yeah, okay, but if they continue past the tip of Texada, we won't follow them since I'm sure they'll be heading back for Comox. My flight doesn't leave until five-thirty this afternoon, so we should have lots of time."

"You'll be lucky if the flight takes off at all if this weather gets much worse," Harry said, looking up at the blustery, dark sky.

Adrianne turned the Zodiac northward as she rounded the tip of Harwood Island. Texada Island acted as a buffer from the wind, and the waters became calmer in the shadow of the large landmass.

"Here, take photographs and video of the areas that look interesting to you while I navigate." Adrianne pulled her phone from her jeans pocket and handed it to Dillon.

She reached under the console for a chart of the area. The detailed chart showed the depths and shorelines of the entire area from Desolation Sound down to Grief Point south of Powell River. She placed it on a flat chart table in front of her electronic and navigation equipment.

"We're here," she pointed as the Zodiac tossed in the waves. "We're going to head along here and circumnavigate

Vivian Island. I don't know how far in we can get in this rough sea, but we'll get as close as we can. The cell is not so good with distance shots."

"I'm going onto the back deck. I can't get clear shots through the wet glass."

"Keep your body center of gravity low, Dillon. I don't want you tossed overboard."

Dillon crouched down, and worked partway down the back of the boat. He kneeled and waved to Adrianne.

"What the hell are those kids doing?" Eduardo saw through his binoculars that the Zodiac had altered course and turned northward.

"Beats me. They're slowing down, though, and getting too close to the shoreline for this weather." Harry throttled back the twin outboards and slowed his approach to Blubber Bay. "There're shallow rocks up here so we've got to be careful." He watched his depth sounder and studied his chart as the boat tossed about violently in the water.

"They're going around that small rock of an island," Eduardo reported.

"Ain't much there … only scrub brush and sea lions." Harry concentrated on his own trek through the rough waters.

"They're off again, heading toward that other long island," Eduardo said. "Pretty shitty weather to go sightseeing."

"They must be looking for something. Probably on the shore. Damn strange though."

Adrianne throttled ahead toward Savary Island. Dillon, now completely soaked, picked his way back inside the cabin.

"You see that fishing boat?" Dillon pointed at the white-hulled Grady-White. "It's a bit rough for coho fishing, don't you think?"

"Maybe they got caught in the storm, and the boat is going to Comox or Powell River." Adrianne turned northward along Harwood Island in the direction of the mainland. "Look at this chart. The reefs are really shallow all through here," she pointed out the marked shallows off Savary Island to the south. "It's too rough to travel around the southern side, so we'll cover only the backside of the island today."

"You're driving," Dillon said, water streaming down his face and hair. "I'll go outside and take photos once we reach Mace Point."

♓

Eduardo wasn't happy with the flight to Victoria from Comox. He knew he was fortunate his flight departed in the nasty weather, but the ride was bumpy and stressful. He had decided not to take the float plane and landed in Saanich instead. This necessitated a cab ride to his car at the Victoria Harbour Air terminal downtown.

He had had time to think about what Dillon and his girlfriend were doing around those islands in the midst of an incoming coastal storm. He realized Powell River had been an important stop for the youth, and he also realized that Selina Archie was from the same community—a fact he wasn't sure he would share with Hamish Firth.

He recalled Hamish's reaction when Pirro Marco's name was mentioned in casual conversation. He was going to be less forthcoming with information he passed on to Hamish—the Spanish escudos were fair game for anyone, even for himself. Eduardo had told Hamish he would arrive from Comox late in the afternoon. They agreed to discuss the trip over a drink and dinner at Pagliacci's, an Italian restaurant on Broad Street frequented by locals.

The restaurant was a converted fire hall and the large front window was once an exit for horse-drawn pumpers. A few people were outside or crowded into the entrance waiting for their tables to be vacated. Eduardo had to press through to reach the front reception. He spotted Hamish, and the hostess guided him through crowded tables in the cozy and charming interior.

"The food here is fantastic. I came here early to ensure I had a table by the time you arrived." Hamish had to speak loudly to be heard over the din. Eduardo jammed his considerable frame into the booth seat. "It's crazy in here on Saturday nights."

"Crazy is an understatement. The food must be exceptional," Eduardo said.

"How was your trip to Comox?"

"The kids went there to scuba dive. I spent two days on a boat following them around the strait. I don't think the trip had anything to do with the coins, my friend."

"It's unusual for university students to disappear on diving excursions at the beginning of a new school term, Eduardo. Where did—" Hamish was interrupted by a cell phone ring.

"Speak louder, Jack, it's noisy here … you are supposed to call every day, Jack. That was our arrangement. Yes, yes …." Hamish sighed, "Not back? You're sure. Okay, every day."

Eduardo took a drink of red wine. "What was that all about?"

"I have someone monitoring activities at the kids' house. I thought I might obtain information about Walter Smith's diary. The kids didn't return from Comox today—at least, not yet anyway."

"The weather was awful. Maybe their flight was cancelled."

Hamish leaned over the table. "Eduardo, I want you to look for that diary. Get into the kids' house and see if you can find it. It must be there."

"Are you nuts? Me do a B&E?" Eduardo took another drink from his wine glass. "Get your friend on the phone to do it for you."

"I don't want him involved in that way. His job is to watch and report, Eduardo. You're getting a cut of the bounty, remember." Hamish glanced about at the crowd. Everyone was engrossed in their own conversations.

"Tomorrow is Sunday. You know what the kids' car looks like, so you'll know if they're home. Wait until the other two roommates leave, and then take a quick look about. That's all I'm asking. In and out. It's an old house. It shouldn't be tough to get into. Do it yourself this time. The last time didn't go so well. We didn't get the quinto."

Eduardo became thin-lipped. "This is the last time I do anything like this. If I don't find the diary, I drop the whole thing. It's a long shot at best. I don't want to risk everything I've built for something that isn't likely there."

"It's there, Eduardo. I know it is."

☩

Moonlight leaked between strands of cloud when Dillon and Adrianne pulled into the driveway of the lane behind Adrianne's parents' house on the south side of English Bay. A large Greek community lived in Dunbar, and the majority had built their fortunes from hard, honest work. Adrianne's parents' home reflected their success. The contrast between

Dillon's home in Sliammon and Adrianne's was beyond comparison.

"We're late, Dillon." Adrianne handed the fare to the Pacific-Cab's cabbie.

Dillon surveyed the rear of the beautiful property, noticing a kidney-shaped pool off to his right. "Yeah … I'm coming." He emptied his and Adrianne's backpacks from the cab.

Adrianne waited for Dillon to join her on the sidewalk before she approached the back door. She flipped through the assortment of keys on her key ring and inserted one into the door lock.

"We're here," Adrianne yelled as they entered a tiled mudroom.

"Adrianne, I'm in the kitchen … dinner's almost ready, dear." A woman's voice drifted into the mudroom as Dillon closed the back door.

Adrianne took Dillon's hand. "Come meet everyone."

"How was your flight from Comox?" Adrianne's mother asked when Adrianne and Dillon walked into the kitchen. She wore an elegant blue, narrow-strapped dress that complimented her suntan and hair. A gold pendant hung around her neck.

"Really rough, Mom. Those commuter planes sure bounce around. Mom, this is Dillon Point."

"I'm Lia," she said, sizing up Dillon. "You're the one sharing the house with my daughter, no? Boys and girls didn't sleep together in the same house when I was Adrianne's age, unless they were family. You are careful and treat her right?"

"Yes, of course," Dillon stammered, at a loss for words.

"Mom," Adrianne gave her mother a big kiss, "I'm glad that we're going to stay overnight. It's so awful to travel in this weather and I want everyone to meet Dillon."

"I told your father and I've made up the spare bed."

Adrianne sighed, "Mom …."

"Don't Mom me. We know you two have shared the same bed, but not in our house. He booked the room for you in Comox, remember?" Lia stirred a pot of gravy. "Grandpa Frank's with your father in the sitting room. Go introduce Dillon while I finish up in here."

"Your mother gets right to the point, doesn't she?" Dillon whispered.

"Your mother wasn't much different."

"Grandpa Frank and Dad, this is Dillon Point," Adrianne smiled as she led Dillon into the inviting sitting room.

"Hello, Dillon. Call me Ted." Adrianne's father studied the young man. "You two want a glass of red wine before dinner?"

Adrianne's father was dressed in a black sports jacket, a casual, light-gray shirt, and gray dress pants.

"Yes, please," Dillon answered.

Ted opened a bottle at the bar. "This is Tselepos, a Greek cabernet." He began to pour two glasses. "I started drinking this wine when I was thirteen. Adrianne tells us you are a First Nations member from up the coast."

"Yes, I'm Sliammon. My people have lived in a village by Powell River for centuries. I took Adrianne to meet my mother this weekend."

"Dillon, this is Grandpa Frank." Adrianne led Dillon to an elderly man sitting in the corner of the room.

"Sir," Dillon shook his hand.

"My daughter says you're reading a diary left to you by your grandfather and discovering your heritage. It's good to know and respect your roots, isn't it Grandpa Frank?" Ted asked, turning toward his father.

"Your heritage helps you learn who you are and gives you your family values." Grandpa Frank's deep-set piercing gray eyes focused on Dillon.

"Come, Dillon, tell us more about you and what you plan to do with your life." Ted handed him a glass of wine.

Both Dillon and Adrianne were glad to go to her room and get away from the family inquisition. She heaved a sigh of relief as she closed the door.

Dillon needed relaxation. "I'd like to read more of the diary."

"Sounds great to me. I have to run to the bathroom first. Your stuff is in the room next door." Dillon watched the slim, olive-skinned brunette disappear into the en suite bathroom, then exited the room to find his.

Dillon took deep breaths and slowly exhaled as he looked at the inviting room with flowered wallpaper. He searched his backpack for the diary until he remembered it was in Adrianne's backpack with her slips of clothing. He changed his shirt, removed his shoes and returned to Adrianne's room to find the diary.

"Hey, what's with going through my stuff?"

Dillon held up the diary.

"My period's started."

"At least you're not pregnant. Your parents would kill me."

"Only after me, mister. They wouldn't even find your miserable body." She wore a cotton nightie imprinted with rosebuds that skimmed her feet. "Sexy, isn't it?"

"It looks warm, anyway." Dillon placed the diary on the mattress.

Adrianne felt strange sharing her bed with a young man in the house where she had grown up. She gazed at treasured photographs of family and friends, and diving artifacts. The familiar surroundings eased her.

"Ready to go," Dillon remarked. "Which side's mine?"

"Side ..." Adrianne frowned, dragged from her memories, "you can have the one by the window." She pulled back the patterned black and white bed cover with diary in hand.

Dillon propped up his pillows on the headboard. "We're almost finished reading this." He took the diary from Adrianne's outstretched hand.

She laid her head on Dillon's chest. "You okay with all this, Dillon?"

"I'm with you. That's what matters." He opened the diary and inhaled the aroma of her sweet perfume.

Wednesday 17th December 1975;

I told Larry and Faye-Elliott that my work was completed, and I had booked a flight from Powell River for Thursday night. They put on a great feast tonight. I feel my dishonest story will haunt me the rest of my life. I had an opportunity to briefly talk with Gloria. She couldn't look at me when she said that Brett had agreed to marry her before the end of the month. Brett glanced at me a number of times during the meal, but never said a word to me. Gloria agreed to see me tomorrow evening. The days were shorter and it was dark by four in the afternoon. We would meet at the big rock on Gibson's Beach after darkness fell.

Thursday 18th December 1975;

> *This is my last entry. I've decided to give this book, and the golden coin, to Gloria in a carved wooden box I purchased in Powell River. It isn't much of a gift. It certainly isn't enough to reflect my love for her. We never determined what to do with the treasure, but I'm sure Gloria will make the right decision. I don't know if Gloria will ever tell Larry and Faye-Elliott the truth about her pregnancy, but I do know my child will be well looked after. I will regret my decision to leave every day. I hope one day my child will learn the truth of its mixed heritage. I trust the coins will make life easier for all.*

Adrianne sighed. "It's tragic, really. Such wasted love and an awful thing for Walter to do—abandon Gloria and their unborn child."

"There's one last entry," Dillon said.

Postscript message for Gloria—my only love.

> *I hope you forgive me one day for my cowardly actions. My love for you encompasses my entire being and soul, but I believe that my decision is the best for you and the baby. Tears are flowing onto this page as I write. I don't know how I will share my life experiences with the Sliammon without feeling the pain I now endure. Forgive me, my love. Qoqoq*

Dillon closed the diary and placed it on the bedside table. He stroked Adrianne's hair without a word.

Fourteen

Sunday morning Vancouver traffic was light. Dillon and Adrianne were travelling to the airport in Richmond. They hoped to be home early enough to get in some study time.

"I feel a lot better after a good night's sleep in my own bed," Adrianne said. "Now that we've finished Walter's diary, do you know what you're going to do, Dillon?"

"One thing is for sure, I have my answers about my family heritage. Certainly nothing I ever imagined. I guess I didn't know what to expect. I see why my mother and grandmother have kept the story from everyone. Obviously Brett hasn't seen the diary."

"I think Brett should be given the opportunity to read the diary. He married your grandmother. In my opinion, he has a right, Dillon."

"I don't know. It was a long time ago. I could talk to my mother, but it's certainly not my call. I don't know what my mother expects me to do now, anyway."

"Your mother said reading and acting on the diary was your choice, Dillon. You must finish your quest, as your mother and grandmother expect you to."

"I don't care about the coins, or whatever was hidden by Walter and Grandmother Gloria, I really don't. I have my answers to my questions; my quest for so many years. I don't need the rest to be content."

"I think you must fulfill the destiny laid out for you, Dillon. It's not about the physical value of the hidden coins, but to close that chapter—do what Gloria and your mother could or would not. They want you to, or your mother wouldn't have given you the diary. You must find the hidden coins and decide once and for all what to do with them—if they're still there."

"Okay then, if you'll help, but this entire thing must remain our secret."

"Agreed. I'll take another look at the diary entries and download the photos and video from my cell phone. I can start at the airport while we wait for our flight."

Adrianne sat at the Vancouver Airport South Terminal waiting for their flight to Victoria with Dillon. She keyed notes into her laptop as she glanced at the diary. Dillon leaned over to see how she was doing.

Dillon let Adrianne focus on what she was doing. She Googled "weather patterns Powell River" and checked the diary for the date. "Early November … let's see."

She nodded her head. "I thought so … gale-type winds … normally northerly up the strait. I'd better look at the tide tables, too." She continued to mutter to herself, engrossed in her research until the boarding announcement was made.

"The clues are here, I'm sure of it," Adrianne said. "I'll go see Nathan at the marina for a marine chart for that area."

♓

Eduardo Dominguez sat in his Escalade a block away from Dillon's Charles Street house. He was still annoyed that he had been pressured into breaking into the kids' house. The fact that Dillon and his girlfriend were poking around the islands off the coast of Powell River led Eduardo to the conclusion that the Spanish coins were connected somehow to Walter's research on the Sliammon peoples.

He agreed with Hamish that the diary was crucial. He watched the faded Jeep back out of the driveway. Adrianne's car wasn't in the driveway when he arrived. He waited a few minutes before he sauntered down the street and knocked on the door. There was no answer. Eduardo decided it prudent to knock on the back door as well. Again, no answer.

He looked around one more time, and then ran down a concrete staircase underneath the back deck that led to the basement. He turned the knob and was surprised to discover the door unlocked. He darted inside.

The basement was damp and musty, lit only by door and side windows that ran along each side of the house. He bent over to avoid hitting his head on the low ceiling, and began to search for the main floor staircase.

The main floor of the house was tidier than he had expected for students. He soon located the master bedroom on the main floor. He combed through the contents of two desks. Eduardo turned to check the bedside tables that contained sex toys and paraphernalia. He realized he was in the wrong room when he saw photographs of the gay couple.

A step creaked as he proceeded to the upper floor. Eduardo walked into the bedroom on the right at the top of the stairs. He began to strew women's clothing from the dresser onto the floor. "Not here. Maybe in the bookcase." He pushed texts and notebooks onto the floor; he scanned the books on the shelf and found nothing of interest.

He rushed into the bedroom across the hall to repeat his haphazard search for the book. "Damn." He pulled books from a small bookcase under the window and let them fall onto the floor. He stopped for a moment when he recognized the black and white photograph Hamish had shown him on his computer. He was now certain that he was in Dillon's room.

Eduardo turned everything upside down, checked under the mattress and through the suitcase stashed in the closet. "Damn it all, no diary. I'll have to see what Hamish wants to do now. Damn." He looked out the window in the room to ensure the kids hadn't returned before making his escape empty-handed.

♓

Adrianne was laughing as she unlocked the door. Dillon chased Adrianne up the stairs.

"Holy shit!" Adrianne stopped abruptly at her bedroom door. Dillon almost ran right into her as she stared at the mess in her room.

"What the …?" Dillon looked around Adrianne's room.

She slowly entered her bedroom looking at everything tossed onto her floor. "Dillon, my stuff. Someone was looking for something." She carefully picked up a few things from the floor.

Dillon rushed into his room and sharply inhaled when he saw the mess on the floor. "My room's even worse than yours." He called for Niki and Josh to come upstairs.

"Hi, Dillon. Have a nice time away?" Josh asked, climbing the stairs, followed closely by Niki. "It was quiet while you two were away."

"Did you guys notice someone has been in the house?" Dillon asked. Adrianne joined the group at the top of the stairs.

"In the house?" Josh asked.

"Both Adrianne's and my rooms have been ransacked. Come look."

"Oh, my," Niki said, as he surveyed Dillon's room. "There was no indication downstairs that someone broke in when we came home today. Nothing's missing that I noticed. We'd better call the cops and leave things as they are."

"Niki, you call 911 and we'll wait in the sitting room. If nothing's missing downstairs, why break in?" Josh asked.

"They're here," Josh said when he saw through the front window a squad car pull into their driveway. Josh went to greet the two constables at the front door.

"Thanks for coming so quickly. Someone broke in, but we don't know what they wanted."

"We need to talk to you before we look around. I'm Constable Harold Taylor, and this is my partner Constable Vivian Barr." Josh invited the strapping constable and his partner in.

"Everyone is in the sitting room," Josh pointed to his right. The constables entered the room and eyed the three sitting quietly. "These are Constables Barr and Taylor," Josh said. He joined Niki on the sofa.

"Everyone okay in here?" Constable Taylor asked. "I don't see any signs of a B&E in here."

"Yes, we are all okay. No one was home when it happened. The rooms upstairs were ransacked, but it doesn't look like the thieves were looking for anything down here. None of the electronics are missing, and our bedroom on this floor looks like everything is where it should be," Josh answered.

"Let's start from the beginning," Constable Barr said. She pulled a notepad and pen from her right pocket. "What are your names, please?"

All four gave their names and birthdates.

"What happened?"

"Josh and I were out most of the day. We came home about four this afternoon. We were studying at Starbucks on Cook Street. Dillon and Adrianne returned home a short while ago from a trip to Powell River, and they found the disaster upstairs. I called 911."

"Do any of you have any idea what the burglar may have been looking for?" Constable Barr asked. The four youths shook their heads.

"The burglar only ransacked upstairs, you say. That sounds strange for a random B&E. You better show me. Harold, why don't you go outside and see where the perpetrator entered, while I look around upstairs."

Constable Taylor went outside. Dillon and Adrianne led Constable Barr upstairs.

"We'll wait down here," Niki said.

The threesome reached the top of the staircase. Adrianne showed Constable Barr her room. "I haven't touched anything." She stood aside so that the constable could take a closer look.

"The perp was certainly looking for something. You have any jewelry in here?"

"No, nothing special." Adrianne walked to the dresser and pulled out a jewelry box. "It's all here.

Constable Barr wrote a note. "Is there anything missing, Ms. Padrino?"

Adrianne bent down to put her text books on the bookcase. "I'll check the rest of the dresser drawers after I put these back."

"Carry on while I check over here." Constable Barr walked to the desk at the end of the room, while Dillon helped Adrianne replace the books. The policewoman bent down to pick up a few pens and a notebook from the floor by the desk. She noticed a black devise lying under the desk by the wall. "What's this?" She picked up the object and examined it closely. "This is a wireless camera."

"What?" Adrianne rushed over to look at the device. "It's a ... a camera?"

"Does this belong to anyone in this house?" Constable Barr asked, glancing over at Dillon.

"It's not mine. I don't know much about computers. A wireless camera?" Dillon walked over to the policewoman to look at the camera. "That does what? Takes pictures?"

"It's a video camera, and it can send a video feed through your wireless Internet," Constable Barr replied. "Show me your room, Mr. Point."

As they reached his room, Dillon explained, "It's a bigger mess in here. I didn't leave anything of value at home. I had my computer, cell phone, and money with me on our trip. Can I begin to put things away?"

"In a minute. I need to take a quick look first. Why do you think someone broke in here, and what do you have that they would want?" Constable Barr asked.

"I have no idea."

"You or your girlfriend stash drugs in the house?"

"Drugs? Absolutely not."

Constable Barr knelt down and carefully looked around the entire floor. "Here we are. Another camera." She studied the area from her place on the floor. "I bet this was placed in that silk tree. I'd better check for more downstairs."

"I don't get it. What are those things doing in here and in Adrianne's bedroom?"

"I have no idea yet. Let's go downstairs and ask the other two boys."

Constable Taylor had returned from his task and was waiting in the front entranceway for his partner. "The back door to the basement was unlocked. There are no other areas that show signs of forced entry, so I suspect our intruder came in through the basement. It's an old door and should be changed or bolted."

"I found two wireless video cams. There doesn't appear to be anything missing upstairs." She showed the two devices to her partner. "Let's talk to the other two," she said and went into the sitting room.

"Anything missing from upstairs?" Niki asked.

"When was your Internet service activated?"

"Over a year ago when Niki and I rented the place," Josh said. "Why?"

"No internet service person since then, or any other service people been here?"

"No, the landlord comes once in a while, but only when we've been home as far as I know. What's the problem, Constable?"

"It appears spying devices were placed in the two upstairs bedrooms before this B&E. Do these things belong to you boys?" Constable Barr displayed the two mini video cameras in her hand.

"What are they?" Niki asked, jumping off the sofa to take a look.

"Wireless video cameras. Someone planted these in the silk trees in the rooms upstairs. Let me look at your computers, boys. I also need to see if there are any cameras in your room," Constable Taylor said.

Josh and Niki followed Constable Taylor, and left Dillon and Adrianne with Constable Barr.

"I see no motive for the B&E. These video devices may not be connected to this event, as they were on the floor. Does any of this make any sense to either of you?"

"No, not in the least," Dillon replied. "What now, Constable?"

"I suggest that all the locks be changed and a deadbolt installed on the basement door. You should also change the Internet password."

"That's creepy—someone watching me in my bedroom. Can you determine anything from those things about who this might be?" Adrianne asked.

"I don't think so. My report and these devices will go to Computer Forensics first thing Monday. That's all I can say right now. Here is my card. Call me if you think of anything else."

"Yes, of course, Constable. Thank you." Adrianne took the card as Constable Taylor reappeared.

"I saw nothing suspicious on the computers nor were there hidden cameras. That's all we can do right now."

♓

Eduardo sat with Hamish holding their customary scotches looking at the clear evening sky through a picture window in Hamish's Oak Bay home.

"Time is running out on our arrangement. We haven't made much progress on finding the Spanish escudos," Eduardo said. "The B&E was fruitless, and I was scared shitless I'd be seen breaking in."

"The timeline of Walter Smith's research of the Sliammon aligns with the suspected Gonzalo Cielo heist of the coins, and possibly the El Rey Dorado." Hamish swirled his scotch and ice. "Too bad you didn't get your hands on that damn diary today."

"The key must be the First Nations kid. I saw the original black and white photo in the boy's room today. He and his girlfriend stayed overnight in Powell River—no, he must've stayed in the Sliammon village because he's First Nations. I'm not interested in chasing fantasy escudo treasure. The coin in the photo must've been purchased," Eduardo said. "Pirro Marco's the real expert on this Spanish escudo stuff, especially the Santa Regio. You may need to talk to him to find out if he knows more about the El Rey Dorado than what's covered on the Internet."

"You said you've talked with Pirro before," Hamish said. "Give me his number, and I'll consider it."

♓

Jack was home late from class and put a pizza into the oven for dinner. He had to review the video footage from the St. Charles Street house before calling Hamish Firth. Hamish was a pain in the ass, but the daily surveillance fee came in handy. He hoped there were juicy bedroom scenes.

He sat at his desk with a can of beer. "Who the hell is that?" The monitor showed a corpulent man ransacking Adrianne's room. Jack heard the intruder speak in a Mexican accent. "Not here. Maybe the bookcase." The video ran for a few moments, then the feed suddenly went blank.

Jack switched to the digital copy of Dillon's room. The invader muttered, "Damn it all, no diary. I'll have to see what Hamish wants to do now. Damn." The video feed ended.

"So Firth hired a guy to B&E the kids' place looking for the diary. He should've talked to me first." Jack's equipment was wrecked, and the cops would be all over the place. Jack took a gulp of beer and plotted his revenge.

Fifteen

Jack was up early and was seated in a workspace at the University of Victoria's library. His flash drive was inserted into a USB port on one of the student computer terminals. He was writing an email addressed to the local Victoria Police Crime Stoppers from a new Gmail account he had set up.

Please find attached videos of a B&E at 2012 St. Charles Street that took place yesterday. The Hamish referred to by the perpetrator is Hamish Firth, who is a rare coin dealer in the city. Regards, a concerned citizen.

Jack pressed send and withdrew his flash drive.

⋊

Jamie and TJ were sitting in Inspector Harris's office waiting for their new assignment. It was a warm, sunny day and didn't feel like the middle of September. The Inspector had left the detectives to wait in his office. His private assistant, Constable Lyndon, had left after delivering fresh coffees.

"How was your weekend, TJ?" Jamie asked.

"Detectives." Inspector Harris entered his office holding a brown folder and closed the door. "I was going to assign you this case this morning," he said, as he picked up a blue folder from the corner of his desk, "but another matter has come to my attention that I think you should handle instead. Our Crime Stoppers Unit received an email with a couple of videos attached. I think you may find them interesting. I believe they may be connected to the case you closed Friday."

"Sir?" Jamie was curious about the connection.

"There was a B&E on Sunday at a house in Fairfield. I have the responding constables' report." Harris opened the brown folder. "University students had their rental house broken into, but nothing was missing according to the students. Constables Vivian Barr and Harold Taylor did locate two wireless video cameras in the two rooms that were ransacked." The Inspector took a sip of his coffee.

"The interesting thing is that the video files received by Crime Stoppers captured the B&E and the perpetrator. I'm assigning this case to you because there is one common thing among all these cases: a Hamish Firth. See what this man has to do with all these crimes." The Inspector pushed the brown folder toward Jamie. "Keep me informed, Detectives."

The detectives reconvened in Jamie's office. "I guess our case wasn't as cut and dried as it seemed on Friday, TJ. Let's look at the videos first. Pull a chair around." Jamie selected the VicPD shared drive on her computer and found the case file. She played the first video, then the second. "What do you think?"

"It's clear Hamish was mentioned in the video, but the specific link to Hamish Firth—I don't know. What's in the file?"

Jamie opened the brown folder. "Here is a copy of the email." She handed the paper to TJ.

"The email is specific to Mr. Firth. What else is in the file?"

"The constables' report at the B&E scene. There were video cameras found in both the girl's room—Adrianne Padrino—and the male's room—Dillon Point. It's the same address as the informant gives. I guess our informant is the person who planted the wireless cameras. I don't get the reference to a diary. I think we need to meet with Adrianne or Dillon to obtain more information on that. It's interesting that Mr. Firth is mentioned by our B&E intruder, though. We need to find out what that connection is, too. I agree with the Inspector that this isn't coincidental."

"Is there any data on the IP address of the video peeper?"

"Computer Forensics guys say that they can't establish a link because the equipment is off-the-shelf, and there is no signature link to the actual person hacking into the home network. I don't understand why this video was sent to Crime Stoppers in the first place. Retaliation or vendetta? Forensics was only able to determine that the file was sent from the University of Victoria."

"I think it's time to visit Firth again, Jamie, and see where that conversation leads. We should also call the contact in the B&E report—Adrianne Padrino—and set up a discussion with her. I think there is more going on than she admits. A camera in her room and nothing missing. Give me a break."

The unmarked VicPD Charger parked across from Firth Coin and Rarities on Store Street. The detectives' entrance into the shop was announced by the doorbell, and following its sound, Hamish appeared from the back room.

Hamish sharply inhaled at the sight of his visitors. "Detectives, what brings you back to my humble shop?"

"We need to talk to you about a video we received this morning, Mr. Firth. Could I show it to you?" Jamie asked. "It won't take much of your time."

"A video." Hamish eyed the smart phone Jamie held.

"We received two clips, but this one is the most interesting." Jamie selected the clip and placed the phone on the counter, turning it so that Hamish could see the screen. The clip played, complete with Eduardo's voice. He was frozen in utter amazement for a few seconds, then rapidly attempted to concoct a plausible story.

"Mr. Firth, can you comment on this for us?"

Hamish slowly raised his eyes from the smart phone. "What help do you think I can provide? I don't recognize that voice, if that's your question."

"The person in that video is referring to you, Sir. He distinctly said Hamish," TJ said. "What diary is the man referring to?"

"You're mistaken. I'm not the only person named 'Hamish.' That video was likely staged for some reason. Your guess is as good as mine about the diary."

"So you don't recognize the man in the video, or know anything about a diary that he refers to?" Jamie asked. "It's interesting that the person who sent this video to us names you specifically. Do you have any idea why someone would do that if you're not involved in the B&E that took place?"

"That video was a B&E? I run a legitimate business. I've been an honorable businessman in Victoria for years."

"Thank you for your time, Mr. Firth." Jaime put her cell phone back in her pocket.

"That guy's involved. My gut tells me that." Jaime said as the women walked toward their car. "There's a few pieces missing, but we'll find them. Maybe Ms. Padrino can tell us something that's not in the B&E report and comment on the diary, too."

"Ms. Padrino and Mr. Point are going to meet us between classes, so we better get a move on."

Hamish Firth watched the detectives leave his shop, and he sighed with relief that he didn't have to answer any additional pointed questions. He couldn't believe Jack had sent that video, and Jack's action had directed the police back to him for a second time. He'd deal with Jack once things cooled off. The S-O-B broke their deal.

Hamish poured a stiff scotch in his office. After the 1979 shooting in Gastown, he relocated to Victoria, to remove himself from any possible association with the victim. Now he would have to deal with Eduardo, too. It was too risky now that Eduardo could be identified in the videos.

The scotch did its work. As he relaxed, his thoughts became clearer. Perhaps the best course was to call Pirro Marco. He likely would be interested in hunting for the escudos and the El Rey Dorado. Hamish fished through his wallet for the scrap of paper Eduardo had scribbled Marco's number on.

⯑

Dillon and Adrianne sat at a table at Village Greens, a casual eatery on the University of Victoria's campus, waiting for the detectives, who were late.

"Adrianne Padrino?" Jamie asked.

"Yes, and this is Dillon Point."

"I'm Detective Steele and this is my partner Detective Kennedy. As I mentioned on the telephone, we would like to talk to you about your B&E statement from last night."

"I told the constable everything I know, and so did Dillon."

"We have some additional information concerning the B&E. Does the name Hamish Firth mean anything to either of you?"

Adrianne glanced at Dillon, then replied. "I sent a photograph to Mr. Firth a week ago, if he's the same man who owns Firth Coin and Rarities."

"A photograph of what?"

"A snapshot of a black and white photograph that belongs to Dillon. There was a coin in the photo. I wanted to see if Mr. Firth could tell me something about it. He said the coin is called an escudo, and that it was minted for the Spanish in the mid-1600s. He asked where the photo was taken, but I didn't reply."

"Do you know anything about a diary?"

"A diary? How do you know about Dillon's diary, Detective?"

"The person who planted the video camera devices sent us a clip of the B&E. The man who was in the video burglarizing your rooms mentioned a diary. It seems that the diary was the motivation for the B&E."

"Did Mr. Firth plant those video cameras?" Dillon asked.

"We don't know who planted the cameras, but we do have a clear image of the perpetrator. Do you know a heavy-set man who might be Mexican?"

Dillon briefly glanced over at Adrianne. "No."

"Adrianne, how is Dillon's diary connected to the coin photograph that you sent to Mr. Firth?" TJ asked, with her notebook and pen ready.

"The photograph Adrianne sent to Mr. Firth was a picture of my grandfather and grandmother holding a coin. We were curious about the coin, since it didn't appear to be a Canadian coin. Mr. Firth said the coin was an escudo. After reading passages in my grandfather's diary, we subsequently discovered there might be substantially more coins hidden somewhere around where I live—the Sliammon, just north of Powell River."

"So there is a hidden bounty of these escudos then?" TJ asked.

"We believe so, but we don't know exactly where they are or even if they are still where they were hidden many years ago. We know that they are rare and made of solid gold."

"They were hidden? By whom?"

"The diary says by my grandfather and grandmother," Dillon admitted. "It's a closely kept family secret. I'm supposed to figure the mystery out myself. I can trust you guys, right?"

"Of course you can, Dillon. How did Mr. Firth discover that there was a diary?"

"I have no idea, but maybe that's why there were cameras in our rooms. We didn't want anyone to know we are looking for the escudos. Can you arrest Mr. Firth?"

"We can't connect him to the B&E or the video cameras at this point. We haven't identified the burglar as yet. Have you ever seen this man?" Jamie played the video clip on her smart phone.

"No." Both responded by shaking their heads.

"If you see this man, call me on my cell phone immediately, but don't approach him." Jamie extracted a few cards from her pocket and handed one to each of them.

"We have classes soon. Can we go now?" Dillon asked. He wanted to avoid further questions about the diary.

"All right, then. Your secret is safe with us. Be careful if you decide to continue your search for those coins. We'll be in touch." Jamie thoughtfully watched the two students walk out of the cafe.

"Jamie, Firth was involved in the appraisal of the quinto, which is made from Spanish golden ingots. Now it seems there are gold Spanish escudo coins, too. That's the connection, and it looks like the video camera peeper was working for Firth. Firth lied about not knowing the Mexican intruder, who he obviously sent to find the diary. I think another visit with Mr. Firth is in order. Maybe we can pressure him into a confession about the B&E. It seems it might be his MO to hire people to break and enter. Collins was a similar case chasing Selina Archie's quinto necklace."

♓

Hamish Firth was elated he had convinced Pirro Marco to fly in from Florida to Vancouver for a meeting. Pirro had been intrigued by the possibility that some of the Santa Regio bounty might be on the west coast, but had told Hamish he was skeptical about the story. He would evaluate the facts once they met in Vancouver. Hamish agreed to pay for Pirro's airfare and overnight stay. Pirro would make his decision before he returned to Florida.

It was only late morning, and Hamish had a pounding headache that he blamed on the cops and Jack Bryce. He poured the remnants of the scotch into his glass. He held his head in his hands as he thought about the phone call he must make to Eduardo.

"Eduardo, it's Hamish. I was visited by the Victoria Police this morning. They have a video of you doing the B&E. I told them I know nothing about it, and that I didn't recognize you."

"A video? How the hell did they get a video?"

"They said the rooms had wireless video cameras. I think you need to disappear for a while."

"Why did they come to you, Hamish?"

"They found out about the photograph from the girl at the house—the photo with the escudo that she emailed me. I guess the cops are fishing."

"I assume you're going to drop the escudo thing now, right, Hamish?"

"Not exactly. I contacted Pirro Marco, and he's coming here to talk. He might be interested in following up …."

"If he does, I still get a cut of the value of anything found."

"Of course. We have an agreement, my friend, but you need to leave right now before the cops link you to me. Go to Sooke and spend a few quiet days fishing until the cops move onto another case file."

"No more fishing boats for me, Hamish, but I will find a quiet place outside Victoria. Keep in touch, Hamish, and don't bet on finding anything. Pirro Marco will be expensive. Cut your losses. It's a long shot so far as I'm concerned."

Just as the phone call disconnected, the shop doorbell announced a new customer. Hamish stood up and realized he'd had a few too many scotches.

"Mr. Firth," TJ said. "We have a few questions."

Hamish sighed. "Now what?" he asked.

"Just following up on our conversation. It appears you left out a few details this morning. You don't seem too busy so I assume now is a good time."

"A few details about what?" Hamish's head pounded.

"An email with a black and white photograph of an escudo coin, to start with."

"Escudo coin—oh, that. I told the Padrino girl it was impossible for a Spanish escudo from the 1600s to show up in this part of the world. As far as I was concerned, it was a Photoshop prank."

"What would a coin like that be worth, Mr. Firth?" Jamie asked. She watched the man's body language closely.

"An escudo like the one in the photograph—if it was an escudo coin—is probably worth about three grand US dollars, if it's in mint condition. There are coins of that type for sale on the Internet. The escudo coins were originally found in 1972 on the Santa Regio, a galleon wreck off the Florida Keys. They were minted around 1656 in Bogotá."

"The quinto necklace was from that wreck as well, wasn't it?"

"A strange coincidence, don't you think? What does the email have to do with the B&E we discussed this morning?"

"The email was sent by a victim in the B&E. That's a coincidence I find intriguing, Mr. Firth."

"That's my business, Detective—rare coins and rarities. I get questions like that all the time."

"So you take the position that this is all a coincidence, and that you weren't involved in this B&E or the one at Ms. Archie's house. Is that right?" Jamie's stance was intimidating.

"That's right. I object to your accusations. I have a reputation in this town. Your implications could destroy what I've spent a lifetime building."

"We are following the facts and the evidence, that's all. We will unearth the truth, sooner or later. If you get another inquiry about anything associated with the Santa Regio wreck or its cargo, please call us."

"Firth is up to his eyeballs in this, Jamie," TJ remarked, as the women walked to their car. "I'd sure like to get my hands on that Mexican guy in the video. If he's working with Firth, then he likely orchestrated the B&E at Selina Archie's place to grab the quinto necklace."

"Perhaps our drug dealer, Sam Queen, knows more than he admitted. He was the last person that we know of who talked to Charles Collins. Maybe Collins said something about the person who hired him. Queen must've asked Collins about the whale key before it was exchanged for the pills," Jamie said. "I'll put a bulletin out on him and hopefully one of our uniforms will spot him."

♓

Dillon lay next to Adrianne in her bed. She was still distressed about the house invasion. She felt safer with Dillon at her side.

"I just about freaked when the detective told us that there were video recordings from those cameras in our rooms. That's all I could think about for the rest of the day. I couldn't focus on my classes, and just the thought about someone watching me … us in bed and … having sex."

"The cameras are gone, and the police are investigating Firth. I agree that it's unnerving. I'm sure the video cameras were to find out about the diary and not to capture us having sex. The cops will find the guy. Cuddle. It'll help you feel better."

"Okay."

"I'm concerned that someone is after my diary and may know about the hidden Escudos. I don't think we read a lot from my diary in our rooms, but maybe we should go to Sliammon and find Grandmother Gloria's escudos before that Firth guy—or whoever—finds them first."

"I called Chuck Williams to be prepared for us tomorrow. He's outfitting our Zodiac with the detail charts that include Savary and Harwood Islands. Vivian Island isn't large so we'll have to deal with the detail of that one once we're there."

"I'll let Mom know that we're coming back. I want to talk to her about what she knows about the escudo coins. Maybe Grandmother told her things that aren't in the diary."

"That's a good idea. Snuggle with me now, Dillon. I just want to rest with you next to me."

Sixteen

Early the next morning, TJ opened the interrogation room door, let Jamie proceed into the room, closed the door, and sat down. Sam Queen sat at the table.

"So what is it this time, Detectives?"

"We've been thinking about the story you told us when we sat in this room last time, Sammy. Your story about that whale key," Jamie said. "I want you to think back and try to recall anything Collins told you when you traded the key for the pills."

"That was some time ago, now, Detective." Sam Queen's eyes rolled to the top of his sockets, "He said something about he was goin' to meet some Eduardo guy, but wanted the pills. Chaz said the guy was Mexican, I think. That's all he said, and we made the deal for the pills."

"Eduardo? You're sure about the name?"

"Yeah. Was that key thing the Mexican's?"

"No it wasn't, but we think Collins was paid by that guy to do the heist. You can leave now, Sammy, and stay out of trouble."

"Well, we have a first name now," TJ remarked.

"Yep, we have a photo and we have a first name. If Eduardo isn't a local, he had to arrive by flight, ferry, or private boat. You check out flights and see if any passengers had the first name of Eduardo and post his photo at the Swartz Bay ferry terminal. I'll check for hotel reservations in town."

♓

Hamish waited outside the arrivals level of the Vancouver International airport to meet Pirro Marco. Pirro was well known in the antiquities salvage community. Hamish hadn't expected Pirro to be interested enough in the escudo story to fly to Vancouver.

Hamish held a sign, "Mr. Marco," written in black felt pen; he was ready to meet the man he was convinced could finally achieve what Eduardo had failed to do—find the stash of the Spanish bounty taken from the Santa Regio in 1972 by Gonzalo Cielo and his partners.

"Señior Firth, I presume." A sophisticated, gray-haired man about sixty years old stopped in the busy, crowded corridor to greet Hamish. "You're so kind to meet me."

"Not at all ... not at all, Mr. Marco." Hamish reached to shake the man's hand. "Call me Hamish."

"Yes, I'm Pirro. Where shall we talk about the escudos?"

Hamish took the man's suitcase. "This way to the Fairmont Hotel. There are some comfortable seats in the lobby. We can go also to the lounge, if you wish."

"Canada. I've never visited Vancouver. It's a beautiful city I hear, is it not?" Pirro asked, as he followed Hamish along a corridor that led to an elevator.

"Yes, it is. I'm so honored you came on such short notice."

"I'd go anywhere to investigate a 1656 escudo that may be from the Santa Regio. You're absolutely positive about your facts, are you Hamish?"

"Yes, of course, I'm sure. I believe some of the cargo was stolen in 1972 from the Capland expedition, and it ended up here on the West Coast. You know about the Cielo murder? I believe his accomplices brought some of the goods to Vancouver sometime in the mid-1970s. I also know the ship manifest was located in '87, and that there were other treasures besides the gold and coins and ingots aboard that majestic galleon.

"You've been reading public articles, I see, Hamish. Yes, you're right, of course. There were other artifacts of greater interest on the ship. That's why I've come to Vancouver. There were items never recovered when Cielo was discovered murdered in Palm Beach. Everyone went crazy when the manifest listed the Necklace of Kings and the El Rey Dorado."

"Let's take those private seats over there." Hamish pointed to a seating area in the lobby of the hotel.

The men settled into their chairs. Pirro continued, "Of course, with four conspirators, those items could be anywhere, if they were, in fact, ever found. After a short while, the whole episode was forgotten."

"Things have a way of reappearing. By chance, as it turns out," Hamish said.

"They do, Hamish … they do indeed. So you want a share in what we find. That was your offer, was it not? You need my expertise. I need your knowledge of this area and the information you've uncovered. Tell me more."

"There are other issues at play, Pirro. The Victoria police are watching me closely. They know I've been involved with a number of items connected to the Santa Regio. I appraised a necklace that was made from gold ingots. I'm sure the ingots are the same as those documented on the Santa Regio wreck. I haven't been able to find out anything about the jeweler who made the necklace, so I don't know where the ingots came from." Hamish paused, noted Pirro's intense look, and continued.

"I also received an inquiry about a black and white photograph with two people holding an escudo coin. The photo belongs to a First Nations kid. It was taken somewhere up the west coast around Comox or Powell River."

"I have identified one of the people in the photograph, a Walter Smith, who was studying the First Nations people in the mid-1970s. The kid is from Sliammon, and Smith published a study about these people. I had someone watching the First Nations boy and his girlfriend, but I haven't been able to obtain a stronger lead on the escudos. That's where you come in, Pirro. I'd like you to follow those kids and discover where the bounty is stashed."

"I'm not a young man, Hamish. I finished legwork activities a long time ago. I haven't wasted my time, have I?"

"There's no physical exertion involved. You just have to follow a couple of kids. I believe they'll lead you to the Regio cargo that reached its way to Vancouver."

"I want half of what's found. No negotiation. I have to traipse around tracking kids and who knows what else."

Hamish sighed. He had promised a piece of the action to Eduardo as well. "I was hoping for a sixty-forty split. I have someone else to share the find with as well, Pirro."

"That's it. Take it or leave it. Your information is persuasive, but I've studied the Cielo case and there is no evidence that supports your theory."

"You drive a hard bargain, Pirro, but I'm convinced that it's here. I purchased an air ticket to Powell River for you and the flight leaves later this afternoon. Nose around and see what you can find out." Hamish checked his watch. "I have a flight to Victoria in ninety minutes, and I have to change airports. We're agreed you will keep me apprised of your progress?"

"Fine. Here is my email address." Pirro passed him a business card. "Cell phone roaming fees are ruinous, so I prefer communications via the Internet."

♓

Jamie was picking at a salad in her office when TJ knocked on her door.

"Jamie, we got a hit on Eduardo. He took a flight on the 13th to Comox with Harbour Air and returned on the 15th with Pacific Coastal. He also took a flight to Powell River yesterday. His last name is Dominguez. The ticket agent at Harbour Air remembers him. I was able to get his credit card number and license plate number for his black Escalade SUV."

"Great work, TJ. We'll send a photo and a note to the RCMP in Powell River, and see if they can get a line on him. The only way Eduardo can get out of Powell River is by plane, private boat, or BC Ferries. We'll find him soon enough."

♓

Eduardo had no intention of hiding out in Sooke as Hamish had suggested. He would return to Powell River and recover the escudos himself. He wasn't going to do all the dirty work and let Hamish take most of the profit. The demand for the B&E didn't sit well with him, either.

He booked a room at the Island View Lodge, which was close to the Sliammon community. He recalled Selina Archie, who was raising funds for the First Nations' essential skills program. He knew that it was too coincidental the quinto and the escudo were both connected to the Sliammon.

He poked around the historic area of Powell River, asking the locals whether anyone knew of a shipwreck in the mid-1970s from which gold coins had been recovered. No one admitted to knowledge of any such shipwreck. Most people told him a find like that wouldn't be a secret for long.

Eduardo learned that if anyone knew anything about a connection between the Sliammon and a shipwreck, it would be Cecilia-Archie Windsor, who owned Sliammon Adventure Charters.

That was his plan for the next morning.

⋈

It was dusk when Dillon and Adrianne arrived in Sliammon. The Georgia Strait crossing had been rough in the Zodiac, and the two were glad to reach Powell River before the thunder and lightning started.

They sprinted from the bus stop to Dillon's mother's house, even though they had both been soaked through already by the time they had moored the Zodiac.

"What a downpour," Dillon said, as he closed the door and his mother rushed to the foyer to meet her son. "ƛatom." Dillon rubbed the dog's ears as the animal nuzzled his way into the crowd.

"Come in … it's awful outside. Give me your coats." Dillon's mother helped Adrianne with her less-than-waterproof jacket. She shook the coat and took Dillon's. "I'm surprised you came across the strait today in this weather. That was a bit irresponsible, Dillon."

"Adrianne's an expert boater, Tan. It was kind of fun." Dillon grinned. "We hope to search for Grandmother Gloria's coins tomorrow if the weather eases up."

"Are you now? Have you figured out where they are, my son?"

"Not exactly. I hoped Adrianne and I could talk about that later with you and Grandmother Gloria."

"I see. Your grandparents have gone out to visit some friends." Robbie's eyes sparkled. "I'll tell you what I know, though."

"Robbie, why do the women have two first names and the men don't?" Adrianne asked.

"Come sit by the fire and warm up. We can talk in a minute. Would you like tea?"

"That would be wonderful, Tan," Dillon said. "You need help?"

"No, but you can take your bags into your room."

Adrianne wandered into the sitting room and sat beside the fire. The scent of cedar impregnated the entire house. She heard Robbie in the kitchen, and smiled as Ⲗaⵜom took a place by her feet. She felt safe and at ease. She wondered what her life would be like if she chose the Sliammon way of life.

"To answer your question, Adrianne, the second name is the woman's maiden name." Robbie brought in a cup of tea. "We believe it's important to recognize one's heritage and blood lineage. My mother's maiden name was Louie. So as an example, if you were to say, marry my son, your name would be Adrianne-Padrino Point in true Sliammon tradition." She watched Adrianne for a reaction to the analogy.

"What happened to Dillon's father, your husband? Dillon doesn't talk about him."

"He was a wonderful man and loved Dillon immensely, like most men love their boys. When Dillon was five, his father was killed by a bear. David and his close friend, Leonard, were hunting for food in the late fall, and well … things happen. He and I were so young back then and we felt invincible, just like the youth of today I suppose. Be careful seeking those coins with my son, Adrianne Padrino."

Dillon returned to the sitting room with his diary. "Can we talk about Walter Smith's diary and the coins now, Tan? I'd like to use the kitchen table, too."

"Yes, all right, Dillon. I haven't started preparing dinner yet so you can come in here. Bring your tea, Adrianne." Robbie moved a cutting board from the table.

"So?" Robbie put Dillon's tea on the table and sat down with her cup. "What would you like to know, my son?"

Dillon spread a marine chart that Adrianne had brought, which showed the area surrounding Powell River and the strait northward to Desolation Sound on the table.

"Sliammon is here, Tan," Dillon pointed. "Walter's diary tells us that on the sixth of November he met the sailor who was shipwrecked on Vivian Island. The sailor told him that he and his brother were with another man in a schooner headed for Campbell River; up here past Desolation Sound. The ship hit a rock and was blown by the storm toward Vivian Island. We believe the rock was Rebecca Rock, and the schooner was blown northward to Vivian Island." Dillon tapped the chart.

"Gales are unpredictable at that time of year. It can be treacherous as the winds head northward around Texada Island. Grandmother Gloria and I believe the sailors were trying to reach Blubber Bay to wait out the storm when the gale pushed the schooner toward Rebecca Rock. Likely some of the crew went overboard at that point, Dillon. Weather similar to today, but more violent," said Robbie.

"The day the sailor died, he gave Walter the coin you have in your box and said there were hundreds more in the schooner hull. He also said the ship broke into pieces on Vivian Island, so the wreckage Walter and Grandmother Gloria found in the shallow water must've been on the southern shore, around here. The sailor told Walter the schooner drifted northward after breaking up on Vivian." Dillon tapped the map again.

"I did some research on the Internet for weather patterns in that area in the last twenty years, as well as the tide movements and levels," Adrianne said. "My guess is that the remainder of the schooner is somewhere between Vivian Island and the eastern side of the Grant Reefs south of Savary Island." Adrianne ran her finger along the path she suspected the schooner had likely been blown. "The strait is deep in some of these parts, but the direction of the tide at the time would've played a big role as to where the wreckage actually ended up."

"Walter tells us that he and Grandmother Gloria found hundreds of coins and hid them. The mystery is where. The poetic entry in his diary entry is the clue, isn't it, Mother?" Dillon asked, studying his mother's face. "They're still on Vivian Island, aren't they?"

'It is a cross I'll bear as I watch the playful sea lions on the north point, nosing at the open crevices of the rocks and croaking in laughter." Robbie recited from memory.

"I know the passage well, my son. When your father passed away, Grandmother Gloria and I agreed we would leave the coins to you and give you the opportunity to decide their fate when you were old enough to make such a decision. I've never searched for them, Dillon. Only Grandmother Gloria knows their actual hiding place, and I never asked."

"You never talked about the coins, or Walter, ever?" Dillon asked.

"I think Grandmother Gloria believes the coins are part of their love affair, and the secret of the coins helps her stay connected to Walter in some mysterious way. I believe this is why she never showed any interest in recovering them. I believe it's now time for her to let go ... for you to help her forgive and move past the endless sadness of her affair." Tears ran down Robbie's face. "We both knew why you returned to Sliammon today. She wanted to avoid this discussion—talking about Walter—so she encouraged Grandfather Brett to take her away from the house while you did what she knew you must. Be strong for her."

"We took photographs and video when we were here last time, Robbie. I've studied them, and there are only a couple of places where the sea lions play by open rock crevices in the area. Here—on the north side of Vivian Island—and here— around the eastern end of Savary Island. The coins must be in one of those two places. My best guess is Vivian Island. We need to find the cross marker the passage tells us about. Dillon and I are going to begin our search at Vivian Island tomorrow morning, weather permitting."

"We now know a little more about the coins, Tan. There are stories on the Internet about coins like the one Walter was given. They are Spanish escudos and were being transported in a large ship to Spain in the mid-1600s from a mint in Bogotá, Colombia. The shipwreck was found in 1972 in the Florida Keys and the ship's manifest was discovered in 1987. Somehow the sailor who the Sliammon saved on Vivian Island had gotten hold of some of that cargo discovered in the wreck in Florida"

"Most interesting, Dillon. More tea?" Robbie asked.

"One last question, Robbie," Adrianne said. "The manifest found in 1987 listed a number of things besides coins and gold ingots. There were two necklaces listed—a Necklace of Kings and an El Rey Dorado. Did Gloria ever say anything about necklaces or things other than coins?"

"No, dear. As I said, we didn't talk about the coins or anything else. When I came of age she let me read the diary and gave it to me to keep for Dillon after he was born. I've read it numerous times, but I never talked to Dillon's grandmother about the entries until it was time for Dillon to leave for Victoria. We agreed to let Dillon discover his heritage through the writings of Walter." Robbie poured herself another cup of tea. "I think we both feel the pain of Walter leaving us, and our feelings are well left unsaid. That's all I want to say on the matter."

"Thank you, Tan, for sharing with us." Dillon gave his mother a hug and a kiss. "I'll do the right thing," he whispered.

Seventeen

Pirro woke up early in the Court House Inn, a Tutor-style hotel built in the late 1930s. It served originally as the Powell River courthouse and jail. Pirro ate his continental breakfast in a quaint study.

"Good morning, Sir, can I help you find something?" A woman carrying a large tray of muffins noticed Pirro thumbing through the local phone book.

"I need to charter a boat today."

"Going coho fishing? We're starting to have a good run this year. We've a number of fishing charters down at the marina, but I recommend Sliammon Adventure Charters. Cecilia-Archie Windsor's a knowledgeable, local woman who runs the outfit. I think you'd like her."

"She sounds perfect to me." Pirro flipped through the pages to find the advertisement in the business phone directory. "Thank you, miss."

"Tell her Amy-Charlie John says hello."

Pirro waited until the woman finished laying out the muffins on a far counter. "Amy, where can I find the marina from here?"

"Just a few blocks toward the water, that way," she pointed in the direction. "It's an awful day for going out in the strait. They say the weather will be better tomorrow."

"Thank you for the advice."

"Ms. Windsor," Pirro called. He stood in light rain on the marina dock beside a white fiberglass-hulled fishing boat with *Kumaqɛn* printed in black letters and *Sea Lion* in smaller letters underneath on the stern of the boat.

"Just a minute."

A bony woman in her fifties popped her head up in the glassed cabin and slid open the rear sliding door. "Do you want to book a charter?"

"Yes, I do. May we talk inside?"

"Sure, come on up. Be careful, the deck can be slippery."

Pirro carefully worked his way up to the bridge of the boat and into the cabin. "A little stormy today," he said, pulling back the hood of his coat.

"Still great for fishing. You want to go out today? Coho are running good right now."

"I would like to look around the area, and maybe you wouldn't mind telling me something about this part of the coast." Pirro shook water from his jacket arms. "I don't know anything about coho fishing."

Cecilia studied Pirro. "Are you Mexican? Your Spanish accent …."

"No, I'm Colombian. From Sincelejo actually, but we do speak Spanish in Colombia."

"If you just want to look around, you might as well put a line or two out—the price is the same. I can tell you almost anything you want to know about the coast. It'll be a hundred and fifty an hour, in advance … Mr.?"

"Call me Pirro. I have cash and a credit card. I'll take the whole day and go from there, Cecilia."

"It's Cecilia-Archie, but you can call me Cilia. I can cast off in about ten minutes. I just have to let the office know. That'll be six hundred. I can take the card with me if you like."

"Sounds like fun, Cilia."

In a short time, Cilia returned from the office. "Okay, we are set to go." Cecilia-Archie handed Pirro his credit card. She started the engines of the fishing boat. "We're on our way, so settle yourself into that seat. The coho love this drizzly weather. We're going to head west between those two islands, Texada and Harwood. I'll then turn southward and run along the coastline of Texada. I usually have good luck there."

"So, Cilia, you Sliammon?" Pirro asked.

Cilia concentrated on maneuvering the thirty-two-foot Campion fishing boat out of the marina before she answered.

"Yes, Tla'amin, from the village of Sliammon, just north of Powell River. It's a small community. Everyone knows what everyone else is doing. The Sliammon people have lived there for centuries."

"I grew up on the coast of the Caribbean, but Sincelejo isn't small and we surely don't know everyone like you say. Our waters aren't like these either, I can assure you."

"The Strait of Georgia is a narrow waterway, and the weather can change here quickly. Navigating these waters takes knowledge and skill when the tides and winds are running strong. There's no other place I would rather be."

"The Caribbean has stories of lost treasures because of stormy weather. Do you have such stories around here, Cilia?"

"We have a few, including the Malahat Wreck off the water's edge in Powell River. It's a five-mast schooner from World War II and popular with divers. You like diving, Mr. Marco?"

"No, not anymore, anyway. When I was young I did. No treasures around here in sunken ships?" Pirro asked. He held onto his seat as the boat began to roll in the slight chop of the open waters.

Cilia laughed. "Not in these waters that anyone has ever heard of, and the Sliammon people would know about it if there ever was. You find gold and treasures in the Caribbean?"

"Me, no. But divers have over the years, usually farther north around Florida. The Florida waters can be dangerous with flash storms."

"Time to put out your fishing lines, Mr. Marco, once we are closer to Texada. Do you want me to do it for you when we get there?"

"Yes, please. I don't want to lose my footing."

⋈

Dillon and Adrianne arrived at the Powell River marina later than hoped, and pitched their gear into the Zodiac.

"Looks like we're stuck with wet weather today, Dillon. Just as well we have wet suits on," Adrianne said. "You untie the moorings. I'll stow our gear in the cabin and start this thing."

Dillon put his thumb up indicating he'd released the moorings, and Adrianne took the lever out of neutral and pointed the boat toward Harwood Island's southern shoreline. Dillon joined Adrianne in the cabin and shut the glass door as Adrianne navigated the craft from the marina.

"Hey, Dillon, could you pull out the chart please? It's in the side of my backpack. I hope it doesn't get too rough out here. Vivian Island isn't sheltered. It's basically an enormous rock. It'll be the wind that might be the problem. The water surface doesn't look that bad right now."

Adrianne cleared the marina and pressed the power lever forward. The bow lifted as the engines screamed. "Let's find those coins, Dillon!"

The *Kumaqεn* started southward when Cilia spotted the Cyril Rock marker off the coast of Texada. "I'll go set your rigging now, Mr. Marco."

Pirro pulled a pair of field glasses from his jacket. A sheltered bay on Texada eliminated the possibility that a ship could founder. He followed the coastline further, but saw no obvious rocks on which a ship could be battered.

"All set, Mr. Marco."

"Cilia, if boaters came up this strait from Vancouver, would they travel this stretch of water?"

"Likely they'd come up the other side of this island. The strait is wider between Vancouver Island and Texada on the southern side." She reached for the boat controls.

"Could we go to that side of the island then? I'd like to look at that coastline."

"The fishing is not as good on that side. It's less protected, and the coho usually run along the inner strait."

"Let's start on that side first, please, and then we can move over here. Remember, I'm not here to fish."

"It's your charter, but I got our lines out now so I must watch my speed." Cilia shook her head and turned the boat around westward. "The water runs faster as we pass Blubber Bay, Mr. Marco, so hold on."

ℋ

Eduardo decided to eat a good breakfast before he looked for Cecilia-Archie Windsor. He wasn't overly excited about another boat trip in the strait, but he was convinced that Ms. Windsor could provide information if he asked his questions properly.

He found the Sliammon Adventures Charters after breakfast. "I would like to talk to Cecilia-Archie Windsor," he told the person in the office.

"Cilia is out with a client right now. It's prime coho season," an elderly man informed him. "The weather's closing in so I don't think that she will be taking another charter out today."

"I was told Ms. Windsor was the best, and I would like to go out with her. When will she return?"

"Charters don't have schedules. Why don't you come back tomorrow and see her then. I don't see anything booked. I could pencil your name in."

"Sure, thank you. Dominguez."

ℋ

"Hey, look, that's the *Kumaqεn*, Cilia's charter boat," Dillon pointed to his left. "She knows the coho usually travel along the northern side of Texada, so I wonder why she has her rigging out heading toward the southern side."

"Beats me, Dillon, you're the local guy around here. There's Vivian."

Dillon continued to watch the *Kumaqεn* as it trolled slowly around Kiddie Point, the furthest western tip of Texada. "Weird." He returned his attention to Adrianne's approach to Vivian Island.

"It gets shallow along here," Adrianne said, pointing to the marine chart. "We're going to look around this piece of the island. It looks to be the most likely place based on Walter's cryptic entries. It's the only area where the sea lions are." She pointed to the mammals in the water and lying on the smooth rocks in the rain.

"Maybe we should find a place that we can anchor or tie up the boat while we look in the water along the shoreline?" Dillon began to strip his outer clothes off down to his wet suit.

"You'll have to watch the depth here as I navigate. These outboards draw more water than you think, and the rocks are unpredictable."

"I can pull the engines up a bit Adrianne, then it's only the hull we have to be concerned about."

Adrianne turned off the engines and let the Zodiac drift toward the rocky shoreline. Dillon leaned over to pull the first engine up as Adrianne steered the craft toward the rocky shallows where sea lions croaked at their visitors.

"Dillon, work your way to the bow and drop the anchor before the wind pushes us out again."

Dillon waved his arm and was headed toward the bow when the boat drifted into a rock and almost sent him overboard. He grabbed the side of the Zodiac and regained his balance as the rear of the boat began to drift sideways away from the island.

The boat continued to drift between the rocks. Dillon lifted the stainless steel anchor and pushed it overboard. When it hit bottom, Dillon grabbed the line and tightly roped it around a cleat so that the boat floated only above the anchor line. The stern of the boat drifted at the mercy of the breeze as Dillon made his way back to the enclosed cabin. "It's shallow here. What's the tide table for today?" he asked.

"We're close to low tide right now. That's good, as it will make it easier to find the marker. I'm going in with water shoes to look about around here. Remember, we're looking for a cross of some type that marks the place that we're looking for. Sure looks desolate to me."

"What a place to become shipwrecked," Dillon said.

"If this is the place, the schooner hit the island on the other side. It's a lot rougher over there. I have knapsacks to put the coins in if we find them, Dillon." Adrianne pulled woven bags from a small locker and handed one to Dillon. "The weather looks like it's coming in. We won't have long to look about." The chop on the surface of the water was becoming higher and the drizzle had turned into steady rain.

"You start looking to the left, and I'll go right." Dillon pulled a scuba mask over his head and left it on his forehead. "A cross. That'll be fun to find in this weather." He had to talk loudly over the noisy barking of the sea lions. Dillon slipped over the aft into the shallow water. His feet searched for footing on the scattered rocks as he fought to steady the boat. "Adrianne, your turn." She slid onto the rocky bottom of the island's narrow coastline.

The barking sea lions drowned out the sound of the ocean as it washed onto the rocky shoreline of Vivian Island. Adrianne began to pick her way toward Texada. She crouched down, inspecting each rock and crevice.

Dillon tried to look through the water at the granite shoreline, but the surface was too windblown to allow a clear view. He removed his scuba goggles and held them on the water's surface to provide a better view of the rocky bottom as he slowly walked toward the shore.

Walter's written passage repeated in his mind.

There was a sizeable crevice between two smooth boulders on the other side of the island that would be submerged at high tide. We put on our wet suits and stuffed our sock-filled treasure into the crevice, camouflaging it with smaller rocks. We returned to our boat to wait for the incoming tide to ensure it flooded our hidden cache.

He stood up to look at the uninviting island, listening to the sea lions as they seemed to laugh at his fruitless search for the hiding place that the lions knew well. Dillon looked for tide waterline markings on the shoreline that might indicate the possible size of the exposed large boulders. Cutting windblown rain hit his face. Dillon pulled his body through the waist-high water as he waved the sea lions away from their observation place. Dillon searched for the cross marking made by the lovers.

Adrianne decided her search area was a less likely hiding place, as the rocky shoreline had begun to drop off steeply. She turned toward back toward Dillon and realized the weather severity had increased. The wind had picked up momentum. The tide had begun to surge in.

"Adrianne." She looked up and noticed Dillon waving his arms about yelling her name as he stood by a large boulder twenty feet or so from the shoreline.

Dillon made sure Adrianne had seen him, and he reached down to grasp some small rocks below. The rocks were slippery, and the stench from the sea lions brought tears to his eyes as he struggled to keep his balance on the rocky bottom.

Adrianne had to yell over the rising wind. "Did you find it?"

"Look at this. It's a totem with eagle type wings on the top." He washed away sea lion excrement from the surface of the smooth boulder with the knapsack in his hand. "Help me move rocks away ... the passage said smaller rocks hide a crevice."

"The tide's coming in—but look," Dillon removed another rock and pulled on fabric. "Damn." The material tore away. He bent over and stuck his hand back into the open crevice. Dillon searched around with his fingers and then grinned. He pulled a couple of gold ingots from the split in the rock and held his hand out to show Adrianne. "We got it."

"The tide table must be higher today than when Gloria and Walter hid the coins here. This place is already submerged, and the tide's started coming in now."

"The socks are tearing. We need to get the Zodiac over here so we don't have to carry what we find too far. Let's go before this entire place floods."

The pair moved as quickly as they could to the anchored Zodiac. Dillon grabbed one of the outboard engines and hoisted himself up. He crawled over the edge of the boat and knelt on the deck. "Take my hand." He reached out for Adrianne. She grabbed his hand and a cleat at the side of the boat and dragged herself into the boat.

"Dillon, get the anchor up, and I'll put the other engine back down. We're drifting in this wind and rain. The storm's coming in—hurry."

The Zodiac began to drift away from the shore the moment the anchor left its resting place on the rocky ocean floor. Dillon heard the roar of the twin engines. The engines fought the wind to keep the Zodiac under control as Adrianne navigated toward the shallow shoreline, where the sea lions had regained their place on the large boulders.

Dillon pushed the anchor overboard again.

Adrianne turned off the engines and watched the craft spin around the taught anchor line in the wind. "No time to mess with the engines."

The tide had risen a few inches by the time Dillon and Adrianne encouraged the sea lions to vacate their place on the boulder that was now partially submerged in icy water.

"I'll pull some out for a few minutes, and then you do a few handsful," Dillon suggested as Adrianne handed Dillon one of the bags. Dillon pulled a few ingots from the crevice and dropped them inside his bag. He withdrew a few handsful of coins until the sock could be tugged out. "There's another sock," he pulled at it. It, too, tore away. "More coins in this one."

"Dillon, let me do some," Adrianne said. Dillon moved a step aside. She pulled out a handful of coins and looked at them closely before dumping them into her bag.

Adrianne pulled handful after handful of coins from the rocky space. The tide, raging wind, and rain made each grasp more difficult than the last. "One more, I think," Adrianne moved to allow Dillon access to the open crevice.

Dillon grasped the last sock. It came lose without disintegrating. It wasn't as heavy as the previous socks. Dillon pulled apart sock fibers. An intricate, six-stone emerald necklace was revealed. He was momentarily stunned.

"That's it. Let's get out of here." He covered the necklace with the sock remnants and put it inside his sack. He slung his bag of treasure—now weighing over ten pounds—over the side of the Zodiac, along with Adrianne's that weighed about five. He worked his way to the stern of the boat, which was moving back and forth in the strong wind and incoming tide.

Pirro Marco had seen enough of the Texada coastline, and asked Cilia to head back toward Harwood Island. The strong winds and increasingly rough waters warned the captain of the oncoming storm, and she left Pirro to steer the boat while she brought in the fishing lines.

"Storm is coming in faster than predicted, Mr. Marco. We must return to Powell River before this weather worsens." She regained the steering wheel.

"I've been watching those people over there," Pirro said, as held his field glasses trained on the kids. "Second World Diving Co. Not the weather to dive in, is it Cilia?"

"Not at Vivian Island, Mr. Marco. I see that company over here sometimes, but they usually go to Saltery Bay and Mermaid Cove when they come to this side of the strait. Look, they're leaving. It's getting rough and, if they want to head back to Comox, they better get started."

"Can we follow them for a bit, please?"

"The weather is turbulent, and we should head back, Mr. Marco. Why?"

"Just to see where they are going. I'm interested."

Adrianne pushed the engine throttle forward to gain control of the Zodiac as she turned southward to head away from Vivian Island. "Hang on, Dillon, we're off to Comox. It's going to be rough."

"See that fishing boat? It's the *Kumaqεn*," Dillon pointed past the stern of the Zodiac. "I think it has been shadowing us since we left Powell River. Turn around and head toward the western side of Harwood. I want to see if Cilia heads for Powell River, or if she is going to follow us around Harwood."

"You sure, Dillon? We may not be able to get back to Comox if we spend much longer out here." Adrianne altered her course.

"There's a lot more gold than I ever imagined, Adrianne." Dillon watched the *Kumaqεn*. "If that boat follows us around Harwood, we've got to put together another plan—and fast."

"They're likely going around Harwood Island to head back to Powell River, Mr. Marco. It's better sheltered for that type of craft," Cecilia said, pushing the throttle open. "We really should head back to Powell River now."

"Just follow them around Harwood. You said it's less rough," Pirro replied, trying to look through his field glasses as the boat was thrown around by the wind and rough sea.

"The *Kumaqεn* isn't turning toward Powell River. What do you think?"

Adrianne looked at the marine chart. "Okay then, we can go around to the north side of Savary Island and leave the coins at the Keefer Bay marker. It's a bit of a trip and rough. Once we clear Mace Point, that fishing boat won't be able to see us for five to ten minutes, depending on their rate of speed. They'll have to follow us around this buoy here that marks the shallow shoal area of Savary Island." Adrianne pointed to the symbols on the chart.

"We can't just dump the sacks in the ocean, Adrianne. They must be anchored somehow, otherwise they won't be there when we return. You'll have to put on gear and secure them." Dillon glanced at the approaching fishing boat. "We can anchor when we reach the Keefer Bay marker."

"You can't stay with me, Dillon. There won't be enough time and the *Kumaqεn* will pass around the point before I can secure the sacks. While I'm planting the sacks you move farther along the coast to say, off the shoal line of First Point. Anchor and wait for me there. It's shallow there and you have to be careful you don't run aground in the swells." Adrianne measured the distance on the chart to a safe water depth.

"I'd say about one hundred-fifty meters off the shoreline, but maybe about fifty from the marker. That way I won't have too far to travel underwater from the Keefer Bay marker back to the Zodiac. I hope this is enough to fool them."

"This is a tough task for you, Adrianne," Dillon shook his head, and looked back toward the stern. "They're still coming."

"It'll be all right, Dillon. I'm experienced in this type of sea. You just watch that depth sounder when you get close to First Point before you drop anchor. The island should shelter you a bit as the wind is driving northward over the land mass."

"Yeah, okay."

Dillon walked to the stern where the sacks lay. The wind-driven rain stabbed his face as he looked first into one sack and then the second. He pulled a partially decayed sock out of the sack.

"What are you doing, Dillon?"

"Let me take over, and you get your gear on," Dillon said, as the Zodiac sped past the buoy marker of the Savary Island shoal bed. "Go."

Dillon stashed the sock fibers and contents under the dash of the Zodiac and looked back at the *Kumaqεn*. The wind speed had increased. Dillon fought the controls of the Zodiac to keep it on course pointed just off the far tip of Savary Island.

"They're going around Savary Island, Mr. Marco." Cilia watched the Zodiac as it disappeared from view. "It's too rough. I'm heading back." She changed her heading toward the far side of Harwood Island.

"What are you doing?" Pirro rushed to stand next to Cilia when he realized that they were turning away from the Zodiac.

"I'm not risking going any further, Mr. Marco. We're going back to the marina. Sit down before you fall. This fishing trip is over."

"Damn."

"They can't see us now," Dillon glanced back, but couldn't see the *Kumaqεn* as their boat passed Mace Point. "We have a short window of time."

"It's time now, Dillon. Drop me off at Keefer Point and head off-shore like we discussed. Wait for me to surface. Keep the nose facing into the wind."

Dillon concentrated on the depth sounder as he drove the diving boat toward the marker. Adrianne knocked on the glass window and gave the thumbs up. She tied the two sacks together with their ties, then added a length of rope. She dragged the waterproof bags toward the bow while Dillon fought to keep the craft headed into the wind. She pulled her goggles into place, lifted each sack onto the bow, turned her back toward the side of the Zodiac, and allowed the weight of her air tank to pull her overboard.

Dillon held his breath as Adrianne disappeared overboard. He watched the bags disappear over the bow and into the choppy sea. He gave Adrianne enough time to clear the engine props, then reversed the boat, and headed off the coastline. He looked for the *Kumaqεn*, but it still hadn't appeared around the point.

Pirro Marco held onto the front seat and watched the Zodiac disappear around Savary Island. "Hmm," he grunted as the fishing boat rocked and bounced into the wind heading back toward Powell River.

It was almost fifteen minutes later before Dillon saw Adrianne's arm pierce the surface of the rough sea. He put the craft's engine lever into neutral, rushed outside the cabin to the deck, and grabbed the yellow life collar as the boat started to blow away from the island. He tossed it into the wind toward Adrianne, but it didn't travel far enough. Dillon pulled the empty collar back into the Zodiac, which had now drifted away from Adrianne toward the shoreline of Savary Island.

"Damn." Dillon ran into the cockpit of the boat, put the engines into gear and worked back toward Adrianne. He fought the steering controls, and struggled to keep the craft in a straight line. He put the engines in neutral a second time when he was a few feet away from Adrianne, but the boat began to drift instantly.

"Shit." He moved the boat further away from the island, dropped it into neutral, and went outside to toss the bow moorage rope overboard. He returned to the helm and pushed the transmission gear into forward. The Zodiac headed slowly toward Adrianne, who was now bobbing in the water fighting the heavy wind and draw of the raging water.

This time Dillon maneuvered the Zodiac so the bow reached Adrianne. She caught the moorage line as Dillon put the engines back into neutral. He rushed outside, trying not to fall, as she unstrapped her air tank. Dillon leaned over the side of the boat and pulled her gear into the boat.

Arianne held the moorage line with both hands as Dillon hauled her up—kicking her feet until she slipped over the edge. She lay breathless on the deck as Dillon returned to the cabin, regained control of the boat, and steered northward along the coastline of Savary Island. He peered through the windshield to check on Adrianne, who was now on her knees and grasping the side of the rocking boat. She inched into the cabin.

"My God," she was out of breath. "That was tougher than I'd imagined." She lay on the cabin floor. "Where's the *KumaqƐn*?"

"It never came around the Point. The sea's too rough for Comox, Adrianne. We have to go back to Powell River." Dillon changed his course.

Adrianne got to her feet. "Great job, Dillon," she kissed him. "What a rush."

She turned on the short wave radio. "Second World Diving … come in, Chuck. It's Adrianne, come in please, over." The radio speaker crackled and then responded.

"Second World Diving. You're late, Adrianne. Are you okay? Over."

"Second World Diving. All a-okay, Chuck. Weather too bad to return, heading back to Powell River. Over."

"Second World Diving. Current weather pattern expected for rest of day. Will cancel your flight. You want to reschedule? Over."

"Second World Diving. Can you book our flight out of Powell River for today? Over."

"Second World Diving. Will advise. Over."

"Second World Diving. Thanks, Chuck, will wait for your confirmation. Over."

Adrianne replaced the receiver on its hook. "I don't want to put your family out again, Dillon, but this storm came in quicker than I expected."

"If we can't get a flight out today, there's a hotel just a few blocks from the marina—the Court House Inn. It's supposed to be a nice place to stay, if we can get a room that is.

We can celebrate our good fortune and adventure without the need to tell Tan."

"What do you think that fishing boat was all about?" Adrianne asked.

"I know the *Kumaqɛn*. Cecilia-Archie runs Sliammon Adventure Charters from Powell River. She's a nice woman and knows these waters well," Dillon said, rubbing his face with his hand. "She didn't follow her normal fishing course. She certainly should've turned back toward the marina long before she did. I think she must've had a customer who was watching us."

"Who'd think that we were doing anything out here but diving, Dillon?"

"I don't know, but someone knows about the diary and who knows what else they know from the videos."

The radio crackled again. "Second World Diving. Adrianne, come in, please. Over."

Adrianne reached for the microphone. "Second World Diving. Go ahead, Chuck. Over."

"Second World Diving. I booked a flight for two from Powell River departing ten-hundred tomorrow. Over."

"Second World Diving. Ten-four, Chuck. Will call landline later. Over."

"I guess we're staying overnight. I'm too tired for a flight to Victoria anyway."

♓

Eduardo Dominguez waited at Sliammon Adventures Charter for Cilia. He decided the weather was too ugly to wander about asking questions about Dillon Point. He had purchased a few coffees and spent the time talking with George.

George was from Sliammon and had worked for Cecilia-Archie for over fifteen years. His deep-socket eyes missed little.

Eduardo learned much about the local First Nations community. It became clear that shipwrecks were common along the rugged coast, but none had been carrying gold coins in George's recollection. George made it clear that it was unlikely Cilia knew anything different.

Time passed. The conversation was a pleasant distraction from the foul weather. Eventually the sound of the *Kumaqɛn* returning propelled George to his feet.

"I must help Cilia tie up," George said. "You can talk to her about a charter when she's done with her current client. I'll be back, Mr. Dominguez." Eduardo watched the boat maneuver in the wind and rain, as it moved into its slip.

"I'm sorry about the weather. Do you want to try again tomorrow?" Cilia asked Pirro when she finished tying up the *Kumaqɛn* to the wooden dock.

"No, thanks. I've had enough rough water for one trip. By the way, do you know Dillon Point? I understand he's from around here," Pirro asked.

"Yeah, he's from Sliammon, like me. His father died in an accident when he was young, and he was brought up by his mother and grandparents. Good boy, why?"

"A friend of mine has a son who goes to school with him. I thought he said the boy was from around here. I just wondered, that's all."

"Have a nice stay in Powell River, Mr. Marco. Call if you change your mind about fishing. You didn't catch a coho," Cilia smiled.

"Yes, I will." Marco pulled his hood more tightly, and began his walk to the Court House Inn.

"That's the second person asking about Dillon today," George said.

"Second person, George?"

"Yeah, there's a Mr. Dominguez in your office who wants to book you for a fishing trip. He asked about Dillon while he waited."

Cilia and George walked down the dock, and George opened the shack door for his boss. "Mr. Dominguez, I understand that you want to book a charter for tomorrow," said Cilia.

"Yes, that was my plan. George told me he needed your approval first, as the weather is getting rough on the strait."

"George is right. My last client found it rough and you likely won't catch any coho. Could you return in the morning, and we'll see if this weather system has passed through? I'm sorry for your wait."

"That's okay, George and I had an interesting conversation. I'll be back in the morning. Would you please book me now? George has penciled me in, but I want to confirm the trip now."

"Certainly. George, schedule Mr. Dominguez. We'll talk in the morning, say seven o'clock."

"Could we make it a little later, about eight thirty?" Eduardo asked. "I'm not the best on boats, and want to have a good breakfast first."

"Eight thirty in the morning then, Mr. Dominguez."

⋈

Pirro reclined on his bed in the Powell River hotel room; disappointment hung heavy that he had not kept track of the Second World Diving Company's Zodiac. He knew it was strange to dive in a storm. The close proximity to the small island also aroused his curiosity. The Zodiac's continued trip to the larger island was what really intrigued his mind; his brain was honed to fit small details into larger actualities.

He reached for a mini-bottle of rum from the guest service pack, and opened his research notebook on the Santa Regio. He pressed the spine of the notebook for ease of writing. He gulped a mouthful of rum, and began to scribble on an empty page.

September 21st, 2012.

Powell River BC, Canada. Met Cecilia-Archie Windsor from Sliammon. She is captain of a fishing boat I hired to explore the coastline. She told me she's never heard of a local shipwreck with gold treasure. Diving company boat spotted at Vivian Island, and then lost sight behind Savary Island when forced to return to marina by foul weather. Strange weather for diving. Don't know if any connection to coins—but gut tells me area could be site of possible shipwrecks due to weather and rocky shorelines. No evidence of this though. Weather can get rough, heavy winds to north and cold.

Dillon Point's Sliammon family: father died when boy young, brought up by mother and grandparents.

Pirro sat back a moment and flipped back several pages. He took another gulp of rum, then picked up the notebook, and read prior entries.

February 12th, 1974.

Gonzalo Cielo found shot to death early today in Palm Beach warehouse. Suspicions he was murdered by other mariners that salvaged gold and artifacts from Santa Regio in 1972. Cielo partner Robert Capland was on camera today saying he had no idea who could want his partner dead; all items salvaged from Santa Regio are recorded according to law.

February 28ᵗʰ, 1974.

Discovered today government officials have suspicions some of the cargo salvaged from Santa Regio may not have been recorded; officials believe that Cielo was involved in the non-disclosure. Officials also believe Cielo could not have removed the unknown cargo alone. No formal charges as there is no evidence of such activity.

March 17ᵗʰ, 1974.

Discussions with Carlos Panay, Capland's cook on the salvage vessel. He thinks four others worked with Cielo to heist the Santa Regio. He told me in confidence Pedro and his brother Benito Narváez, Rene-Robert Jolliet, and Fernando Diablo are close friends and were seen talking to Cielo frequently.

March 19ᵗʰ, 1974.

Research of crew register of Capland's salvage ship revealed: Narváez boys from British Columbia, Canada; Jolliet from Quebec, Canada; and, Diablo from Veracruz, Mexico.

Pirro considered the facts he'd collected over the years. A likely scenario might be that the salvaged items were split among the partners in Palm Beach in 1974 when Cielo was murdered. Possibly the half belonging to the brothers from British Columbia was what Firth was on to.

He decided to return to Victoria and give Firth some facts. The gold had to have been converted to cash by the Narváez brothers somewhere to purchase a boat. Pirro needed to know the Narváezes' destination.

⊀

Adrianne and Dillon were finally in a room at the Court House Inn. Dillon kissed Adrianne as soon as the door was closed.

"Sit, I have something for you." Dillon walked back to his backpack. "Close your eyes … it's a surprise." Dillon unzipped his bag and pulled out a partially disintegrated sock. "No peeking." He took the sock into the bathroom, withdrew the necklace, and pitched the sock into the garbage.

"What are you doing, Dillon?" Adrianne obediently kept her eyes closed, but she could hear water running in the bathroom.

"Just another moment … don't peek." He dried the necklace with a towel, walked back into the bedroom, and draped the necklace around her neck. "Okay."

Adrianne looked down at the stunning piece of jewelry and gasped. "Dillon … it's … so beautiful." She got off the bed to look in the mirror. She began to cry as she turned to face him.

He pulled her into his arms and kissed her. "I love you … I want you to have it, and remember I had one of the best days of my life with you today. I wouldn't have found it without you."

She kissed him. "I'll treasure this all my life, Dillon. Are you sure, really sure, you want to give this to me? Maybe you should give it to your mother or even your grandmother."

"It's mine to give, and there is no one else … please accept it. You look stunning." Dillon stood back from her and smiled.

"Where was it, Dillon? I thought we recovered only ingots and coins," Adrianne asked, as she turned to admire herself wearing the elegant necklace.

"It was in the last sock at the bottom of the crevice. I never imagined anything like today. My mother will never believe it. We found an absolute fortune, Adrianne."

Adrianne put the necklace on the dresser and joined Dillon on the bed. "I want to clean the dirt and the mess off this before I wear it again. I'll wash it in the sink later."

"What are you going to do with the coins and gold bars, Dillon? It's an enormous decision. Those coins must have historic value. I'm sure the necklace has." Adrianne put her arm around Dillon's waist.

"I haven't a clue. I need your help, but one thing's for sure—my family will never go without again. We never had any money and life was often tough. I wonder why Grandmother Gloria never used any of it to make life easier."

"Maybe this is the 'becoming a man decision' your mother talked about. Surely something for the Sliammon community is a consideration. You've got time, and you need guidance. The right answer will come to mind, I'm sure."

"Maybe all the stuff belongs to someone else, and I'll have to give it all back …."

"Let it wait a few days, Dillon, and go from there. We've figured out almost all the clues in Walter's diary, except one that has been gnawing at me. There was a comment in the entry about something the sailor said to Walter—'Diablo,' I believe. I Googled the word and it means 'devil.' Why would the sailor refer to a devil?"

"Diablo, huh?"

"Get the diary. I'll show you."

Arianne flipped through diary pages. "Here we are. I'll read only the pertinent part." She ran her finger down the handwritten entry:

Wednesday 5th November 1975;

> *I didn't know what to do and leaned down to hear his labored voice. He whispered he had something for me, and he struggled to give me a gold coin from his pocket. No one saw him pass it to me. He told me there were hundreds more in the hull of the schooner. The bounty was his gift to me for my help. I asked him what 'Diablo' meant, but he was too weak to answer. He died later this afternoon on the stretcher before he reached the hospital.*
>
> *I told no one of our conversation or the gold coin.*

"I didn't pay attention to that the first time we read it," Dillon admitted. "I should call Tan to let her know we recovered the coins."

"Dillon? I'm concerned about the fishing boat that followed us today. I don't think we should go back to Victoria tomorrow. I want to have the police involved when we recover the bounty."

"A wise suggestion, Adrianne, but I don't want the local RCMP involved. Nothing stays a secret here. How about that policewoman we met after the burglary? Do you still have her business card?"

"I don't know if a Victoria policewoman would come to Powell River, Dillon, especially if there is RCMP here."

"Can you call and see? She already knows about the escudo and the diary. She might come if you ask her, especially since we are taking the gold to Victoria."

"Okay. It's unfortunate that Cilia shut up business before we got back to the marina. She might be able to tell you why her charter customer was following us."

"That's another thing the police can handle. I don't want to ask questions around town right now, especially of Cilia."

"I'll make the call and ask Chuck to cancel our flight, too. You can talk to your mother after I know what our plan is for tomorrow."

Eighteen

Eduardo thought about his scheduled boat ride all night. He didn't want a repeat of his last experience. After chatting with George, he didn't consider a trip with Cilia worth the effort. The howling wind and choppy ocean helped him make up his mind. He decided to cancel the charter.

He waited for George to open the office before the planned charter start time to tell him he had changed his mind. Eduardo noticed the Zodiac was tied up close to the charter's space, and asked George about the Second World Diving's boat. Eduardo recognized the craft from his Comox experience and knew that it belonged to Dillon's girlfriend, Adrianne Padrino.

George didn't tell Eduardo anything he didn't already know, so he asked the Sliammon elder for a recommendation for the best place to talk to other long-term residents.

"Shinglemill Pub," answered George.

♓

Dillon and Adrianne walked into the Court House Inn breakfast room. It was raining heavily outside, and the weather pattern appeared stalled over the coast. They found a cozy table by a fireplace. Adrianne sat as Dillon walked to the counter, poured coffee, and piled plates high with chocolate croissants and sticky buns with fruit.

"Hi, Dillon. Who's your friend?" A husky-framed woman in a service uniform stopped at their table.

"Amy-Charlie," his face flushed. "Adrianne, this is Amy-Charlie John."

Adrianne glanced at Dillon. "Good to meet you, Amy-Charlie. This is such a quaint room."

"You aren't staying with your mother, Dillon?"

"It's a surprise, Amy," Adrianne said. "These croissants look wonderful. Are they made here?"

Dillon watched as Amy-Charlie walked toward the kitchen. "The whole town will know I'm in this hotel with you before noon."

"You said it was a small town." Adrianne took his hand under the table. "It'll give them all something to talk about."

"Should we stay again tonight or go to my mother's house?"

"We'll have to make that decision once Detective Steele calls this morning. We have a romantic room, though. Considering last night, we best stay here tonight if we must delay our expedition. By the looks of outside, it might be for the best anyway."

♓

Jamie and TJ were in the Inspector's office discussing the call Jamie had received from Adrianne Padrino. It was a miserable September morning and the rain pelted down the Inspector's window as he sat contemplating the facts of the

"Firth Investigation" case. "You don't have anything new on Dominguez, and now you have a request to go to Powell River?"

"Yes, that's correct, Sir," Jamie replied. "We know Firth and Dominguez are connected to the attempted robbery of the quinto necklace, and that Firth is a prime suspect in the Point B&E. Point allegedly has a gold coin Firth wants. Ms. Padrino told me she and Mr. Point did uncover a bounty of escudo coins. She requested police protection while the coins are recovered in Powell River and returned here."

"The RCMP has an office in Powell River. It's their jurisdiction. Why should we get involved?" her boss asked bluntly.

"Ms. Padrino said Mr. Point doesn't want local police involvement. It has something to do with a family secret, and he wants things to be handled by an outside agency."

"This is highly irregular. I contacted the Powell River RCMP office and outlined the situation. They have agreed to keep this situation confidential. We agreed that they will lead the recovery, but you, TJ, will participate as a gesture of good faith. Detective Kennedy will escort the pair back here with whatever they discovered."

"Detective Kennedy, Sir?"

"I selected Detective Kennedy, as she is comfortable in a marine environment, and I wish to see how well she can perform on her own. I want you to continue to look into Dominguez and Firth, Detective Steele.

"Remember, Detective Kennedy, that Powell River is the RCMP's turf. Your role is to assist in the recovery and safe return of the escudos, along with the safe return of Adrianne Padrino and Dillon Point. Is that understood?"

"Yes, Sir, understood."

"Make the arrangements. Detective Steele, you advise Ms. Padrino of our course of action. Detective Kennedy, be careful. It seems there are a number of people trying to abscond with the escudos."

"Absolutely, Sir. Thank you for your confidence."

"Dismissed."

♓

"Give me Colombia, or even Florida, any day of the week." Pirro tipped his rum glass as he sat with Hamish in the late afternoon. "Damn, it was cold and wet up there."

"Your trip was productive, Pirro?"

"The Sliammon woman had nothing to say that helped us with Dillon Point. If there were any escudos found by that kid's family, no one is admitting to it. If the escudos were on a boat, a storm could easily have destroyed it and the sailors drowned without a soul knowing."

"By sailors, you mean one or more of the accomplices who worked with Gonzalo Cielo?"

"Yes. I spent years researching the Santa Regio and the Cielo murder. I know there was a strong likelihood there were four others involved with Cielo. Two crew members on the salvage expedition that I believe might have been with Cielo, were from British Columbia."

"I didn't know that." Hamish leaned forward in his chair. "That information has never been published that I know about."

"There were other details not reported because there was no proof, and Robert Capland didn't want speculative conjecture printed. My research indicated that there was a Mexican and a Canadian sailor from Quebec, as well. If the brothers from here were taking their share of the cargo up the

Georgia Strait and became shipwrecked in a storm, then there might be some bounty to recover as you surmised, Hamish."

Hamish considered the new information. "A Mexican, you say."

"I believe we should focus on the two Canadians from around these parts. The Mexican likely skipped back into Mexico, and who the hell knows what happened to the French-Canadian? All reported 1656 Spanish escudos sold in Mexico or Canada originated from Capland. We should see what we dig up on Narváez and his brother Benito."

"Just for interest's sake, who were the other two sailors?" Hamish asked, and held his breath.

"Rene-Robert Jolliet and Fernando Diablo. Why?"

"The saga is fascinating, and if we find some of the cargo, it would be nice to know the entirety of it." Hamish was shocked to finally learn the name of the Mexican who he'd dealt with in Vancouver.

⚓

Eduardo took a taxi to the Shinglemill Pub and Bistro, a short distance north of downtown Powell River. The pub sat on wooden pilings that suspended the cedar-sided eatery over the Powell Lake shoreline. The pub was busy, and Eduardo found a seat at the bar. He ordered a draft beer.

"Awful day to visit the lake," said the bartender.

"I expected it might be nicer since it's only September," Eduardo replied. "I'm in town to do some fishing, and I was told this is a great place to meet the locals. I'm writing a book set in the area during the 1970s."

"You should talk to Arnie over there. He's from the Sliammon, and was a young man back then. He'll have stories for you."

"Thanks." Eduardo looked at an elderly man sitting alone by the window, and then, beer in hand, sauntered over. "Excuse me, the bartender said you could tell me tales from the seventies. I'm writing a book."

The man with graying hair slowly looked away from the window. "Mainlander?"

"Yes, I'm here for coho fishing and research about the local people. May I sit down?"

"Fishing. What kind of stories about the seventies?"

"What it was like around here back then, shipwrecks, and such. I was fishing yesterday when the weather turned ugly. I'm sure there have been boating accidents and deaths." Eduardo noticed that the man's mug of beer was almost empty. He stood up and waved at the bartender. "Another beer for Arnie, please."

"I guess it was more dangerous when people didn't need boating licenses."

Arnie laughed. "Boating licenses. People are just as stupid with licenses these days as back then. People thought they knew about these waters, but they didn't. A license doesn't fix stupidity. I do recall one poor soul, though, back in the seventies. He was shipwrecked on Vivian Island and died shortly after. The Tla'amin buried the man on Harwood Island. It was unusual to bury a man not from the Sliammon on Harwood."

"A shipwrecked sailor. How many of them were there?" Arnie had Eduardo's full attention.

"I don't know. Just that poor soul survived, I'm afraid. I was there to help bring him back to our village, but he died of exposure. No one knew what he was doing out in that storm. He should've known better and headed inland earlier. A license wouldn't have helped him none."

"Did you see any of the ship or was anything washed ashore?"

"No, nothing much really. Ships or boats can't survive our November storms if the crew isn't familiar with how it blows up here."

"I heard that there was a jeweler from Sliammon back then—Archie or something like that. Is he still around?"

"Lawrence Archie. He's passed now, maybe three years ago. His wife Clara-Meyers passed just over a week ago from cancer. You could talk to his sister, Cecilia-Archie Windsor. She operates a fishing charter business in Powell River." Arnie finished his first beer. "The rumor going around back then was that Lawrence's daughter Selina was betrothed to Brett Paul's grandson Dillon Point, but there was some type of falling out between Brett and Lawrence. I don't think the two kids were ever told as the arrangement was called off. Nice kids, though. Both have left the Sliammon. Selina is an artist and Dillon's at university so he can become a council member for the Sliammon. If you're interested in Lawrence's work, you should talk to his sister."

"Are pre-arranged marriages still a custom in Sliammon?"

"For some families it's important, but the Sliammon are slowly changing with the times. It's not as common as it once was." Arnie glanced toward the pub entrance. "Some friends are coming. I hope I gave you something for your research."

⽊

Adrianne and Dillon were having sex when her cell phone rang. "No, not now," Dillon gasped. Adrianne leaned over to reach for the phone on the night table.

"Dillon, it's likely Detective Steele." She lifted her body off his.

"Adrianne Padrino."

"Detective Steele, Adrianne. Sorry for the late call, but it has taken time to get approval for a Victoria Police officer to come to Powell River. As we discussed yesterday, you should have contacted the local RCMP."

"But …."

"I understand your situation, and since you need an escort back to Victoria, the local RCMP has agreed to our participation in the escudo coin recovery. My partner, Detective Kennedy, is coming. Her flight is scheduled to land in Powell River at eight fifty-five tomorrow morning. Please tell Dillon that the RCMP has been advised to keep this situation confidential, and a Constable Reid will pick you two up from your hotel at eight in the morning."

"What did she say?" Dillon asked, as Adrianne put her cell on the table.

"There's a jurisdictional issue and the local RCMP must be involved. Detective Steele said the local RCMP will keep this confidential and her partner, Detective Kennedy, is coming to participate and take us back to Victoria."

"I didn't want the entire community to know what we're doing, but I guess I have no choice. I don't think I'll tell Tan about the police until we have recovered the escudos and bars."

"What about this necklace?" Adrianne fingered the emeralds around her neck.

"I wasn't going to tell her about that," he pulled Adrianne's body towards his.

♓

Eduardo unstrapped his Beretta Jetfire ankle gun from his right leg, and placed it on the dresser next to his wallet and room key. He realized he needed to visit Cecilia-Archie in the morning, after all. If he played the conversation right, he might find out more about her brother's jewelry business and maybe the quinto. It wasn't surprising that Lawrence and Dillon's grandfather Brett had a tight relationship, and that it had encouraged them to betroth their children. The question was, what happened and why was the arrangement terminated? Regardless of that situation, there must be a link with the quinto and the escudos. Eduardo was determined to discover the truth—the truth he was convinced would lead to a payout of escudos and ingots.

It was imperative that he talked to Cecilia before she took another charter out. He called the front desk for an early wake-up call and turned on the television to distract his mind. He had to be fresh and alert to manipulate Cecilia into divulging what he wanted to know.

Nineteen

It was a bright and sunny morning when Hamish appeared in his kitchen.

"What are you doing so early in the morning?" he asked Pirro.

"Surfing the Internet for Vancouver newspaper articles. I'm running the names we talked about yesterday."

"Any luck?"

"I've looked at all the West Coast Canadians, even the French guy. I'm waiting for the results on Diablo. It's a long shot, as I'm sure he disappeared in Mexico long ago. This whole thing's a long shot, but I love mysteries."

"You never said whether you are married, Pirro. When are you expected back in Florida?"

Pirro snickered. "My wife left me years ago. I was away chasing some treasure or artifact, and she was screwing my neighbor. I like it this way anyway. I have a few señoritas on the side. I have sex when I want it and it's cheaper than a wife. Use it or lose it, my friend."

"I lost my wife five years ago to heart failure. Heart was an oxymoron in her case. I have no desire to chase the young stuff. Too much effort." Hamish turned to pour his coffee.

"Here we go," Pirro muttered. "Yes, I know the Spanish word for devil is Diablo ... Diablo video game ... El Diablo Restaurant ... Louisa Diablo birth announcement."

"Nothing? Let's spend time on this later. What do you want for breakfast?"

"Hang on." Pirro selected the birth announcement. "Diablo's an unusual surname hereabouts. Maybe our sailor married and had a kid."

"Lots of Mexican immigrants move to Vancouver, Pirro. You're wasting time on this."

"I'm curious. Remember that's what I do—spend hours looking for clues and pieces of puzzles."

Pirro read the newspaper article.

December 12th 1979;

Louisa Diablo announces the birth of baby girl Mandy at a healthy 8pounds, 2ounces at Vancouver General. Prayers sent to murdered father Fernando as Louisa knows that he is watching over his beautiful new daughter.

Pirro glanced up at Hamish, then returned to the list of links. "There're no articles about a murder investigation. Why murder Diablo, and what did the killer want?"

Hamish inhaled silently and held his breath for a moment. "Obviously the police didn't resolve the case or the name 'Diablo' didn't get picked up in some obscure article." Hamish walked away from the counter. "We should work on a different tack, Pirro."

"No, no. This tells me our Fernando Diablo was definitely here, and he had a family. His wife may have some of the Regio bounty … the Necklace of Kings or even the El Rey Dorado." Pirro's eyes widened in anticipation. "Messing with Dillon Point isn't leading anywhere, so I say we follow up on this Diablo clue. I'll bet Diablo's murder is connected to the Santa Regio cargo, just like Gonzalo Cielo's five years earlier."

Hamish laughed. "You think Diablo was murdered by the same person who killed Cielo?"

"I doubt it. Five years is a long time, and the murders were at opposite ends of the continent. I think someone else got a line on Diablo's participation in the Santa Regio heist. Who knows, Diablo might've been trying to sell some of his share to pay the bills for that baby," Pirro mused. "All the coins and ingots found on the Santa Regio were stamped or marked by the Colombian and Mexican mints. If someone like you who notices that type of detail saw the bounty, they might've asked questions."

"Yes, or murdered him because it was gold, nothing more."

"Why not go after the wife then?" Pirro asked.

"Maybe they did, and she had nothing."

"I don't buy that. The coins or ingots would surely have shown up, even on the black market. The coins are worth a lot more than just the melted down gold. Even the ingots are, for that matter, with their unique stamping." Pirro leaned back in his chair. "We have to find the wife, Hamish. She'll likely know more about her husband's murder. She must still have some of the Regio cargo since none has apparently surfaced."

"Yes, on the supposition that Fernando even told her about it. It's probably hidden, and she doesn't even know that it exists." Hamish rubbed his chin. "That's why it hasn't shown up, Pirro."

"Then we'd better find her. We have the wife's name, Louisa, and the daughter is Mandy. I'll start looking on the Internet for marriage and birth certificate documents. We need an address."

"Great idea, Pirro. It's Friday, and I have a few pressing things to do at my shop. You work on your theory. I'll be back around lunchtime."

⯑

Eduardo couldn't believe the hotel had forgotten his wake-up call. He knew Cecilia took fishing charters out before eight if she could. He was in no mood to wait another entire day, and he was in no shape to hike the trip from his hotel to the marina more often than he had to.

The weather that had appeared to be clearing the evening before hadn't, and storm clouds once again engulfed the coast. It had also begun to sprinkle. Eduardo pulled up his coat collar as he walked toward the Powell River docks.

"I appreciate you picking us up, Constable Reid," TJ said as she climbed into the front seat of a Powell River RCMP squad car. "Good morning, you two," TJ greeted Dillon and Adrianne sitting in the back seat of the car.

"It's going to be ugly on the water today, Detective," said Constable Reid.

"Yes, it looks like that's the case. Have you lived in Powell River all your life?"

"Born and raised." The brawny policewoman glanced over at TJ. "I understand you're on classified security detail?" She glanced at Dillon in the back seat. "Our RCMP boat isn't large enough and, since I'm to be the only local RCMP presence during this mission, I decided to wait until you arrived before discussing a course of action."

"That's right, Constable. This trip is classified, and that is the arrangement. We sent information regarding an Eduardo Dominguez to your office. We know he's here, and we need to talk with him. He's a B&E suspect connected to this case. Is there any report on that inquiry?"

"Sorry, I don't know anything about that request. We can check when we're finished later today if you wish."

"Detective Kennedy, Dillon and I have been talking about the storm that's approaching. We've been out in the strait in this type of weather before," Adrianne said. "The Zodiac's cabin we used the other day is tight for four. I think that it would be best to rent a boat that's more appropriate."

"I was thinking about calling Cecilia-Archie Windsor. She runs a charter company and owns boats that would make this trip easier for everyone." Dillon leaned forward from the backseat. "She runs her business from the marina."

"That sounds like a good suggestion, and you two know the situation here. I didn't realize that your company kept diving boats in Powell River," TJ said. "My briefing told me your father's company operates from Comox."

"Yes, we do, but Dillon and I left from Comox and moored our Zodiac here in Powell River. We intended to use it on this trip, but didn't expect passengers."

Constable Reid turned the white squad car into an RCMP designated parking space at the marina. "I'll go talk to Cecilia-Archie and make the arrangements for a boat. You all wait here."

Eduardo was walking on the wooden dock toward Cecilia's shack when he noticed the RCMP squad car park.

"Shit." He darted past the shack for a place to hide. He eyed the boat he had taken on his prior charter. He dismissed it as a possibility immediately. He glanced behind him and saw the RCMP constable vacate her car. "Damn." A larger boat with *Sliammon Adventure Charter* stenciled on the side was moored in front of the Campion. He climbed aboard and concealed himself under a white tarpaulin that covered a dinghy on the upper deck.

Everyone in the squad car watched the RCMP constable walk away.

TJ turned to face Dillon. "The entire community's going to know something's going on once Ms. Windsor tags along on this diving trip, Dillon. You guys best figure out a story if you still want to keep this entire thing a family secret."

"We thought that would be the case last night. This whole situation is becoming more complicated than I'd imagined. My grandmother Gloria will never forgive me if her secret is exposed. But the entire world will know once the escudo coins are on the market. I want them to finally do something good for my family and my Sliammon community."

"Why not just say we found them on Savary Island during a prior diving trip? We're going there anyway, and no one needs to know about Vivian Island. Besides, if anyone wants to go looking for the wreck, they'll be in the wrong place," Adrianne suggested.

"That sounds like it might work. Let's see how today plays out. I like the idea, though. One thing is for sure—once Cecilia-Archie is involved, we need a plausible story."

"Okay, here you all go," Constable Reid pushed a handful of yellow slickers into the squad car. "Ms. Windsor has recommended we take her thirty-six-foot boat."

260

TJ smiled. "Let's get this stuff on and go and see Ms. Windsor."

They donned their raingear, and the foursome headed down the dock.

"Hello, Ms. Windsor," Dillon called.

"Good morning, Dillon. Come aboard." Cecilia stood on the deck of a Grand Banks fishing trawler. It had *qoxʷɛɑn* printed in large black letters and *The Reef* in smaller letters underneath on the stern of the boat. "There's lots of cabin space inside, and we can talk in there."

The cabin was immaculately maintained with a pair of couches and a teak mini-bar.

"Constable Reid tells me you want me to take you on a diving trip," Cecilia said. She looked at Adrianne. "I saw you and Dillon get out of the Second World Diving Zodiac here a couple of days ago. Why charter my boat, and why is the RCMP along?"

"We can't say at this time," TJ intervened. "I hope you understand that you must keep our activities confidential until I advise you otherwise. This is a police matter, and we need a boat to take us safely to our destination. Are we clear on the criteria?"

"Of course ... call me Cilia. I see you are from Victoria. Is the Victoria Police Department paying for this charter?"

"No, I am," Dillon fished out his wallet. "Visa okay, Ms. Windsor?"

Cecilia looked surprised. "You can pay later, Dillon, once I know how long we're going to be out. It's 175 dollars an hour. Where are we going? The tide is low, so I have to be careful because this boat draws a fair bit of water."

"We'll discuss that when we're ready to go, Cilia," TJ said.

"We have to transfer the diving gear from the Zodiac first." Dillon got up from the sofa. "Adrianne and I will do that. Detective Kennedy, maybe Cilia can tell you why she was shadowing us the last time we went out. I'd sure like to know."

"I didn't even know that you were in that Zodiac at the time, young man," Cecilia barked. "I was running a charter for a Colombian man. He wanted to travel the coastline ... well ... he was interested in watching that Zodiac of yours, Ms. Padrino, once he saw you guys at Vivian Island and later at Savary Island. It did seem strange to go on a diving trip in that weather."

"Let's go, Adrianne, we have work to do." Dillon nodded his head toward the aft door.

"We should be ready to cast off in about ten minutes. See you shortly," Adrianne said. She pulled up her slicker hood and followed Dillon.

"Can you describe the Colombian for me, Cilia?" TJ pulled out her notebook.

"Tall, early sixties, gray hair all slicked back. Good-looking guy," she paused to think. "He did ask questions about the coastline and whether any shipwrecks were ever found here. He also asked about Dillon."

"Dillon?" TJ looked up from her notebook.

"I didn't say much about Dillon or his family ... what's up with Dillon, anyway? Did he do something wrong? He's a good kid. His family has struggled all his life. I don't know how they did it. If it wasn't for his scholarship, Dillon couldn't have gone to university."

"Is there anything else you can tell me about your Colombian customer?" TJ continued. She got up to see how the kids were doing in getting their gear aboard.

"He paid with a credit card, so I could find his name if that helps, Detective."

"Yes, that'll help. I think everything is almost aboard. Let's get ready to go, please." TJ saw the couple head for the cabin.

Cecilia started the inboard engine.

Eduardo peeked from underneath the tarpaulin and watched the young people load their gear. He pulled the tarpaulin down again.

Cecilia navigated the fishing boat off Mace Point.

"We want to be as close as you can get to that marker in Keefer Bay," Adrianne pointed toward the northern coastline of Savary Island. "Just find a suitable place and drop anchor."

"I wondered where your Zodiac was going the other day when you skirted around this point." Cecilia kept a watch on the depth sounder readings. "It's really beginning to blow. Be careful with the currents."

Eduardo felt ill. He made a scraping sound as he pulled himself a little further from under the dinghy. He froze. He listened to see if anyone in the cabin had heard him, but the conversation below continued. He decided to stay where he was.

"I'm going to put my gear on now," Adrianne said.

"Hey … I'm going. I didn't take a diving program to sit on the deck. Besides—"

"Remember it's rough and dangerous down there, Dillon, and this weather's going to make it difficult to maintain control. You can't let the current get control of you. Stick close to me. This isn't worth getting anyone hurt. We can always come back."

"Not a chance. Let's go."

"Detective Kennedy, you take the helm and try to keep the bow pointing into the wind. I'm going to drop anchor. We are close enough to the shoreline in this low tide."

"I was with the navy at Esquimalt. I can handle this, Ms. Windsor."

"Constable Reid, could you please help when those two get outside? I'll do whatever Cilia needs me to do in here. If you need help, I'll join you."

The constable followed Adrianne and Dillon onto the deck at the stern of the boat.

"I've come to help," Constable Reid said. "What can I do?"

"Go back inside for a moment. We need to get wet suits on first." Adrianne grabbed a pair of duffle bags from the pile of supplies that had been transferred from the Zodiac. "You can help when we're ready to get into the water."

"I have this bag." Constable Reid had to yell over the rush of the wind as she picked up a duffle bag.

They all returned to the cabin and Cecilia asked, "How you doing there, Detective?" Cecilia wiped water from her face with her hand.

"I got it."

"Now, Dillon and Adrianne," Cecilia made sure she had their attention, "because the props on this boat are exposed, I'm going to put it into neutral while you're in the water. The wind will force the stern of the boat to come around while we're anchored. You come back toward the boat from the stern. If I'm forced to engage the engines, stay clear of the props. They are not far from the diving grid. Understand?"

Cecilia turned to TJ. "This vessel rolls badly in heavy seas and winds. When we see either of the divers, I want you at the stern with Constable Reid to help pull them aboard. I'll handle everything in here."

"All right, then. Let's go," said TJ.

Dillon and Adrianne went downstairs to a bedroom to pull on wetsuits.

"We'd better hurry," Adrianne said. They struggled into the wetsuits and reemerged into the cabin in record time.

"We're going to get our tanks set up and strapped on. Constable Reid, you drop the swimming ladder from the grid at the stern. Dillon and I are going to retrieve two waterproof bags we left tied together by the marker. We'll hand you the rope that each one has tied to the end, then you pull the bags up onto the swimming grid," Adrianne said. "Can you manage?" she asked.

"Don't worry about me, just be careful," Constable Reid said. "Detective Kennedy will be close by when you return."

Dillon and Adrianne crouched on the deck to keep their balance. Constable Reid worked her way to the stern. She could hear the throaty sound of the inboard engine idle as she climbed over the edge of the boat, and knelt down to drop the swimming ladder into the water.

"Hold on while we climb over," said Adrianne. The drivers clutched flippers as they climbed over the stern of the rocking boat.

"Watch for us," Adrianne told the constable, as she and Dillon sat on the edge of the swimming platform, pulling flippers onto their feet. "It will be tough to see us in these swells."

Adrianne pulled down her facemask and put her thumb up. She checked that Dillon was ready, then pushed herself off the grid. Dillon followed closely behind, and the divers disappeared from view, swallowed by the sea.

⋈

Hamish was in his office contemplating his course of action now that Pirro had discovered the demise of Fernando Diablo. Pirro had surprised him with how easily he had made the connection; but, then again, Pirro knew the names of the conspirators whereas he hadn't. Hamish wondered if things would've worked out differently if he had known ....

He twisted the dial on his safe, pulled a PMS pistol out, and placed it on his desk. He stared at the elaborate, unique carvings on the grip of the pistol. He couldn't take the chance of Pirro filling in the pieces of the puzzle.

⋈

TJ watched the Savary Island shoreline, looking for signs of Adrianne and Dillon in the water.

"They haven't been gone that long. It's a bit of a swim to that marker and back in this rolling sea," Cecilia remarked as she, too, looked out the window "What are they looking for?"

"We'll talk about it when they return, Ms. Windsor." TJ held tightly onto a counter in the cabin as the boat continued to roll and yaw. "How long have they been down there?"

Cecilia looked over to the clock on the dash, "Seven minutes," she replied. She felt the gusting wind pick up speed as the trawler pulled at the anchor.

"I see them." Constable Reid pointed to an arm sticking out in the ocean about five meters from the stern of the boat.

TJ went to join Constable Reid at the stern.

Eduardo heard Constable Reid's shout, and he lifted the tarpaulin. He was in a quandary. He knew that if he stayed where he was, he likely wouldn't be discovered. But the anticipation of laying his hands on the escudos overshadowed common sense.

He slowly reached toward his ankle and withdrew his weapon from its holster. He decided to wait for the right opportunity, a time when the policewomen were in plain sight.

The diver's head disappeared under the waves again as TJ joined Constable Reid "Where did the diver go?"

The diver's head then reappeared by the swimming grid holding up a rope with one arm before the Constable could answer. TJ leaned over the back frame of the trawler to steady the constable, who was now lying on the diver's grid ready to grab the rope from the divers. TJ couldn't quite reach the constable's sprawled-out body.

Constable Reid decided that she couldn't grab the rope from her position, so she crawled across the grid toward the diver who had disappeared once again. Constable Reid stared into the darkness of the rolling sea. Moments later a diver grabbed the grid with one hand and a second diver appeared alongside. They both clung to the rocking boat for a moment, and then one of them raised an arm and tried to hand over a rope twisted through their hand to the outstretched fingers of the Constable.

"I got it," Constable Reid yelled as she grasped the rope while hanging onto the swimming grid with her other hand. The weight of the bag on the rope was unexpected and it almost pulled the constable over the edge of the platform as the boat pitched. "Shit," she groaned as she stabilized her balance.

The constable pulled on the rope and dragged a bag onto the swimming grid. The diver went to help the other, still clinging to the edge of the narrow platform. The fishing boat continued to roll heavily as Constable Reid reached out for the second rope now held up by both swimmers. "Got it." she yelled. The divers let go of the rope, and the woman yanked the second heavy bag onto the grid.

Constable Reid leaned back against the backside of the stern to catch her breath while the divers threw their fins onto the grid. The first one grabbed the stainless steel ladder, while the other clung to the diving grid.

"Man, that was crazy," Adrianne said. She pulled off her diving mask, climbed onto the grid, and slid over the rear of the boat's hull onto the deck. The second diver grabbed onto the metal ladder and climbed out of the rough sea.

"I'm sure glad to see you, Constable," Dillon said. He pulled himself from the water and grabbed Constable Reid's hand. He pulled off his facemask and spit salt water.

Eduardo knew this was his chance, and he scrambled out from under the tarpaulin, pistol in hand. He stayed on his knees and pointed the weapon at the two women, who he assumed were police constables.

"You and you … toss your weapons into the sea. Now." For emphasis he shot into the air.

All four below twisted their heads and stared at the heavy-set man on the upper deck.

"I said toss your weapons overboard."

Cecilia poked her head through the rear of the cabin door.

"You, Ms. Windsor … join us." Eduardo waved his pistol.

TJ stayed motionless as the boat rocked unattended in the rough sea. "Dominguez, put your weapon down. I'm Detective Kennedy of the Victoria Police."

"I'm not screwing with you two. Dump your weapons or someone might get hurt." Eduardo tried to keep his balance. "You first." He aimed his pistol at TJ.

TJ assessed the situation. "Okay, okay. Don't do something stupid." She slowly pulled up her slicker and extracted her Smith and Wesson.

"Dump it," Eduardo demanded, with his Beretta pointed at TJ.

TJ tossed the weapon overboard. "Okay now?"

"And you. Toss yours, Constable," Eduardo redirected his weapon. "This is no time to be a hero."

Constable Reid slowly extracted her weapon, glanced over at TJ and understood when TJ nodded her head. She tossed her weapon into the sea, and twisted her body around to face the large man. "You haven't a chance. Surrender your weapon before this situation gets worse," she yelled at Eduardo, who had begun to climb down from the upper deck.

"You, Dillon, get lifejackets for these police constables," Eduardo demanded. "Cilia, get away from that cabin door. Don't do anything stupid, Dillon. Your girlfriend's out here."

Dillon's heart pounded in his throat as he climbed over the back of the boat.

"They're under the seats in the lounge, Dillon," Cecilia said, as Dillon slipped past her.

Eduardo stood in the rain, drenched as he waved his pistol. He held onto the side railing of the rocking boat. "You, constable—lift those sacks off the grid and place them on the deck. Then put your cell phones on top."

Constable Reid glanced at TJ for a moment, then sighed and grabbed the first knapsack. She lifted it over the lip of the boat, trying to keep her balance.

"Come on, I don't have all day," Eduardo yelled, as the second bag was placed next to the first. "Your phones."

Once both cell phones were added to the pile he took a calming breath, eyed Cecilia, then returned his attention to the two policewomen. "Constable, go up onto the upper deck and untie the dinghy. Detective, you help her get that thing in the water. Your life depends upon it."

Dillon reappeared with two lifejackets and stood by the open cabin door as the policewomen climbed to the upper deck. Eduardo watched the two women while occasionally glancing at the others standing in the wind and rain. The small dinghy was lowered onto the rear deck along with two wooden oars.

"Each of you take a lifejacket, then I want you to put that thing in the water and get in. One of these kids will hand you the oars once you're aboard. Get on with it."

"What about the others?" Detective Kennedy asked, as she climbed down to the main deck.

"The two kids are going to put on those tanks and join you in the water. Ms. Windsor and I are going for a ride. You've got two minutes, then I'm going whether you're in your boat or not. You better move it."

The policewomen pulled on their lifejackets and the dinghy was lowered into the water. They got into the small lifeboat and Adrianne handed them the wooden oars. "Wait for us to get our gear on, then we'll all head for Keefer Bay."

TJ grabbed the diving grid as the couple strapped on tanks and pulled on flippers. She looked at the captain standing outside of the cabin door as Dillon and Adrianne reentered the waters.

Eduardo waited until the dinghy with the divers clinging aside slowly drifted away from the fishing boat. "Okay, Ms.

Windsor, get the anchor up. I'll run this thing. Make it fast, or you'll end up overboard without a lifejacket."

Cecilia began to maneuver toward the front of the boat, while Eduardo entered the cabin and picked his way over to the steering wheel. He watched Cecilia as she knelt to prepare to raise the anchor. He pushed the engine speed throttle a little forward and engaged the drive. The boat began to twist around in the heavy wind and ocean swell as he pushed the engine throttle further ahead trying to control the boat.

"Shit." The boat was pushed toward the rocky shoreline of the island, where the dinghy could be seen bobbing over the large swells of the ocean waves.

"Give me that," Cecilia reentered the cabin. "You'll run aground."

Eduardo moved aside to allow her to take the helm of the drifting boat. He stepped back farther as she regained control and pushed the throttle further forward.

Cecilia-Archie's heart pounded in her throat as she momentarily focused on her abductor. The boat was now moving away from the dinghy and headed north-westerly toward Mace Point. She knew she was in real trouble, and that she had better devise a plan to gain control of Eduardo's weapon.

"So, Mr. Dominguez, I see that you were fishing for something in those sacks out there. That wasn't nice leaving those people out there. Can I call for the Coast Guard for them?"

"No. They're on their own, at least for now. Head for Comox. Turn on the heater in here."

The fishing vessel rolled as the boat headed into the enlarging waves. Eduardo clutched a railing as the boat pounded ahead in the heavy swell.

"Comox is a long way in this weather, Mr. Dominguez."

"We have lots of time. I know how far Comox is from here," he replied as the fishing boat passed the point. "Come on, Cilia, turn this thing over there." He pointed to the right of Harwood Island that loomed in the distance. "No, maybe stay closer to this island and the ride won't be so rough."

Cecilia didn't say a word, but turned the boat in the heading Eduardo suggested. She knew all too well about the rocks and shoals around Whalebone Point, but didn't say anything. Savary Island began to block the heavy wind. The water was less rough and choppy as the boat plowed through, running ever faster as Cecilia eased the throttle forward.

"We should make the time when we can," she explained her increased speed as she watched every motion of the armed man. "What's in those bags that's so important, anyway?"

Eduardo eyed the woman, and then glanced at the shoreline with rocky cliffs. "Gold escudo coins and ingots. Ingots just like the ones your brother used to make that fancy necklace."

Cecilia scrunched her face. "What are you talking about?"

"You know exactly what I'm talking about. Your brother Lawrence made a necklace using ingots from the Santa Regio. I know, I saw it."

"Ingots from what?"

Eduardo was about to answer when the fishing boat struck a partially submerged rock with a loud bang, knocking him to the floor. Cecilia had anticipated the collision and ensured she was prepared for the large jolt that sent the boat careening toward the shoreline.

She lost her grip on the steering wheel, but saw the pistol was knocked out of Eduardo's fist. It had spun around on the floor and ended up at the rear of the cabin.

"What was that?" Eduardo spit out.

Cecilia cut the power and rushed toward the gun that was now sliding around on the floor by the rear door. The boat listed in the choppy water as Cecilia scrambled to grab the gun. The fishing boat continued to be pushed by the heavy seas, its stalled engines allowing the uncontrolled craft to be swept toward the shoreline.

Eduardo tried to regain his balance as the boat rolled again, its upper deck pushed by the wind. His bulk slid on the wooden deck. A loud scraping sound vibrated through the hull as the boat was dragged along the gravel shoreline of the island by the wind and incoming tide.

Cecilia sprawled out and snagged the weapon from the floor as the fishing boat stopped all motion, now grounded on the shallow seabed on the shoreline of Savary Island.

Dillon and Adrianne were exhausted as they helped the two policewomen to shore at Keefer Bay. The group pulled the dinghy onto the rocky shore and found a protected rock face that sheltered them from the weather.

TJ was trained for such an event and knew exactly what to do, but there wasn't the standard emergency pack on the dinghy. She had everyone huddled together underneath the life raft for protection from the elements and to share body heat.

TJ grasped the mooring rope of the dinghy to keep it from being blown away by the driving wind. She wondered what Jamie would think. It was her first assignment with the Victoria Police Department. She had lost her weapon and cell phone, and let a suspect abscond with an innocent woman and the coins.

She turned her thoughts to the young adults in her care. She would try to explain to Jamie later. Her survival and that of the three others with her was her only priority.

Cecilia's hands shook as she pointed the gun at Eduardo, who was now staring at the woman. "Move over there." She waved the gun unsteadily. "I'll use this, make no mistake."

Eduardo studied the woman as he tried to get to his feet on the sloping floor of the grounded boat. He leaned on the side of the fishing vessel. He remained quiet and picked his way to where he was directed, while Cecilia crawled to the opposite side. She grabbed the edge of the lounge seat, got to her feet, and continued to point the weapon at Eduardo.

"Sit where you are and don't move." Cecilia turned on the boat's radio microphone. "Mayday. Mayday. This is the fishing boat *qoxʷɛɑ̃n*. Come in, please." The radio crackled, then a response came from a small speaker in the ceiling of the boat.

"Come in, *qoxʷɛɑ̃n*. What's your distress?"

"I've run aground at Whalebone Point. Send RCMP. I have a man onboard with a gun. There are four stranded people at Keefer Bay. Send Coast Guard. Over."

"Anyone injured, *qoxʷɛɑ̃n*? Over."

"Stranded policewomen and two young adults at Keefer Bay likely have exposure. Over."

"Ten-four *qoxʷɛɑ̃n*. Will deploy RCMP and Coast Guard. Over."

Cecilia replaced the microphone and clutched the boat's inner frame. She leaned on the back side of the boat with the handgun pointed at Eduardo.

✳

Hamish decided to take Pirro Marco on a boat cruise to see Fort Rodd and Fisgard Lighthouse. The fifty-foot Tiara yacht was sleek and the salon was elegant, finished in custom, natural cherry wood. The men were standing in the cockpit as Hamish navigated the boat past the large Canadian Forces naval base at Esquimalt.

The partially sunny day showed signs of giving way to a cloudy evening, threatening that the early fall's weather pattern would return to rain. The air began to cool down in the early afternoon as the clouds rolled in from the north, and a breeze began to remind the tree leaves on the shoreline that it was time to alter color.

Hamish placed the yacht on autopilot, then turned to face his guest. "I found the article about Diablo interesting. I didn't know the Mexican's name that came to see me in 1979. He didn't have any ID on him." Hamish sipped scotch. "Your research has been extremely useful."

Pirro stared at Hamish. "He didn't have any ID on him. How do you know that?"

"Because," Hamish put his scotch on the front console and pulled out a Soviet PSM pistol from his jacket, "I shot him by accident, and I looked for his identification. Cagey bastard, not carrying standard identification in his wallet. I bought Santa Regio ingots from him twice. He said he planned to go on a belated honeymoon, but he never mentioned a baby."

Hamish raised the barrel of the pistol and pointed it at Pirro. "I wanted to purchase everything he had from the Santa Regio, but he said the ingots I purchased were the last of the lot he had. I didn't believe him. I also didn't know about the Necklace of Kings or the El Rey Dorado back then, either."

"You knew all along that the heisted Regio cargo ended up in Vancouver. When you killed Diablo and couldn't find his ID, you had nothing else to lead you to the rest of it." Pirro stood frozen, staring at the barrel of the gun.

"That's right. I wanted the names of the others with him, but the Mexican pulled this pistol and tried to escape without telling me who they were. We struggled for control of the gun and I shot him, took his gun, and ran.

I looked through the newspaper for weeks to see if there was anything on his death, but there was nothing—not a word—so I was forced to let go of the Regio secret. I was convinced it would resurface one day, but it didn't. All I had was dead ends."

"So you got the names from me and a new starting point. How fortunate. That gun is old, Hamish, are you sure you—" Pirro lunged at Hamish, knocked him to the floor of the enclosed cockpit, his hand clenched with Hamish's on the pistol grip. The gun fired and shattered a side window as the two men rolled around on the floor of the yacht.

Hamish slowly overpowered the older, weaker man. The gun exploded twice and Pirro's hand relaxed its grip on the pistol; blood oozed from Pirro's chest. Hamish lay on the floor catching his breath as the yacht continued on course. Hamish got to his knees and emptied the dead Colombian's pockets.

Hamish clambered to his feet and stuffed his gun and Pirro's wallet and cell phone into his jacket. Hamish looked around as the yacht slowly headed past Saxe Point Park portside. No boaters were within sight. He dragged Pirro's body to the stern of the boat.

Hamish looked around once again and—satisfied that there weren't any witnesses—pulled the corpse over the lip of the boat and pushed it overboard. It floated on the surface of the calm ocean toward shore, propelled by the ocean current.

Hamish returned to the cockpit, released the autopilot, and pushed the throttle full ahead. The yacht's dual Caterpillar engines roared and the yacht swiftly headed for Victoria Harbour.

♓

It was mid-afternoon when the Coast Guard returned to the Powell River marina. The policewomen and the couple were draped in red blankets as they climbed off the Coast Guard vessel. A police constable had Eduardo shackled inside a squad car, and Cecilia was giving her statement to a uniformed RCMP constable.

"Where's Ms. Windsor?" TJ asked. Constable Reid joined her and the women went in search of Cecilia. Dillon and Adrianne were taken to an ambulance waiting in the marina's parking lot.

"You two need to be checked out," a paramedic told the women, as they walked briskly down the dock.

"Give us a few minutes, then we'll join you in the parking lot," Constable Reid said. "We have immediate business to conduct first."

"Hi, Kate," the constable said when he saw Constable Reid enter the office. "Are you okay?" he asked, as he put his clipboard down.

"Yes, John, thanks. This is Detective Kennedy of the Victoria Police Department. May we have a few minutes with Cecilia please?"

The constable rose from his chair. "Sure. The captain was concerned when the emergency call came in. We recovered a couple sacks of gold from the *qoxʷɛɑ̀n*. I put them in the trunk of the squad car. I'll wait in the car with the prisoner."

The policewomen waited until the constable left the office. "Are you all right, Ms. Windsor?"

"I think I sprained my ankle, but I'm fine. That's more than I can say about my fishing boat, though." She forced a smile. "I was scared to death he was going to kill me. I purposely headed into the shallows and rocks. I couldn't think of anything else to do."

"I'm sorry we couldn't help. You were very brave. This expedition was supposed to be kept confidential, but it is complicated now." TJ clutched her warming blanket. "I will ask the local RCMP office to keep details of this event confidential, and you must do the same. Mr. Point needs time to deal with family issues. He requested that the contents of the bags remain between us until he decides how to handle the public disclosure."

"Dominguez told me my family is connected to that gold as well. It somehow involves my brother Lawrence, but I don't have all the facts yet." Cecilia looked exhausted.

"We wanted to see how you are and apologize for not protecting you. We'll deal with your fee and damages." TJ was concerned about the entire event.

"You did your best under the circumstances, Detective, and no one was hurt in the end. I expect to be told at some point the details of what is in those bags, though."

"We will advise you when we can Ms. Windsor." TJ turned to face the wet Constable standing next to her. "We have a couple of hours or so before our flight leaves for Victoria," TJ said. "Maybe we can all get dry clothes. I want to take those two kids to the Point house before we leave."

Constable Reid parked her squad car on the street outside the Points' house. Dillon expected his mother's neighbors were watching, but he didn't see anyone. Dillon and the three women walked to the front door and he knocked. His dog barked when his mother opened the door.

"What's wrong, Dillon?" his mother asked, as she spotted the RCMP squad car and the policewomen.

"It's okay, Tan," said Dillon. "We need to talk."

"ƛatom." Dillon rubbed the dog's head while he held the door open.

Robbie took a deep breath, and smiled politely, "Come in."

"This is Detective Kennedy from the Victoria Police Department and Constable Reid from the RCMP office here in Powell River," Dillon said, as the group of women entered the house. "Are Grandmother Gloria and Grandfather Brett home?"

"No, son, they're visiting the neighbors down the street. What's this all about?" Dillon's mother asked, noticing the scraggly hair and outfits. "Let me take your coats. We can talk in the sitting room."

"Thank you, Mrs. Point," TJ said, as she pulled off her coat and handed it over. "Your son asked us to help him, and he wants to let you know what's going on."

"It's about the coins, isn't it, Dillon?" Robbie asked. "You found the coins, didn't you?"

"Yes, we did. Dillon's concerned about how to deal with the publicity once the discovery of the coins becomes public knowledge, Mrs. Point. We've had a difficult day that your son and Adrianne will tell you about later, but the entire community will know something took place out in the strait today that involved him. We have a story we would like to discuss with you that Dillon and Adrianne have concocted." TJ took a seat by the fire in the small sitting room.

"Concocted?"

"Yes, Tan. I don't think anyone in the family wants the story of Walter and Grandmother Gloria known publicly. I believe the escudo coins are of no value unless they are sold, and the money then used for the good of the Sliammon community and our family. Once the discovery and sale of the coins is announced, we need a story to satisfy everyone's curiosity and to deflect questions suggesting that the discovery was anything other than a random find.

"I'm going to say Adrianne and I were diving around Savary Island and found a chest of coins. We searched for several days after the initial find, but no more coins were found. We had Cecilia-Archie take us to a location where Adrianne and I moved the coins a few days ago, so it looks like the find was on the north side of Savary."

"That was clever," Robbie mused over the story. "Selling the coins to help our community is a noble thing to do. I'm proud of you, my son." She put her hand to her mouth. "Your grandmother has been torn for years about her secret, and your solution will certainly preserve her dignity and respect."

"Few people know yet about the find, but I'm afraid Ms. Windsor does. She has been instructed to keep what she knows confidential until I tell her otherwise. Everyone in the community will know that something was pulled from the ocean floor by the island, and that we are here at your house with your son, as well." TJ warmed her hands by the fire.

"Everyone in your family must tell the same story; you didn't know anything about the coins until we came here today to tell you. The find was a fortunate accidental discovery that your son and Ms. Padrino made while practicing their diving. Ms. Windsor won't know anything different from that story either, as today's circumstances align with that explanation."

"If you agree, Tan, you must talk to Grandmother Gloria when she comes home," Dillon added, looking at the floor. "I hope she won't be upset with me about how I handled this."

He looked back up at his mother. "You said I would become a man and understand what that meant when you gave me Walter Smith's diary. I had no idea."

"You're more of a man than I had ever hoped you'd be, Dillon. I already knew it long before I gave you that diary. You just had to discover that for yourself." Tears formed in Robbie's eyes. "It will be a test for all of us to deal with the publicity in the coming weeks."

"I hope that Grandmother Gloria will be able to move on now, and let Walter fade into her past. The knowledge of the treasure must've been such a burden."

"I'm sure you're right. As for the rest of our discussion, do what you feel's right, my son. I think using the northern side of Savary Island is questionable, but it will likely keep all the fortune hunters up around Lund rather than around Powell River, and I like that."

Dillon got up and gave his mother a big kiss. "Arianne and I expect to be back here tomorrow. We need to take her company's Zodiac back to Comox, and we must get the coins back safely to Victoria tonight. Tell everyone I love them and will see them tomorrow, likely after lunch."

"Good to meet you, Mrs. Point," TJ stood. "You should be proud of your son, and Ms. Padrino has been supportive. We have a plane to catch and the constable here has other business to attend to."

"It'll be an emotional talk with my mother tonight," she said softly, with a sigh.

♓

Selina was in her bedroom getting ready for her art exhibition. Her debut as an artist was less than ninety minutes away. She opened her dresser drawer. She had decided to wear her mother's quinto necklace as a personal tribute.

She put the carved box on the top of the dresser and opened it. Her father's envelope sat on top of the necklace. She typed a number on her cell.

"Hello, Aunt Cecilia?"

"Selina, I was just thinking about you. I've had an extraordinary and crazy day."

"Really? I've got to run in a few minutes. My art exhibition is tonight. You'll have to tell me all about it, but I just wanted to let you know I have the whale key back."

"Oh dear, the key … we have a few things to talk about, Selina. Could you fly up here tomorrow and bring the key? I'll pay for your ticket."

"I'd like that, Aunt Cecilia. We can talk about my show. I'll bring the key and Dad's letter that Mom gave me. We can open it together. I would like you to be with me when I do."

"I didn't know that your father left you a letter, Selina. Call me when you arrive at your mother's house. Have a safe trip and a successful art show, dear."

♓

It was past eight in the evening when TJ, with Dillon and Adrianne in the backseat, reached the police station on Caledonia Avenue in Victoria. She parked and called dispatch. "This is Detective Kennedy. I'm in the parking garage, and I need a couple of constables down here, please. I have evidence that needs to be logged tonight, and I need assistance."

Two uniformed constables exited the elevator and approached the Charger.

"I won't be long," TJ popped open the trunk of the car.

Dillon and Adrianne watched the coins being carried into the elevator. "They are finally safe. I don't know how I'm going to sell them," Dillon rambled on. "Cecilia-Archie wrecked her boat, too. I should pay the repair costs. I was worried about you and—"

"It will be all right, Dillon. Chill," Adrianne interrupted. "I can't wait to get home into my warm bed. I'm exhausted."

Adrianne said no more, and Dillon stared out the side window. The silence lay unbroken until Detective Kennedy reappeared at the elevator and got into the car. "Okay, time to go home. I'll call you in the morning, Dillon, as there is paperwork that must be completed."

"What kind of paperwork, Detective?" Dillon asked.

"We need to determine whether you can keep your find, which means that first we must confirm it isn't considered stolen goods. You must have the legal right to sell or do whatever you wish with the coins, and any buyer must be assured you have the right to sell them."

"But I recovered them. They were found by my grandmother over thirty years ago."

"I know that, Dillon, but crown counsel must review the case first. I'll get that ball rolling in the morning."

"What will happen to the Mexican?" Adrianne asked.

"He's in RCMP custody in Powell River. That will be sorted out next week. My partner will be happy he was collared, but I'm not so sure what she will think about the rest of my day."

Twenty

A Victoria Police squad car, a coroner's SUV, and an ambulance were parked in a cul-de-sac outside a rancher home on Plaskett Place in Esquimalt. A body located at the bottom of a rocky cliff of a home overlooking the ocean was on a stretcher. The homeowner had seen the corpse mangled between the rocks early that morning and called 911.

Jamie and TJ were assigned to the case. The coroner reported two bullet holes in the chest of the male victim.

"Inspector Harris called me this morning. He said our Dillon Point case is nearly closed, so we've got this assignment," Jamie said. "You'll have to tell me more about your day in Powell River, but right now let's see what we got."

The detectives walked over to the stretcher. "I understand our vic has a couple of gunshots to the chest," TJ said to the medical examiner who was with the body.

"I'll have to take him to the lab, but it looks like a pair of 18mm slugs," the medical examiner replied. "I'll know for sure at the morgue. The shot was at close range, a struggle by the looks of the entry wound and bruising. The gunshot residue was washed away in the salt water."

"Eighteen millimeters isn't common these days. Any guess how long this guy's been in the water?"

"Less than a day. Based on the currents and weather yesterday, he was probably shot in the Saxe Point area. I'll get prints and see if I can ID him. I'll call when I've got something for you, Detective Steele."

"Thanks, Doc." Jamie turned towards their car. "We're done here for now. TJ, tell me about your day yesterday."

♓

Hamish was in his yacht stateroom surfing the Internet at the Oak Bay Marina. He had spent most of the prior evening cleaning up blood from the cockpit and rear deck. He had covered the broken window with a piece of cardboard. It had been a long night, short on sleep.

Hamish picked up his cell phone.

"Yes, madam, I'm looking for the widow of Fernando Diablo. Would that be you?" He smiled when he heard the woman's answer.

"I'm an historian and writing an article about the Santa Regio. I understand your husband was a crew member on the salvage vessel that discovered the wreck off the Florida coast. I also understand his murder was never solved. May I come and talk with you? ... Wonderful, I'll see you early this afternoon then."

Hamish stared at the Soviet pistol lying on Pirro Marco's notebook, which he'd found earlier while packing Pirro's belongings back into the dead man's suitcase. He leaned forward and slipped the notebook from under the gun. Firth opened the book to the last marked page and read part of the last entry again:

> *Diving company boat spotted at Vivian Island, and then lost sight behind Savary Island when forced to return to marina by foul weather. Strange weather for diving. Don't know if any connection to coins—but gut tells me area could be site of possible shipwrecks due to weather and rocky shorelines. No evidence of this though. Weather can get rough, heavy winds to north and cold.*
>
> *Dillon Point's Sliammon family: father died when boy young, brought up by mother and grandparents.*

There was still work to be done. The El Ray Dorado and Dillon Point required further investigation. But, first he would take care of his meeting with Louisa Diablo. He shoved the gun, articles, and Pirro's belongings into his safe and locked it.

♓

Dillon rolled onto his back. "You've been quiet since we left my mother's house. Is something bugging you?"

"Do you think we should've told Detective Kennedy about the necklace? It's part of the stuff we found."

"I guess so, but I gave it to you. Let's talk about it when we hear what crown counsel has to say about the rest. I can't believe they'll make me give it back. It's been lost since Walter and grandmother found it in '75."

"I still want to look for the rest of the wreck, even if we have to give up anything we find." Adrianne looked up at the ceiling. "It's about the adventure of the search, and the rush you get when you find something."

"Ah, are you sure …." Dillon tried to caress her.

"Dillon … no … that's enough." She pushed his hand away.

"I'm going to get cleaned up then," Dillon snapped, and got out of bed. "We have to get ready to go to the police station, anyway."

Adrianne watched Dillon stomp off to the shared bathroom. She thought about how Robbie had looked at her when she explained why Sliammon women had hyphenated first names ....

♓

Hamish moored at the marina outside the Bayshore Hotel in Coal Harbour. He had rented a car at the hotel and paid his moorage fee for the day. The cloudy day had cleared, and the sun brought out strollers along the promenade by the hotel, most in the direction of Stanley Park.

Hamish entered the lobby of the Summerhill Retirement Residence in North Vancouver. The receptionist gave him Louisa Diablo's room number. He went up the elevator to the second floor and knocked on number 211. There was no answer. He knocked again.

"Yes?" a woman said softly. She opened the door a crack to see her visitor.

"I'm Mr. Firth, I called earlier." He smiled. "I wanted to talk with you about your husband, Fernando."

"Yes, come in. I haven't talked about my poor husband for years. The police never found his murderer."

Hamish entered the single-bedroom apartment.

"I have bad arthritis and my hands don't work well these days. I've been living here for a year or so now." She closed the door. "Come and visit in the sitting room. I can make you some tea, if you wish."

"No, thank you. I won't take much of your time, and I can't stay long." Hamish sat in a Victorian chair. "I'm doing an article on lost Spanish treasures, and wanted to know if you can recall anything about your husband's adventures when he was a working hand with Gonzalo Cielo on a salvage ship in 1972."

"I'm afraid that he didn't tell me much about that expedition. I met Fernando here in Vancouver and we married in 1977. He was a private man, but obsessed with finding his fortune, I'm afraid. We loved each other, but he always seemed to be looking for something. It wasn't another woman, but I don't know what it was. He did get something from the wreck—a handful of beautifully cut emeralds that he gave to me when I became pregnant with our daughter."

"Do you still have them? They would be of great interest to my readers if I could describe them."

"I gave them to my daughter for her twenty-first birthday. I had them strung into a beautiful necklace, but you know young people these days, the style wasn't modern enough so my daughter's having them reset."

"I've heard that crew members may have received small gold bars that were recovered from the wreck. Did your husband receive any of those besides the emeralds?"

Louisa laughed. "Those emeralds were everything to my husband. He thought they contained a secret, but he never had a chance to follow that dream. He was murdered trying to raise money so we could pay for a few things after our daughter's birth," Louisa said. "I told him that we would find a way to get through the tough times, but he said that he could fix it and left the house one morning to meet someone he'd met before. I don't know who it was, but my husband was found murdered the next day. The police said that they had no clues as to the identity of the person who shot him." Louisa's eyes brightened with pooled tears.

"It was so long ago … I'm sorry, but there's nothing else to tell you."

"Your daughter …."

"Mandy, well, really Manuela Rosita Princeton now; but I always called her Mandy."

"Can you give me her phone number? I'd really appreciate seeing those emeralds. They are a new piece for my article that I didn't know about."

"You'll have to talk to her about that." Louisa pulled open a drawer in a round side table. "I have her husband's business card. He owns a construction company and his home phone number is on the card." She handed Hamish the business card. "Good luck with your article. I'd love to read it when it's published."

☧

Selina was at her mother's house drinking tea with her aunt Cecilia-Archie. The whale key lay on the table in the sitting room, and her father's unopened letter lay underneath the key. The room felt empty with her mother gone. The house was now Selina's, but she didn't care. She missed her mother and father.

"I have something for you, Selina. I've had this for a long time and forgot all about it until you reminded me about that whale key." Cecilia picked up a paper bag from the floor and put it on the table before her. She reached in and pulled out a similar whale key to the one on the table. "I think these two keys slip together and make one master key."

Selina put her teacup on the table, picked up the two keys with diamonds on one side and a flat edge on the other. She glanced over at her aunt, removed the chain that had been left on her key, and fiddled until the two keys slipped together on the flat sides. "Did Dad make this?"

"Yes, Selina. That key set is designed to open this box," Cecilia replied, and pulled a carved box from the bag. "Your father told me this was to be your wedding box, and that I was to give it to you when you became betrothed. I thought, under the circumstances, that you should have it now."

"This box is just like the one my mother gave me that contained the quinto necklace."

"What quinto necklace?" Cecilia asked.

"It's a long story, but it's a gold necklace my mother gave me before she died. I have it in Victoria. The jeweler who appraised it for me named it the quinto necklace, as it appears to be connected to a Spanish treasure. I have the document that explains it."

Selina's aunt inserted the key set into the custom designed slot. She twisted it, and the lid popped open.

"Selina," Cecilia gasped.

Selina pulled back the wooden box lid, and she sat with her eyes wide in astonishment. The box contained a necklace similar to the quinto, except that it had five ingots instead of three. It dangled from a thick gold chain. "It's like the quinto, except it's bigger." Selina sat for a moment.

"Wedding box?" Her eyes welled with tears.

"That's what your father said, Selina. I've never seen what was inside. Maybe his letter explains." Cecilia pushed the envelope towards Selina. "I think it's time you opened this."

Selina wiped the tears from her eyes, then took the letter. She sat and looked at the words *Selina* and *χaʔnomeč* in her father's handwriting. She slipped a finger under the flap, tore the envelope, and extracted a paper. She unfolded the page and read the handwritten words.

My dearest Selina.

I made this gift for you, as well as another larger one that I gave your aunt Cecilia to keep until your betrothal. Brett Paul and I have agreed that you and his grandson Dillon Point will marry, and this necklace is for you to wear on your wedding day, as the other larger one will be Dillon's to wear.

These gifts are made from gold that bears a rich tale, as I hope that you and Dillon will create your own life story together. May the unique impressions of these bars represent the unique impressions that you will give your children.

I hope to share in your special day but, if that isn't possible, may these necklaces represent me when you make your vows to each other.

With all my love, your father.

Selina put the letter down and began to cry. Cecilia picked up the paper and read the note in silence, then put the paper back on the table and put her arms around Selina.

"Dillon Point. I don't even know Dillon," Selina choked out the words.

"I know Brett and your father had a falling out many years ago. I don't know what happened. Nobody knows now, except Brett."

♓

Jamie told TJ to go back home. They would resume their work on the case Monday. She decided to go back to her office to follow up on the Dillon Point case. She looked at photographs of the escudo coins and ingots that had been recovered. She pulled the inventory sheet that listed the number of each item now stored safely in the locked evidence room.

Her office phone rang, and she promptly picked it up. "Detective Steele."

"Detective, I expected your voicemail. It's the coroner. I'm calling about the body washed up in Esquimalt this morning."

"What have you got for me?"

"Another case for you to look into. Those 18mm slugs match a cold 1979 murder case in Vancouver. A Fernando Diablo was murdered on the docks on the east side of Vancouver with the same gun as our victim here. Our victim is Pirro Marco according to his passport print file. He resides in Florida. I'll send my report Monday."

"Thank you, I'll look into the connection between the cases."

Jamie turned toward her computer and Googled "Pirro Marco." A number of links appeared. Jamie selected one that appeared to be of interest, waited while the page loaded, and then skimmed the information. Pirro Marco was an expert on the Santa Regio, which made him a possible connection with Firth. Jamie opened up her contact list and scrolled down to "Vancouver police." Tomorrow was Sunday, but she needed that file.

⛢

Dillon was in his room. He hadn't spoken to Adrianne since dinner. Adrianne decided to talk with her downstairs roommates, who, when she walked through to the kitchen to pour a glass of wine, she saw were watching television.

"Hey, guys, you want a glass of red wine? I would like to talk with you. I need some advice."

"Sure, Adrianne." Niki jumped up from the sofa to follow her into the kitchen. "We'll have a glass of wine. I'll help you carry the glasses." Niki smiled. "We're here for you."

Adrianne poured the wine and the pair rejoined Josh in the sitting room. Josh turned down the volume of the television. Adrianne sat between Josh and Niki.

"Problems with Dillon?" Niki asked.

"How's it going? I haven't spoken to you guys in a while." She wasn't as ready as she thought to share.

"Josh and I are working on this dummy at class. It's part of our training ...."

"Yes, and it acts like it's a real body. Its eyes flutter when you touch it in a certain way ... all I could do was laugh and Niki kept poking it so that it would keep flashing its eyes at me," he laughed. "Kind of like when he touches me, I guess."

"You flutter your eyes ..." Adrianne started to smile, "like the dummy?"

"You don't know the half of it," he replied, and winked at Niki.

Adrianne laughed. "You guys are great, but ..." she looked down at the floor, "Dillon wants more than I can give right now," she said softly.

"What do you want Adrianne?" asked Niki.

"I like him ... but he's getting intense ... he gave me this really expensive gift and ...."

Niki put his arm around her. "It's okay. Be friends for a while. Tell him, he'll understand."

"I don't know, we had sex and he ...."

"That's not necessarily a long-term commitment."

"I know, but I don't want to hurt his feelings," Adrianne sniffled.

The room was silent as all three sipped their wine.

"It will work out okay in the end. Josh and I knew right away that we were meant to be together, but that doesn't happen all the time. Tell him, and you'll feel better."

Adrianne took another deep breath. "Okay, thanks. I'm glad that I'm here with you guys, and that I can talk about this stuff."

Twenty One

Jamie stepped off the Harbour Air flight at the Bayshore Hotel in Coal Harbour. It was a sunny day in downtown Vancouver, and the flight had been smooth and on time. She was greeted by Detective Sommers of the Vancouver Police Department's forensic unit, and the pair drove to the Vancouver Police archives on Main Street.

"Case 79.VR139. That's the case where you say that your 18mm casings matched our thirty-three-year-old unsolved murder." Detective Sommers began to hunt for the brown, cardboard storage box containing the file. "Here we go, Detective ... Case file 79.VR139." Richard Sommers pulled the box from the shelf and wiped dust off the lid before removing it.

Jamie's cell vibrated in her pants pocket. "Detective Steele." She momentarily listened to the caller. "TJ, I thought you were taking the day off," Jamie said, as she pulled the contents from the cardboard box. "Hold on a moment." Jamie pressed mute on the phone and put it on the concrete floor.

"An escudo." She looked at a coin in a sealed plastic bag.

"An escudo?" Sommers picked up the coin.

"Yes, it looks like one I've seen in my active case in Victoria. I see that they both were minted in 1656. They both have the same markings and cross on them." She rifled through the case file. "There isn't much information about the murder in this file other than the 18mm ballistics report and this coin that was in the victim's pocket. The detective at the time had no leads until a few days after the murder. A woman reported her husband missing, which led to the identification of the corpse. The victim had no ID on him, but was shot at close range."

Jamie continued, "A Louisa Diablo married the victim Fernando Diablo in 1977, and according to these notes, Fernando was a crew member of the expedition that discovered the Santa Regio in 1972, a Spanish Galleon wrecked off the coast of Florida. Apparently, according to his wife, Fernando received a portion of the cargo as payment for his services and was selling some of it to support a new baby in 1979. Mrs. Diablo believed that the person her husband was meeting murdered him. She had no idea what exactly he was selling or to whom. She said the coin was his lucky charm."

"Doesn't that sound rather strange to you, Jamie? I've never heard of crews being paid with salvaged cargo, especially anything like rare historical coins. His wife must have known something, too."

"If this coin is from the same cargo that Dillon Point's grandfather had, I wonder where Hamish Firth fits into all this. It sounds like the cargo wasn't paid as services rendered, as Mrs. Diablo says. It appears as though there are two identical coins from a salvaged shipwreck that happened on the U.S. east coast in 1972. We need to find Louisa Diablo."

She picked her cell up and turned off the mute. "Sorry for the delay, TJ. I'm investigating the DB that washed up in Esquimalt. The vic was shot with the same weapon as another man in 1979. Guess what—this vic had an escudo like Dillon Point's. I'm going to check that out. I'll call later."

Jamie looked at Richard Sommers. "It's Sunday. Do you want to follow up with me today?"

"Sure, why not? I'm here and this case sounds intriguing. Maybe we can score a double-header."

♓

TJ was called into the office by Inspector Harris as Dillon was anxious to talk with her. She sat in a meeting room with Dillon and Adrianne looking over some documents.

"Okay, Dillon, here's the listing of what was logged into the security room last night. There are 832 Spanish gold coins and eleven gold ingots. When Detective Steele and I spoke to Mr. Firth about the escudo during our early investigation, he told us that each coin could be worth about three thousand dollars. This entire find could be valued at over two and a half million dollars if you can find a buyer."

"You've got to be kidding!" Adrianne exclaimed as Dillon sat shocked.

"I want to sell them if the crown counsel says I can keep them, Detective Kennedy. They're no good to me as they are." Dillon slid the document back to TJ.

"Last night I advised Inspector Harris of your situation. He's dealing with legal. I also have some contacts in the government, so I've asked one to see who might be interested in buying the coins. I sent her photographs of the coins and the ingots. I hope this is all right with you. I didn't tell her anything else other than that I had a case involving those pieces."

"Thank you, Detective Kennedy, I appreciate it. I wouldn't have a clue as to the best way to sell them. While we were waiting, I found another page in Walter Smith's diary that I hadn't noticed. It's in the middle of these unused pages." Dillon slid the open diary over to Adrianne. "Look at the notations on the right side of the page."

"The diary notes here say that there are 832 coins and twenty-one ingots." Adrianne looked up after she read the note. "That's ten more ingots than we found according to the police documentation. How could ten ingots be missing?"

"Exactly. I don't remember taking as many as twenty-one ingots from the crevice on Vivian Island. Tan told me she never knew where Grandmother Gloria and Walter hid the sailor's bounty. Do you think Grandmother Gloria took some of them after all? It makes no sense as she's so concerned about her secret."

"I don't know, Dillon. Gloria said she never told Brett about the diary, so he couldn't have taken them. If it was someone else, why was the rest of the gold still where the diary said it was?" Adrianne looked at TJ.

"Don't look at me," TJ said, shaking her head. "What's this notation about an emerald necklace? Is that missing, too?"

"Dillon gave that to me. I have it."

"We can talk about that later. I see a passage entry here, Dillon. It sounds as if it was written for your mother." TJ said, sliding the diary toward to Dillon.

"Yes, I read it a couple of times." He took the diary back and looked at Adrianne.

A knock on the conference room glass interrupted the conversation. Dillon and TJ twisted around in their chairs as Inspector Harris entered the room.

"Good news for you, Mr. Point," Harris said, with a smile. "I pulled in a favour and talked to the Crown counsel. He thinks that you'll get to keep your find. There's no evidence the goods you found were stolen since Robert Capland, who ran the Santa Regio salvage operation, never reported stolen goods in 1972. In short, you found it; you get to keep it."

"Would that mean that if there were more items located in the future, the find would belong to whoever found it?" Adrianne asked. "Who knows if there's more where Dillon found his?"

"I assume from crown counsel's advice that another associated find would be considered fair game, Ms. Padrino," Inspector Harris said. "There would have to be a formal ruling in court, though. Our legal counsel is sending forms for you to complete so that the goods can be legally declared yours, Mr. Point. I'll have Detective Kennedy bring them to you before you leave today."

"Thank you, Sir. I'd like to get back to Sliammon as soon as possible. I need to talk to my mother about all this. Adrianne and I must return her diving boat to Comox before it gets dark, as well." Dillon grinned ear to ear as he shook hands with the inspector.

"I'll always appreciate what the Victoria Police Department has done for me, Sir."

⋇

Hamish dialed Louisa's son-in-law's home number. "Manuela Princeton?"

"Yes, what can I do for you?"

"My name is Hamish Firth, and I'm writing an article about a Spanish galleon that was discovered off the coast of Florida in 1972. Your father was a crew member on that ship. I just spoke with your mother about her recollections of the story."

"I don't know anything about that, Mr. Firth. My father was murdered before I was born."

"Yes, your mother did tell me about your father, but she said you have an emerald necklace that once belonged to him. I would appreciate it if you allowed me to see it, for my article, of course."

"Mr. Firth, I'm on my way to do errands. It's Sunday, and those emeralds were just restrung."

"Could I just see them for a few minutes? Anything that was recovered from the Santa Regio is of interest for my article."

"My mother met you and told you about the emeralds?"

"Yes, that's right. She gave me your husband's business card. I need just a few minutes, that's all, Mrs. Princeton."

"I have to run, Mr. Firth, but will two thirty this afternoon at my house in Shaughnessy work? I've a prior commitment at three thirty to meet my husband. All I can give you is thirty minutes. Will that suffice?"

"Absolutely, thank you."

"The address is 2297 Angus Drive, just west of Granville Street."

⚸

"Ms. Louisa Diablo, please," Jamie inquired at the front desk of the Summerhill Retirement Residence. She showed her police shield.

"We're just finishing up lunch in the dining hall. She's sitting with that group of five by the window." The receptionist pointed across the room.

"Richard," Jamie grabbed his arm, "let me talk to her alone for a moment. We might be intimidating if we both march in there."

"I'll wait here."

Jamie worked her way through the myriad of tables and stopped at the group of five elderly women. "I'm looking for Mrs. Diablo," she said quietly.

"I'm Louisa Diablo."

"I'd like to talk to you in your room when you're finished. Would that be all right?"

"Certainly, I'm done here anyway. We'll talk later, Dorene." Louisa rose from her chair with difficulty. Jamie lent her arm for assistance. "What do you want to talk about?"

"The man over there and I would like to talk about your husband, Fernando."

"You're the second person that's come today asking about my Fernando," Louisa said.

Richard Sommers joined them in the front lobby.

"Mrs. Diablo, I'm Detective Steele from the Victoria Police, and this is Detective Sommers from the Vancouver Police Department. You said someone else was asking about your husband, Mrs. Diablo?" Jamie asked.

"Yes, there was a man here earlier today." She pressed the second floor button and the elevator door slid closed. "He said that he was writing an article on a shipwreck found in Florida back when Fernando was a sailor. I told the man that I didn't know much about those days, and that Fernando had been paid with recovered cargo. I'm in room 211." Louisa unlocked her door.

"Come and find a seat." Louisa sat on a small love seat. "Detectives, why do you want to talk to me about Fernando?"

"We're working on a case that's connected to your husband's murder in 1979, Mrs. Diablo," Jamie said. "What did that man who was here earlier look like?"

"He had broad shoulders, was in his late fifties I'd say, and spoke with a Scottish accent. He was interested in a necklace I gave to my daughter when she turned twenty-one. Fernando gave it to me, but the emerald stones hadn't been set into a necklace back then." Louisa took a framed picture from a side table next to her seat. "This is my daughter, Manuela Rosita Princeton. She's thirty-two now."

"She's attractive, Mrs. Diablo. How can we contact her?" Jamie asked.

"There are business cards in the drawer of the round table. Her husband owns a construction company and their home number is on that card." She pointed at the round table.

"What can you tell us about your husband's murder, Mrs. Diablo?" Richard asked. "There wasn't much in the police file."

"He was murdered in a warehouse along the waterfront in the Gastown area. Back then, Gastown wasn't as it is now. I was pregnant with Manny when he was shot and killed. I think he was trying to sell gold ingots that he'd been paid with for his work on the shipwreck. I didn't know about the ingots until after my husband's death. The police found a gold coin in his pocket. I told them Fernando thought it was his lucky charm."

"Could you tell us more about the ingots, Mrs. Diablo?"

"Some months after my husband's death and the birth of our daughter, I decided to finally sort through Fernando's things. I found a notebook with an envelope containing a key taped inside the front cover. The key belonged to a safety deposit box at the Royal Bank on Hastings Street. I showed the bank my husband's death certificate and was allowed access to the box. I couldn't believe what was inside. There were seventeen gold ingots. Of course, I didn't know what to do with them. I often forget I have them these days."

"Did you report your discovery to the police?" Jamie asked.

Louisa rose and stood before a bookcase.

"No, I didn't. Where is it? Anyway, I noticed the ingots had stamps on them, and thought that my husband's killer would come after me for them. No one, not even my daughter, knows about them."

Louisa smiled. "Here it is." She pulled out a dirty hard-covered notebook.

"So you never sold any of them?" Jamie asked. "Didn't you need the money, Mrs. Diablo? No husband and a new baby?"

She sighed. "It was tough in the eighties for many. Lots of single mothers had to juggle their lives, but I was lucky and had a boss who understood."

Louisa handed the book to Jamie. "This was my husband's. He was looking for something. There are math formulas and cryptic notes written in Spanish about some Dorado … but I never figured out what that was. There're even drawings of the emeralds I made into a necklace. They have funny symbols cut out of the gold backings. I always thought that it was better for the light to come though the cut emerald, and never could understand why they were set with a gold backing. When I took the stones to be made into a necklace, the jeweler thought I should reset the emeralds, but it didn't seem right. I wanted to keep them as they were given to me by Fernando." Louisa looked sad for a moment. "My daughter's now having the necklace restrung. I hope her jeweler doesn't press her into resetting the stones."

"So you said that the man that was here today was interested in that necklace. Was he going to talk to your daughter then?" Richard asked.

Jamie flipped through the pages of Fernando's notebook.

"Yes, I gave him the same business card I gave you, Detective."

"May I borrow this book, Mrs. Diablo?" Jamie asked.

"Yes, of course. Do you think it'll help you find Fernando's killer?"

"You never know. Thank you. Your safety deposit box key is still in the envelope inside the book cover. I should take it out for you."

"Please, no, Detective. I'll never find it otherwise. Just tape the envelope flap shut. I like to leave the key where my husband kept it."

"I notice your daughter's cell phone number is not on this card, Mrs. Diablo. Could you give me her cell number, please?" Richard asked. "Could you also give us her home address, too?"

"Yes, it's on a note under my phone on the kitchen counter. I'll get it for you."

♓

Hamish rang the doorbell of 2297 Angus Drive. A dog barked, and Hamish saw the shadow of a figure approach through the frosted glass imbedded in the front door.

"Mitsy," the woman said, as she partially opened the door. "Yes, good afternoon."

"I'm Hamish Firth. We spoke on the telephone earlier."

"Mitsy, go lie down." She turned back to face her caller. "I'm Manny Princeton. You wanted to look at my mother's necklace. Come in, but I must leave in thirty minutes." The trim woman opened the door.

"You mentioned that you spoke with my mother this morning. I'm going to see her this evening to show her the necklace. I had it restrung, and she's worried I was going to ruin it."

"Thank you for letting me see the piece," Hamish said. "Your mother's a nice woman and quite young to live in a seniors' residence."

"It's her arthritis. She worked with her hands when she was younger. I guess that might have something to do with her condition. My husband and I fund her residence there. She sacrificed so much when I was growing up."

"May I see the necklace?"

"It's still in the jeweler's box. I left it in the sitting room because I knew you wanted to see it this afternoon. I'm told that the emeralds are of a high quality from Colombia." She led Hamish to the sitting room. "My mother told me the twelve emeralds were once loose and not originally strung into a necklace."

"Loose, really," Hamish said. Manny handed him a blue box. Hamish lifted the string up with both hands, and then turned the necklace around and studied the back side. "Wow. I've never seen stones mounted like these before, Mrs. Princeton."

"I know. The jeweler wanted to reset them, but my mother would be devastated if I altered their settings. The gold backing looks like a symbol or backwards letter that is pressed out. You can see the clear emeralds shine through the opening if you hold them up to a light."

"Yes, I see that." Hamish held one of the stones up to the light. "One of the emeralds doesn't have a pressed out symbol and the impressions are different."

"I know, strange." Manuela looked at her watch. "I couldn't believe what the necklace is appraised for. My mother will choke when I tell her."

"I'll bet, and that doesn't likely include valuation for its historical value. I'd like to study this piece a while longer." Hamish pulled out a notebook.

"I'm sorry, Mr. Firth, maybe another time. I must leave now. I'm sure you've seen what you need for your article." Manny reached to take the necklace from Hamish's hand.

"No ... I must study this now. It's important. You do know that these stones are special? Historically, I mean." Hamish turned away from Manny so that he could study another stone. "I think these stones must be the El Rey Dorado."

"Mr. Firth, I don't care what you call it. I must go now. Call again, and you can look at it another time." Manny tried to reach for the necklace a second time. "Mr. Firth."

"Back away." Hamish pulled his Soviet pistol from his pocket. "There's no time to come back again, Mrs. Princeton. I'm sorry, but I must unravel the mystery of the El Rey Dorado right now. These stones were cut in the 1600s and describe the location of El Dorado, the largest undiscovered gold treasure of the New World." Hamish stuffed the necklace into his coat pocket.

"What are you doing?" Manny screamed, and the dog ran barking into the sitting room.

"Quiet, and shut that mutt up, too." Hamish kicked towards the yapping dog. "I must study these ... ah," he looked around the room bewildered for a moment, "ah ...."

"You don't have to hurt my dog." She tried to snatch her necklace from his fist.

"Where's the bathroom?" Hamish gripped Manny's arm. Mitsy disappeared into the kitchen, yapping.

"Why?"

"Just show me where it is, and you won't get hurt."

"Toward the kitchen."

Hamish pulled her toward the open bathroom door. "Stop and put your hands behind you."

"I won't tell anyone … just take the necklace and go."

"Shut up." Hamish slipped his gun into his coat pocket and pulled the coat belt from around his waist. He tied her hands with the belt. "Into the bathroom, now."

"This isn't smart, Mr. Firth. The police will find you." Hamish turned on the bathroom light, grabbed a facecloth, and shoved it into Manny's mouth. "That's better." He pulled the toilet lid down. "Sit."

Hamish locked and closed the door, then stood in the hall for a moment to gather his thoughts. The dog was still barking. The phone in the kitchen rang. Manny's cell phone rang immediately after. He had to get out of there. The racket was driving him crazy.

⚓

Jamie and Richard sat in Richard's unmarked police car outside of Louisa Diablo's retirement home. "No answer on either the house or her cell," Richard said. "We'd better drive over there. It's a Shaughnessy address, Jamie, a good half an hour from here." Richard started the car.

"The description that Mrs. Diablo gave us sure sounded like Firth to me. How did Firth find out about Louisa Diablo, and why now?" Jamie said. "And why the interest in those emeralds?"

"Who is Firth?" Richard asked.

"A suspect who we think is involved in a murder in Victoria that could be connected to your cold."

Richard Sommers pulled into the driveway of 2297 Angus Drive. "There's a car in the driveway, Richard. It looks like Mrs. Princeton is home now. Pretty nice digs."

Yapping greeted their arrival. Jamie rang the doorbell. No one answered, but a dog continued to bark. She cupped her hands and tried to peer through the frosted glass.

"Richard, listen. I hear thumping," Jamie said. "I can hear muffled banging."

Richard knocked on the door, and put his ear against the door. "It's the dog, Jamie."

"I don't know, Richard, I heard banging." Jamie walked into the front garden to look through the front window. "I don't see the dog, Richard. Let's go around to the rear ... the woman's car is here and the dog hasn't stopped barking. Something's not right."

"I'll call her cell again," Richard said. They could hear the phone ring faintly in the house. The glass in the back door was clear.

"I see the yappy dog scratching and clawing on a door inside," Jamie said. She looked at Richard. "What do you think?"

"I'll break it in."

⚓

Hamish drove back to Coal Harbour. He knew he had botched this one. He climbed aboard the yacht, and put the pistol and necklace on a seat in the stateroom. He decided to stop at Galiano Island for the night. He'd figure out a plan there. The cops would be hot on his trail now.

⚓

Dillon and Adrianne were outside his mother's front door. He knocked on the door. "Tan ... we're here."

"How did it go with the police yesterday? Come tell me all about it while I make you lunch. Dillon tells me that there's never any food on those airplanes." Robbie grabbed their coats.

"Only a few neighbors came to ask about the RCMP car yesterday. I expected more. Maybe this won't be as bad as we all thought."

"Is everyone here, Tan?" Dillon whispered. Ⱦaⱦom tried to nuzzle his way into the crowd. "What have you told Grandmother Gloria?"

"I told her you were coming today, and we would talk about what's going on when you got here. She knows it's about the coins, but I didn't say anything specific. She and Grandfather Brett are in the kitchen."

"Would you take Adrianne into the kitchen and ask Grandmother Gloria to come out here, please? I should talk with her right now."

Robbie looked into her son's eyes for a moment. "Certainly, son." She nodded her head. "Come, Adrianne, you can help me make something to eat in the kitchen."

Dillon waited silently for his grandmother in the hall. He smiled when she appeared.

"Dillon," Gloria asked softly, "what's this all about?"

Dillon gave his grandmother a big hug. "I love you. Can we talk for a bit in my room, please?"

"What's wrong, Dillon?"

He picked up his backpack, took her hand and they walked down the hall to his room. "Join me, Grandmother," he said, patting his hand on the bed beside him.

"I know you and Tan gave Walter's diary to me for a number of reasons." He wiped a tear from his eye. "I'm sure that you must know Adrianne and I have recovered your secret treasure. I respect your concern about privacy for you and Tan." Dillon tried to smile as he looked at the woman who sat solemnly silent. "The secrets need to be over now, Grandmother. It's time to let all the secrets in our lives go."

"What do you mean all the secrets, Dillon?"

"I mean the diary. Grandfather Brett doesn't know about it, right?"

"That's right, Dillon. I didn't feel that it was anything that I could or should share with him. It's my private life with Walter ... it's not about the coins, it's—"

Dillon interrupted, "What did Grandfather Brett say about the story we are telling about the discovery of the coins?"

"He believes the story, Dillon. Why wouldn't he?"

"Yes, of course. I'm going to sell the coins for the benefit of our family and the community. I gave the emerald necklace to Adrianne. I wanted her to have it. Is that all right with you?"

"The necklace is beautiful, Dillon. It's your heritage to do as you see fit. I didn't know what to do with what Walter and I found. I was worried those coins would ruin everything. You do the right thing, my grandson. I'm proud of you, Dillon—for caring so much. Your mother told me that you went to see Walter." Gloria swept tears off her cheeks.

"I would like to have a few words with Grandfather Brett. Some man advice. Okay?"

"You stay here. I'll send Brett to talk with you."

Dillon pulled Walter's diary from his backpack and placed it on the bed beside him.

"Dillon … your grandmother said you wanted to talk to me." Brett stood by Dillon's open bedroom door.

"Yes, Grandfather Brett. Come in and close the door, please. I need to talk with you in private."

"There aren't any secrets in this house, my boy." Brett left the door open and joined Dillon. "What's on your mind?"

Dillon closed his bedroom door and sat next to his grandfather. "Secrets—that's what I want to talk to you about." Dillon held up the diary. "Grandmother Gloria thinks you have never seen this diary, but I think that you have. I love you and know how much you've sacrificed for us, but you know what's written in here." Dillon hugged his grandfather. "I'm not going to tell Grandmother that you've known about it all these years."

"Please read this passage for me, Grandfather Brett," Dillon opened the diary to a page that he had marked.

Brett looked at Dillon, took the book and read the words:

My Dear unborn child;

I'm sitting by myself at the Court House Inn making arrangements to leave Sliammon with tears that won't stop. I thought that I was a man of many words, but they fail me now as my heart is heavy that I will never know you … the kind of person that you'll become. I cry these tears with mixed emotions about the choice I made. Brett will be the father that I should've been, and he has shown the courage that I lack. I sit and contemplate the gift that I hope will be taken by your mother to sustain a healthy and happy life for you all. Adults sometimes do things that are difficult to understand, and one day I hope you will see in your heart that my leaving wasn't totally a selfish act. I do love your mother and I do love you, but love can't always overcome everything. I believe that our cultural differences will destroy our love in the end. Your mother will grow to love Brett, even if it's just because I know he will care for you as his own; a debt I can never repay and will never be able to thank him for. When you grow older, I ask you to express my gratitude to Brett. Walter Smith, your father.

Brett sat looking at the words scribed on the page. "You're right. I have read this diary, but I never saw this page before." Brett looked up from the diary with teary eyes. "You are now a man, and … I must admit I found this diary just before your mother was born. Gloria asked me to fetch a few things from our room to take to the hospital in Powell River when her water broke.

"Later, after your mother was born, I read about the love your Grandmother Gloria shared with Walter Smith—the type of love she never had for me. I love your grandmother. I never told her I found her secret diary."

"I understand how personal the diary is, and how special the love that she and Walter shared together was, but you chose to be with her and stay with her baby that wasn't even yours, even though you both said that it was. I respect you for that."

"You know there is more to the story, don't you, Dillon? I mean about the ingots at Vivian Island? I knew about the coins and tried not to think about how much better your life—everybody's life—would be with the money they'd have brought in. I decided to look for the hiding place and take some of it to pay for things. It was difficult in those days, Dillon. The community was having a hard time; I was having a hard time with a baby and your grandmother."

"I figured you must have been the one, Grandfather Brett, who took ten ingots. Walter made this note on this other page, listing exactly what he and Grandmother found. When I got the listing from the Victoria Police this morning detailing what we recovered, I realized some ingots were missing. The ingots were at the top of the pile that was hidden away in that covered crevice. Since nothing else was missing I knew what had happened. I'm surprised Grandmother never wondered where the money came from."

"I was careful with the money I got from those ten bars. I used a little at a time, sometimes just enough to keep us going. A Sliammon jeweler friend of mine in Powell River gave me good value for the gold when I sold them to him. My friend never asked me where I got the gold bars, and kept my secret until he died a few years ago," Brett paused. "That friend was Lawrence Archie."

Brett sighed. "I wasn't a good friend in the end. We had an argument. Lawrence was a good man and friend. We decided we wanted our families to bond together, so … we agreed that you and his daughter Selina would marry when you both became of age. Lawrence made two necklaces in celebration—one for Selina and one for you. They were made from the ingots that belonged to your grandmother. I became angry. I wanted them destroyed, but he said they were beautiful and unusual—like his daughter—and he made them for your wedding day. You were about one at the time, I think."

Brett inhaled, then let his breath out slowly. "Anyway, I saw the smaller necklace only once, around Clara-Meyer Archie's neck at a special celebration. Your grandmother never saw it, and I'm thankful for that. I regret the whole episode and lost a great friend."

"So, I was to marry Selina Archie. Does Tan or Grandmother know this?"

"No, I never told them. How could I? The story about the ingots would have been revealed. Anyway, what little money was left from the ingots I used to help you with your trip to Victoria. I'm not sorry I took them. They made a difference over the years. I think the hidden gold was partly her way of keeping Walter's memory alive. She could look out at Vivian Island and know he was still there. I love your grandmother very much, but I don't think she will ever let go of Walter."

"I don't know about that, Grandfather Brett. I'm sure Grandmother and Tan knew in their hearts what would happen when I was given the diary. Grandmother needed an excuse to let her secret out, and she hoped that I would know what to do because she didn't." Dillon took back the diary, closed it, and placed it onto his lap. "Only Adrianne and I know about the correct count for the ingots we found. Grandmother will never know that you took any. I'm not telling her that I showed you the diary either. It's to be the only secret left in our family and that's okay with me."

"So what are you going to say to everyone when we leave this room, Dillon?"

"I will say we talked about being a man and the responsibilities that it entails."

"I'd like that, Dillon." Brett hugged Dillon. "What about the young lady with you?"

Dillon sighed and looked at his grandfather. "I thought I knew the answer to that … but I'm not sure anymore. I don't know if things have changed much from grandmother and Walter's time here in Sliammon. I'm still working that answer out. Let's join the others. Adrianne and I must return the Zodiac before dark."

$$\text{⨉}$$

Manuela Princeton cradled her poodle on her lap in an interview room at the Vancouver Police building.

"Your husband will be here shortly, Mrs. Princeton. I have Tylenol for your headache." Richard sat next to Manny. "We have an APB out on Mr. Firth. Could you please sign your statement, Mrs. Princeton?" Richard slipped the document onto the table and placed a pen on top.

"I thought he was a nice man and just wanted to look at my necklace. He called it the El Rey Dorado and went nuts." She signed the document and started to cry again. "He kicked my Mitsy, too." She hugged the little dog.

"My jeweler appraised the necklace at 110,000 dollars, but didn't indicate the stones were of historic value."

"We'll find Mr. Firth and the necklace, too, Mrs. Princeton. We're drawing up formal charges on Mr. Firth right now." Richard took the signed document.

"My mother will freak when she hears the necklace has been stolen. I was supposed to show her the new setting later tonight."

"You may want to postpone your visit with your mother for a few days to give us some time to find Mr. Firth and your necklace. It may be best not to tell her about the theft right now," Jamie said. "Try to relax while you wait for your husband."

♓

"I'm exhausted," Adrianne said, as Dillon followed her through the front door of their Victoria house. "It's good to be here."

"I thought we should've stayed in Comox, myself." Dillon dropped his backpack in the front hallway and closed the door.

"Dillon, we've already gone over this. I didn't take clothes with me. It was a one-day trip. Besides, I think Dad's paid enough money for us to bounce around the province, don't you?"

"Well—" Dillon was interrupted by a voice from the sitting room.

"Hey, guys," Niki joined Dillon and Adrianne in the foyer. "It's great to be back, don't you think?"

"I need to go to bed. Let's catch up tomorrow." Adrianne started up the stairs. "You guys can visit if you wish."

Niki glanced over at Dillon, and then up at Adrianne who had already reached the top of the staircase. "What happened to her?"

"I don't know, but she's been like this since we left Sliammon." Dillon scratched his head. "Women … I'll never figure them out, I swear." He grabbed his bag and headed for his room.

Dillon sat in his briefs on the side of his bed while he waited for Adrianne to finish with the bathroom. The door was closed. He tried to figure out what was going on with her, and his thoughts turned to the message Walter had written to his mother, Robbie.

Adults sometimes do things that are difficult to understand, and one day I hope you will see in your heart that my leaving wasn't totally a selfish act. I do love your mother and I do love you, but love can't always overcome everything. I believe that our cultural differences will destroy our love in the end.

He hadn't shown Adrianne the passage in the diary yet, and couldn't decide if he should.

"I'm finished," Adrianne said, and closed the bathroom door to her room.

Dillon followed Adrianne into her room. "What's wrong, Adrianne?" He tried to kiss her.

Adrianne turned away from him and sat on the edge of her bed. "Dillon … I can't do this … having sex with you and leading you on. I've got my own life to follow."

Dillon sat beside her. The room was silent as he searched for the proper words. He sighed.

"Yeah … me, too. I figured it was something like that. We're different in many ways, but in many ways we're not," Dillon paused as Adrianne began to cry. "I said I loved you and that's true. It's not about sex—even though that's great. It's Walter and Grandmother's story, isn't it? You feel we're like that?"

"I guess so. I want to be with you Dillon, but, as friends, I think. Can we do that?" Adrianne raised her head to look into Dillon's eyes. "You're a great and caring guy. We need to experience life before we commit to one person … putting the values and the cultures aside."

Dillon gently took her face in his hands and kissed her. "Friends then … diving buddies, to find that shipwreck."

"Yes, diving buddies. I like that, Dillon," Adrianne smiled. "By the way, I get half of what we find." She gave Dillon a hug.

Twenty Two

Hamish was anchored in Montague Harbour on Galiano Island. He was having his coffee in the galley on a sunny morning. The harbor was quiet. He was relaxed after a good night's sleep.

The more he thought about it, the more he was convinced that the Santa Regio heist was larger than anyone had anticipated. The emeralds lay on a table in front of him. Why did Diablo have them, and did they hold the answer to El Dorado?

He opened Pirro's battered notebook to a fresh page. Hamish picked up the necklace, and one by one, held each stone so that the morning light illuminated the image pressed into the gold backing. He wrote the individual letters in the notebook.

There were eleven letters scribbled in the notebook when he finished. One of the twelve emeralds did not have a letter impression. His next challenge was to make sense of the letters to formulate a word—in Spanish.

A bottle of scotch later, Hamish was no closer to solving the riddle. The golden city had remained hidden for centuries, it would wait another few weeks. His ass was in a sling now, and he had to get out of town.

Pirro's notebook and his pistol taunted him. It wasn't his fault. Diablo and Pirro made him do it; he deserved the Regio spoilage after more than thirty years of watching and waiting.

He called Eduardo's cell. It went into voicemail. "Eduardo, Hamish. I got a job for you. No B&E, just get a few things from my office safe. You're right, Point is a waste of time. Call me."

He checked the pistol. Five shells spent. He must be careful with the rest.

⋇

TJ sat down in Jamie's office. "You didn't call back yesterday. You find what you needed in the case file?"

"Sorry about that. I'm convinced Firth is our man. He attacked a woman yesterday in Vancouver and stole a piece of her jewelry—a piece connected to the Santa Regio. Firth owns a yacht that he keeps at the Oak Bay marina. It's gone, so I've asked the Coast Guard to keep a lookout for it. It shouldn't be that tough to spot from the air."

"If he has his weapon with him, we can't spook him. He'll toss it overboard and your key evidence is lost."

"Yes, I know. I don't have a plan for that yet. I got this notebook from Louisa Diablo, the wife of the man who was murdered in 1979. It turns out that her husband was a ship-hand on the salvage ship that found the Santa Regio. She still had his notebook, and I was about to take a look. There must be something useful in Fernando Diablo's notes."

TJ pulled her chair around to sit next to Jamie.

"The first page has names with what looks like math: Rene-Robert, 44 ingots; Benito and Pedro, 832 escudos, 21 ingots and Kings necklace; me, El Rey Dorado, 1 escudo and ~~27~~ ~~22~~ 17 ingots." Jamie looked at TJ. "The crossed out numbers must mean he started with 27 and ended with 17. I bet he sold them and that's why Louisa Diablo said there were 17 at the bank. The single escudo was found on Fernando's corpse."

"Louisa said that she still has ingots?"

"Yes. The key to a bank safety deposit box is taped inside an envelope in the front of this book." Jamie pushed the pages back and showed TJ the taped envelope. "Mrs. Diablo said Fernando was selling something to a man that he'd met before, so that's why there are two strikeouts for 5 each. Fernando's murderer purchased 5 ingots the first time, and took another 5 at the murder scene. I guess he did the math before the sale."

"The other entries sound like the split of the remainder of the Regio cargo heist," TJ said. "We know about Diablo's share now, and we have a list of what the kids found. Those amounts are close to Benito's and Pedro's. That leaves Rene-Robert's share still unaccounted for."

Jamie flipped through a number of other pages then stopped. "There are quite a number of pages that have drawings of shapes and letters. See this entry, with these scribbled letters?" Jamie pointed to the note, "'P, a, m, v, r, a, s, a, e, L, c, blank.' These same letters are rearranged in different sequences on following pages, TJ. It looks like Fernando was trying to shuffle them. It goes for pages."

Jamie put the notebook down and thought for a moment. "Manuela Princeton said Firth was peering through the cut emeralds when he was inspecting the necklace. So maybe each stone has a letter. Those letters likely spell something …

something Firth is trying to decode, and according to that notebook, Diablo was trying to figure out the same thing."

TJ flipped through a few pages. "There are only single words or phrases in here. Nothing is organized." She stopped at a page. "Wait. 'Parime Lacvs' is underscored, and the word 'Chinga' with 'Muisca shit' is scribbled in big letters across the bottom of the page."

"I wonder what that means."

TJ's cell phone rang. She grabbed it off Jamie's desk and answered, "Detective Kennedy." She listened, then said, "Hold on Constable Reid, please." TJ put the call on mute.

"It's the RCMP in Powell River. They heard Eduardo Dominguez's cell phone ring and listened to his voicemail. It was from Firth who wants Dominguez to get some things from his office safe. He's going to run. Obviously Firth doesn't know that Dominguez has been arrested, so maybe we can use Dominguez to lure Firth off that yacht."

"You got an idea?"

"How about making a deal with Dominguez? If Dominquez convinces Firth to meet him in town, Firth won't be expecting us. Once he's off the yacht, we can nab him. We can locate the murder weapon after."

"That works for me—set it up if you can."

TJ smiled, turned off the mute key, and explained the situation to Constable Reid.

After a lengthy discussion, TJ put the phone down on the desk. "Constable Reid will call me after she talks to her captain. She thinks they can work a deal with Dominguez, but we'll see."

"Great. I'll advise the Coast Guard to hold off until this is confirmed. There's no sense in spooking him now."

⋈

Hamish heard back from Eduardo, who agreed to help him. They were to meet at Harbour Air in Victoria, where Hamish would give Eduardo the shop keys and safe combo. Eduardo would then retrieve the items from the safe and return to Harbour Air with all the cash and ingots from the safe. After that, Hamish had told Eduardo he could fend for himself. Hamish was United States-bound.

⚥

"I received a call from Constable Reid, and everything is set up. Eduardo arranged to meet Firth in the Harbour Air terminal. Firth is going to tie up his yacht in the harbor."

"We'd better go in a minute then. While you were out getting lunch, I was on the Internet. I was curious about that scribbled note in Diablo's notebook about letters inside the emerald necklace. It turns out that the Muisca were people who lived in Colombia, South America, during the time of the Spanish Conquest. The Muisca made gold items. They performed human sacrifices to a goddess at a lake or lagoon, and the sacrificial offering wore the all the gold they had made."

"So, the mystery is about the location of that lagoon," TJ smiled. "It's always about the money, Jamie."

"The interesting thing is that the Muisca tried to keep the sacred place a secret and misdirected the Spaniards with false clues. That sacred place was called El Dorado."

"El Dorado is the word the Spaniards named the sacred lagoon, then."

"Well, not exactly, according to the info on the Internet. El Dorado actually means 'gilded person,' but it's often referred to as the location. The real surprise here, is that the name of the place the emeralds spell is 'Parime Lacvs.'

Fernando Diablo figured that out as shown in his notebook, but apparently that place never existed. It was a false clue."

"Diablo must've recognized that word, and knew the entire El Rey Dorado set of emeralds was a big hoax, a five hundred-year-old hoax. That's why he scribbled Muisca shit under the word."

"I bet he was really choked when he finally figured it out," TJ said with a laugh.

"It's going to be a joke on Firth, too. What do you think about Firth using the same 18mm gun he used in that Diablo shooting, TJ?"

"It seems to me that Firth is a bigger idiot than he appears. I would've tossed it after killing Diablo. I bet he shot Marco on his yacht, and that explains why Marco's body was floating in the strait."

"Ah ... but he is a collector of antiquities, TJ. The weapon is an 18mm, and no longer a common caliber. I bet he kept it, like last time. The only stupid thing was to use it again. Killing Pirro Marco makes no sense."

"He's obsessed, that's why, Jamie. He's wanted the Santa Regio bounty for himself for so long that he can't let it go. That's why we'll get him. Obsession."

"Firth has the emerald necklace stones, likely knows what he's got, and hasn't had time to work on the clues like Fernando Diablo did. He's going to disappear and let things cool off as he unravels the mystery."

TJ poked Jamie. "Firth is maneuvering his yacht into the harbor." She pointed to the fifty-foot Tiara as it began to align with a berth. "We'd better get ready to move on this guy." TJ looked around to confirm that the terminal was empty, as the clerk had promised.

The two detectives watched Firth go through the motions of docking the yacht, then disembark, and walk down the pier. She pulled out her service revolver and unclipped the safety.

"He's almost here. When do you want to take him?" TJ asked.

"We'd better take him just as he comes through the front door," Jamie replied. She pressed her body close to the wall by the door to stay out of sight. Jamie held her breath as the door slowly opened. She saw Firth's reflection in the glass and pointed her gun at his face.

"Police. Stop right there, Mr. Firth."

"Hands where I can see them," TJ demanded, her gun drawn as she appeared from the other side of the doorway.

"What's the problem, Detectives? Here to harass me some more, I suppose."

"Hands where we can see them, Mr. Firth," TJ repeated. "Take your hand out of your pocket slowly so that we can see it."

"Stay back from me." Hamish stepped backwards away from the door.

"Hands out where we can see them ... this is the last warning, Mr. Firth." Jamie followed the man outside, but Hamish continued to step slowly backwards. "Don't move any further," TJ repeated, while her gun remained pointed at the broad-shouldered man.

"What's going on out here?" A voice came from inside the terminal as the glass door opened. Jamie and TJ turned their attention momentarily toward the voice behind them. Hamish pulled his pistol from his pocket. A shot pierced the air as he aimed at TJ, knocking her to the ground.

Hamish shifted his focus to Jamie. Two shots rang out as bullets spat from her service weapon, hitting Hamish in the chest and upper shoulder. He fell backwards from the force of the two slugs. He landed on his back on the concrete pad of the terminal, blood seeping from his body. Jamie rushed toward Hamish and kicked the man's weapon across the pavement, a few feet away.

"You okay, TJ?" Jamie yelled as she checked Hamish's condition.

"Yes ... luckily he's a bad shot." TJ got off the ground and joined Jamie by Hamish's sprawled body. "Bloody stupid move."

"You or him?" Jamie asked. "I'm glad you had your flak jacket on, Detective. I'll call a team out here. He's dead."

An hour later, TJ and Jamie were in Inspector Harris's office. "You two are restricted to desk duty until you've been cleared. You have reports to complete anyway. That was a good job in my books, Detectives. We recovered the emerald necklace and have notified Vancouver. Ballistics has confirmed Firth's Soviet pistol was the murder weapon for both the Diablo and Marco cases."

"Stupid man," TJ said. "He knew he didn't have a chance, and that we had the drop on him."

"My guess is suicide by cop."

"I wonder if he knew the El Ray Dorado was a fake."

"We'll never know. I have Louisa Diablo's notebook to return, sir. It's on my desk," Jamie said. She looked at TJ "How's the shoulder, Detective? Must hurt like hell."

"Yes, a first for me. I hope my last."

"Do you think that you're going to like working here, Detective Kennedy?" Inspector Harris asked with a twinkle in his eye. "I realize it's a big adjustment."

"Things started off slow, and I did question myself about my decision, but I'll stay."

"That's good news. Someone has to keep Detective Steele here in line. Dismissed."

⋇

Adrianne lay in her bed listening to her iPod play as she thought about her discussion with Dillon the night before. The music reflected her state of mind. Adrianne pressed replay for the third time. She didn't hear the knock on the front door downstairs.

"I'll get it," Josh rushed to the foyer.

"I understand that Dillon Point lives here." A young woman with jet-black, arm-length hair stood on the covered porch. "I'm Selina Archie."

"Come on in and I'll get him." Josh opened the door to let Selina, who was carrying two carved wooden boxes, into the front foyer.

Josh skipped over a number of stairs on his way to the second floor. Dillon's door was closed, so he gently knocked.

"Come in."

Josh opened the door. "You have a pretty guest downstairs. She said her name is Selina."

"Selina!" Dillon jumped off his bed and followed Josh down the staircase.

"I don't know if you remember me. I'm Selina Archie. I have something to tell you. I hope now is a good time."

Dillon smiled. "You bet. Come in. We can talk in the sitting room."

The End

List of Characters

- Clara-Meyers Archie – Tla'amin; mother of Selina Archie
- Lawrence Archie - Tla'amin; father of Selina Archie
- Selina Archie - Tla'amin; artist and daughter of Clara-Meyers and Lawrence Archie
- Vivian Barr – Constable, Victoria Police
- Josh Bruno - Gay roommate of Niki Lukas
- Jack Bryce - University of Victoria student running Geek IT Services
- Robert Capland - Ran salvage operation in Florida, discovered Santa Regio
- Gonzalo Cielo - partner with Robert Capland
- Charles (Chaz) Collins - Drug addict
- Monica Davies – Owner, Vanessa Jewelers
- Fernando Diablo - Co-conspirator on Robert Capland's crew
- Louise Diablo - Wife of Fernando Diablo
- Eduardo Dominguez - Supplier of rarities to Hamish Firth

- Hamish Firth – Owner, Firth Coin and Rarities
- Stephen Harris - Inspector, Victoria Police
- TJ Kennedy - Detective, Victoria Police
- Nathan Lenox - Manager, Esquimalt branch of Second World Diving Co.
- Niki Lukas - Gay roommate of Josh Bruno
- Larry Louie- Tla'amin; father of Gloria-Louie Paul
- Faye-Elliott Louie- Tla'amin; mother of Gloria-Louie Paul
- Pirro Marco - Expert on Santa Regio Spanish ship wreck
- Adrianne Padrino - Daughter of Lia and Ted Padrino
- Caroline Larose – Owner, Dales Gallery
- Brett Paul - Tla'amin; grandfather of Dillon Point, husband of Gloria-Louie Paul
- Gloria-Louie Paul - Tla'amin; grandmother of Dillon Point, wife to Brett Paul
- Mason Perez - Contractor for rehab center
- Dillon Point - Tla'amin; son of Robbie-Paul Point
- Robbie-Paul Point - Tla'amin; mother of Dillon Point, daughter of Gloria-Louie Paul
- Sam (Sammy) Queen – Drug dealer
- Manuela Rosita Princeton - Daughter of Fernando and Louise Diablo
- Dr. Wallace Redding – Director, Museum Anthropology, UBC
- Kate Reid – Constable, RCMP Powell River
- Chelsea Roberts - Waitress at Brasserie L'ecole restaurant
- Dr. Sanders - Coroner at Royal Jubilee Hospital in Victoria
- Walter Smith - Social-cultural anthropologist, birth father of Robbie-Paul Point

- Richard Sommers - Detective, Vancouver Police, Forensic Unit
- Jamie Steele - Detective, Victoria Police
- Harold Taylor - Constable, Victoria Police
- Cecilia-Archie Windsor - Sliammon; sister of Lawrence Archie, owner of Sliammon Adventure Charters

Acknowledgements

There are not enough words to express my appreciation to my wife Diana, who has supported me during my journey as a writer. Without her love and support, this novel would never have been written.

A heartfelt thanks to my fine editors, Darlene Elizabeth Williams and Karen Kibler, whose dedicated work has been invaluable in the production of this book. I would also like to acknowledge Vivian Davis who has provided her time and support in the review of this story.

A special recognition to Dorothy Kennedy and Randy Bouchard who have dedicated their lives documenting the culture of the First Nations peoples of British Columbia.

Other novels by G. R. Tigg

The Detective
Kelly O'Brian Series

Go to www.rushingtidemedia.com for further information.

CPSIA information can be obtained at www.ICGtesting.com
Printed in the USA
LVOW08s0739160414

381842LV00001B/3/P